On the cusp of his senior year at Mercy High, Elliot Donahey, an out but terminally shy gay young man who keeps to the shadows—never wanting to be seen or noticed—suddenly finds himself in the arms of the highest profile jock on campus, local star quarterback, Marco Sforza. Their lives, and the ones of those closest to them, will never be the same.

Set against the backdrop of competitive sports, this character study work deep dives into the lives of these young men who each must "play the game" so Marco can play the game he loves. They are just trying to find some small slice of happiness to call their own amidst their hellish final year of high school.

MY SUMMER OF LOVE

Angels of Mercy, Book One

SA Collins

A NineStar Press Publication

Published by NineStar Press
P.O. Box 91792,
Albuquerque, New Mexico, 87199 USA.
www.ninestarpress.com

My Summer of Love

Copyright © 2019 by SA Collins
Cover Art by Natasha Snow Copyright © 2019

This is a work of fiction. Names, characters, places, and incidents are either the product of the author's imagination or are used fictitiously. Any resemblance to actual persons living or dead, business establishments, events, or locales is entirely coincidental.

All rights reserved. No part of this publication may be reproduced in any material form, whether by printing, photocopying, scanning or otherwise without the written permission of the publisher. To request permission and all other inquiries, contact NineStar Press at the physical or web addresses above or at Contact@ninestarpress.com.

Printed in the USA
First Edition
June, 2019

Print ISBN: 978-1-950412-85-3

Also available in eBook, ISBN: 978-1-950412-84-6

Warning: This book contains sexually explicit content, which may only be suitable for mature readers.

To the two J(ay)s in my life: My husband, JL, my Marco Sforza in every way imaginable. You are my light, my stars and the foundation that allows me to take flight and pursue my dreams. And to out queer musician and bard extraordinaire, Jay Brannan (jaybrannan.com), whose music, particularly the album "Rob Me Blind," inspired the Angels of Mercy series. His brilliant words and melodies are the true soundtrack of this series. I am forever in his debt for allowing me to quote from his works.

On the Tropics of Angels
—as above, so below...

*"The Angels were all singing out of tune,
And hoarse with having little else to do,
Excepting to wind up the sun and moon
Or curb a runaway star or two."*
—Lord Byron

*"We are each of us angels with only one wing,
and we can only fly by embracing one another"*
—Luciano de Crescenzo

*"The wings of Angels are often found on the backs
of the least likely people."*
—Eric Honeycutt

*"Subnormal people do supernatural things,
in a world full of demons
with white feathered wings."*
—Jay Brannan

Chapter One

For the Love of the Q

MY DAY AT the Q went pretty much like any other day. I prepped the machines to churn out the requisite soft ice cream Dairy Queen was known for—a pale mixture not too unlike frozen liquid paper (and probably contained quite a few of the same ingredients, come to think of it)—a heart-stopping coagulation of fats and chemicals. That broad assertion of its core ingredients was made by my mother, Kayla Donahey. As a bona fide health nut, she had the irony of owning the local DQ franchise she'd inherited when her father dropped dead—in the store, in front of customers no less—only two short summers ago. Coincidentally, and much to my chagrin, the very same year I was able to legally work. You can just imagine my euphoric bliss. This was how one Elliot Donahey entered the workforce: a by-product of a family franchise transfer. Sometimes I marveled at how my grandfather had timed things so precisely to check out of life so everything could change hands with nary a wrinkle in the process.

That fateful hot summer day, Taylor Campbell, a wiry six-foot three tall man, was the sole employee manning the store. As with most people, he had no way of knowing that day would be his last. At the time, he was sixty-three years, four months, twenty-two hours and thirteen minutes old (I did the math later—hey, I was bored), and was busy running the local shop he'd had for the past thirty years—working on probably his two millionth Oreo Cookie Blizzard, never realizing it was *his* number that was up.

At exactly 4:57 pm he dropped dead on the job. The only reason anyone knew the exact time of death was because, as the aneurysm burst in his head and his body took its death plunge to the floor, his right arm caught the electrical cord of the store clock, yanking it out of the wall and thereby fixing the time of death for all to see. By six that evening a distraught and frantic Kayla, with a disheveled and confused me in tow, had the store operating while she tried to coordinate calls to the family advising them of the change in ownership and what time the funeral services were going to be held. Meanwhile, she left me alone to do battle with the obtuse workings of the fryer.

I would've thought she'd have closed the store due to a death in the family. But you'd have to know my mother, practical to a fault. And she was worried about money—so the store stayed open. She said she'd grieve later, in private, alone in her room. I tried to comfort her. She told me she was going to be all right but needed some time alone to process it. It was a very lonely night for us both.

Other than the steady decline of customers due to the recent downturn in the economy, not much had changed in the two years since my familial indentured employment began. I was now on the cusp of turning eighteen on the second day of August. You know, that momentous occasion in a boy's life where I was supposed to blossom into manhood. Where I—I dunno, like sprout hair on my chest, grow a huge cock, and want to bang a gaggle of women—or *something* like that. Sadly, since it was only Tuesday, July 17th, I still had a couple of weeks before I could claim the status of being a pseudo-adult American male. I couldn't legally drink, not that I had a hankering to do so, but like all red-blooded American males, I was working on it.

This particular Tuesday, though, seemed like any other. In fact, since we'd taken over the Q, all of my days stretched out before me like the blank white walls of the shop. It was just one boring set of non-events meandering into another. I had no way of knowing how this particular day's events would drastically change my life forever.

For today was the day I would fall in love.

I'd like to say, looking back on it later, the air smelled different, the sun was a bit brighter, and I was greeted by deer and birds on my walk to work, but no—no change. Same ol' boring Mercy day. I'd always imagined what it'd be like to have a special someone in my life. There'd no doubt be challenges ahead for us: the thrill of the chase, the incredible emotional highs and hopefully, very few lows. But for now, I refilled condiment containers, had buns queued up, and stocked the requisite food supplies for another thrilling adventure-filled day at the Q...

...then proceeded to wait four hours for my first customer.

Sometimes, I wondered why my mother even bothered sending me to the shop. There was a Baskin-Robbins only a few doors down the same strip mall practically stealing all the ice cream business. And, honestly, who really wanted a grilled cheese from the Q anymore?

Even though my taste in food often ran contrary to Mom's overly crazed health-conscious experiments with our home meals, I often dreamed of settling down to a basic meal of steak/protein of some sort, potatoes (because I have a particular affinity for them), and a veggie or salad (because rabbit food is good food—or so they tell me). Hey, it wasn't like I was demanding a gourmet feast straight from Tyler Florence's recipe box, but I didn't fancy having to compete with the local rabbit or avian population in foraging for my next meal. I just wanted real food, not the corporate-processed shit I was forced to serve up to our barely existent customers.

On most days, there was nothing to pass the time other than a continuous round of stocking and cleaning. True enough, I could play my favorite XM radio station in the store—not like anyone else was around to protest my taste in music. Way I figured it, if I was working for nearly free (Mom did give me some money so it wasn't legally slavery), then at least I could listen to whatever the hell I wanted. Musically, I was all over the map. Country (especially the new "sexy" gay country singer Steve Grand who'd recently gone viral on *the inter-web thing*, as Mom calls it) to show tunes (I swear this will become clearer to you in a moment) to classic rock or even disco (okay, that one might've been a dead giveaway). I did it all.

I even liked to play coffee house fave Jay Brannan cranked up and do my own little fake video shoots in the store. I mean, who needs *High School Musical* or *Glee* when you could have me bouncing around from table to table in the seating area wailing at the top of my lungs to Jay Brannan's song "La La La"? Haven't heard it? Well, Google it, dammit—do I need to bring you up to date on everything?

Go on, I'll wait...

See what I mean? Broadway'd only be so lucky! And you certainly ain't lived until you've walked in the Q and watch me pour a mean Blizzard while hearing

Tchaikovsky's Piano Concerto No. 2 gushing forth over the fairly adequate sound system. Right now, though, it was Donna Summer extolling the virtues of *working hard for the money*. My disco mood was running rampant.

I looked around—knowing I'd spent the better part of the day revisiting the things I'd already done. Some stocking had to be put away from this morning's delivery, but I wanted to save it for later, just to give me something to do this afternoon. The sad stark truth was the place was so well cared for you could eat all the fatty chemical-laden food right off the floor and not have to spare a thought of catching anything that could remotely kill you. There was still shit to do, but being the clever guy I am, I spaced out what there was. Otherwise, I'd be done in about an hour and a half and completely mental by the time the first customer would show up.

Bored beyond tears, I leaned against the front counter in a huff—elbows firmly planted on its surface, smooshing my face into my hands and sighing to no one in particular, for there was no one in the store at the time.

"I'd just like something spectacular to happen just once in my life," I sighed as I spared a pointed glare at the ceiling trying to seek god's (I'm using a little "g" until I find out if s/he really exists) assistance. I contemplated my options. Hell, I'd take the offer of entertainment from just about anywhere. Not hearing anything from the Big Kahuna upstairs, I looked at the floor and bellowed to his fallen comrade, "Just once, and then I swear I'll never complain and accept my lackluster fate!"

I know, *be careful what you*...yada, yada, yada...got the memo. Hey, as bored as I was, I was willing to roll the dice on a zombie apocalypse if that's what it took to shake things up a bit. At least it'd be something to take the boredom out of the day. Besides, I had enough Q food on hand to distract the rowdy beasties if they did show up.

I sighed again, resigning myself to the solitude of working at the Q. Deciding I'd spent enough time staring at these particular walls, I heaved myself up and walked—really it was more of a shuffling of zombie-like feet than the actual lifting of them. I even amused myself by making zombie sounds and moving my arms about stiffly as I did so. I ambled with all the glorified zombieness I could muster around the wall separating the cooking area from the front counter. You can imagine my surprise as I turned the corner to hear the door alarm go off in its slightly slurred manner, sounding like it was on one helluva bender. To my shock, I had my first real customer for the day.

Or sadly, just someone who was lost again.

It happened...*a lot*.

As potential customers go, being lost these days was happening far more than the reverse of actually having someone who wanted something to eat. I had a sneaking suspicion Mom should start charging for the free advice; it might help pay the bills in the joint. I knew she was worried about how slow business was lately. I was glad she hadn't resorted to putting me out on the highway in some goofy getup to drag would-be customers into the store to see what non-spectacular things we had on offer. Of course, this extended to the pink goo frozen into disks the marketers at the Q's HQ bravely called hamburger patties. Once cooked up, they sort of resembled the real deal, but I still had my suspicions as to their quality or if they, in fact, contained any real meat, beef or otherwise.

But I suppose, for the sake of my family's financial stability, I should make peace with the marketing demons and hoped they would cook up some spectacularly irresistible offer soon so we wouldn't be out of business before my birthday rolled around. Hey, I had my priorities too.

I couldn't blame the nonexistent crowd—I certainly never ate at the Q, not even when I'd forgotten to bring something from home. To put it into perspective, I'd rather brave my mother's health-conscious foodie experiments than chow down on some grilled-up Q goo. Just the thought had me imagining I'd keel over on the job like Grandpa had. The mere thought of coagulated arteries pumped full of the soft ice cream chemical fats was enough to make me retch, even if I had to admit it did sort of taste good. Okay, I had some once. And it was good. I felt guilty. I don't do it no more.

Uh-uh, nothing doin'..., I'd thought as my eyes narrowed on the steely beast churning the white lie we passed off as soft ice cream. It gurgled and slurried, unheeding my pointed gaze.

As the echo from our drunken doorbell faded, I shuffled back around to the front counter, not really expecting an actual sale. Instead, I found myself staring into the prettiest green eyes I'd ever seen. They were dramatically set off by dark dreamy lashes that could paint a door from at least a foot away. I knew these eyes, though I'd never had the opportunity to view them this close. The fact they were attached to one hellacious rockin' bod never failed to hold my gaze spellbound at school whenever he was near—well, that was just the cheese on the beefcake standing in front of me as far as I was concerned. I stood there wide-eyed, like a deer caught in headlights, watching his glorious face framed with the longish dark brown curls making him look so romantic.

Kit Harrington—Jon Snow from *Game of Thrones* romantic—a fucking wet dream of a face.

Oh yeah, I should probably fess up here—not like you had to work hard at it, I'm sure: I'm gay. Get over it. I have. Not like it means much—cue the static loudspeaker announcement: *Whoop! Whoop! Virgin alert on the sales floor, ladies and gentlemen.* I mean, it's not as if there'd been any takers. I once thought maybe Stephen Lowry, who'd been my best buddy since my elementary days, would entertain being my first boyfriend. But after 2.67 milliseconds of deep consideration by said pre-pubescent boy, probably due in part to any lasting loyalty Stevie had for me as a friend, he said no. We don't talk much now, if ever. But the boy in front of me here at the Q, this boy, I always dreamed would be in front of me.

Just.

Like.

This.

Marco Sforza, the star quarterback of my high school varsity football team, the Mercy High Avenging Angels, stood at the counter with a look of trepidation and awe as he gawked in enraptured glazed wonder at the backlit menu above me. I was silently thankful my long straight raven bangs (homo-aesthetically bleached with white tips along the fringe, thank you very much) fell across half of my face. It meant I only had to concentrate on keeping one of my silver blue wolf-like eyes schooled, thereby keeping my faux teenage noncommittal cool intact.

Yeah, here's the deal—I'm not very good at getting my body to do what my brain thinks is a good idea. So instead, I mumbled the first thing popping into my head.

"Wow...fucking sex-on-a-stick Marco."

My eyes widened to where I thought they'd pop from their sockets as my face flushed eight shades of red because I realized I didn't just think it—my fucking mouth got ahead of me again and it spilled out.

Way to go fuck yourself, douchebag! Fuck, I'm a dipshit moron. Seriously, my own worst fucking enemy!

This seemed to bring him out of his mesmerized stupor brought on by the offerings glowing above. His husky baritone voice went straight to my dangly bits when, at last, the heavens parted, the glow from the perpetual halo surrounding his head glowed brightly, and he spoke.

"Hey, uh, Elliot, right? We go to the same school?"

I mean, could more golden and breathtakingly brilliant words ever be spoken? He was such a fucking genius. I nearly fainted—found I had to grip the counter a bit harder than I thought just to keep my legs from giving out underneath me. I know, I know—googly-eyed teenage girl, much?

"Uh, yeah." I swiped the bangs out of my face once more—only to have them immediately come cascading back down to obscure my left eye again. I hoped it looked cool, though I was 90 percent sure it didn't. I had only my sole unobscured eye to watch him. Wonder of all wonders, my eye caught Marco's—and *held*! We were having a moment...*weren't we?* Then I really had to maintain focus because of what he did next—he smiled warmly. At me! Who'd a fucking thought?

Keep it cool, Donahey—you could still so fuck this up.

"So, uh, you want to, uh, like, order something?" Yeah, that came out cool enough.

Maybe...

"Oh hell, yeah. Was just toking with some of the guys on the team out by the cliffs."

I tried not to drool. My eyes widened as he absentmindedly ran his fingers along the ridges of his eight-pack abs—seriously, the dude had an eight-pack, whereas all I had was at best a pull tab. Thin as a rail, I was. Hell, on a good day my abs could be mistaken for skin covering the underside of my spinal column. I couldn't help but become riveted to each bump of his T-shirt fabric pulled tight against him as if it were a size too small. I stared dumbfounded as he traced his fingers over his taut stomach.

"Got an incredible craving for the munchies. There's just so much to choose from. How do you do it?"

Did he just ask me, "How do *we* do it?" *We* were going to do it? *Anyway you want to, baby. Oh, wait...dammit, fooled again.* Cue the noncommittal face.

"Huh? Oh, the menu...Yeah, I usually don't."

"Oh? So...why do you work here, then?"

"Family owned and operated." I tilted my head to the side in an off-kilter way and put on a fake practiced smile then let it drop and rolled my eyes—schooling my features again into passivity.

I swear I nearly blanched when he giggled nervously at my small pantomime. *What the fuck was that about? Marco I-am-fucking-sex-on-two-legs Sforza actually giggled? At something I said!* I found I could ponder our little moment for hours and never tire of it. The absurdity of the situation had my head turning slightly like a dog hearing a high-pitched tone.

"Oh yeah, that's right. The original owner died on the job here, huh? Like a couple of years ago, wasn't it?"

God, he had such a brain on his shoulders, such a memory on this guy. Einstein should have been so lucky. Okay, I freely admit my hormones were doing the talking here.

"Yeah, that woulda been my grandpa."

We stared at each other. The only sound in the room was from the low hum of the air conditioner and the steely white-lie-churning beast while France Joli cooed the slow part to my new come-hither disco anthem for Marco, "Come to Me."...Yeah, baby!

"Oh, wow, uh...awkward—eh, sorry," he said softly.

And for some reason I couldn't fathom, he looked it too. This was sooooo fucking surreal. Black-and-white TV *Twilight Zone* surreal. I didn't know what to make of it. Was I being *Punk'd*? That was so Ashton Kutcher circa 2003. I didn't know quite how to respond, so I just used the de facto teenage response when you don't know what to do: I shrugged off the apology.

"Nah, it's cool. I only saw him on occasion. We weren't really that close. Not on that side of the family, anyway. Now my Aunt Tilly on my dad's side, she's an A-1 whack job. *We're* close."

He looked at me with an amused curve to his lips. I thought better of the over-sharing. "Sorry, I know, WTMI."

He shrugged he understood—it was cool. It was a brief male bonding moment over family oddities. We both lapsed into silence. His eyes searched mine with an intensity that went straight to my crotch. I can't tell you how thankful I was I had the counter to hide the sudden tightness in my jeans.

Change topics, you goof-less fuck, right fucking quick!

"So, uh, can I serve you something?"

Yeah, like me, ass up, naked on a platter, perhaps? I couldn't believe the bold thoughts popping up in my head with Marco so close. My gaze darted to his large hands as he placed the palms of them onto the counter and leaned forward. His eyes became a bit softer. Did they dilate as he came forward?

What the fuck?

He looked around and noticed how underwhelmed the business seemed to be today. *Barren* was the word that sprang to my mind. *Normal* was another one. *Ghost town* could work too.

The quirk at the corner of his lips pulled all of my focus—never had one tiny square inch of flesh been as appealing as the small dimpled curve of those lick-worthy lips. I wanted to flick my tongue in that little curve to see what it tasted like. Probably sunshine and puppy breath, I allowed myself to imagine. His next words brought me out of my fixated stare at his mouth.

"Well, there is something I'd like to have...but I don't seem to find it on the menu."

My eyes narrowed a tiny bit. The hairs on the back of my neck prickled like a rabbit under a fox's gaze. And he was such the fox. Okay, even I realize how lame the reference was—but I was flustered, dammit! His gaze made me nervous as hell; my survival instinct was trying desperately to kick in—and Marco's gaze had warning written all over it. Gayboy Red Flag Number Two on my warning list—I realized this could so be a setup to get pummeled by a jock.

I flicked my tongue along the small ring piercing at the left corner of my lower lip. I couldn't help it. It was a nervous tick I'd acquired whenever I saw a boy I liked.

And I liked him very much. For far longer than I was willing to admit just then, hence the near involuntary rapid-fire flicking at the corner of my mouth. Truth be told, I'd had a hard-on for Marco for a couple of years now, since I first spied him on campus and realized my predilection ran to the male of the species. But then again, who didn't like Marco? If I had to guess, the line currently went around several blocks. I was just a nameless face in his book, one of his many adoring fans. He was extremely well-liked in Mercy, a real golden boy in town. Removed, untouchable, and heartbreakingly stunning.

Unbelievably, the look in his eyes mirrored my own. Our gazes locked—neither of us flinched. A flirtatious game of chicken. Without breaking his gaze, he rested his elbows on the counter and beckoned me forward by curling a finger of his right hand (he had big rough-looking hands), suggesting I lean in too, as if he were going to share the most scintillating secret known to man. I paused for a second, then figured, *what's the worst that could happen?* There were cameras in the store—not that anyone actually viewed the damned tapes, but hey, none of the customers knew that. So, curiosity getting the better of me, I gave up and leaned forward.

For fuck's sake it's Marco Sforza—when am I ever going to get another opportunity at something like this?

"Actually, smoking also gets me completely horned up too. I'd much rather take care of that then have a burger and fries. What I really came in for is, uh"—he narrowed his eyes, desperately searching my own—"you."

Before I could even process his tantalizing bit of information, he leaned even closer and his lips brushed mine ever so softly. I froze on the spot. As the kiss caught, it was as if his tongue was laced with a muscle paralyzing neurotoxin. I found I couldn't move. *Fuck me, I couldn't even breathe!* As if connected to Marco's brain, my lips parted on some unspoken command and he softly chuckled with little puffs of his breath punctuating into my mouth. A swipe of his tongue along the crevice of my lips, and I nearly came from the sensation.

Without missing a beat in the kiss, like a crocodile, he glanced to the left and right of us with half-lidded eyes and then slipped his tongue further into the warmth of my mouth. Our kiss probably lasted for a little over a minute—each time I thought it would end he found a new way to paint my mouth with his formidable and talented tongue. If you asked me, I'd tell you the kiss went on for hours. The taste of him was beyond anything I could have imagined.

While sunshine and puppy breath weren't on offer, there was the stale stench of pot—he hadn't lied about it, but he had evidently chewed some gum on the journey from the kids' local partying spot along the cliffs to the Q. Hands-down, spearmint and marijuana was now my absolute favorite flavor combination. Though in hindsight, it may have had more to do with the bone in my jeans that wasn't getting softer anytime soon.

He gradually withdrew and I yelped a little at the parting—leaning forward like I could continue to kiss if I just followed him across the counter. I couldn't help it. I think it might have been the lack of air pressure escaping when we parted. Yeah, I'd like to go with that.

Embarrassingly, a small strand of saliva linked our mouths as he withdrew. He swirled his tongue languidly, circling around his lips—severing the liquid link we shared. He smiled, before wiping his mouth with the back of his hand, watching carefully for any signs from me.

What he was looking for was beyond me—he'd just given me something that would keep my hand and cock very happy for the next decade. Full-on jerk material, the kiss was.

He whispered gently to my bliss-filled face, "Fuck, Elliot, you've got me all kinds of hard up here, boy. I knew you'd know how to kiss. Those full sexy lips were just begging for me to kiss you."

I fought like mad to regain some sense of composure. I shook my head and the small trail of spittle dangled from my lower lip onto my chin. *So not cool, Brewster.* Yeah, I had devolved into paraphrasing Evil from *Fright Night* now. I needed to man up here.

Marco bent his head down slightly, looking at me with such desire from under his brow. He calmly reached out and, with his thumb, gently wiped the trail of spit from my mouth, before bringing his thumb to his mouth to lick it off. He chuckled softly, the air from it puffing against my face, his eyes flashing brilliantly. I flushed. I smiled so widely I knew I looked like a dork in front of the sexiest guy at our school.

"Ooh, and he looks adorable when he blushes. I think I just may have fallen in love, Donahey," he purred softly, his voice dark and raspy.

"What? Huh?" I mumbled in a dizzying daze.

In some weird way I could hear what he was saying to me, but it seemed so far away—so from left field. I had to be dreaming. Yeah, that was it. I got so bored I fell asleep from lack of any customers and this was some sort of erotic hot dream. It would surely explain the absurdity of the situation.

Like the twat I was, I just nodded lazily, whispering in a soft, drawled mumble, "Yeah, has to be a dream, 'cause there's no way 'Come-fuck-me-now Sforza' would do that to someone like me."

"Really?"

His smile—so warm and inviting—pierced my soul. It felt so right it hurt. It stole my breath. And I'd so let him do it to me again and again. He laughed softly, only this time he walked from around the front of the counter, trailing the middle finger of his right hand along the counter top. I didn't move. I couldn't. Suddenly, as if by magic—only because everything was such a fucking blur—he was right behind me. I felt him tug at my belt—pulling me around the wall to the prep counter and away from any passersby. He turned me around gently so my back was pressed into the counter. Marco slipped his arms around me, coming up along my way-too-skinny body and hooking his hands up onto my shoulders. He ground his hips into my own, making sure our hard cocks were rubbing against one another through our clothes. Both of us sighed heavily into the other. Marco shuddered from the pressure between our erections.

"Fuuuuuck, does it feel like a dream to you now, Els?"

Involuntarily, I convulsed like I was having some sort of seizure. I tried like hell to contain it into small spasms. But fuck me, with the feeling of what the hottest guy at our high school was doing to me I was so out of my element. This simply couldn't be happening. I bit my lower lip at the sheer pleasure he was causing.

I shook my head, managing to get out, "No, uh, it feels pretty real. Ah, fuck, Marco. Christ, please, I'm close."

A dark purring laugh bubbled from his lips. A long slow breath slipped from his nostrils, bathing my face. Without a thought I breathed him in. The best fucking scent on the planet.

"Yeah, I thought you'd feel the same way."

Despite all the physical sensations he was causing he was keeping a watchful eye to the door as the seduction went on. Some small warning was raging in my head signaling this had to be a setup of some kind. His buddies were going to walk in and catch the fag trying to put the make on their star quarterback and then beat the fuck outta me. He was just watching the door for the signal to flip the situation around on me. As if sensing a building reticence on my part, he stopped rubbing so intently. He put a finger under my chin and gently lifted my face—my icy steel blue eyes to his verdant green.

Riveted. Electric. Our gazes clashed—combined, held.

"When I watch you, you don't look away. Understand?" His eyes were dark, probing—tearing away any defenses I had like tissue paper. I solemnly nodded. "It's how we are. How we'll always be. Can you do that for me? For us?" He said it so softly, with such conviction, that I knew, *I just knew,* this was right. It was how it was supposed to be. Everlasting.

Always.

I wanted to believe what was happening was the real deal but every fiber in my young gayboy body was telling me it couldn't be. It went against the laws of nature, or whatever governed shit like this. What I did know was football players and little artistic fagboys don't mix—and they sure as hell don't fuck. It was in that unpublished but oft-known rule book all teenage kids simply had memorized. But then there was the look of lust in Marco's eyes, not to mention the feel of his bone-hard cock rubbing against me, sending me nothing but mixed signals. Confusion laced with desire. But there was no mistaking—Marco was hard. Very hard. His gaze held mine and we simply regarded each other, panting slightly from the pointed exertion. He leaned in so our foreheads nearly touched.

"I know you think this is sudden, Els. But I've observed you for two years now. I know what people say; I've heard the rumors too. But I can't deny it anymore; you do it for me, Donahey. Always have; from the moment you walked into my life on my first day at Mercy High. I even adjusted my schedule last year so we'd have PE together so I could watch you naked in the shower. I know it sounds *so* fucked up. I know. But you have no idea how hard I had to flirt with ol' Miss Crabapple in the front office to get her to change my schedule. But you're so worth it."

He kissed me softly again. Twice.

"I don't know why it's you, but it is. I've been working up the courage to get closer to you all summer. I'm sorry it took me all of June to figure out what day was the absolute slowest in your week. You have no idea how many Tuesdays I've spent nearly my whole day watching the store, making sure you'd be alone for me to ask you out."

We kissed again. He stole my breath when he pulled away. Sweet torture.

"Please tell me you won't disappoint me by saying no. I don't think I could bear it."

"You want...to go out...uh, with me?"

He nodded and chuckled, his eyes flashing brilliant green like freshly cut grass on a spring morning.

"Yeah, now he's getting it."

It had to be a trick of some kind. Just had to. Maybe on this "date" Marco was proposing, things would turn around. Yeah, I'd be alone with Marco and then his buddies would spring from the bushes or from outside the car and all be ganging up on me. But the look in Marco's eyes. He couldn't possibly fake it, could he? And the prodigious bone in his pants hadn't been a mistake either. *So maybe...?*

As if to quell the unspoken wave of worry, he leaned in again and our mouths met in a clash of teeth, lips, and tongues. Marco's hands became frenzied, lustful. After a few harried moments where our hormones got the better of us, we settled down and eased into really enjoying each other. As we kissed, he slipped his hands deliberately down to pull me from the safety of the counter and cup my ass in his big paws. I just held onto the belt loops of Marco's cargo shorts with a white knuckled grip as Marco did magical things with our tongues. We parted after the long tortuous kiss.

"Yeah," Marco panted, leaning his forehead against mine—his breaths like a soft summer breeze—circuitous heaven. It was shredding me raw—and don't think it's lost on me how over the fucking top I'm taking it. But you have an outrageously unattainable hunk of man flesh you've drooled over from afar suddenly professing their love for you and see how well you do. Yeah, I so didn't think so either.

But what he murmured next fucking nailed it for me. There was no doubt—I was his.

"I think I love you, Els. I know it's fast for you, but you'll see. I've kept my eyes on you for so long." Another soft kiss, our lips barely touching—achingly pleasurable. But it seemed he wasn't through with professing his feelings for me.

"I've been such a coward. Those eyes, the way your hair moves across your face, not to mention that it fucking slays me every time your eyes search me out. I tremble when you look at me. I know it's all new for you. But for me, it's weighted; it has history. I've waited for so long to do this."

He kissed me softly again.

"Just to taste you. Please say you'll go out with me. We can go to Carmel or somewhere else—you name it. I got a car, I got money. We can get away. I just want to spend some time with you. Please say you'll come. Please, Els? Please come."

I swallowed audibly. If Marco kept up what he'd been doing, then I would definitely be coming, and not solely in the manner he was suggesting either.

"Uh, well, I don't have today off. But I can get away tomorrow. Mom watches the ss-st..."

"Store on Wednesdays and Thursdays. Yeah, I know. I've been watching, Els, remember? I know your schedule."

"Wow, it just hit me. I have a boyfriend stalker! How fucking righteous is that?" I blushed at how forward it sounded, and maybe a little bit whacked. You can imagine my surprise when his eyes brightened—a dazzling flash of intense green. I marveled openly how I'd got that reaction out of him.

In awe, as if I'd just given him Christmas in July, he asked, "Di...di...did you say *boyfriend*?"

Fuck me. Scramble, dude, scramble. He's panicking, you fuck! You're so going to lose him!

"Too soon? It's just, hey, I'm aware of where we live. I thought I was the only one, ya know? Small town, averages of there being more, well, uh, not so great, you see. But hey...we can just call it friends with bennies if it's what you want...I don't..."

He cut off my ramble with a deep kiss, holding my face in his large rough hands. We parted and he was smiling broadly, dazzling perfect white teeth showing brilliantly against his olive skin.

"Nah, I was dreaming you'd say we're boyfriends. Fuck, I know I did it all wrong, Els. I just couldn't wait any longer. God, you must think I am really a whack job, huh? So not cool, Sforza. So not cool." He guardedly shook his head—as if he were ashamed of how he handled this. His glorious eyes were cast down to the floor—so not where they belonged. Those eyes deserved to be seen.

"Hey." It was my turn to catch his chin so we could find each other's eyes. "*Boyfriends* it is. Life's too short to sweat the long courtship thing, right?"

"Yeah, okay." He smiled and I knew right then and there I'd do anything to keep a sexy smirk on his face.

"So, uh, did you really want something or was it just the make-out and date thing playing on your mind?" I quirked a brow, already finding myself testing the waters of this new budding romance. Fuck, *me* and...*romance*. Two words I totally never thought I'd associate together about myself.

"Well, I guess I could eat something. I really was toking out in the car. Not with the guys on the team. Hell, I haven't seen any of them since summer vacation began."

"Oh, so you don't have to get back to them?"

"Well, I could just go back to what I usually do on Tuesdays, but hey, it's actually much more comfortable to be inside the store than in my car all day."

We laughed. I blushed at how Marco had been trailing me all along. I was way not paying as much attention as I thought. Then it truly hit me—I really did have my first boyfriend stalker! It had to rank somewhere on a gayboy's list of things to do, right?

"You're welcome to hang, but I sorta got some things I gotta do to stay busy. Mom may be the boss, but she's a little Nazi when it comes to the store being kept up."

"I don't mind helping."

I couldn't help it. I looked at him like he was from Mars.

"What? Can't I stay around my guy while he's at work? Isn't that what boyfriends are supposed to do?"

"Fuck all if I know. You're my first."

"And I better be your last, if I've got anything to say about it."

I flushed again. Between my dick and my face I didn't think there was any more blood to circulate and keep the heart going. *Wouldn't it beat all to drop dead on the cusp of finding my first boyfriend?*

"Fuck, Els, when you blush I just want to fuck the daylights out of you."

Okay, his remark struck me so hard my eyes went really wide. I couldn't help it. From the moment we'd agreed we were boyfriends, I knew what our positions were going to be in bed, primarily because I couldn't ever imagine Marco being a bottom sort of guy. And truth be told, I had bottom written all over me anyhow. So, the proposed arrangement was already working for me. Thankfully, I was resilient enough, so I wasn't down and out for long.

"Yeah, well, I'm sure we'll get to it soon enough. For starters, let's just concentrate on getting the stock that arrived onto the shelves in the stockroom, okay?"

"Okay."

We walked to the back of the store with little regard for any would-be customers mistakenly finding their way to the Q today. I didn't care if they ate the store out from top to bottom. I had my *first muthafucking boyfriend*! The world could just go fuck itself.

"Ya know, I hear stockroom sex can be wicked hot," Marco said as he reached for my hand.

"Yeah, well we're so not using the hamburger spread as lube on *my* buns, big guy. So, we'll table it for now."

"Spoilsport."

Chapter Two

Of Kisses and Unspoken Dreams

AS WE GOT to know each other, as couples no doubt do, Marco and I talked about a lot of things. I know it seems so obvious. Couples talk; not a foreign concept, I'll grant you. But for me, who had been alone for most of my teen life, having someone to confide in, to lay every fear bare, was such an amazing thing to discover. Even though I was completely smitten with his good looks and infectious charm, I found, to my overjoyed surprise, he really was a very thoughtful and considerate person. And it wasn't just my raging teen-boy hormones kicking in to do the talking. It pleased me beyond my wildest dreams to discover how deeply he felt things. You have no idea how much I needed that from my boyfriend: compassion.

I guess some secret part of me always wished the jocks had more to them than the beefcake image they projected. Though they were a constant thorn in my fae-boy side, by and large I had a begrudging admiration for them. I mean, men were the object of my desire, so I had to cope with the whole love/hate relationship with them. It was even nicer to discover my guy didn't disappoint. In fact, he exceeded every wish I could have for him.

"One thing sort of did surprise me about you, though," he said as I rolled from lying beside him in the backseat of his car onto his chest. I rested my head on my arm, my eyes searching his in the waning light of dusk, noticing the amber flecks highlighting the rich green, jewel like eyes. We had parked out along the cliffs along Big Sur late one afternoon just to spend some time together and talk.

"What's that?" I purred as he trailed a hand along my spine, before carding his fingers languidly through my hair. I relished every time he did. I fucking loved it when he touched my hair. He knew, so he did it often.

"The randomness of the way you express yourself. At first I thought it was random, but there's a calculated genius to how you employ it. I knew you were smart, sweetheart. Just didn't realize how smart."

I gave a mock gasp, but my eyes were alight with the humor he had goaded me with. Realizing he wouldn't buy any of my bullshit, I sighed. "I know I tend to be random—going left when right is the more likely choice. Not that I am purposefully contrarian by nature. It's not my intention, I swear. Shit happens. I panic, and brash decisions are made. I'd like to think I think things through; I don't know if I am always so successful."

He rolled his eyes and nodded but blew me a kiss anyway.

"Okay, I can suck at it. I'm a teenage boy on the brink of manhood. Freaky shit is going on in my head and body and sometimes it scares the crap outta me, okay?"

He chuckled and wrapped his arms around me. He pulled me up to him and kissed me passionately, rolling me around to where he could eclipse me—wrapping every bit of him over me. Heaven. You'd think my mind would've been obliterated by his passion. Typically, it was true. Yet my trap just kept on flapping. I needed to expend nervous energy, I guess. It happens.

"I know it's a bit weird. I learned early on in life that since I wasn't a fighter, words could become my shield—I find I often need them. I have a tendency to cultivate words most kids my age wouldn't use. Ya know, to mess with their heads while I make a getaway?"

He arched a brow, though I think he took me at my word. "Honey, I could show you how to defend yourself."

"I've done well enough without the need for violence, thank you very much. *Words* are my weapon of choice. Let's just say I'd be very comfortable being dropped into a Jane Austen novel. It's my wit what gets me by, Mister Hottie McHottie." I poked at his chest, making him giggle a bit at my mock indignation. "They're what allow me to smokescreen myself out of trouble."

He sighed, resigned to let it drop. We'd sort of had this conversation before. He wanted me to learn how to defend myself. But it's what I had him for, wasn't it?

"Okay, okay. I believe you. Whatever works for you, lover. I just want you safe and sound. Whatever it takes."

"Well, it's my über-awareness of all things around me that has kept me safe, hasn't it? Though, I'll admit, it *is* random when I employ them. I try to keep it in check. I'm not always so successful."

"Oh, I dunno 'bout that. It brought you safely to me, didn't it? So, it can't be such a bad plan. You've obviously made it work for you. But—" He held a finger up in front of me and leveled it squarely in my face. "I'm here now. I will watch over you and protect you. You are the most precious thing I have in my life. Nothing is more important or valuable to me than you and your continued safety. I mean *nothing*. I would give everything up in my life except for you. *Never* doubt it."

Conversations like that impressed me most; the reasoning he employed when we talked about how we felt about things. I flushed, amazed at how vehement he could become over the way guys like me were treated by society—as if it didn't apply to him. His passion was truly impressive to behold. He told me he often pushed back against the other guys he hung out with on the team over their internalized homophobia—pointing out how they were just parroting their parents' bullshit and they needed to grow a pair and get to know someone who was gay and deal with it for themselves. He said he wasn't always so successful, but generally, the guys had sort of given him the benefit of the doubt on the topic. He was still one of them, so I guess they thought he was enlightened in some way that escaped them.

If they only knew...

On more than one occasion he told me he often thought about us in the long term. Not just in years, but in decades. He said our love was a forever kind of love. Beyond the ages. It was poetic, if a bit smarmy. But that was my guy. He didn't write the gooey romantic stuff found in Hallmark cards; he was the guy they wrote about. There was a subtle but very important difference. I thought it was sweet of him to think about us like that, but I really didn't know whether to put much stock in it or not. I mean, we were young. Things can change. While I wanted desperately to believe, I kept a careful eye to any deviation in his quiet confidence of all things us.

"I know you think I am just springing this all on you, Els. But you have to understand I've thought about it for these past two years. It was a constant conversation I've had going, trying to anticipate every possible response you'd have to what I wanted for us. I get my telling you this might seem bizarre or so completely whacked-out crazy. But for me it is *very* real. I can't tell you how much having you in my life means to me. I could walk away from everything that ever mattered to me if I could have you."

I mean, what do you possibly say to something like that? Had I not been so wrapped up in all things him I probably would've thought it was a full-on cray-cray moment and bolted for the hills—except, I knew in my heart of hearts he'd find me. Marco was intense. And he was *very* intense about me. There was so much passion in him I could feel it coming off him in waves—the ebb and flow of how much I seemed to mean to him. At times he'd just sigh while he held me close and his eyes searched every tiny facet of mine. Marco was deeply intoxicating to me—I was absolutely powerless against him. I know how over the top and romantic novel this shit sounds. I get it. But having experienced the way he could shred me with a single look, I understood those words more plainly than my own name. It was an immersion into my soul he had complete and unfettered access to. I would deny him nothing. Wouldn't you?

"You can have me as long as you want. I'm yours for the taking, as they say," I told him though I completely put my foot in my mouth with the very next thing falling out of it. "To be honest I don't know why you'd want me. It still doesn't make any sense to me whatsoever."

My man wasn't one to take my self-berating attitude lying down. "Elliot Donahey, I've wanted you even before I knew what it meant. Now I have you I won't ever let you go."

He said this as his gaze burrowed deeply into my own, his lips speaking softly against mine, sending little tremors of passion across my skin. I shivered in his arms which only drove him to become more possessive, more protective of me. I never thought I'd willingly let go and trust someone else so completely. Dreamed about it, sure. Thought could it remotely happen? Not a chance in hell, though it seemed Lucifer had answered my secret desire of all desires by sending Marco my way. Not that I believed for one second in all the religious mumbo-jumbo. But there was a certain poetic license in how I thought about why he came to me—mythic and monumental as his love was to me. Make no mistake, Marco was legendary to me. A god. A man whose love I would worship and submit to whenever he asked, wherever he desired. I was completely his.

As clichéd as it may sound, shortly after we got together, he confessed he knew I was *the one*. He said he would definitely marry his high school sweetheart—it was just in the cards for us. Not a question of it happening—only when. Even though I'd secretly allowed myself to ponder the idea, I never in a million years thought it'd come up so soon.

Marriage.

The word carried a lot of weight. In California, I knew it was a very real possibility for us. It was then I realized how long term he thought about us. He told me he wanted the whole thing: a big house filled with kids. He observed me with an analytic eye as he spoke. His gaze tore through me, laying me bare while I pondered what he said.

Kids, obviously, were a major point with him. To be honest, I'd never given it a single thought. It wasn't as if I didn't like kids. They were fine enough. I played with my little cousins and such at family events. But hell, I never spared a thought of ever having my own. It never seemed to be in the cards for a gay guy like me. Or so I thought, anyway. I guess along with some other misconceptions, perhaps I had that one wrong as well.

He told me with the way technology was now, we could both be donors with an anonymous egg donor and the kids would really be ours, of our blood. He'd researched it; said it's what Neil Patrick Harris and David Burtka had done. He said it's when he realized his feelings for me wouldn't deny him anything in life. He could have it all with me. There was a long, tension-filled pause while I contemplated what he said. I knew he was watching. It was most definitely a make-or-break moment.

As I thought about it, I tried to imagine him and me years from now. The big house he wanted—*a cleaning nightmare*, I thought, and immediately made a mental note. A maid or two better come with the enormous house we were going to share because I could barely keep my room clean. But it was then I realized what he undoubtedly saw in us: an older version of ourselves in bed on a crisp sunny morning. A child or two running in and crawling up on the bed, toys in hand, squealing with the delight of a new day. I found myself warming to the idea. I actually liked knowing he and I would make decisions to help these children prosper and grow.

I told him, much to his relief, I could definitely sign up for it. In a wave he came at me—hugging and kissing me relentlessly for nearly an hour after. I knew I had the power to make him deliriously happy. I would dedicate my life to doing just that, no matter the cost to myself. He became my everything. No price was too high to see his eyes light up and the smile illuminate his brilliant good looks. God was he ever good-looking. And wonder of all wonders, he said he was mine.

There was something else I'd come to understand about his being such a fixture in my world. Marco calmed me. He soothed me in ways I wasn't even aware I was being so random or spinning out on my own shit. When we locked gazes, I immediately became still. Green to blue. Weighted, all-encompassing, and immersive. I marveled at the power his simply being in my life had over me. I found myself clinging to him because of it. He was my rock. My guardian angel. My verdant light.

We'd spend many a day lying safe in each other's arms, our fingers playing against one another—twining in and out as we both silently watched them. He told me he wanted me in every way imaginable. He said I had him spellbound in everything I did—in the way I moved, the way I thought about things, the touch of my ridiculously slender soft fingers upon his heated skin. Yeah, I was there with him on that one. I fucking loved running my fingers all over him, especially his chest and abs. He even said he liked the fact I would break into song when we rode in the car. It made his heart soar—he said he never tired of it, suspected he never would.

Of course, I suppose the fact that, despite his many talents, Marco couldn't carry a tune if you put it in a bucket probably had something to do with it. Okay, maybe it was a bit of an exaggeration. It's not like Marco didn't like to sing or was particularly bad at it. Actually, he *could* be quite good; he just never had the time to concentrate on it, especially now I was in the picture and could serenade him so beautifully—or so he said. He told me he marveled at how those things came so easily to me—the creativity, the way he said I shone when I felt safe enough to let it show. I was always safe with him. I never had to fear because my angel, my rock, was there no matter where I went.

He followed me around like a lovable puppy, as if I were air itself to him. It was sort of cool and a little bit frightening—mostly because I didn't know what I'd done to warrant it.

One afternoon, near the end of the first week we met in July, I had to make a day trip to Carmel with my mom to buy some things for me to wear. A girlfriend of hers was getting married. So, she got my Aunt Marsha, who was married to her winner of a brother—the town's deputy, Nate Campbell—to cover the store for us. She was adamant despite my reminding her about our money situation—or lack thereof—I should have something nice for the event.

Marco tagged along from a distance the whole day, acting like he was shopping in the same stores. I could tell he was amused. We both were. A knowing smirk plastered on our faces even though we were several feet apart, eyes darting to the other when we thought we could get away with it. One of the best afternoons on record for me. When I went back into the dressing room to try things on, he was there to give me his opinion. We managed this only because I told my mom I wasn't ten any longer and I could decide for myself if something was right for me or not.

The funny thing about our little trip was it was my *boyfriend* (I was still getting used to referring to him as my boyfriend) who chose what I ended up wearing. I thought he was shopping for himself. Silly me. He pulled a complete outfit from the racks and brought it with him as he followed me into the dressing rooms. You can imagine my mom's surprise when I walked out with what he'd picked out for me. I had to say, it wasn't what I would have chosen for myself, but I looked pretty damned good in it. My baby knew what was best for me. It was a turning point in our relationship. My trust in him and what he thought was best for me, for us, had begun to be absolute.

NOT LONG AFTER our shopping trip I brought him home one night. My mom was watching the store, so we were alone, and I gave him the grand tour of my bedroom, such as it was. He was practically giddy to behold the inner sanctum of my world. He blushed as much as I did while I revealed my little domain. I blushed with how he could sense my embarrassment at my small room and the few things I could show him. It was awkward because I knew he wanted to say something to ease how uncomfortable he thought I was. I suppose he wanted to set straight whatever misconceptions I may have of his world. I was sure his room was grand by comparison, but I could tell the preconceived idea of who I thought Marco was had very little to do with the man I'd come to know. I once thought he was a product of his parents' obsession with presentation, a cardboard cutout of a beautiful looking guy—two-dimensional at best. I never realized how much I had short-changed him. My Marco was considerate, caring but very low key when we were alone. He could just look at me and I'd melt, a big puddle of emotional paint he could dip his fingers into and sweep into his deepest desires. No words need be spoken. He was the greatest gift he could ever give me. I really required nothing else.

Before I got going too much on bringing out every little thing I thought would interest him, he said he wanted to show me something. He said it was important. I knew I looked amused by his being so cryptic; he had a shy smile across his face paired with such an intensity in his eyes beckoning my interest to be easily piqued. I mean, what could he possibly show me near my house I didn't already know about?

He took my hand and tugged me along.

"Um, how do we get out back?"

His eye roved over to the kitchen where I could tell he knew there was a door leading to the backyard. I quirked a brow. He had already sorted it out but for some reason he was being coy, wanting me to take the lead. I didn't understand the need for it, but it looked so damned cute on him—this shy and nervous boy. I mean, he already looked like a man, but in this particular moment I could see the little boy in him, quietly seeking my approval. I indicated the way with a wave of my hand. Smiling shyly, he walked us over to the door, opened it, and we went out into the yard.

We stood there for a few minutes in the gloaming, a magical time when the light made everything seem enchanted. It was all softer, more romantic at this time. Out of all the hours in the day, I loved this the most, the point where the sun just dipped beyond the horizon.

Magic time...

On him it was nothing short of breathtakingly beautiful. Dusk made love to my boyfriend in ways I could scarce imagine; he practically glowed in the waning light. A Maxfield Parrish kind of glow. Heroic, titanic in its godlike etherealness. There were no other words to describe him: he was transcendently beautiful. But it seemed his words were not about him just now. This was about me. About *us*.

"This is where I fell in love," was all he said as we faced my backyard and the rising hillside covered in oaks and conifers lying just beyond.

"What? Sweetheart, I don't understand."

He smirked a crooked grin at something he found infinitely amusing. His eyes darted to my own in a flash of deep green and amber before finding the safety of the ground once more.

"Well, not here, silly. But up there a ways, just beyond." He tossed a hand without really looking, indicating somewhere along the hillside, but kept his gaze pointed at the ground and kicked at a small rock with the right toe of his trainers. He shrugged in an *aw, gosh* sort of way. When I didn't have anything to say in response, confusion no doubt plain upon my face, he sighed, resigned he had to explain further; he held out his hand to me and said, "C'mon, I'll show you."

He tugged me along and we began to scale the hillside. It was a little risky what with the dew of evening starting to settle in and the leaves carpeting the forest floor from the previous fall. The night's chorus of bugs, bats, and an owl or two began their evening tune-up. There was some small part of me overjoyed with being on this hillside, holding his hand and disappearing further into nature with him. I slipped a couple of times and he was always there to catch me. After the second time, I felt his grip, strong and firm about me. I knew it would always be this way. If I ever faltered, he'd be there.

I looked to the trees; though late in the season they seemed ready to shake off the vestiges of summer already. As I took in the surrounding landscape, I was really confused where this was all leading. Marco glanced back as he helped me scale another slippery part of the slope and realized he better say something to alleviate the confusion I still wore.

"You kidded me about stalking. But I guess you could definitely make an argument for it after I show you this."

He took me to a small stump of a tree that had long ago been cut down. I recalled my dad had chopped it down for firewood back when we were being a bit frugal with money but needed to keep the house warm on those cold wintry Mercy nights. We came to a stop at the stump when he pulled me around so we could see my house in the distance below.

"Here's where it all happened," he simply said.

"What?" I looked around, unsure of how those words could have any real meaning here.

He waited patiently while my eyes drifted from the stump down to my house, connecting the imaginary dots from where we were to my bedroom window.

"You spied on me from here?" I huffed in complete surprise. It was a good surprise. His eyes were guarded, unsure of how I was going to react. "But, *why*, sweetheart?"

With his eyes cast down to the ground in front of him he shrugged. He was very quiet now. Reserved. Pensively so. When he spoke, his voice was hoarse with emotion as he whispered to me. It was so soft, pillows of dark, punctuated tones on the air, I had to lean into him to hear.

"It was the only way I could be close to you. At least, back then, you see. You didn't make it very easy, you know." He was kicking the stump with his trainers, like a small boy embarrassed by something he'd done he didn't think I would approve of. I noticed the area he was kicking. There were tiny notches etched into the backside of the stump along the bark. There had to be several hundred of them along it. Some were so old that moss had begun to fill them in. I knelt down and ran a finger along the mossier etchings.

"Sweetheart, are these what I think they are?"

He shrugged and sort of nodded very rapidly, fearful of what he was admitting he'd done, still so unsure of what I thought. The anxiety colored his face, speaking volumes about his worries over what I'd do. I stood back up, brought him into my arms, and I kissed him fiercely—with more passion for him than I'd ever expressed. I poured everything I thought I had into our kiss. As the kiss deepened, his face became wet with tears. So did mine. After quite a few minutes of my eating his face (it wasn't a stretch, either—I practically devoured him), he giggled softly as I let my passion loose on him. We finally broke, panting heavily, our breaths lingering in the night air. He waited until he caught his breath before continuing—ever so quietly. This was his heart, completely vulnerable, open, wanting desperately to be fearless. But it was me. The one person he was so afraid would cut him deeply. His next words only confirmed what I thought.

"I was so afraid to show you this, but it's important. *This* is why I say our love has weight. This is *how* it has history. I was fearful of what you'd think of me, but I was caught, you see. You already had me. One step behind, one heartbeat away. I know how corny that sounds, but I can't help how I feel. I spent many an afternoon and, on some occasions, nights out here, watching for a glimpse of you. Anything you'd give me. I know it was foolish. I know it sounds so whacked. But it was all I had. I wanted you so much, Els. You've no idea how much. But I heard what you thought of the football jocks. I didn't think you'd give me a chance. I was terrified of how it would be. What you'd say."

He ran his right hand along the side of my face, wiping a tear long since fallen. He kissed my nose before bringing me into an embrace, my head into the crook of his neck.

"I was such a coward. I know you think I'm smart, that I'm brave. But I didn't know what else to do. I was petrified of how you'd react. Being here, tucked up on the hillside was safer. It was okay, for me at least. It gave me peace, allowed me to sleep at night, dreaming one day you'd look at me and love me for me. I can't tell you how many tears I've shed just thinking about that day." We separated only a little so I could look at him. Glorious.

He wiped his eyes with his free hand, the other firmly tucked into the front pocket of his jeans. He sniffled a bit before letting out a puff of air. It billowed softly from his lips. He tried to crack a smile through tears threatening to spill over at any moment, his eyes finding a way to glisten in the waning light. He was so nervous, it pained me to see him like this. His breath caught in a light mist as it left his mouth. The cold was settling in now. He smiled, his eyes so radiant, a light from within. But it was clear to me he was still very afraid of what I'd say about all of this.

"Say something, please. I know it's..."

I never let him finish. I pushed us both to the ground, with my body collapsing on top of his, not caring about the mess we'd get ourselves in. I kissed him over and over—punctuating each kiss with whatever random feeling made itself known to me.

"Thank you, Marco. Thank you, sweetheart. I just never thought...more than I'd ever hoped for..."

We rolled in the leaves as I took his mouth with a ferocity I'd never had the courage to do before. But really, what was that compared to what he'd just shared with me? It was nothing. Not even a small flickering candle to the torrential fire and light he brought to me. I finally relented in my mouth's onslaught upon his, leaving soft chaste kisses in its wake—a tangle of limbs and leaves, of kisses and unspoken dreams. He was so, so incandescent in the gloaming and receding light. A radiating warmth coursed through me as he gazed upon me, basking in embers of everything him. Bracing himself above me in the looming twilight, framed by the burnished orange and pinks as they receded into blue, haloing him in the cloak of night. *Magical.*

"Then, uh, you're okay with this?" He looked down at me with such wonder and amazement at how I'd taken all of it in. My verdant light. My angel.

I told him of course I was as I moved to get up, pulling him along with me. I dusted him off as we went down the hillside to the warmth of the house below. He still had a few leaves in his hair, but it sort of looked sexy on him, like some powerful satyr who fell in love with a boy. We gradually made our way back into my room, stopping every few steps to kiss again.

I knew he was trying to be gracious about my little world; he just couldn't find any words to soothe what he thought was my unease with it. I didn't know what the fuss was about, I was okay with it. I made peace long ago we weren't rich. We weren't poor either. I'd go so far as to say we were downright average. I was good with average, though it did give me pause for thought if he ever took me home to meet his parents. With the talk of marriage and kids, I knew the possibility was nearly a surety. I prayed I could pull it off without embarrassing him or myself in the process.

I know the revelation of my small world only drove Marco to be more protective of me—as if it were remotely possible. It was not a complaint, mind you. I was good with whatever Marco thought best. Luckily, I was nimble enough to change direction—choosing to let Marco view what few ever had. In fact, it was the only thing I had any abundance of—my drawings. Marco found out about my secret wish to be a comic book artist. I couldn't believe myself when I told Marco I'd been developing a character of my own but it wasn't ready to show him yet. I didn't say it was based on him, even though it was, but I had mixed feelings about what he'd think about it. I meant it as a tribute of how much good I saw in him, but he could take it the wrong way and be very upset. But I really wanted to know what he thought.

In the end, though, I chickened out. I told Marco there was a real reason why his opinion on the matter was really important to me. Marco pressed to see the early sketches but I was adamant—he'd have to wait until it was ready. But I promised I'd share it with him soon. Marco was so touched by the gesture. He said that I would even consider his opinion on my artwork warmed his soul. Within seconds the drawing portfolio was on the floor and he had us both stripped, with some of our clothing in tatters on the floor, and we made out on my bed for the better part of two hours. We both came multiple times—we were teenage boys, producing cum was not an issue. It's one of the things teenage boys do best.

I confessed to Marco I'd wanted to do it since we started going out. Now I could say our relationship was solid—my bed had been christened. Jerk-off fantasies had a whole new meaning for me and my bed. I could trust it was real for me. I don't know why I can be so slow on the draw, as they say. Before he left, we made out one more time very leisurely. Marco eyed me carefully, absorbing every subtle nuance of how I responded as I writhed in pleasure to his ministrations of my body. It was as if he burnished every whimper, every line and curve of my face, those icy steel blue eyes (as he called them) watching him with such love as he ravished me. Kitschy, I know. But that was my man. Not the greatest poet with words, but what he lacked in poetic license, he more than made up for with his more amorous inclinations. I was the man of words; he of love and passion. I thought it was a good match—even if I found at times hard to trust in it completely. I wanted to, I did. He never gave me a reason to think it wasn't true. One thing I was certain of, this was a man I could love all of my life. I didn't know why it worked for us; in truth I didn't care. He said my touch crackled along his skin like nothing else did. Electric.

When we had to be apart Marco said he ached for anything he could take away from me, anything he could cling to, just to know it was real, promising I loved him back. Thus began the odd tradition of my giving him something from my room. The first night it was a pencil. I know, romantic, huh? Okay, it was one of my art pencils. He said he would put it in a very special place in his room. It was enormously silly, but I loved him for it. Every time he secretly came over, he'd leave with something from my room. One night, it was a wayward sock of mine. I wasn't even sure if it was washed—he said he was cool with it. I thought, *uh, eeew*. But then I realized I'd so be the same way with him. I'd probably be one hell of a sniff freak with his laundry. So yeah, he got the sock. Gay or not, we're boys, it's what we do.

Chapter Three

Shadowboxing and Champagne

OVER THE NEXT couple of weeks of summer, our love was a blissful whirlwind of peaks and valleys. Our relationship was like one big roller coaster ride neither of us wanted to stop. It was exciting, thrilling, and at times we marveled at the quietude that would suddenly and unexpectedly consume us. Eyes meeting eyes, followed by mouths and tongues as our bodies learned how to mold ourselves into each other. Those were the peaks.

The valleys threatening to undo me shook me to my core.

Work became a distraction, leaving me very frustrated. The blow was lessened only when Marco would show up like the great big gift he was and hang out in the kitchen area while I waited out the one or two customers who lost their way to our store. He never complained about my summer schedule. He hadn't lied when he said he just wanted to be near me. Once he told me every time he left me he had to fight with his desire to run back to me because he just couldn't stand to be apart from me. I blushed so hard at his words. I couldn't fathom why he felt the way he did. I told him as much, to which he simply said it wasn't for me to understand. It just was, and I better get used to it 'cause he wasn't going anywhere.

I said something about moth to a flame, you know, that old adage or proverb or whatever. And he said he'd rather risk being burned alive by me, thankful for whatever few moments I would give him, and if his life were to end (my heart lurched at the very thought of his being taken away from me—even in jest) he would die a very happy man that I had given him anything. He cherished every moment I could spare. I found I wanted to keep precious little to myself. I'd gladly give him every moment of my life if it would please him.

He said it would.

Given the small town with its roving and prying eyes (his words, not mine, though I knew them to be true), we were very careful to plan our getaways with minimal detection. Was it a pain? Sort of. But I didn't focus too much on it. I guess I was just soaring so high the man in my arms, the one who searched my soul for confirmation proclaiming we were one, had my focus all wrapped up in him—I didn't necessarily spare a thought for how or why we were doing the things we were doing.

It just was, and it was glorious.

He spent a fair amount of money on me—for which I felt enormously guilty. I mean, I knew his family was rich. After all, his dad was the local doctor in town with a thriving practice—hell, my family even went to his father. He said the money didn't matter to him. I guess it didn't if you had it in abundance. When he noticed how much it bothered me, he relented and allowed me to pay for some things for us. Though I spied him once or twice slipping some bills into my wallet to replace what I'd spent. I could have made a big deal about it, but I knew it was coming from his heart. He just wanted to make life easier for me. For us. It bothered me, but I understood why he did what he did. I think he knew I knew. We just never talked about it. We didn't need to.

After a while, I purposefully would leave my wallet around where he could get to it. Not because I wanted a sugar daddy or anything like that, but because it *mattered to him*. Hell, I didn't care if he *took* my money. I just wanted to do whatever made him happy. His providing for me in whatever way he could think of made him deliriously happy. So, I made sure I was never the one to stop him.

As for our getaways, we were all over the map. Well, any place other than the small confines of Mercy. He entertained me just driving to Carmel, Monterey or Santa Cruz—far enough away so we were reasonably safe from the intrusive world we called home.

While money wasn't the issue for us—he constantly kept telling me not to worry about it, to just enjoy myself— it was awkward at times, though I endured it because it was my guy. He'd never intentionally hurt me or cause me pain or grief. I knew that. He had my back. He was my rock. All we wanted was away time. Together time.

I'd say I was in a whirlwind romance but, in all honesty, I didn't have anything to compare it to—other than the fact it was all happening so fast. Even the slow moments, those moments when there was very little separating us, his face millimeters from my own, his breath caressing my skin, seemed to flit by far quicker than we'd like.

That was always the feeling we shared. No matter how long we were together, it just wasn't enough. It never was. The ache for him would begin the moment our bodies parted when we'd say our goodbyes for the night. I wouldn't even make it to the door before he'd be calling my cell phone so he could talk to me on the drive home. It was invariably followed by talking as we prepared for bed and then at least an hour or two until we became too drowsy with sleep to go on. We talked about everything. The topics I'd prattle on about were so random he never had to struggle to come up with a subject. He said he liked the surprises I'd bring him when we talked. It made me blush every time he commented on something he liked about me. He was my constant companion.

His was the first voice in my morning, and the last at night.

Oh, baby. Was I ever in *luurrve*.

But it's what terrified me the most. The absolute horror to think it could all be taken away. I was metaphorically holding onto "us" with a white-knuckled death grip. I often found myself desperate with worry, just thinking about losing him. I tried to never let it show. I'd like to think I was successful, but of course, I never really knew if he sensed it. He never said he did. Maybe he didn't. Maybe.

I knew my fears were completely unfounded. He'd never given me any reason to worry about us. If I went by what he said and did, it was real. And it was forever. I held onto his confidence in the power of us. I needed it, I needed him. I was my own worst enemy. I knew it—didn't mean I could do much about it, try as I might. I wasn't stupid, though, because I realized I needed to check the doubting bastard inside me and beat him back into the darkest depths of my psyche if I had any hope of keeping Marco in my life. No one, no matter how much they said they loved you, would want to deal with a basket case. It would wear them down. Then I really couldn't blame him for ditching me if I went jack-shit crazy. My own fears would drive him away, into someone else's arms. I couldn't let that happen, but I could definitely see how it could all get away from me.

But like I said, he never gave me any reason to doubt him. He was a rock when it came to us. For him, we simply were. For him, there would always be an "us." And I have to admit, at times I could see it. The way we could just look at each other and say absolutely nothing. We didn't need to. He completed me in ways I never even anticipated I needed. I'd thought, off-handedly in the heat of our first meeting, he was fucking brilliant. I found out over the next couple of weeks how prophetic the statement truly was. He was smart, no dumb jock for sure. But he was brilliant because he was so perceptive. I guess it had to do with his football training. He hinted as much. He knew what I wanted before I could put a word to it. He just knew. How? I had absolutely no idea. But it was automatic between us. He reached and I was there. I'd want and he was there, every time, without question, without fail. He knew what to do to make me feel like the center of the universe.

We had sex.

Many times.

I can't put too grand an emphasis on this aspect of our relationship. We were teenage boys who didn't have to worry about pregnancies or the like. So, we made out whenever the moment made itself available to us—and we made sure we had plenty of opportunities to make love. His having a car and money didn't hurt either. You'd think the familiarity of doing it as often as we did would've lessened the need over time. Nothing could be further from the truth. Every time he took me in his arms, he filled me in ways I never dreamed were possible—not just with the prodigious gifts his anatomy afforded him, but with the enormity with which he relished everything about me. His love was monumental, awe inspiring. So much so that when he left, I physically ached from the loss. I don't know why he craved me, but I completely understood why I craved him, nearly pined for him when we were apart.

But then again, being horny all the time wasn't difficult. We were at the age where contemplating bathroom tiling made us hard. Marco was a voraciously demanding lover. Funny thing was, I discovered I desired his voracity, and he made sure I never wanted when it came to making love. But so far it had been a lot of rubbing, sucking, jerking—and okay, I know how it sounds. Like we didn't really know what we were doing, right? Well, we were still trying to figure things out between us. I mean we knew what two guys could do. There is the internet for Chrissake—it wasn't like we hadn't sorted out what could go where.

But he was such a thoughtful man about it. He had needs but he was so contemplative about when our first time was going to happen, our first time when we'd actually do *it*, where I would truly give myself to him. He was so loving and careful when he could have easily thrown me in the back seat of his classic Impala and boned me to his heart's content. Truth be known, I probably would have been okay with it. I just wanted him. I would do anything he asked, no matter the pain it might cause me. You can imagine my surprise when what he asked of me was patience. What he asked of me was to love and trust him.

And so, I did.

But that's not to say he didn't know how to woo. He definitely knew how to lay it on, and lay it on thick, at that. When my eighteenth rolled around the second day of August, he prepared a romantic picnic dinner and drove us out to a secluded area in Big Sur where his family had a cabin. We ate dinner along the wiry cypresses jutting out dramatically from the cliffs. Could we have stayed closer to town? Sure, but he didn't want to spend such an important day in my life (no matter how much I told him it was no "big deal") by simply hanging out closer to town. He was such a romantic at heart. Who knew? I even got flowers as part of the deal.

He shook his head in complete disbelief in how easily I was writing the whole thing off. He explained as we shared strawberries with Champagne he snuck out of his home, letting me know in his book of all things me, my eighteenth was a fucking national holiday. *Banks should fucking close, for Chrissake*—or so he claimed. Then, wonder of all wonders, he did something which completely turned my world upside down. Literally. My stomach flipped; my heart raced and then stopped abruptly. I thought I was going to vomit. *Now ain't that a pretty picture?* Now you can see how I might have reason to worry in driving him away.

It was such a simple act, really. He'd obviously put a great deal of thought behind it. I pondered afterwards how much he rehearsed it so it would go so smoothly. As with all things in his life, he did it with such grace. But lord, did he make my heart stop when it happened.

We were laughing after he said something funny and I snorted on a piece of strawberry and the Champagne ended up bubbling out of my nose. Embarrassed, I put a hand up to my face to wipe myself. In the middle of our laughter—through tears I might add, which is the best kind of laughter—he simply took my hand. I blinked or something, not really thinking anything of his taking my hand in his. We did it so often it was natural.

That's when he brought my world to a complete standstill.

I swear the air became thick, viscous, even. The wildlife paused—I thought even the waves stopped beating upon the shore. The silence of the moment had weight. At first, I didn't know what that strange feeling was: a simple circle of metal, cold, weighted on my finger. A ring.

He gave me a ring. A band of silver-looking metal (which I found out later to be platinum—nothing but the best from my guy) comprised of intertwined vines culminating in an inflamed heart made of garnet. It was slightly Goth-looking, sexy, and in no way a chick ring even though it kind of sounded like one when you tried to describe it. Something a rock star would wear.

Okay, I cried.

Like a fucking Tesla going from zero to sixty, I went from laughter to downright heart-wrenching tears in less than five seconds. You would have thought he actually proposed. I guess, in a way, he had, which is what touched me so. I don't know why it completely undid me, but it did. He pulled me to him, smothered me with kisses and soft murmurs of how much he loved me. His eyes were glistening; he was full of love. I could see it. I didn't understand it. How could someone as amazing and as confident in life even notice me, much less than give me a ring declaring to me I was his and he was mine?

And you'd think he'd be golden, right? That it was enough. I mean, flowers, a dinner, a muthafucking ring for Chrissake! But it wasn't the best part of my eighteenth birthday. That distinction went to when he took me in the bedroom of the family cabin and made slow, arduous, and soul-wrenching love to me. He possessed every inch of me—made love to the man he said he wanted for the better part of two long years. *Muthafuckin' me! Elliot Donahey has snagged himself a man! Whoo-doggie, the girls back at the office are so gonna hear about this!* 'Cept of course, there were no girls. Nor did I work in an office. But those are pesky details. It didn't take away from the moment. Not in the least.

I already surmised Marco was a man full of surprises. He was thoughtful, gentle, and very passionate. But the most surprising thing about him was his patience. I was a jumble of nerves and conflicting emotions. Not about him. I knew I loved him. I was overwrought inside, concerned if I would make the grade, be an adequate lover the way he would wish me to be. Turns out, I needn't have worried.

He was so sweet-tempered, taking his time to undress me slowly, gently batting my hands away anytime I tried to help him. With a lone small table lamp on the nightstand next to the bed, our bodies shadowboxed on the wall behind us. In our silhouette I became ultra-aware of how inadequate my body was in comparison to his. I tried to hide it, painfully aware of how glorious he was, and how not I was.

He smiled and said I was perfect for him in every way. He reminded me gently of how long he'd observed me, how his desire to have me for himself had built over the past two years. Then he said the most amazing thing to me: he told me he hoped he would be everything I wanted in a lover. What I thought mattered to him so much he was a bit nervous. He hoped it would be good for me. His hands were trembling and there was a slight quiver to his voice. My heart melted for him.

I heard the words; I knew what they meant. But for the life of me I couldn't make them make sense. He was becoming pensive, being so vulnerable with me about his insecurities. There was no way I was going to let him think he would ever be inadequate.

I pulled him to me and we fell onto the bed with a ferocity I didn't know I had. We tangled; we writhed, our bodies becoming slick with the passion we felt for each other. And it mattered to me he was just as unsure as I was. Marco, my confident, sexy-as-hell boyfriend, was vulnerable with me. He allowed me to see the fear in him. And it mattered. It mattered in ways I couldn't even fathom in our moment of passion. I would ponder this from time to time thereafter. Truly astonished someone like Marco, who seemed so sure of himself and his place in the world, was worried about what I thought of him, of whether he'd measure up to what I wanted. If anything, it made my heart flutter thinking about it, the way sentiment from him did. But after his admission, I could see it in his eyes. Tucked there, in the furthest reaches, along with his abiding love for me was the fear he'd fail me. Absurd. Completely absurd to think he could ever fail me.

His kisses brought me back to the moment.

He whispered he loved me, every inch of me, proving he did by covering every inch of me in soft kisses. I tried to return each of his ministrations, but he wouldn't have it. He said it was my night. He wanted to spend the night making love to me, pleasuring me, letting me take from him what I wanted.

And make no mistake, I *wanted* him.

When the moment arrived, he looked into my eyes, and he spoke of our love again, and how he knew how much trust I was putting in him. I had reason to be concerned—he was no shrinking violet. Italian Stallion didn't begin to cover it. But there was no way I was not going to do this. With an ample gob of lube, he worked his fingers into my ass to get me used to it. I knew he didn't have to; after all, he was a hormone raging teenage boy— as was I. He could have just plowed me for all I was worth. But he didn't. That's not my Marco.

After a few minutes of his fingering me because we'd watched it on a porno once (exchanging charged looks between us as we did so), I told him I thought I was ready. He leaned down and we kissed very tenderly. He asked me again if I was sure. He wanted me to have a way out if I was worried. *No way.* I was in all the way. I wanted him to take me, no matter the pain, no matter the cost. He slicked up his sizable condom-sheathed cock, my eyes wide at how much of him there was. I wasn't sure how all of him was going to fit in so little of me. But I'd remembered the porn videos where twinkish guys like me were able to take some massively hung men—so in theory it was possible. A part of me was inflamed with the possibility, but the more reasonable part, the part speaking fairly loud at this point, wasn't so sure.

He paused, unsure if we should do this. No going back. I reached down between my legs and gripped his slicked-up monster cock and pulled him to me, letting him know we'd passed the point of no return, the moment we became a couple. I wanted him to know I was good with it. I wanted it. I wanted him.

I don't know if he thought it would be sexy or if he was trying to distract me from his impressive cock, but when he pressed into me, kissing me while he was shaking it a bit with his hand as if it would get me to loosen up further, precious little would have distracted me from what I was feeling. There was no denying it. It hurt, far more than I was prepared.

With my sharp intake of breath and a deep moan, he stopped, his eyes soft with fear, saying over and over how sorry he was, and we should stop. When he began to withdraw, something within me clicked. I didn't want him to stop. I hooked my feet around his back and drew him forward. I was already committed to being there for him. I would endure anything for him—even if it meant enduring the pain as if he were cleaving me in two. I was determined my body should learn of his passions and not only accommodate them but become adept at pleasuring him. I never wanted to become so good at something as I did in that moment.

I once read somewhere online Linda Lovelace had commented fucking John Holmes was like squatting on a telephone pole. Sister Linda was preaching to the choir here. But he meant everything to me, so I begged him to continue, biting my lip as he pulled me to him. His next few thrusts into me burned, and I hissed—part in pain and part in a blossoming raw erotic pleasure. Then before I realized it, his fucking me caught fire, ignited an inferno of desire, and then I couldn't get enough of him. My legs had moved from being at his side to finding their way onto his shoulders as he brought our bodies together in a thunderous clap of sweat, flesh, and passion. My toes curled from the largeness of him moving deep within me. I moaned—loudly. I tried to keep from calling out his name, afraid he would think he was hurting me. And he was hurting me. Each time he withdrew, it hurt—aching he wasn't there anymore, and I needed him to be there.

He chuckled softly at my pleading for more. He picked up the pace—only because I told him I wanted it to be rougher. Before long I was demanding he give me his all. And he did. He poured every ounce of his body strength into fucking me, and I met every thrust, hoisting my hips to meet his with a resounding clap of flesh. Panting with exertion, he asked me if I was sure I hadn't ever done this before. For his cheekiness I clenched my ass tightly around his cock, causing both of our eyes to bulge at the sensation. Hands down, that became our new favorite thing. He began begging me to bear down on him as he fucked. I was a quick learner. I could tell he was pleased.

"So good, baby. You're so fucking beautiful. I just want to make love to you. It's all I want to do," he murmured as we kissed between his impassioned words. I nodded. I was beyond words to tell him what I was feeling for him. I hoped like hell he recognized it in my eyes.

Without much in the way of warning he leaned forward and bit down on the tendon from my neck to my right shoulder as he continued to take me. His teeth gripped that taut piece of flesh, rasping his tongue against it—the pull upon my skin burned while he fucked me with reckless abandon. I was in heaven. I was shuddering with how deeply he burnished his way into me. I was on fire. I didn't want him to stop; I wanted his burn to consume me. I would always want him this way. There was no going back. He sucked very hard upon my tendon. I knew he was leaving a mark. Marking me—making me his own. I'd wear it proudly. I was putting the world on notice: *I was Marco Sforza's*. It put an extra spark in our fucking, making me abandon any pretense of being quiet. I'd become a dirty little bad boy and I begged him to keep fucking me.

Surprisingly enough, he came after only a few seconds of my dirty talk. Leaning forward so our foreheads touched, he giggled and told me I got him so hot when I said those dirty things to him. I felt sort of cheesy saying them, like I was some sexy porn star, but fuck, he was doing me good and it seemed to spill out without much thought on my part. I told him if he fucked me like that, I'd always remember to do it for him. He smiled as we kissed. His erection waned a bit, though he never really slipped from me, but as the kiss blossomed in the afterglow, his cock stirred to life and we went for another round right on the spot, laughing as we did so. Ever laugh while you fuck? I can tell you now, I highly recommend it.

Hours later on the drive home I told him I'd never felt anything so moving. True enough, my ass ached—not from pain but rather from his absence. I wanted him to fuck me again, stopping short of begging him to pull over to the side of the road so he could. I was so hot for it. He smirked in his uniquely sexy way because he appeared slightly embarrassed I made it sound like a dirty little porno scene we'd once watched. Then I confessed to what I was really feeling inside. It had moved me—when we made love it was like he'd kissed my soul. And I told him I wasn't fucking around—I meant every word I said. I could tell Marco wanted to smirk, but one sideward glance my way and he could see my eyes moist with heartfelt emotion. I couldn't help it. I had a glistening ring on my hand, I'd made love (more than once, I might add), and I was madly in love with the star quarterback of Mercy High. It just didn't get any better. I knew this moment was golden. I was trying like hell to commit every single second of it to memory, trying desperately not to forget a single breathtaking moment.

I told him it was hands down the best damned birthday I'd ever had. Then I ended up breaking the awkward spell with a nervous laugh. He eventually joined in, but I think in the deepest part of his heart he was truly touched. It seemed that way when I spied him from the corner of my eye as he drove. We held hands in the car on the way home. He radiated warmth from his large rough hands. Mine were frigid. Holding his leeched away the cold, made me feel whole again.

Glancing at our joined hands, he told me he'd come up with a secret sort of way for him to let me know he wanted to make love to me. He said if he rubbed his thumb along my palm the amount of pressure he applied was like a scale. The harder he rubbed, the more intense was his desire to fuck me. I flushed from head to toe, then rolled my eyes if only to hide how much I loved the idea he could convey with touch how much he wanted me. So, what I told him was I thought it was the sexiest thing he could say to me. We laughed softly—letting ourselves enjoy how sexual we could be with each other, how safe it was to be with each other. The time we made love back at the cabin he swore to me it was something he'd never forget. As he said this, he was rubbing my palm so hard I think he bruised my hand.

We fucked again in the back seat of the car, nestled between some trees, about a block from my house. He soothed the ache away—filling me with everything he had to give.

Chapter Four

The Elephant at the Aquarium

BY MID-AUGUST I had the ring, the wildly hot sex, the ever-attentive hot quarterback boyfriend (even if I couldn't talk to anyone about it), so I had finally accepted none of our dating was a setup and allowed myself to relax and fall wholeheartedly in love.

For Marco, it had been love for some time now. He focused on trying to get me to see it for what it really was. And there was no mistaking it: he did love me with every fiber of his being. I felt it. It was raw; it was powerful. It was all-consuming. But no matter where we went, however far we ventured from the small town with prying eyes and ears, we seemed to tow a big elephant along with us.

Neither of us wanted to address it. But our reticence to talk about what it symbolized—how we didn't want to face the start of the school year having the potential to change everything in our new and fragile little world—loomed large. Ignoring our damned elephant only seemed to swell it to the point where it was beginning to make his '67 black Impala seem rather cramped.

On one of our day trips, which we had to work in between his football practices which had already started up, we visited the Monterey Bay Aquarium. Standing in front of the large jelly exhibit, I couldn't bear to tow the elephant along for the ride any longer. I knew we were both dancing around it but someone needed to break the ice, to call it out.

"So, uh, school's only a week away," I said with my head down looking at my shoes, noting how scuffed up my trainers were. My hands were tucked firmly in my jeans pockets though I really longed to hold his hand as we gazed at the jellyfish bobbing along in the large floor-to-ceiling tank in front of us.

Fearful of his response, I wanted to be one of those jellies. The idea of being cared for and tended to and not have the worry eating away at my gut while I broached the painful subject we'd been avoiding as of late, was like a balm to soothe what ailed.

"Uh-huh," he acknowledged. The sadness eking into his comment made the churning in my stomach much more pointed.

He'd been thinking about it—whether we wanted to talk about it or not. He finally tore his eyes away from the jellies to watch my single visible steel-blue eye gazing intently back at him. He smirked. My lips curved in response. This always happened when my other eye became obscured in what he called my "sexy bangs" constantly falling over my face. I told him once I should probably cut my hair. It nearly started our first real argument. He said in very unequivocal terms I wasn't to change a single thing about me. He loved that my hair kept falling forward. He said it was like a magnet for him. It would draw him closer each time it fell. Even now I could see him resisting the urge to lovingly slip the lock of hair back from my face. I could see his heart swelled every time I focused on him.

There was no mistaking it, he had it real bad. He told me once I controlled his every move without so much as lifting a finger, my pull on him was so strong—like iron filings to a magnet strong. He said the classic song "Magnet and Steel" reminded him of us. He'd often play it in the car. It was a great song, I was cool with it, even if Walter Egan sang about a woman. Marco and I could adapt it—make it our own. It was the first song I taught him to sing with me.

I brought our elephant into the conversation, making it important for him. He could no longer avoid the topic altogether. His brow furrowed as he considered school was most definitely going to be harder this year. But he said he'd figure out something, 'cause "there's simply no way I am ever going to let you slip away from me. No fucking way." I got hard from him whispering his vow to never let me go.

The noise of the Aquarium and all of the people milling about the exhibits brought him back out of his reverie. "Yeah, we're going to have to figure something out, that's for sure. C'mon, let's go get somethin' to eat and talk."

It was a rather late lunch, nearly dinner actually. He made sure I called Mom at the store to tell her I had dinner covered. She made some inquiries on where I was and what I was doing. She seemed surprised I had a friend to pal around with on my days off. I could tell he was a bit perturbed I didn't appear to have anyone else in my life. I told him I did, but he'd better not freak 'cause it turns out I was gay and had an über-hot football-playing boyfriend who was probably wicked jealous so he better watch himself. We laughed. He agreed, with a very pointed look, how he could see why this über-hot boyfriend would be wicked jealous if anyone even remotely *hinted* at getting with me. I nodded I understood what he was saying. We walked for a bit and he said it still bothered him no one else could see what he saw—how no one else was in my life. I told him not to worry about it. I had the only one who mattered to me: him.

We walked from the Aquarium to a nearby restaurant where we grabbed a quick bite of fish and chips to momentarily satisfy our hunger. Bubba Gump, I think it was. I noticed he kept looking around but I couldn't quite make out why. It wasn't like we knew anyone there. I chose to let it go. We ate in peaceful silence—eyes meeting eyes with warm smiles conveying anything we could ever say to each other. After we'd finished, he fired up the Impala while his hand reached for mine. I returned the squeeze while the car rumbled down the street. A smile slinked along my mouth; he caught it out of the corner of his eye. "Carry On Wayward Son" by Kansas was the song on the stereo. Usually I sang along. Not this time. I was too wrapped up in us at the moment to care.

"What do you find so amusing now, Els?"

"This car. It's so you."

"Yeah? You think?" He couldn't help but smile whenever I approved of something in his world.

"Hell yeah, big guy. Classic muscle car. Not to mention the pop-culture tie in. I get it. You're so Dean Winchester."

He smiled broadly. He told me it was his favorite show. I knew it was why he bought the muscle car. The Impala suited him as much as it did Jensen Ackles' character on *Supernatural*. I could see how the demon hunter on the show was a role model for how Marco carried himself in the world. Though I could certainly do without all the blood and guts present in Jensen Ackles' portrayal of Dean Winchester, but I got it. We'd even curled up on my bed one Thursday to watch an episode or two of the reruns on TV. I understood Marco's fascination with fighting evil. He was definitely one of the good guys.

"You really know how to make a guy get all gooey inside, don't cha?" We squeezed hands again. He grazed his thumb lightly but purposefully along my palm. He wanted to fuck.

"Really? Now? How the hell are we gonna manage that? It's still daylight out. I don't fancy getting hauled into the police station for lewd behavior just 'cause I got you all boned up. That would so not help our situation."

"And just what is our *situation*, Donahey?" The caress along my palm was harder now. By now I knew the scale; as the pressure increased so did the desire to fuck me. On the Sforza fuck-o-meter, as I'd come to call it, we were at about a five out of ten. There was still room for a cool down, but I'd have to work fast if I was going to get him back home before we could do it.

"Our *sitch*, Sforza, is I don't know how we're going to carry on being boyfriends while you have the whole star quarterback thing going on at school and I am a virtual nobody, the quintessential persona non grata, if you will. Christ, it makes my head hurt to think about how we're *not* going to manage next year after the summer of love you've had me on."

"The summer of lo...?" His pressure on my hand increased slightly. He knew what I was doing. He knew my little tactic. Definite end-run around what I knew we both wanted; what we both knew would bring the day to closure. There was no way he was going to let me talk him down from what he wanted. He wanted me, plain and simple, legs parted, feet on his shoulders on my back on the back seat of the Impala. He'd always want me and I had begun to lose count of how many times the backseat had served as our little love nest.

"I get what you're doing, Els. It's not going to work. You know I get what I want from you. And you give in. That's how it works, lover boy. And you *like* it."

"Yeah, I know. It's not that I don't want to, sweetheart. It's not. I'll always want to. I'd never deny you. You know that." I looked sheepishly out of the window rather than face the heated lust building like a furnace between us, continuously stoked by the persistent pressure of his thumb across my palm. By the feel of it now, we were definitely approaching seven on our F-O-M scale, *point of no return.*

Hell, I knew I was going to give in. Like it had a mind of its own, my ass was doing the happy dance—already twitching for him in anticipation. Marco chuckled softly. He tugged on my hand to get me to look his way.

"Hey, you trust I'd never willingly put you in harm's way, right? C'mon. I love you, Els. Mind, body, and soul. It's all yours, babe."

Babe.

The solitary golden word I'd been waiting to hear since we started this epic romance. It was the first time he'd used it to define our relationship. Up to this point it had always been "Els." It was his term of endearment of choice. I'd noticed it from day one when Marco seduced me back at the Q so many weeks ago.

Wow, that was *weeks* ago...I silently marveled how the time had flown by. Marco had been there nearly every day, whether at the store or together on some far-off getaway. But now I'd achieved the blessed *babe* status in Marco's life. Surely, it deserved some kind of reward, didn't it? And Marco said he'd never put me in harm's way.

"You called me babe," I murmured softly. Over the rumble of the muscle car's engine I wasn't sure if he'd even heard. He pulled our hands up to his lips and kissed the back of my hand.

"You'll always be my baby. You're it, Els. Ain't nothing gonna keep me from you. We'll figure something out for school. But we'll do it together, so no one gets hurt. I wanna be on the same page with you. 'Kay?"

Ding! Ding! Ding!...And we have a winner! The thumb has reached ten on the scale, ladies and gents! No going back now. I sighed, a dark smirk quirking my lips.

"Well, find some place secluded for Chrissake. If I am gonna drop trou, I'd rather it not be entirely in public."

He smiled, let go of my hand, and gripped the back of my neck to bring my head in for a quick kiss along my temple. "That's my boy. I knew I'd win you over."

"Yeah, then why does it feel like I'm going to the dark side, when you say it like that?"

"Baby, it gets fun when it's dark." He wiggled those beautifully arched brows in his wicked way, sending all my blood rushing to my dick.

I rolled my eyes. "Well it's a good thing I rinsed before we left then."

We'd made out in the back seat of the Impala before. Truth be known, the back seat was just the right width to accommodate my backside with the perfect distance between the back seat and front to allow my feet to rest on the small shelf along the back window and next to the head rest of the driver's side while he fucked the daylights out of me. And let me tell you what, he was one aggressive fuck—leaving no doubt when the Impala was a rockin' in anyone's mind. He poured all his muscled body into fucking me. I liked how we fucked. Whether it was slow and agonizingly gentle or a balls-to-the-wall slam fuckfest, either way I was down with it all. If I had my druthers, though, I liked it when he was a bit on the rougher side—the biting, nipping, and low growls he emitted as he took his pleasure did it for me. Sent me over the fucking moon for him.

There was something to be said for liking the feel of accommodating how powerful his body was when he took me. And surprisingly I found he relished when I released my more aggressive side to meet him halfway. I think he got off on how my thin waifish body absorbed the thundering crack of his lust. There was no doubt our first few love sessions had some pretty pointed moments of pain. Marco had no shortage when it came to producing the beef. He was bona fide stallion material, and I was in horse heaven.

Driven by Marco's lust, we found as secluded a spot along the waterfront as any we'd seen so far. It was late in the afternoon; there weren't any other cars in the parking lot. He said we'd have to be quick about it but with the danger of being caught it was either going to be a very quick one or we would cave under the pressure and nothing would come of it. Literally.

There was some fumbling with clothing, and we giggled while we fought to wrestle each other out of just enough clothes to get the deed accomplished. If I was honest with myself, I didn't really care if we got caught. Well, maybe a little, but the thrill of having my guy fuck me again was worth just about any price I was more than willing to pay.

Turns out, we were going to put it to the test.

Midway through our lust-driven body-slamming fuck, there was a persistent tapping on the glass behind

Marco. It brought our actions to a complete halt. He turned his head, his eyes widening with what he saw. I tried to lean my head to the side to take in what he was seeing because the look on his face said it might be our worst nightmare come to life.

He brought his cold stare back to me. "Els, it's the cops. Fuck!"

"Uh, yeah, it's what we've been caught doing. Well, pull out so we can get sorted." We hastily composed ourselves while the officer stood there patiently with his hands on his hips. I peeked out of the corner of my eye at the muscular cop. He leaned in and looked into the cab of the car, the mirrored lenses of his sunglasses not giving us an ounce of comfort—but reflecting our lust-crazed hormonal mess back to us. When he was satisfied we'd pulled ourselves together—Marco hadn't even tried to pull off the condom, just hiked up his pants and zipped up—he opened the door so we could crawl out of the car.

"You boys know what you were doing was against public decency laws, do you?"

The sheriff's car was parked slightly behind the Impala—the lights thankfully *not* flashing. I observed the man as unobtrusively as I could. I couldn't help but notice the small quirk at the corner of his lips as he spoke in rough tones to us, admonishing us for our public lewdness. Was he amused by this? I found it a teensy bit curious. I didn't know if we were among family or not.

The officer dutifully checked our IDs and collected the registration and insurance information Marco retrieved for him. He walked back to his car to run a check against it. Thankfully, I'd turned eighteen and Marco had just before the end of the previous school year. So, we were both above the age of consent—that wasn't an issue.

But it was also the wrinkle in our little fuck-up. We were legally adults which meant a couple of things, and with Marco's penchant for screwing whenever we could get away with it, I'd made it a point to look it all up on the net. We'd be charged with indecent exposure which was a misdemeanor and had a fine of $1,000. It was bad in and of itself, but certainly not the worst part. If convicted, both of us would have to register as sex offenders for the rest of our lives. I didn't think my boyfriend had any idea of what we were up against.

Thankfully, a small quirk of Officer Langley-Pierce's lips saved us the aggravation. He handed back both of our IDs and Marco's registration and insurance card.

"Now, I know you boys seem like good kids who just let their other heads do the talking." Officer Langley-Pierce pulled those terrifyingly glaring glasses from his face and the humor in his eyes was undeniable. With his thumbs tucked into the top of his formidable belt, he stepped into our personal space and leaned forward to provide some privacy in our conversation. We leaned back a bit; he would've been rather overwhelming if it weren't for the gleam in his eye coupled with a devilish smirk on his face.

"And, off the record, my husband would kick my ass for writing you both up. We nearly got caught when we were your age too. So, consider this a warning. And count your lucky stars it was me who found you. It might not swing your way again. And for Chrissake, do a little research before you decide to fuck like rabbits in public. It ain't all that hard to do." Officer Langley-Pierce was my new hero, and his point was sayin' something to me 'cause I generally distrusted cops seeing how my dick of an uncle Nate was everything I despised in law enforcement. He felt entitled by the position, above it all. Not Langley-Pierce; I could tell he was solid good cop material. From the relief on his face Marco felt the same fucking thing.

A call came over the officer's talkie thing. Radio? Cellular? I didn't know what it was. In stern efficient tones, Officer Langley-Pierce acknowledged it. He then told us where we could go to get a little bit more privacy. He shook hands with each of us and proceeded to walk back to his car.

"Heya, Officer...?"

The cop turned around, eyeing Marco's call in surprise. "What's the hubby's name?"

"Frank. Frank Pierce." He tapped the name badge on his shirt.

"Yeah, well, give him our love, 'kay?"

He smiled a kind of sexy smile, slipped those mirrored specs back onto his face, and nodded once to both of us.

"I will at that. You boys be careful now. I wouldn't want to see you back at the station. Okay?"

We nodded and waved him off as he swung out from the parking lot.

"Ya know, I think his husband is the Monterey County Sheriff," I mused to him as I slipped an arm around his shoulder.

"What? No way. Now I know you're making it up."

"Uh-uh. I think I saw him on the TV news one time when they had a big crime thing here in Monterey. He's a good-looking guy. Bit older but still can see why Officer Langley would go after him."

We gazed at each other for a moment. Much warier of our surroundings, I looked around and didn't spy a single person in the area. Not caring who else was around as the worst had obviously happened, I pushed Marco against the car and kissed him deeply. "I'd risk almost anything for you, you know that, right?"

Marco nodded, "Ditto. Right back atcha, babe."

WE FOUND THE secluded spot the officer had told us about. As we got ready to go at it again, Marco whispered how Officers Langley and Pierce probably fucked out where we were doing it now back when they were young. I offered that maybe they still did it out here. He smirked before saying it was sort of like a tradition, and if one of our kids turned out gay, we'd have to tell him about it.

One of our kids.

I tried to wrap my head around it. A fucking father. A father who still liked to fuck. Too much. I smiled, not knowing if he knew why I was doing so.

We climbed into the back seat of the car to resume fucking again—though this time we had to pause first to have *the talk* about it beforehand as he'd only had the one condom on him and it had broken in the scramble to clothe ourselves in front of Officer Langley-Pierce. I acknowledged the danger but told Marco honestly he was the only person of either sex (he couldn't help but quirk his lips at the remote idea of my *ever* being with a girl) I'd been with. He was my first, and more importantly, was my only. He told me he'd played around once before, with a guy and a girl at the same time. But it was like a year before. There had been no one but Rosetta Palm and her five boyfriends since then. He wiggled his fingers as he said so. We both agreed we wanted to be exclusive and he said if I had any qualms about it we could always drive back into town to buy some more condoms.

Okay, time out. Serious moment time. I mean, I get it. Life or death sort of commitment going on here, you know? What would *you* do? Way I saw it, this was literally "taking a bullet" for the one you professed to love, right? The ultimate commitment/sacrifice. No getting away from it. I completely understood in that frozen moment what I was playing with here. Marco's pointed gaze said we both did. Yet buried in there, in his gaze I beheld so many times before, was hope. In every way he was extending his hand to me forever. If I took it, there'd be no going back. It's a lot for a boy like me to take in. That second, that frozen moment, cleaved its way into my heart. The defining moment of our love.

I thought about it. I did. I told him it wouldn't be necessary. His eyes glistened a bit with how much trust I was putting in him. We kissed quite a bit over my decision. He promised me between kisses he'd never stray. I was it for him; he knew what a big leap of faith I was taking, how much I was trusting him. He'd vowed he would never fail me.

This time we fucked intensely, eyes burning into each other. He whispered how lustfully crazy he got whenever he was around me. I flushed at this but could never quite see what the fuss was about. I was a skinny, average looking guy. I had an ample-sized dick which seemed to excite him, so yay team, there. And he raved about my ass, which, for a skinny guy, was a bit on the meaty side so that was a plus. I had enough junk in the trunk to keep him happy. It was all well and good, I guess. He gradually built up to climax. His moaning became rather loud and I bit my lower lip as he spent himself deep within. With the final shudders of his juices flowing into me I felt incredibly close to him just then.

"Hon, you know I love you, right?"

"Ah, baby, I got you on this. I love you with all my heart too. It was so special what you just did. I can't tell you how happy you've made me. Just knowing I'm there. In you. I know it's weird. It's crazy even. But..."

"No, you're right. I feel the same way. I think I'll always want it this way now. I like how you're giving me something for it."

We were talking about his baby batter being inside me. I knew how strange it was, how totally insane this whole conversation was, but what I'd said was equally true—I was wildly ecstatic he'd spent himself *in* me.

We lay there for a bit before I let slip what I'd been mulling around in the back of my head. "I think I should start working out a bit. You know, put some more meat on these bones."

He pulled back, his look one of confusion. "What? Why? You're the most beautiful thing I've ever seen. You're perfect. I wouldn't change you one bit."

"Yeah, but look at me; I'm all skin and bones."

"No you're not. Yeah, okay, you're a bit on the thin side."

"Like Karen Carpenter or Kate Moss thin."

"Not even. You've got like a swimmer's build or a dancer. But you're not all skin and bones—not even close. 'Sides, I happen to love you just the way you are."

"Like the song?"

He nodded, his eyes alight with love. Yet my mouth decided to toss damage control to the wind yet again.

"Yeah, well, not accounting for good taste, you just wait until you see some sexy buff dude in college and then it'll be Elliot who? I know I've got competition already, even if you don't see it."

He sat up, his eyes dark, a burgeoning menace to them.

"I would *never* look at another guy, or girl even. I wouldn't do that. Ever, Els. Not ever! You're it for me, babe. Total bim-bam, *no thank you* ma'am sorta shit. I can't believe we could make love like and you let me...God, Els!" He slammed his fist against the back of the driver's seat for emphasis. "Sometimes I don't know where you get these hare-brained ideas of yours!" He was hurriedly getting dressed again. I lay there, mouth agape, completely floored by how he raged about the remote possibility of his eye ever straying.

"Baby, I'm sorry. I just..."

But he wasn't having it.

"No, Els, I know what *you were just*...and let me tell you so we're clear, it's crystal. I. Love. You. You! You hear me? That's it. I ain't ever, *ever* gonna stray. Fuck! I watched you for *two years* before I made my move. You think I didn't have opportunity to stray? Hell, that one time I messed around with a guy *and* a girl? I learned two things. One, the girl held no interest for me at all. So bing, right out the gate—gay! And two, and you better listen in on this one baby, 'cause it's the meat of the matter here, the guy was too muscly or built or whatever. I wanted you. I was already fixated on you. Your body, your look, your...well, arrgh, everything! Christ, Els, when I tell you it's you, it's only you. Forever! I ain't playing around here. For fucksake I staked out your store for three weeks watching to see when the exact perfect time would be to make my move. Doesn't *any* of this ring a bell with you?"

I panicked. I couldn't hear anymore. It hurt far too much that I angered him like this. I cut him off with a kiss pushing him to the other side of the car. I tore at his clothing again, pulled him back onto the seat, stroked him to hardness again. It didn't take long. I pulled his cock to me and gripped his ass, forcing his way back in.

"Then fuck me like you mean it. Burn your way into me, lover. I want you to fucking own me." My voice was thick with passion. The fire ignited in his eyes and we fucked. We hollered, moaned, and shook his Impala like a six point on the Richter scale was rocking the west coast. When we erupted, it was together, me splashing up my chest with a few spurts making it as far up as his chin. We laughed as he dashed his tongue out in a vain attempt to lap it up. He spent himself deep within me. We lay together for a while, kissing softly, followed by more murmurs of love.

WE NEVER DID get rid of the elephant that day.

Chapter Five

Montgomery Clift, Pachyderm

I'D TAKEN TO calling the large invisible pachyderm in our life, Monty—ya know, after Montgomery Clift, of the golden age of Hollywood? I know it seems a bit obtuse, but my mom was a big time old-fashioned movie queen (and I suppose by extension, so was I—how cliché, right?), and well, Monty was in the closet throughout his whole career so the name seemed apropos at the time, seeing how Marco and I sorta kept our elephant in the closet.

I know Marco struggled with it sometimes, but my love of old time Hollywood movies colored how I viewed my world. Mom and I watched them all—across all genres and big time studios. It was one of the few things binding my mother and me. She gave me my love of history, and in particular, cinema history. She knew all about those classics, down to the gossip which had run rampant during their making. She collected old Hollywood biographies—we had just about every movie star's story in my dad's den. My favorite was Rosalind Russell's story *Life is a Banquet*. Hands down, the funniest damned autobiography on the planet. It was out of print now, so I valued it above all the others.

But these movies provided a foundation for me. They're what taught me about people and how they relate to one another (hell, I could pick just about any drama or musical as an example). Then I found a couple of documentaries which provided me with a virtual hit list of gay films throughout history. You can bet I consumed every damned one of them. Those films became my guide on how to navigate and survive in this world.

Like how bullies taunted boys like me and the repercussions stemming from such an exchange (my first influence was *Rebel Without A Cause* with James Dean and let's be honest, I was so Sal Mineo's Plato in *Rebel*). Those movies and the men in them taught me about love. I had a particular affection for one I watched over and over—more than any other, 1996's *Get Real* had that impact. I know, it's hardly a bona fide classic by Hollywood golden era standards, but it was a classic of gay filmmaking nonetheless. It certainly was the most instructive to my young burgeoning gayboy sensibilities. Probably because now I could relate to it seeing how the main character was in high school and had a boyfriend who was a jock, though I wanted my story to end far happier than Stephen and John's relationship from the movie. I wanted to know why the jock was the weak one in those stories. Marco certainly has far more balls than John did.

This was the kind of stuff populating the whole gayboy pop-culture reference index I had stored up in my head. It allowed me to pop out with the really esoteric references about such well-known luminaries as Maria Ouspenskaya—ya know, shit nobody who didn't reside in a retirement community would get. So helpful at parties with kids my age. You can see why my dance card was so full. I was in constant demand for my witticisms and plucky bon mots. And if you believe that, I got some oceanfront property in the middle of Florida I'd like to talk to you about.

I suppose I could have asked my mom and dad about those things, but heck, they were parents—what the hell would they know about anything? They were still trying to figure out Facebook and Skype, say nothing of what we kids were into. Instagram? Twitter? Forget about it. It looked like they were making it up as they went along anyhow. So why the hell couldn't I?

I'd often mention Monty being neglected to Marco, who shrugged it off with a slightly annoyed look. He couldn't figure out who this Monty character was because he knew he was the only guy in my small social world. Well, him and Greg, though I didn't talk to Greg nearly as much as I'd like.

He asked if maybe this Monty was some imaginary friend from my past who I'd brought along for the ride. I could tell it sorta bothered him when I didn't directly respond to his line of questioning. It was what it was. Though I didn't talk about Monty a lot, he'd been mentioned off and on over the past couple of weeks with the frequency increasing during the past couple of days. There was a slow increase in panic in the fact our time was running out. All of this led to our current effort to ignore Monty while I took one of my many breaks at the shop. Marco finally owned up to the realization this Monty guy had to be dealt with.

"So, I gotta ask, who the hell is Monty and should I be worried?"

"He's no one in particular, and yes, you should definitely be worried. We both should."

"Okay, like that made any kind of sense, Els. Care to enlighten me?" He broke into a poor impersonation of a dumb jock/Ricky Ricardo. "I mean, I just knows I ain't as edjoomacated as you is, but hell, if you 'splain it to my little ol' pea-brain, I might be able to connect the dots enough to warrant a cause for concern."

"You a…" I playfully smacked him upside his head.

"Hey!" he retorted. We laughed for a second before I finally fessed up. "It's the name I gave the elephant we keep tugging along for the ride. Ya know? The one we don't want to discuss though I keep bringing it up and you keep screwing my brains out so we avoid it for another day."

We were sitting at one of the tables at the Q on the last Thursday of our summer vacation, just before closing time. He held out his hand, and as if his touch would sting me, I retracted mine far up above my shoulders, reacting to his gesture like the righteous black woman I wanted to be from time to time.

"Uh-uh, lover boy. I know what you're up to and where *that* will lead." I indicated his hand with one of mine. He pouted.

Goddamn him.

He flexed his fingers on the table, just waiting it out till I caved. I always did. And don't think it wasn't lost on him, either. He wiggled his fingers again—more pointedly this time—for attention, his lip quivering playfully, and made those puppy dog eyes which never had failed him before. And cue the big time collapse of my resolve.

I sighed, put my hand in his 'cause there wasn't anyone else in the store who'd see. Thumb to palm, a full out ten on the F-O-Meter gate. He wanted it, and right now. He'd tear my clothes off and bone me on the table if I'd let him. I pulled my hand away.

"See, there you go again! I mean it, babe. We gotta sort it out. It's our last weekend before school begins and we still haven't discussed how it's going to go down."

Marco's eyes brightened visibly. "Ooh, you wanna go down, do ya?"

"Yes, er, uh, no! Dammit, Marco! Please pay attention. You're killing me, Smalls!" We often used that line from one of our favorite kid movies, *The Sandlot,* to signal a timeout.

Marco pulled his hand away hesitantly, sincerely reprimanded for his libidinous actions...though only for the moment. He was never truly ashamed where his lust for me was concerned. On the contrary, he wore it quite proudly. He still had it on the back burner there in his eyes. Like my knight in zero armor, naked to the world, the return of Marco, brandishing cock in hand, was still on the horizon. It was already a ten. No going back now. I knew the rules of engagement.

Fuck! I can't believe I actually used Marco's words for it.

The guy had permeated every nook and cranny of my life. He had it all. Well, I'd told him to go ahead and do so—take it all. So, he did; and he hoarded me with a fierce intensity that sometimes threatened to overwhelm me. I didn't understand it, thought I never would. The only thing I knew was I never wanted it to end. I feared it would end and what would be left?

My beast of a Gollum-like voice rattled around in the back of my mind: *Best not to think about it, precious. Best not to give it any thought. Make it a possibility, it would.* Okay, maybe he was more like split personality with a wicked Yoda twist? Either way, the little fucker needed to shut his pie-hole.

Despite what he had to say on the topic, and Marco had plenty to say on it, he'd never wavered *once* since we got together back in July. The football practices were starting to influence our get-togethers, though—eking their way and eroding our time together; further proof school was looming large, and it was clear Marco didn't want to deal with it.

"Okay, lover. I hear you," he said softly.

"Yeah, well, good because Monty's been trumpeting the school alma mater for a week now and you've just been blitheringly going about your bidness."

"Well, doing *you* has *been my bidness*," he countered.

Okay, I blushed. I couldn't help it. I always did when he reminded me of how often we were doing it. All I can say is it's a good thing we have to do shit like eat and sleep or we'd always be boning. He craved it that much. *Who am I kidding? It's not an indictment of his desires of all things me, and if it were, I'd be just as guilty only in the reverse.*

"Anywho, we need to sort this shit out, because these past few weeks have been the best of my life. I don't know how I can crawl back into my little world without your being there." I hiked up a foot onto the bench seat I was sitting on and absentmindedly picked at a frayed tangle of threads from a strategically sexy tear at the knee in my jeans, trying hard not to meet his intense stare. "I'm sort of scared, to be honest."

"Hey now. You think I'm not?"

That was unexpected. I found his confession refreshing. He could've easily lapsed into some sort of macho he-man position that while he loved me unconditionally, I'd have to sort out my shit on my own. Here I was, thinking he had bigger fish to fry in the social elite stratosphere he circled in. Just knowing he was just as worried as I was gave me some courage we would work it out, together, as he'd said.

"Look." He put his hand out again and I took it without question. There was no stroking of the thumb along my palm, but I could still see it lingering in the back of his eyes, but he was all serious now. "I know we move in different circles. I get it."

"*You* have a circle. *We peons* gotta scurry between rocks and hide in obscurity. Let's not forget your world is not mine."

"I. Am. *Your*. World," was his only defense, his eyes pointed, dark, lusty.

He smirked darkly at this, but I knew he knew what I was speaking about. It's the way it was. Marco was golden—a god among men; he was untouchable. Well, in my small social world, at least. And therein lay the rub, as they say. I had touched, and touched quite a bit, that which for all intents and purposes should have been completely untouchable for me. Outside his circles, I was a pustule-ridden vagrant meandering along the fringes of existence we called high school, my prince's frog who would always remain a frog in their eyes, despite how many kisses the prince in question plied me with, so to speak.

I had no illusions to being anything more. The roles were long defined before any of us had arrived on the scene. Hell, our parents, and our parents' parents before them no doubt, had played by the same hard and fast rules. No bucking the system at this point in time. It is what it is. Sure, there were videos on YouTube claiming for kids like us, "it gets better", but what they didn't say, though maybe it was implied, was *only* if you survived the horror of high school to begin with. The land of "better" opened up if you successfully made it to get your diploma and move onto work or college. The dismal reality was better *never* happened while you were in the microscopic climate of high school. Only *after*. You'd have to be a fool to think otherwise.

From where I was, I had to look forward to nine months of hell in school followed by equal dosage of it at the Q. Either way, it didn't look all sunshine and roses. The only bright light, and it was a fucking brilliant one, though I worried it was about to be taken away from me lock, stock and barrel, was Marco. And it all hinged on his next words.

"Babe." He used that marvelous word to let me know we'd get through it—together. "I know it will be weird you think we're not gonna be around each other but, think about it. It's nine months of pure hell, right?"

I nodded, because he hit it square on the head and it was the literal truth.

"Yeah, well okay, but not really."

"Yeah? How do you figure?"

"My season is over in a couple of months at the earliest—if we have a crap season."

"Oh, yeah. Right. And the Angels always have a crap season under your command. So...?"

"Okay, but let's say we did. By mid-November, it could technically all be over. If we have a regular season as we normally do, then maybe a month more if we go onto playoffs or championships. After that, I lapse into upper-class jock obscurity. Once football falls out of the spotlight, I am off the radar. So really, we're only talking a few months at best. Not the end of the world. And I promise, baby, I'll find a way to make time for you during the day at school. I haven't figured it out totally, but I did do something. I hope you're not going to be angry about it."

I eyed him suspiciously as he let go of my hands and pulled out a wrinkled piece of paper from his letterman's jacket. Once he'd unfolded and smoothed it out I realized it was his class schedule.

"It seems my charms still work on Crabapple, 'cause I was able to sync up 90 percent of my schedule with yours. We even have PE together, again." He wiggled his eyebrows over his little ploy and I flushed a bit over the unspoken suggestion in his comment.

It was true, with the exception of one class, right after lunch when I had art and Marco had Spanish, our schedules were in perfect sync with each other.

"The beauty is, if we bring our lunches we can shower fast after PE and get out and be at the bleachers or somewhere for lunch. Hell, we're eighteen now so we can actually leave campus. We can even get in a nooner every now and then..." His wicked smile blossomed across his face as soon as he finished making his case.

I rolled my eyes. "Yeah, I get the nooners, big guy; I am sure there'll be plenty of those. You know I never deny you when it comes to it, though we gotta easily be pushing triple digits when it comes to fucking now with as horned up as you get."

He chortled. "Oh, yeah, like you aren't getting something in the process? Do tell, Donahey. I'd just *love* to hear this..."

I blushed nine shades of red. "I'm not complaining."

He snorted.

"*I'm not*. You're an exceptional lover."

He nodded curtly, confident in his amorous talents and prodigious gifts. I couldn't resist teasing him about it, though. I knew it was slightly evil, but his cool confidence was begging me to do so.

"To be completely honest," I sighed dramatically in my best Scarlett O'Hara way. I knew I was driving him bat-shit crazy with lust already, clearly playing with fire. I loved it. "I don't really have anything to compare it to..." I shrugged as noncommittal as I could. I knew the small smirk along my lips and the sideward glance was enough to give me away.

Marco's eyes flashed intensely with my flirtatious mention of playing the field—even suggesting he let another boy manhandle me brought out his deep sense of possession about me. But I played it cool. I held my hands up in surrender. "And I am not saying I want a comparison. I am a card-carrying member of the Sforza bone-of-the-day fan club. So, no worries there." I slipped the small tube of lube from the pocket of my shirt and placed it in his hand before continuing. "I've already been sorting out where we're going to do it in the shop tonight already. So, yeah, I'm just as horned up for us to fuck as you are, big guy. You haven't lost any ground on that front."

A grin broke across Marco's lips, wickedly dark and with no small degree of libidinous nature coloring them. He slipped the travel-sized tube into the inside pocket of his jacket. We had a lot of those tucked around us. He never wanted it to be an impediment to sex. Lately, our lovemaking had evolved into a prolonged passionate meeting of mind and body—something more akin to an athletic push and pull between sexual gladiators. There was no more harried or rushed fumbling with quick orgasms brought about with the early stages of our relationship. Now, Marco had taken to driving our passions fully so our climaxes were well-timed and deeply gratifying. He'd learned to master his passions and control mine—he wasn't satisfied until I panted, quite literally begging him for a full release before he'd give in and bring me home. Marco reveled in all things me, taking his time to learn what pleased me as I learned how to return those pleasures tenfold.

I had no complaints in the lovemaking department, and if I did, it would only be because we couldn't do it as often as Marco wanted due to his football commitments and my work arrangements. We were spending what little of our free time we had together fucking just to make sure we never missed an opportunity. I swear I had to have the cleanest ass on the west coast for how many times I used an enema wand in the shower—another necessity I'd added to my list of daily grooming routines. It was either feast or famine depending on the time of day or whether or not he was boning me. We were horny boys—it's what we did. And *we* wouldn't have it any other way.

I regarded his face, really taking an interest in what was playing there. The good thing was Marco met my gaze and never faltered, never flinched. He was in it for the whole enchilada.

"Babe, I know it's sorta scary, but it's only until mid-November. After that, I don't really give a flying fuck if everyone finds out about us. Just get me through to then, okay? I promise you I'll make it as easy as I can for the both of us. I don't want to hide, either. I am not ashamed of what we have. I just don't want the drama on top of everything else. Let me get the season out of the way. Snap, snap the photos for the yearbook. Once that's in the can, then we can focus on us. Our life, together. Can we do that much? Together? I want this to work for us."

For my part, I roiled with a mass of conflicting emotions. On the one hand, I could see the value in resuming our normal roles in school. It was known territory. It would take the edge off what to expect. Life would be as it was before. The other hand wasn't one I wanted to spend too much energy thinking about, because no matter how you sliced it, we were straight-up hiding.

As if he could read my thoughts, Marco stroked the top of my hand. "Hey, I won't go out of my way to deny you, if that's what you're thinking. I got the same classes so we could see each other, and we will, nearly every hour. I didn't have to do that, you know. I wanted to."

I nodded. I was trying to put aside the confusion, the hurt, that came bumbling along with what Marco had said. I knew it was silly. Marco was here. He would always be here, in one way or another. And he was only asking for a couple of months. Not so long in the grand scheme of things, really. I knew he was right.

"I know. And I appreciate it. I just have to wonder, with the other peeps you hang out with, if it will only make it worse to have you so near but, in reality, be further away from me than you think."

Marco scrunched his lips a tiny bit. "Well, we'll just have to stage an impromptu meeting at our first class together, then. It might explain how we can talk a bit before and after. I mean, we're seniors, for Chrissake. It's not like we're some mealy-mouthed freshman or something. We call the shots, okay? *That's* the rule."

"Mmmm, yes, sir!" I saluted. We both smiled and blushed at each other.

Chapter Six

A Matter of Trust

I COULDN'T BELIEVE it when Mom said Aunt Marsha would cover for me on Saturday so I could spend the day with my boyfriend. Okay, well, they didn't know *why* I wanted to have the day off. That part I was careful to avoid. I told Mom I wanted to head up to Monterey for the day for some quality *me* time. Of course, I meant quality *Marco* and *me* time.

It was the weekend before school was to begin. So, this time it mattered a great deal to me I was able to do this, my last weekend completely unfettered by work or the terrible soul-wrenching storm I called school pounding at the gates of the romantic world I shared with my boyfriend. I needed *quality* us time. One last hurrah before hell ensued for another year.

I didn't ask for time off from the store too often, so I usually got it when I did. But this time it meant a lot to me. I guess my mom and my aunt figured it would be a day at the Aquarium and then I'd make the trek back home. One last vacation splurge before the drudgery of school descended. Mom asked if I wanted to borrow the car but I told her I had it covered. I could see she was puzzled but when I didn't offer to clarify, she surprisingly let it go.

Small miracles. That's what I was thankful for these days.

So northbound with my hottie of a boyfriend I went. It turned out he had the whole day planned out for us. I just had to hang on for the adventure to come. Oddly enough, our time hadn't been the usual chatty give and take. We seemed to be satisfied with being together—hand in hand, side by side, a gentle caress of his thumb across my palm. Nothing overwhelming, just gentle reminders how much he loved being with me. The feeling was mutual.

THE WHOOSH OF the ball as it slipped through the net was the only sound to punctuate our time together. Well, that and children screeching over on the jungle gym a few yards away beyond the grassy knoll we had planted ourselves on. Marco was being rather quiet today. Something was on his mind but I could tell he was still sorting it out. I wasn't one to rush him into anything, so I think we both knew he'd say it when he wanted to.

We picnicked at a nice park along the waterfront. He brought along a basketball and we were shooting some hoops. I was fairly decent with it. Dad had spent a fair amount of time honing my skills in various sports when I was younger. It was before I dropped the G-bomb on him. We hadn't spent much time on sports after my little announcement. I sorta missed doing that with him now. Funny how you don't realize you love something until it's gone. I couldn't figure out for the life of me why it had all had to change, or more importantly, how to correct it. It was too awkward to deal with over Skype, so I let it go. It was easier that way.

Our date so far had consisted of my spending the majority of the time either sketching Marco in my small sketch book or munching on some of the food he had packed for us—which left little in the way of missing much. Chicken, fried *and* roasted, fresh fruit of literally any kind you could think of (*guavas*—he even thought to bring my favorite fruit of all), along with chips and any other snacky munchies I could desire. My guy was a provider, he was, saying he wanted all of my time devoted to him and not having to make runs for anything I might crave. Silly boy, I had him. He was all I really needed. The rest was superfluous. *He* was the only requirement.

"Whaddya thinkin' 'bout, babe?" he asked as he did a nice layup to slip the ball into the basket yet again.

He hadn't missed thus far and he'd been at it for well over thirty-five minutes. He was one of those guys who could figure out a sport very easily and his body began the road to perfection on it. I marveled at that about him as I sat there at our picnic table finishing a peach he'd brought along for me. I had exhausted the entire bag of guavas in a matter of minutes. He told me he would make a mental note going forward about that little favorite of mine.

"Only how sexy you are," I replied. He smiled the wicked smile that made my danglies not so dangly.

I set the drawings aside and got up, dusting my hands off onto my shorts, and moved closer to him. He passed me the ball and I did a small run up to the hoop, glancing once to see if he was watching my technique, or not. He was. He was always watching me; even when he was concentrating on making the perfect shots for the better part of an hour he was always attentive to me.

After I made the shot and it ricocheted off the backboard without slipping through he retrieved the ball and came up to me. He got behind me to work on my technique a bit. I knew he secretly loved this part because it meant he got to put his hands on me in public. That was always a thrill for him. He loved showing the world he wanted to touch me.

I let him guide me through how to make the perfect basket. After it connected to his satisfaction—a near silent whoosh as it gently slipped through the hoop—he smiled and patted my butt in a big ol' bromance way before going to retrieve the ball again.

He tossed it back to me and I dribbled it up just like my dad had worked with me countless times in my youth and made the shot with nearly as much grace as he could. Marco smirked as he retrieved the ball and did a perfect layup of his own. He grinned, thinking he had already made a vast improvement in my shooting skills.

Truth be known, I had spent the better part of an afternoon as summer vacation started shooting hoops with my only friend from school, Greg, and his older brother, Kevin. It had been a surprise visit when Greg had stopped by the store one afternoon and invited me over for lunch. I didn't get why then; it seemed so random, but I really had a good time with them that afternoon. Now I thought about it, Greg had spent a fair amount of time talking Marco up since he and Kevin were on the team together—until Kevin graduated last year. It seemed fairly innocuous at the time, but now I wasn't so sure. Greg seemed to know an awful lot about my boyfriend for being the brother of a fellow team member. Or maybe I was reading into it too much.

Marco shot the ball in my direction and I signaled I was out. I started to dribble the ball away from him and he called out, "Hey, where ya goin?"

"I need a drink," I said with my back to him, the biggest Cheshire Cat grin snaking across my lips, knowing full well if I could pull this off he'd fucking lose his shit over it. I bounced the ball one more time before I tossed it high over my shoulder, trusting in my blind aim like my father taught me, and smirked as it slipped through the hoop with very little sound.

"*What the fuck?* Elliot! Oh my god!" He lunged for the ball and came trotting up behind me. I playfully glanced back at him and winked.

"You little fucker!" He body dove me and we both crashed onto the small grassy knoll next to our picnic table. He playfully jabbed at me and we giggled as we tussled in the grass. After a few moments, I had to beg off the tickle session because I was having a hard time breathing. He had ended by straddling my waist while he pressed my arms above my head as he looked down at me with wide, lust-filled eyes.

"Babe? How the fuck did you learn how to do that? *I* can't even do that—well, not always. No, fuck it, I can't. Period."

He was grinning so wide, I could tell my little surprise pleased him enormously. I was happy I could give that to him.

I shrugged, looking to the side so I didn't have to acknowledge openly how this little scene had supercharged my lust for all things Marco. He ground his ass down on my groin. He knew anyway. *Damn him.*

He leaned forward and we kissed—out in the open and everything. I broke it off after giving into it a bit.

"Sweetheart..." I murmured, scanning around us.

His eyes flashed with his big shit-eating grin plastered across his handsome mug. He was very into the moment and oblivious to everyone around us. He got up and pulled me up after him. It was then I noticed the knoll had provided us a certain degree of cover from those around us. Smart guy. After the ordeal with Deputy Langley-Pierce, I should've known better.

We took a seat at the table as I grabbed a couple of bottled waters he had in the cooler and tossed one to him. He ran a fair amount of it over his head before guzzling. I gaped rapturously as the water beads dripped from his sexy curled hair onto his sweat-laden T-shirt. I fucking loved the smell of him all sweaty. I'd secretly wanted to make love to him after a hard practice session—*before* he showered. Manly, it was, and a definite turn-on. I could sniff his musk all day long and never tire of it.

"You never did answer me," he said finally, water cascading over the multitude of curls crowning his face. Rain never looked so sexy.

"I know," I said softly as I continued to take a long pull from the bottle.

He eyed me intently. When it got the better of him, he nudged me verbally. "So?"

"What?" I asked in the most neutral tone I could.

Exasperated by me, he groaned and placed his forehead on the picnic table.

"Okay, before you get all gooey boyfriend on me, it was my dad, all right?"

His head popped up. "Your dad? But I thought..."

"In Alaska. Yeah, you remember it right. But this was before. Before G-day."

"G-day? I don't..."

"Gay Day. When I dropped the big ol' G-bomb on my parents. Things changed drastically after my little revelation."

My expression soured just admitting it to Marco. I resolved to put a smile back on my face. No reason to bring what had been a wonderful day down with that small failure in my life.

"But before, Dad and I did a lot of sports together. He wanted me to try soccer, lacrosse, baseball, tennis, and basketball." I indicated the courts behind him. "We did them all. He was adamant I become at least proficient enough I could hold my own. I've even been known to toss a football or two back in the day."

I knew this was a huge reveal to him. Up to this point I'd let him think he was the sportsman in this couple. I was cool with it. This was all ancient history in my book. I had my art now. That's what mattered to me. Marco could be the brilliant athlete in the family. It's just how I saw it. Still did, in fact, despite my recent revelation. He didn't seem to think so, however.

"Yeah, but babe"—there was the golden word that made me all mushy inside whenever he said it—"why didn't you ever tell me? All this time I..."

"You, what? Thought I was the quintessential gayboy who was some father's worst nightmare out in left field screaming like a little girl as the fly ball came my way?" I shrugged. "I'm cool with it."

"I'm not!" His brow stitched, telling me he didn't want me keeping things from him. I'd crossed a line somehow. "I'm the one who should know everything about you. It's why I'm with you. No secrets. My life is completely open to you. I expect nothing less from you. Okay?"

I shrugged again; I really didn't see the point to all of this. So, I forgot to tell him about my playing sports at an earlier stage in my life. Was I supposed to rattle off the first time I learned to use the toilet for myself and not crap in my diapers? Or how about the first time I discovered my cock was for something other than peeing? Falling off my bike like eighteen bajillion times before I got the hang of riding without training wheels? It was simply ludicrous to expect so much from me. I mean, the way I'd figured it those reveals would happen over time.

As if he could read my thoughts his next words stopped me cold.

"I don't expect you to tell me everything at once. I don't need to know how many times you fell off your bike or when you learned how to jack off—though one of those might be of great interest to me. It's a sidebar you need to tuck away for later, 'cause, yeah, anything having to do with your body and sex totally has my attention. Just sayin'..."

I smiled at him as I reached for a carrot and a celery stick and swiped them through the ranch dressing before taking a bite out of them.

"Don't try and be cute and coy with me, hon. I'm bein' serious here," he said as he arched a brow at me, pressing his point.

"You're making this into a big ol' mountain when it's just a molehill, babe."

"Not in the least. I mean, I like you can surprise me, but sweetheart, you gotta see your being athletic gives us a whole new avenue I didn't know I had with you to explore. Don't you see how it could mean something so amazing to me?"

Again with the shrugging. I seemed to do it a lot when I didn't know how to respond.

"Yeah, okay. Message received." I put up a hand in a mock oath. "I promise to reveal all things to you that could make you all gushy about me. Are we good?" I rolled my eyes with a smile to let him know his needling me was an okay thing. I got what he was trying to say.

"I know you were kidding just then but know I took it as a solemn oath. You better keep up your end of our promise, babe."

"Yeah, yeah, big guy. I getcha. No more withholding." I sighed as I beheld the sun slipping further toward the horizon. With a deviation in our moods, I assumed our day was coming to a close. Silly me.

"So, what now?" I asked, bringing my gaze back around to him.

"How about we pack it into the car and take a walk along the beach?"

"If you like, I guess I could sign up for that."

He seemed pleased enough with my going along with this new proposal. In truth his whole mood seemed a bit off, like there was something rolling around inside him he didn't know how to get out there.

"Babe?" I asked as we began gathering things up from the table. He smiled warmly, liking how I referred to him using my preferred term with such ease now.

"Yes, life of my love?" he replied, his eyes flashing to mine—such love there. I flushed with those simple words.

"Is there something bothering you today? You just"— I stopped putting away the fruit back into their containers—"I dunno, seem a bit distracted. Distant. Is it something I've done? Because I'd be the first to say I am sorry. I don't want to do anything that might upset you."

"Elliot, stop." His eyes became a little harder. "Why do you do that?"

"What?"

"Assume whatever is going on is something you've done. You've done nothing of the sort. I know I haven't been myself today."

He came around to my side of the table and sat down with his back to it on the bench next to me.

"It's not you, sweetheart. It's just"—he sighed—"home."

"Something I can help with?"

He shook his head slightly then stopped and looked at me.

"You already have, just by being mine. You've no idea how much I've come to count on you. You are in no small part the whole reason I have any happiness in my life. Before you I thought I was happy. After being with you, I realize how utterly boring and dictated my life was. I know how flowery and Jane Austen-y it sounds. But, life at home isn't what everyone thinks it is. Sometimes it can be quite hard."

"Not abusive, I hope."

"What? Oh, no. Not like that." He smirked. "Wow, I guess it did sound a bit, how is it you put it, maudlin?"

I nodded. "I guess. You, on the other hand, while I like to think we've gotten to know each other quite a bit. And I am looking forward to keep on doing it—for the rest of my life if you'll let me."

"Always," he confirmed and I nodded.

"Anyway, the point being there are a great many things we still don't know about each other."

"Yeah, like blind hoop shots over the shoulder that you've kept carefully hidden from me?"

"Well, it's hardly hiding some deep dark secret, lover boy. But yeah, I guess it's in there too. There's a lot for us to find out about each other."

"Like how you think your parents don't get you or you drove your dad to 'the wilds of Alaska'?" He made finger quotes in the air.

I quirked a brow. "Yeah, *just* like that though you'll have to trust me and remove those quotes you put there."

"Babe, I observed your father watching you back the first day we met. I was spellbound watching him watching you. He loves you *so* much."

"I know he does. He just can't bear the thought I've disappointed him, so he had to seek a life somewhere else, that's all. *And* let's drop it," I said to him as he opened his mouth to protest. "Because it will only lead to a disagreement and pull focus from what I know we were talking about and you cleverly diverted it to me. Nice try. This was about you and your mood. *Not* me and mine."

"Yeah, okay. Look, let's get this packed and then hit the shore before the sun goes completely down. 'Kay?"

"Sure."

FIFTEEN MINUTES LATER with the items safely stowed in the trunk of the Impala, we made our way down to the shoreline, parked the car, ditched the shoes, and walked barefoot down to the beach in an area called Lover's Point Park. I held his hand, not caring in the least who saw us. Though to be fair, no one really seemed to care we were two teenage boys holding hands and walking with our feet ankle deep in the water.

"So, tell me something," I said to him after a rather long period of saying nothing to each other, a quietude we both relished. Marco and I simply liked being together. We didn't always have to fill it with words. In truth, sometimes the most intense moments we had together involved no speaking at all, just looks, touch, and the reveling in all of our senses coming alive without the complications of jabbering at each other.

"What's that?"

"Tell me something you want for us, down the road a ways."

He sighed. "Oh, babe. I have so many. You just don't know. You forget I've had two long years to daydream about what I would do with you once I had you all to myself."

"Okay, so spill something. I want to know what you see about us."

He stopped us and turned to face me, taking both my hands in his.

"That's easy. Married for starters. That's non-negotiable. I want it legal and everything. I want us protected in every way imaginable. I want to bind you to me unequivocally and profoundly. I want every day to be a revelation of some sort. I want to know your dreams and find ways to make them happen. I want to please you every day we're together, finding ways to peel back whatever protections you've put up against the world and let me in there. I want to fortify you, protect you, make you utterly and completely mine till I take my last breath on this Earth. How's that for starters?"

"Wow, okay, you certainly have had time to think about this, haven't you?"

"Uh huh. I told you. Two years. I've thought about nothing but you. I meant it, baby. You have occupied every single thought away from school work, the team, and all the other things that pull my focus from you. And even in them, I still find ways to tie it back to you." His eyes searched mine. I knew better than to look away. Marco thrived on my keeping his gaze.

The sun was no doubt striking the water's edge on the horizon—a dazzling array of oranges, pinks, purples and blues, framing him in such splendid glory. He was positioned just where the sun was obscured from view. He was so radiant at dusk. I always want to watch him in this light. His lips, so soft and full yet with a profound sculpted edge to them, parted and his voice bathed me with such warmth I came close to losing myself and kiss him in front of everyone.

"I love how you've learned to keep your gaze locked to mine. It's like you let me in to know your soul. Nothing moves me as much as when you do that. Babe, I love you. Utterly and completely. You consume me, leave me shredded and raw. When you look at me, like you're doing now, I feel so vulnerable and so incredibly strong. You feed me in ways no food ever could. From the first moment your words broke from your lips, cursing at your mother, I was overwhelmed. Those first five minutes completely and utterly changed my life. Up until then I didn't realize I didn't have focus in my life. I had my football. I had my family. I had friends. But all of it pales when compared to you. I don't know why; I don't think I ever will. But when you said we were boyfriends back in the store when I finally worked up the courage to come to you and say I loved you, that moment?"

I nodded.

"That moment changed me forever. *L'amore della mia vita*, Elliot Donahey, *tu sei tutto per me; morirei se mi lasciassi.* I'd simply wither away. *You* are my life; *you* are my love. *Tu sei le mie stelle, la mia luna, l'aria che respiro, eternamente.*"

A few silent tears fell from his eyes. I was a mess, crying like a baby at his soft words of love. I didn't care who saw. I didn't care if anyone objected. To be honest, I didn't even know what he actually said. I kissed him passionately. He pulled me to him, crushing me as if he wanted to fold me into him so I'd be a part of him forever—I was good with it. After a few seconds, he picked me up and swung us around at the edge of the water. His footing became a little off and we started to tumble over but my guy, ever the brilliant athlete, righted us again to set me softly down. We shared the smile between our barely touching lips.

An elderly couple sitting in a couple of chairs with a small dinner picnic between them applauded our little display of affection. Hardly what I'd thought would happen. The old man's wife was wiping her eyes and beaming.

"That was truly lovely to watch. You boys make quite the couple, you know that?"

Her husband, a rough and tumble looking man, though still quite handsome with a carefully combed silver mane and a white closely trimmed beard, looked on with a smile as well.

"Our Jeffrey has a husband. With children no less," she said. "Married a doctor. Good catch his boy is too."

I looked over at Marco and he had just as big a smile as I did.

"You boys gonna get married now it's all legal?" she asked as she poured her husband another glass of Champagne. She held up the bottle in our direction. We both held up our hands to decline the offer, but thanked her nonetheless for her generosity.

"We're celebrating our fifty-second anniversary tonight. You boys made it bang over the moon for us."

"Yeah, my guy can really lay it on when he wants to." I nudged Marco with my shoulder as he wrapped me up with my back to his chest, leaving his chin on my left shoulder. I turned and kissed his temple.

"Not so hard when I have great inspiration," was all he offered.

"Ah, see, that's what I tell the missus. I tell her, Clarice, what's so hard about telling you how much you mean to me when you're looking so hot over there? She gets all flustered—even to this day." He waved his hand at her in mock dismissal. She just beamed.

"Well, we can't help ourselves, now can we, Clarice?" I winked at her and she winked right back. They were an adorable couple.

"So, your son is gay and married?" Marco asked.

"He is. To a lovely man. Marcel. French. Quite the looker too. And I am totally comfortable sayin' it being a straight guy and all," her husband responded as he sipped his Champagne.

We chuckled. They were truly amazing to be so cool with the whole gayboy thing. I guess it really *could* get better for us down the road.

"Why don't you boys sit down and keep an old couple company for a bit?"

"Clarey, they probably want to be alone, hot studs like them. They don't need a couple of old farts to chat the night away."

I glanced at Marco, his eyes all alight with these two marvelous people right there in front of us. His mood brightened considerably. If talking to them made him happy, I was all in.

"We'd like nothing better than to sit a spell and talk," I offered happily.

Clarice, tapped her husband's shoulder. "See Morty, no harm in asking."

"You're right there, Clarice," I replied as Marco and I took a spot on the edge of their blanket.

"So, what do you boys do?"

"High school," we both chorused at the same time.

Clarice's eyes went wide, and she looked a bit sheepish at her cheekiness in assuming we were older. "Why, you're just babes! So young and already in love. It's sweet!"

Morty shook his head and chuckled. "You'll have to forgive Clarey. Ever since our Jeffrey came out to us and got hitched she's all into the men-on-men romance thing. Her Nook is simply packed with them novels."

"I like men. Who needs to cloud things up with a female in there? But you boys know what I am talking about, right?"

Marco shook his head and chuckled right along with Morty. I decided Clarey needed some reinforcements against our two guys.

"You've got a point there, Clarice. I can definitely see how a female would muck things up."

Marco rolled his eyes but said nothing.

"See." She batted at Morty's shoulder again and I thought he must have a never-ending bruise from all the tagging she must've done over their fifty-two-year-long marriage. "This one has the balls to admit what he wants and gets what I am talking about."

"Damn straight!" I added and held a hand up which she promptly high-fived me.

Everyone broke out into a chuckle at our blossoming camaraderie.

"So, high school? Which school? Here in Monterey?" Clarice inquired.

We shook our heads, but it was Marco who did the clarifying.

"Mercy High."

"You're looking at the varsity quarterback." I lifted one of the hands wrapped around my knees and indicated my guy with a finger. I leaned my chin onto my knees with my eyes all bright drinking in how beautiful Marco truly was, so handsome and charming, those soft dark curls circling his face, dreamy.

"Stop gushing, babe," he murmured to me with a half-lidded gaze. I witnessed the flame burning there if no one else could.

"Really? Wow, you certainly did well for yourself, sonny." Morty smirked in my direction. I blushed and everyone had a bit of a laugh at my expense. I was good with it.

"Is this a closed party or can anyone join?" came a dark baritone voice from over their shoulders.

"Jeffrey!" Clarice shrilled and scrambled to get her slightly pudgy body out of the folding beach chair.

We turned to see Jeffrey, a tall handsome man of thirty or so, and an even more striking tanned man with a carefully groomed five o'clock shadow on his sharply angled face. Both were dressed in khaki shorts showing off their shapely legs and well-formed bodies encased in matching jewel-toned polo shirts. Between them were two children, a boy and a girl, of about the same age. They were barely beyond the toddler phase because of the way they had to work to get through the sand to where we were all sitting. The boy was in a white and blue tank with khaki shorts mimicking his fathers' while the little girl had on a pale flowered sundress. I couldn't help noticing how much the children looked like these two men. Were they actually their children?

My mind immediately went back to Marco's discussion about our being married and with children of our own. Here was proof enough it could work.

Morty rose and greeted their son and his husband and their grandchildren. Marco and I got up thinking it was probably best we took our leave of them as it appeared it was now a family event.

"No, please don't leave on our account. We're a tad late because Marcel got held up at the hospital."

"Trouble?" Clarice asked as everyone got settled. Jeffrey indicated Marco and I should retake our places and he and Marcel and the kids would settle in around us. Marcel planted the four tiki torches equally around the blanket he'd had in his hand and lit them up.

Clarice doted over the two very well-behaved children who took up the center of the large blanket we were all sharing.

"Jeffrey, Marcel, this is...oh, my word, I don't think we've ever gotten around to knowing your names—isn't it silly of me?" Clarice exclaimed, bringing her hand to her mouth in complete surprise. It was then I spied the enormous rock of a wedding ring she was wearing. Liz Taylor would have been proud.

"No, we didn't, and that's our fault," Marco offered, smiling like the charming diplomat he could be. "I'm Marco Sforza, and this is my boyfriend, Elliot Donahey."

Marcel's eyes lit up. "Vincenzo's son?"

By contrast Marco's eyes narrowed a tiny bit, a thread of concern weaving its way through them before returning to their normal brilliant gaze. "The very one."

"I didn't realize Vincenzo had a gay son."

"He, uh, isn't aware," Marco responded flatly.

I shrugged in an "oops" sort of way.

"Ah. Well, no worries, I won't be enlightening 'im about it," Marcel said, with a very sexy lilt to his slight French accent.

"I'd appreciate it," he sighed softly. "I mean, I am not ashamed of what Elliot and I have. It's just new and we're still trying to sort out how all of it will come out. But I plan on making an honest man of him as soon as we're able."

"You should've seen the two of them a few minutes before you got here. Charming display of love there. In Italian, no less. A little foreign boy-on-boy romance—I didn't even need subtitles. I could tell what he was saying to Elliot from the way he was looking at him. *Amore*, right, Marco?"

Marco blushed making me smile broadly.

"Mom, wow, give the boys a break," Jeffrey pleaded. Then to us, "She gets a little over-zealous with the whole PFLAG thing ever since Marcel and I became a couple. She can lay it on a bit thick."

Marcel chuckled and shook his head, rolling his eyes and nodding in complete agreement. The men removed their deck shoes and I noted how handsome their feet were. Nicely manicured and manly, like my guy's. It seemed I had a thing for men's feet.

"You don't know the half of it," Marcel added but blew a kiss in Clarice's direction as a peace offering. "We love her all the more for it." Yeah, like my boy, he was quite the charmer.

"Well, in case you hadn't sorted it, I'm their son, Jeffrey Greenbaum, and this is my husband, Marcel LaCroix, and our two children, Beatrix and Henri."

He indicated the two children who were busy taking their toys out of a small carry-on bag Jeffrey had slung over his shoulder. Marco took no time and slid forward onto his belly to engage the children and their action figures. I smiled watching him act like the big kid he seemed to be, his eyes all alight with the way the children responded to his joining them. He fit right in.

"Glad to meet the both of you." I nodded with a small wave.

"Marco's just telling us he's the quarterback of the varsity football team over at Mercy High," Morty offered.

"Quarterback, huh?" Marcel asked and Marco nodded as his Superman did battle with Henri's Batman. Henri squealed when he got in a good whack with his Batman figurine and Marco played like Superman went flying back and crashed into the ground with a ton of sound effects he happily supplied from his mouth.

"Yeah, seems when I woo 'em I shoot rather high," I deadpanned.

"I haven't spoken to your father in months. Please tell him I said hi the next time you see him for me, will you?" Marcel opened the small cooler he had carried down with the tiki torches. He produced a medium-sized dark brown box rather nicely packaged with a big pink ribbon.

"Absolutely," Marco said.

Marcel handed the box over to Clarice who just squealed in surprise. "Oh, Marcel, you didn't!" She clapped her hands in rapid succession until the box was handed over to her, her face completely lit up with whatever was inside it. "You both are in for quite the treat!" she practically cooed at us.

"Marcel had them overnighted from Clarice's favorite candy maker in Paris," Jeffrey clarified.

"What is it? Some sort of chocolate?" I inquired, licking my lips in anticipation.

"Only the most decadent petit fours you'll ever taste in your life! And they cost a fortune!" Clarice gushed.

"But they're worth every penny!" Marcel chimed in. "The Greenbaums, not the sweets," he added as Clarice placed a soft kiss on his artistically sculpted whiskered face. "How long have you two been together?"

"Since July seventeenth, though Marco's evidently been smitten with me for the past two years. Or so he tells me."

"Two years?" Clarice gasped. "My, that is a long time to pine over someone. They should write a romance story about you two."

Her menfolk shook their heads at her obsession with all things gay romance related.

"Oh yeah, it'd be a *real* best seller!" I chuckled. "Somehow I don't think our little love fest would make for good book fodder. There's just a lot of kissing and stuff. Not much drama there to troll, I'm afraid."

"Oh, I dunno, give it time," Jeffrey said, gazing pointedly to Marcel who was right there for the hand off.

"'E likes to keep poking me about a little trouble I 'ad with a stalker at ze beginning of our relationship. But 'e has a point. You never know where zat drama will come from. Sometimes it is entirely beyond your control."

Jeffrey rolled his eyes at the shared recollection as if there were no small amount of anguish rubbed deeply into it. Though without missing a beat—and I had to hand it to these two, they were quick—he leaned over and kissed Marcel on the side of his face and countered with a conciliatory remark on the whole affair.

"But...I can totally see why she was all wacky crazy for my guy. I mean, look at him—he's hella sexy, right? Isn't that how you kids say it now?"

"Only since 1997 but yeah, I get it." Marco winked at them both and they smiled.

"Zat's my Jeffrey, keeping up with ze kids, circa *last* century." Marcel beamed warmly at his husband.

"She?" I asked, not quite willing to let that little nugget of information go. The fact the stalker was a woman was a twist I hadn't counted on with two gay men.

Marcel nodded while Clarice ogled the petit fours before selecting one and passing the box to Marcel.

"A friend of 'is sister's no less," Marcel offered as he passed the box to Morty without taking a treat for himself.

"Now, bear in mind, my sister was studying abroad and just happened to meet her at a boulangerie and became *fast friends*. Little did she know, Amalie was a number one whack job." Jeffrey chose a simple dark chocolate morsel wrapped in the same pink ribbon as the box's decoration.

Looking at the small treat, I couldn't help making the comparison to those Russian dolls—you know the big wooden hollow dolls containing another and another one inside it? The, uh, oh shit, I hate it when I can't think of something and it will nag at me until I remember it at two in the morning and have absolutely *no one* to tell. While I went on with my internal mental search, Marcel completed the tale.

"She stole Genevieve's passport, 'ad a dupe made because she was basically ze same build and height, and used it to follow me to America where she knew I was going to study."

"What he's not telling you is Marcel went through a 'straight phase.'"

I loved how these two used implied air quotes—then I mentally got off track wondering if all gay men did that.

"It was *not* a phase. I was *straight*."

"What he's trying to avoid telling you is Amalie was his *only* girlfriend and what a doozy he chose in her."

"'Ow the 'ell was I supposed to know? She seemed normal at first! It's not like zey come with warnings stapled to zeir sides—watch out! Thees one will kill you."

"Now boys, bygones, right?" Morty chimed in. It was clear this *discussion* had been had many times before and still seemed to be a sticky one.

"Of course!" Marcel gasped, a little too flamboyantly I had to admit, but then Jeffrey's eyes softened considerably and he took Marcel's hand and kissed the back of it and leaned into it a bit, pressing his cheek against it, before letting it go.

"So? *Reader's Digest* condensed version?" I asked, wanting to get on with the end of the story.

"Hmmm?" Marcel queried, totally not following along. Seriously, these two were hot and cold with the gay references and shorthanded lingo. Must get rusty when you have the love of your life at hand. Who needs quick and witty bon mots when you have the one who occupies your every thought sitting right next...to...you. I looked at Marco. I could tell he was thinking along the same lines. *Damn him.*

He pointed a finger at Jeffrey and Marcel as he crawled away from the kids to come alongside me and wrap his arms around me.

"That's what I want, babe." He pointed at the whole Greenbaum-LaCroix crew. "All of that. Only more kids."

"It's work. We won't lie to you," Marcel said, his eyes searching for his husband.

"But it hardly seems like work when you're with the one you're supposed to be with. *That's* passionate sort of work. Work you love to do. If it isn't, then get the hell out. The world is too freaking weird and life is too short to not be with the one person who means most to you," Jeffrey added.

There was a beat where we all just regarded each other.

"*So?*" I exclaimed, still exasperated neither of them had finished the story.

"Oh." They all laughed but Marcel took pity on me and continued, "Yeah, back to ze drama. So, Amalie got over 'ere on Genevieve's fake passport and weaseled her way to ze west coast and found a way to earn money under ze table. She'd been 'ere for *months*. Now mind you, I'd broken it off well before coming to ze States."

Marco nestled closer to me, nuzzling my neck a bit as we continued to listen to their little domestic—er, uh, international drama. I spied Clarice beaming at the two of us. She really did seem to like seeing two boys together. Who knew mothers could be like that? I certainly didn't think my mother would be a card-carrying member of the gayboy fan club.

"Well, I'm like, what was it, hon? Six months into med school?" Marcel asked.

Jeffrey nodded. "Uh huh. Just about."

The treats finally made their way to Marco and me and we each took one and traded bites of each other's, our eyes flashing in the tiki light at how good those little Parisian treats really were. Marco gently closed the box and returned it to Clarice's hands.

"Well, she shows up and begins to follow me around. Won't leave me ze el…"

"Language…" Clarice chided.

"Hell, won't leave me the *'ell* alone. Zen she found out about my dating Jeffrey, seriously I might add. It was clear to anyone seeing us together zat I was over ze top in love. I was buying 'im things all ze time. It was ridiculous. Even I can look back on it now and see how thick I laid it on 'im."

"He did too. But he was so damned…"

"Language..." Mort, Clarice, and Marcel chorused. Marco and I snickered.

"Darned cute..."

"Darned cute..." the two children echoed while they mashed a treat into their mouths, only succeeding in getting more of it mashed in their little hands than into them.

"Anyway, long story short..." Jeffrey went on.

"Too late..." Morty chuckled, shaking his head slightly and smirking.

"She pulled a full-on Glenn Close freakfest almost down to the rabbit in the pot, if you know what I mean."

"Only 'e was going to be ze rabbit," Marcel indicated.

"What?" Marco and I exclaimed.

Everyone nodded, including the kids. Marco and I sort of laughed and gasped all at the same time. This whole thing had to be rehearsed. I mean, even the kids knew their lines and blocking.

They all laughed at our expressions.

"We can laugh about it now, but that bi—"

"Language...," we all said, Marco and me included, which only brought around another fit of giggles.

"That *woman* was a real piece of work."

"Piece of work..." Henri practically sang it.

Yeah, they'd all heard this story many times, it seemed. I was good with it; it gave continuity to their lives. It had a history. Even the children knowing their parts said so.

"I love that the kids know how it all happened," Marco whispered into my ear, and then promptly took my lobe between his lips for a few seconds. "It's not just history, babe. It's family."

I nodded.

"So, let's just say after some pretty awful encounters between 'er and ze love of my life..."

"One of which had me in the hospital because she ran me off the road and into a ditch,' Jeffrey cut in. "It nearly cost me my life."

"Whoa, really?" I exclaimed.

Marcel nodded, his eyes losing the light that had been there only a moment before. A dark time for them all it seemed.

"But thankfully she wasn't as clever a girl as she thought. Rental, credit card, license plate, need we say more?" Jeffrey said.

"Well, that and I 'appened to walk Jeffrey out to his car zat night and as 'e took off I noted Amalie pulling out in a car further down ze street and giving chase."

Morty shook his head. "A right piece of work all right."

"Piece of work..." the kids chimed musically.

Even with the four tiki torches, it was starting to get a bit dark.

"Suffice to say," Jeffrey said, "I recovered and she was promptly arrested and deported after standing trial here. Twelve years to nearly the day."

"Right near our anniversary—the nerve of that witch," Clarice exclaimed.

"Language..." Henri called out.

And we all broke out in laughter.

THE GREENBAUM CLAN asked us back to their house for a nightcap (even though they knew we couldn't drink) to help them wrap up celebrating their anniversary complete with cake and coffee they had waiting for us at home.

We tried to beg off. Not that we wanted to, because they were all quite lovely and for a short while Marco and I were able to watch how it could all work for us. It was right there, plain for us to see. So, in the end the Greenbaum-LaCroix boys charmed the hell out of us and we caved and followed them back to Morty and Clarice's.

Marco was sure to have me call my mother to let her know I was fine and would be home a bit later than I thought.

"What could you possibly be doing at this hour in Monterey?"

I chuckled. "You wouldn't believe it if I told you."

"What's that supposed to mean?"

"Nothing. Look, I am all right. I am actually celebrating the fifty-second wedding anniversary of Morty and Clarice Greenbaum." I had a big ol' shit-eating grin on when I said it, knowing full well she wouldn't get the humor of the situation. Sometimes I marveled at what truly tickled my funny bone.

"Morty and Clarice who?"

"Greenbaum. And before you ask, no we don't know them. I happened upon them along the beach and they invited me back to their place. Turns out their son is gay."

"Oh."

"No, not what you're thinking. He's like thirtysomething and married and has two really delightful children."

"I wasn't..."

"Uh huh. Nice try, Kayla Donahey, but your suspicious feathers are showing."

"Elliot, you're my only son. I have reason to be suspicious."

"No. You don't. You take liberty with being a doting mother and *behave* with no small degree of suspicion. I will accept it because it's just how you are. But a reason to be suspicious? No. You need to get used to it, Mother. No matter how difficult it may be for you. I am now eighteen. I will be sexually active and will have *boy*friends. I will associate with men of my kind and will enjoy myself immensely while doing so. I just don't want you to think I am being coerced into anything. All right?" I couldn't help darting my gaze to Marco as he approached me. I couldn't quite read the look smoldering back there, in the darkest part of his eyes.

She huffed. She did a lot of that since I'd come out to her and Dad. She had taken to huffing so much I gave it a little nickname: *dragon breath*. Mostly because I knew I was the source of exasperation on her part—and I knew like her reptilian counterpart, if she could, her breath would scorch the world around me if I got onto her bad side. Not that I tried hard to be. I knew I wasn't that sort of son to her.

But the gulf between the boy I was earlier and the man I was becoming now was growing ever wider. Half the time I didn't know how to bridge the gap. Sometimes I think she didn't know either. It was how it often was with my mother and me—on two continents with an ever-widening gulf of water between us. The Pacific seemed like a puddle most of the time by comparison. I didn't want it to be that way, but I didn't see how I could do anything to span the distance. It just was what it was, I suppose.

The others were moving about quietly, looking like they were all settling in for a nice quiet celebration of cake and coffee. I wasn't fooled. They were all on pins and needles about what they'd overheard. Marcel and Marco had put the children down and returned from the guest bedroom while Jeffrey helped his mother get the coffee and cake ready. Morty was busy cycling through his smartphone—checking emails or some other social media thing grandparents did these days. Yet with all of them, I was keenly aware they were all being silent while my little tirade with my mother pressed on. We were center stage and no doubt about it. My mother brought me out of my dark contemplations.

"I know you're *gay*, honey. That's not the issue."

"Well then what is, mother dearest? 'Cause I'd really like to know. If my being gay isn't the issue as you say, then what could it possibly be?"

"You know I don't like to talk to you when you're like this, right?"

"Like what? I said I was spending the evening with a lovely couple and their gay son and suddenly I am smacked with an *oh*... Dangling out there naked as the day I was born. So, what else am I supposed to do with that little sentiment? You tell me, 'cause I am dying to know."

"Els...baby, please," Marco pleaded with me in the barest of whispers, his eyes rolling back to the room behind us indicating everyone was listening.

"Look, I can't do this right now. I was just calling to let you know I am fine and I'll be home a bit later than I thought. We can chat about what I've said later."

"I suppose...you have your key or do I need to leave the door unlocked?"

"I have my key. I'll let myself in. See you in the morning, Mom. Please try not to wait up for me, 'cause that would be like eight buckets of over-caring. Good night."

I rang off without waiting for a reply, not too happy with myself or the spectacle I'd made. I was sure I'd just spoiled the evening for everyone involved. I needn't have worried, though. My guy was on me within seconds wrapping his arms around me for a big ol' hug and nearly cracking a rib or two in the process.

"Omph, yeah, babe. Ease up a bit. Let your lover breathe a little. I hear breathing is the new black these days," I said, smiling as warmly as I could with the worry running rampant in his eyes. I knew he hadn't witnessed enough conversations with my mother to know if this one was normal or not. I thought I should set the record straight for everyone involved before it all went to shit.

"Sorry you all had to hear that. My parents and I have a rather unusual relationship. I'm queer and therefore unusual, so awkward conversations ensue."

Marco began to turn me back from the living room to where everyone else had gathered at the dining room table in the next room. My eyes continued to roam about the house. The Greenbaums truly had a lovely home, tastefully furnished in deep earth tones. A brilliant flow of wood and plaster. Classic color schemes—not the wild over-the-top craziness so many interior decorators ran to so they could "make their mark," thereby guaranteeing in a couple of years when the trend had worn out its welcome, they'd have a repeat customer. The Greenbaums hadn't been taken in with that scam.

There were pictures tucked everywhere among books and carefully placed knickknacks and tchotchkes, but not too cluttered, tastefully arranged in a *we're a big ol' loving family—deal with it* kind of way. I guessed quite a few of them were of Jeffrey's sister Genevieve and her boyfriend/husband. I hesitated in classifying their relationship from the get-go, only because I didn't see any wedding photos of them. But they were easily outnumbered by the images of Marcel and Jeffrey. This was a boy who was deeply loved by his parents. Marcel as well. One particular black and white print dominated the room—large-as-life portrait sized. The two men were shirtless on a black as pitch background, lying head to head in opposite directions where each of the men's heads was in the crook of the other's shoulder. On each of their chests were the new-born babies—they were twins after all. Henri on Marcel and Beatrix on Jeffrey. The image hung over the fireplace with Jeffrey's torso in the normal upright position and Marcel upside down with the rest of his body pointing up toward the ceiling. There were others in this same vein though on a much smaller scale, and a couple of Marcel and Jeffrey holding each other. All very sensual. Morty and Clarice fully embraced their gay son and his husband in a way I truly found quite touching. There was nothing salacious or suspicious about it. Simply family.

I held Marco for a moment, keeping him back near the fireplace so he and I could admire the large print there of these two men and their love for each other, complete with children. Marco's dream, and in a very real way my own too.

"I want to give that to you, babe," he whispered to me as he kissed the side of my face. I leaned into him a bit.

"I know. I want to give that to you too, now I see it for myself. I am totally on-board."

"You boys gonna have some cake and coffee or are you just gonna absorb some hot man-on-man love in our living room all night?" Clarice asked. I smiled at her inflected pronunciation of coffee like any good Jewish

New Jersey woman—very Mike Myers. I broke from Marco's grasp and we walked hand in hand back to the dining room.

Morty and Clarice were marvelous hosts. They shared the story of how Jeffrey's parents met, followed by how Jeffrey and Marcel found each other. What I didn't know was while we were officially celebrating Morty and Clarice's anniversary, it was only a week until Jeffrey and Marcel were to celebrate theirs. They were heading out tomorrow afternoon for a week of anniversary child-free bliss. The grandparents' gift to the boys: a Hawaiian trip and babysitting the grandkids all rolled into one.

"My guy will be on pins and needles—and not just because of the hospital calls he's turned over to his team while he's out. He simply dotes on the kids. It's gonna be our first break in two and a half years. They've just turned three and they've spent the night before here without us so we think we might be able to get through a week with Mom and Dad at the wheel."

"Are you kidding? 'Enri already wanted to know when we were leaving because *Grand-mère* had big plans for zem and zey couldn't get started until *we* got out of 'ere." He shook his head. "'E can't wait to get us out of 'ere fast enough." Marcel whipped it up thick with the French accent to mimic his son's penchant for speaking with one at so early an age. They all chuckled.

"Well in all fairness, we did promise him a trip to Great America so I think the theme park is raging big in his mind. Beatrix too for that matter," Morty countered.

"This cake is really good. Where'd you get it?" I asked as I savored a delicious bite of it.

Clarice shook her head though it was Jeffrey who clarified, "Mom's a retired pastry chef. *This* is home made."

"You have no idea how hard it was for me not to balloon over the years when she kept having me taste so many of her sweet confections. I'm still amazed by how trim I've been able to keep myself. She cooks like a fiend sometimes. Savory as well as the sweets now. I'm inundated with foodie goodness." Morty chortled, enjoying teasing his wife. Her wry smirk made me giggle a bit inside. That was so going to be Marco and me at our fifty-second anniversary, I could just tell.

I carefully navigated the waters of my relationship with my mother to them all. Not that I didn't want to talk about it but in reality, I found it all so terribly boring and so not what was needed as a topic of conversation for an anniversary celebration. Instead I toasted, with coffee since it seemed to be the beverage of choice tonight, to Morty and Clarice. The cake was really marvelous as was the conversation, but I knew I didn't want to overstay our welcome. Watching Marcel and Jeffrey together, I really wanted to get my guy alone so I could tell him how on-board I was with his dream for us. How in this strange and slightly off-kilter day of discovery, I found myself really finding a path to Marco and my life together. It was just there—slightly out of reach but clearly attainable, nonetheless. I needed to tell him that. But I wanted alone time to let him know.

About an hour later, after some more small talk, I feigned becoming tired so we could make our excuses and say goodnight to this lovely, lovely family. I was truly touched by their warmth and generosity, even if it did highlight how much of it was missing from my own life.

"You know you can always have your mother call me and I could get her involved with the local PFLAG. We're a great group of parents and friends. Might be what she needs," Clarice said.

I hugged her as warmly as I could. I wanted her to know how much being with them all had touched me.

"I will think about it."

She passed me a business card from the PFLAG group and made a point to tell me her number was on it and I should pass it along to my parents and they could call her night or day about it. She didn't have to do it. I knew she didn't, but her thoughtfulness made this whole afternoon and evening so important to me.

"You can't imagine how happy you've made me...er, uh..." I looked at my guy, who squeezed my hand gently, letting me know he was there for me. Always. "I mean, how happy you've made the both of us. Really."

She smiled and rubbed my arms. "We're so happy to have met you both as well." Then to Marco, "I'm glad you've met one of your father's friends. I know it meant a lot to Marcel. It all seems like fate, doesn't it?"

Morty rolled his eyes at his wife's over the top dramatic sentiment.

"There she blows, in all her gayboy-loving glory. I swear sometimes she's more consistent than Old Faithful when she gets around your lot." He shook our hands and patted us on the shoulder. We made to move off and onto the front lawn where Jeffrey and Marcel were waiting to walk us to Marco's car.

We casually approached the two of them as they stood next to a tree in their parents' front yard. An old tire swing hung from one of the large oak's gnarled branches.

"Wow, is it the same swing you grew up with or did your dad put it up for Henri?" I asked as we approached them. That seemed to break them from whatever small conversation they had going between them.

"The very same actually. Hard to believe I actually fit in it." Jeffrey eyed it with no small degree of suspicion on whether or not it'd hold him now. "You should see the two of them battle it out over who gets to ride it first. You'd think it'd be Henri, but Beatrix can be a little battle-ax when she wants to be. Henri's going to have his hands full when they grow older," he commented as we all ambled over to the car.

Marco wrapped his arms around me again, my back to his front as he leaned against the side of the Impala, the muscles of his large biceps flexing against my own frail looking arms. I mean, they weren't entirely like matchsticks, but against his they might as well have been. He could always tell whenever I got into comparing his body against my own. I guess I tensed up every time I went there.

"Stop. You're perfect," he whispered into my ear. I sagged and relaxed into him, my only way of letting him know I wasn't going to fight him on it. At least not right now. "Let it go, babe. It's no use. You will never win that debate," he continued, knowing full well I was only tabling the issue.

"I am glad I got to finally meet you, Marco. Your father and I were very close when we were both in medical school at Stanford."

"Yeah, I seem to remember hearing your name once or twice in my past. Finally nice to put a face with a name."

"Well, I wanted to take a moment to say thank you for indulging my parents. I know my mom can be quite a bit to deal with, but she means well. And you'll never find a more vigilant ally than her."

"And 'e's telling ze truth on zat one," Marcel said, though with the only light coming from the Greenbaums' porch, it was hard to tell if that was heartfelt as it sounded or a bit snarky by his expression.

"Don't let his sarcasm fool you. He's smitten with my mother and how she dotes on Marcel and the kids. I'm almost an afterthought now."

Marcel snorted and this time I detected nothing but mirth in it.

"If 'e's an afterthought, than I am ze Archbishop of Canterbury. And you know how we French feel about ze British."

"Only about the same as they feel for you." I quirked a brow at him.

"Oh, I *like* zis one..." Marcel chuckled and patted Marco on the shoulder. Then his mood became a bit more serious. "Marco, try not to worry too much about how your father will react to finding out about you and Elliot. I know I am not your father, but 'e and I were very close when I was going through zat shit with Amalie and Jeffrey. 'E was there for me in ways I couldn't ever imagine. Your father is an amazing man. Trust me in zat. If it's one thing I know, it's how to judge character."

We all began to open our mouths to protest.

"*In men!*" he added in his defense.

We had a bit of a laugh at his comment. Then he continued, "Vincenzo will be there for you. I don't have a single doubt about zat. Your mother on ze other hand..." He just shrugged.

"Yeah, therein lies the rub, as they say," Marco agreed.

"Sofia is, well..." Marcel diplomatically bowed out before he said something he would only regret.

"A piece of work," Marco finished for him. "Yeah, don't worry. You aren't thinking anything my father's mother hadn't drummed into my head as a child. And I've certainly witnessed it enough myself to know what she's capable of. And really, she is the one reason I have held out thus far. I've always sort of known my father would have my back. But she's the big unknown."

"And zat makes it all very touchy. I get it," Marcel finished.

Marco nodded.

"I take it you speak from experience?" I asked.

"All too well," was all he said.

It seemed Marco was ready to shove off.

"Well, thanks again for the delightful evening. We had fun. You both have given us something truly amazing. You have what I want Elliot and me to have. Now he's seen it front and center. He knows what's possible. So, thank you, thank you, thank you. You don't know how much it means to me to have that for Elliot."

"Well, sweetheart, I am not such a total imbecile I couldn't imagine it for myself, but I get you. Yeah, thanks for sharing your lives with us. Seeing it for myself gave me a complete page to work from to help make our own dream a reality. So, thanks."

We shook hands and gave hugs with Euro kisses on each cheek and they watched as we climbed into the Impala.

Just as Marco was about to slip in Jeffrey called to him, "Helluva muscle car you got there Marco. Guess you're a *Supernatural* fan?"

"Buddy, you don't know the half of it..." I chimed in before Marco could respond. He slipped inside the car and slapped a firm hand on my leg and gave me a good squeeze. I knew it meant he was good with my teasing him on it.

Jeffrey leaned in, resting his hands on the window frame. "Yeah, well, that just means he's one of the good guys. We can all use more of them in this world. You boys be careful going home and getting back to school. I know it won't be easy."

"We will. And you both have a safe and enjoyable trip!" Marco called back as he started up the ol' gal. Marcel whistled at how she rumbled.

"Oh, don't worry." He glanced back at his husband. "We will have an amazing time." He wiggled his eyebrows and we all laughed while Marcel just shook his head.

I leaned forward to peer around Jeffrey at Marcel. "Yeah, well, give him a flourish from the two of us, will ya?"

Marcel laughed. "I will at zat! *Count* on it."

Jeffrey stood up and gripped his hubby tightly and they kissed for a second. Then we waved off and Marco pulled out away from the curb and we made our trek back to Mercy.

THE RIDE HOME was quiet. Marco had the iPod running but it was turned down low, more ambient rock music in the background. He was in a full on Stevie Nicks Fleetwood Mac sort of mood. Contemplative, thoughtful. That's my man and I wouldn't have him any other way.

"You know having seen it I want it right fucking now. You know that, don't cha, babe?"

I nodded. "I know. And you know I never deny you on anything, sweetheart."

He nodded. I could tell he was fairly itching to just ditch everything and run off and do it now. Wouldn't *that* be the wake-up call our parents would just die over? Given what I heard about his mother and knowing how hard it was for my own to grapple with, I was fairly sure dying over that bit of news wasn't too remote a possibility.

"But...?" he asked, knowing I had distinctly implied as much.

"But we need to be thoughtful about this and not just give into our baser desires."

"Sweetheart, there's nothing salacious about how I want us to become a couple, legally, matrimonially. Elliot, I want to bind myself to you in every way possible. Seeing Marcel and Jeffrey. Damn babe. I dunno. It just felt so fucking real. Right in front of me where I could scrape it with the tips of my fingers. Like a football you can feel slip into your hands. That fucking close. You have no idea what it did to me. Did to what I feel about us. I'm serious as a big dog, babe. I'd fucking marry you right this fucking instant if you'd agree."

I smiled and kissed the back of his hand where it was firmly laced with mine. "I know and it means more to me than you can possibly know. But as I said, we have to be thoughtful about this, if children are going to be involved, and I know now they will be, so no worries there. I am totally on board with marrying you, having babies with you, raising them and providing a home for our family. Totally, nineteen bajillion thousand percent behind you on that one. Yeah, after Marcel and Jeffrey, it's bang on. I am so down with being your husband."

He had the biggest grin on his face. I could tell how happy I was making him by saying all of this.

"But," I voiced softly while I stroked the back of his hand with my thumb, "since children are going to be involved, I want to be very careful about how we do things. It will color how we approach caring for them. I don't want to act rashly or give in to impulsive thoughts. I mean, surprises and impulses are good and all, but when we're talking about our future, about our lives together and with children, Marco, babe, sweetheart, we need to take it slow. I get you want to get started. Believe me, seeing it now, even I am having to push back on not going for broke right now. But you know what?"

He lifted his chin up a bit to get me to finish.

"It wouldn't be right. I know it, and deep down, in your heart of hearts, you know it."

His mouth became a grim line as he contemplated my words. After an agonizing minute where I didn't know where we were emotionally, he finally broke with a big audible sigh.

"You're right, babe. You're absolutely right. And I am so proud of you thinking enough about us and our future family to talk me down. It just proves to me you are the absolute right person for me. No question at all, babe. It's gonna be you and me."

"And baby makes three?" I asked him, not bothering to hide how much I wanted to fuck him right now.

"...And babies make ten or twelve."

I grinned. "Wow, it's a...um, a whole lot of baby batter there."

"Uh huh. Guess we better make sure the plumbing is all in working order then, huh?"

"Well, we're not too far from the Langley-Pierce fuckpoint."

He pulled his hand free from mine and gripped the back of my neck and brought the side of my head to his lips and kissed me.

"I fucking love you, Elliot Donahey." Then he rolled down his window and yelled it again out loud for the whole damned world to hear. I sank down into my seat as red as the tip of Rudolph's reindeer nose while the Impala sped its way to our little makeshift love nest where I'd show my future husband just how committed I was to him and the dream he had for the two of us.

Chapter Seven

The Man in the Mirror, Biotch!

IT WAS THE morning of the first day of classes and my stomach was doing a series of flip-flops. Seriously, it was like the entire US gymnastics team had been using my stomach as a springboard.

I awoke an extra half hour early just to have time to change my clothes eighteen million times; the shatters of those experiments lay in a tangled heap at the bottom of my closet. I only hoped my mother wouldn't wander in and find half my clean clothing on the floor. All the while I tried to soothe my frayed nerves by listening to my musical oracle Jay Brannan and his "Ever After Happily," extolling the evils and lies in fairytales for gayboys like us while I hummed along, off and on trying like hell to get my nerves under control.

You go, Jay. Feed my black and dark soul this morning. I needed a healthy dose of his cynicism and gayboy sensibility right now to get me psyched for my first day back at school.

I jumped back into the bathroom. As I was struggling with sorting my hair out, the cell phone buzzed, interrupting Jay in the middle of "Half-Boyfriend" and vibrating like a woodpecker on meth across the vanity counter in the bathroom. I barely managed to snag it before it tumbled into the trash can.

"He-hello?"

"Hey beautiful, time to rise and shine. You ready to hit this up?"

"Fuck, no. I think I'm calling in sick."

"Like hell you are. C'mon, babe. We can do this, right? I got your back on it. I won't let you get hurt. Okay? Trust me?"

"Yeah, you know I do. Always will, I 'spect."

"So, get that rockin' look I am so hooked on going and I'll see you in English Lit. Cool? Love you, babe." There was a rustle on Marco's side. "Look, I gotta go. I'll see you there, bye."

He didn't wait for me to say anything. Just *love you* and *bye*.

Well, it was better than nothing, I guess. I looked at myself in the mirror. I knew that fearful face—I'd used it off and on all my life, but I'd never seen the weight of what I stood to lose before. This was new.

I sighed. "One more year of flying under the radar ain't so hard, is it, Els? You can do this." Yeah, somehow it didn't sound as convincing as I'd hoped. I would have to trust Marco on it. The sad part was I didn't know how it was going to play out. It was a whole lot easier when I had no one to react to. I only had to contend with myself before—that was easy. And since it was only myself, I knew exactly what to expect. A whole lot of nothing. I had to face facts: my life before the glory of Marco was boring. My existence was one bland, beige day followed by the next, where nothing ever changed. Well, I'd hoped for something spectacular and the universe had responded post haste. Marco was my world now, and what a glorious world it had been these past few weeks.

"Elliot! You're gonna be late!" came the battle cry of the time-Nazi down the hall.

"We can do this," I said with as much confidence as I could muster. Why did the guy in the mirror still not look so convinced? I glared at him. *"Bitch..."*

MERCY HIGH WAS like most nondescript schools built in the latter 1950s in Northern California. At one time it had been run by the Catholic Church, though that era ended in the late 1970s. It had become unconsecrated and secular. The theatre now occupied what had once been the church itself. No doubt the acoustics lent themselves to no other purpose. The main building of the school was a two-story oblong boxy structure with the PE and sports facilities on the far side of the open courtyard occupying the space between them.

Actually, the nicest part of Mercy was its landscaping. The open courtyard was multi-layered and beautifully landscaped, verdant and lush greenery that was completely wasted on teenage youth of the techno-world generation. It was heavily peppered with tall thick redwoods forming fairy rings on various parts of the campus, giving way to wildly controlled English gardens with a large English oak here and there. About the only good thing the students thought of the courtyard was it made for a killer backdrop for school group pictures for the yearbook.

I loved that part of the school. Many sketches of it graced the sketchpad I always kept close at hand. Now I'd have to keep it even closer as it had numerous sketches I'd made of Marco, several of which were of him sleeping peacefully, albeit completely naked. His beautifully sculpted body made for an excellent male nude study. As his boyfriend, I figured it was fair territory. My territory actually, if what he'd said was true. Now, knowing what my sketchbook represented within the context of being in my backpack, and on school grounds, it carried an ominous tone I wasn't so sure about any longer. I made a mental note to buy a new one this afternoon and swap them out before the worst could happen.

My mother looked sideways at me. "Aren't you ever going to cut that hair? It's never out of your eyes."

"That's the look, Mom."

"Yeah, well, I didn't realize English Sheepdog chic was back in fashion."

"Better than the Day-Glo love fest with Doc Martens from your fly-girl era, Mom. I'll take the canine chic any day."

She rolled her eyes and clicked the turn signal to bring us onto the senior lot.

"Ya know, I asked your dad about a car for you this year, seeing how you're going to graduate and will need one for college."

"Mom, we don't even know if I'm accepted anywhere yet. Besides, we can't afford it. Not the way the Q's been lately."

"Oh, with your good grades, I know you'll be. Any school would be proud to have you as a student; don't worry about the money part of it. Your dad said he would see what he could arrange for you. It won't be a Beemer or anything like that, 'cause we ain't the Sforzas, but I can probably swing it being one of the newer models that will still catch someone's eye."

"Someone, as in?"

"Well, whomever. I don't pretend to know all of your secrets, but I have noticed you seem to be more concerned with how you look, haircuts aside."

"Yeah, well, maybe they like the way I look."

"Oh, ho! So, there is someone special! Why haven't you told me about him, yet? It is a guy, right? I didn't miss a memo on a change of heart, did I?" I heard both sides of our recent family dilemma. Dear ol' Dad had accepted a job off-shore drilling in Alaska rather than face the fact his only son was a fairy. Not that I thought for one minute my pop didn't ultimately love me. I knew he did. But I also knew the big manly guy needed to put some major distance between us to deal with me and my fae ways. The money was good, which helped to balance the failing Q business and keep us financially afloat, but it was putting a strain on the marriage and our family life. To compensate for his absence, my dad did Skype with me once a week and he'd no doubt signaled to Mom he suspected their son had someone special in his life.

"Your daddy figured it out, you know."

"Fabulous. And yes, it's a guy. But I ain't sayin' who just yet. We gotta fly under the radar for a bit."

She pulled up to the drop-off point and threw it into park for a second. Her hand stalled me from pulling the handle on the door that would allow my freedom from the twenty questions I knew she was speedily assembling.

"Oh, he isn't out to his family, yet? You know sweetheart, that's not a very good foundation to start a relationship."

"Yeah, we know. And he's not ashamed or anything like that. It's just, well, who he is would bring a lot of drama down on both of us if it came out. We don't need it right now. We decided this together. I've got him on this. We talked about it. We're good."

I tried a smile on for my mom but it didn't quite fit right. I knew she cared and was trying to see things from my perspective, but she simply wasn't a gay teenage boy. She could empathize all she wanted to; she was one down by not being male, and two, for not getting the whole gay thing. I loved her for trying, but it really wasn't much for me to work with.

"Do you love him, baby?"

That word—*baby*, not the L word—sort of rattled me. It sounded odd coming from her now, though she'd used it all my life. It had a different context than when Marco used it. I supposed it was the way it should be.

"Oh yeah, Mom. It's real. We've been talking about…"

Wait, best not to say anything about marriage just yet. Might jinx the whole damned thing.

"Well, we've been talking."

"That's good, sweetheart. You need me to pick you up for your afternoon shift?"

"Nah, I got it, Mom. I'll be there at three."

"'Kay, love you."

"Yeah, me too," I mumbled drolly as I finally made my escape into the jungles of academia.

I MADE IT to Mr. Crowe's English Lit class well ahead of the other students. As an A-level student, I had no reason to hide with the other kids from the eagle-like gaze of Thomas Crowe's love of all things literary. But, given how the jocks tended to congregate at the back of the classroom, I thought I'd, at least symbolically, meet Marco halfway by taking a seat at the long tables midway up the center aisle along the second story windows overlooking the quad below.

A few minutes later and the other students started to file in. So far no one who looked remotely troublesome had wandered in. Maybe I could look forward to starting off my morning with my new boyfriend with no one around to put a damper on it. I turned slightly in my chair and stared out onto the quad. I spotted Marco chatting with some of his teammates. A couple of the guys already had cheerleaders hanging off them like leeches. *The tarts*, I thought.

I looked on silently as Cindy Markham sidled up to Marco and slinked an arm around his waist and leaned her head on his shoulder. He turned in surprise, smiled in greeting, although I noted how he gently extracted himself from her embrace. His gaze floated up to the English room and noticed me looking down on the gathering. Marco turned to the others and said something, allowing him to beg off the group and make his way toward the building. Within the matter of a few seconds he slipped from view, leaving me to stew in frustration juices over Cindy's pawing of my man. I knew it was totally unwarranted. Marco gently but deftly navigated those waters to rebuff her advances, but he also knew there'd be a whole lot more of this as the school year got underway. I wasn't so sure how to deal with it. A warm, rich familiar baritone snapped me from my thoughts.

"Hey there, uh, Elliot, right? Uh, is this seat taken?"

I allowed my gaze to nonchalantly drift up the length of the body I knew intimately, careful to school my features into that shy mode I knew so well. I shook my head softly, the hair falling into my face (knowing how this affected him), and murmured, indicating the chair between us, "Uh, no. Help yourself."

Marco smiled warmly. His eyes seemed to flash brilliantly as he took the seat, tossing his backpack onto the table we shared.

"Thanks."

He leaned back in his chair, the iconic requisite jock pose. He thrummed his fingers onto the tabletop to some non-existent song, expending nervous energy—it's what they did. I realized when I was nervous, I turned inward, but Marco seemed to work in the reverse. Opposites attracting, right? For some reason, I wasn't so sure. Marco looked around the room; so far, no other jocks or cheerleaders had bothered to show. At least for now, the coast was clear.

Marco chanced a quiet whisper in my direction. "You okay, baby?"

I stared down at the desktop. I found I couldn't meet Marco's eyes even though I knew it was exactly what he wanted. This was all so strange. I didn't know which way was up or down. I felt sick, queasy, over this whole game. I just nodded twice in rapid succession.

"It'll be okay, babe. I promise. But you gotta work with me, 'kay?"

I shrugged. He regrouped and sighed at how uncomfortable I seemed to him.

"Yeah, 'kay," I murmured.

Marco seemed to let his eye rove for a bit before picking up a louder conversation with me. "So, uh, you any good at this whole English Lit thing? 'Cause I might need some help with my writing. Despite what you smart kids think, we jocks aren't all brainiacs."

"Says you, Sforza," bellowed my worst nightmare: Beauregard *The Fag-o-nator* Hopkins. Tall, dark (in that deep russet-colored African-American variety—not that there's anything wrong with it, just an observation), and imminently foreboding. Beau walked around with an air of the last pussy he'd just banged and an ax to grind over anyone weaker than him. And for him right now, it spelled my faggoty ass. For once, I was so thankful I had a jock on my side.

I'd had one class last year with Hopkins and had the unfortunate opportunity of being his lab partner in Chemistry. It was a match made in Dante's ninth level of hell. Beau Hopkins, despite being the local Baptist minister's son, could be cast perfectly in the role of Lucifer. He was blessed with a beguiling beauty but with a heart as black and unfeeling as if it were made of coal, through which it pumped not blood but the sludge of tar. The man knew how to bring Hell's rain for weaklings like me.

The cocky bastard bumped fists with Marco as he passed and then stopped, turned, and looked at Marco with a quizzical stare.

"Somethin' the matter wit choo, Sforza? I think you bettah check your ticket stub. You know we all sit at the back. Or did you decide to get ringside homo seats or somethin?"

I caught the flash of anger moving through my boyfriend upon hearing the word *homo*. I silently marveled at how expeditiously he schooled his gaze at Beau. It was a word I was well accustomed to hearing because it had been thrown my way more times than I cared to count. But for him, it cut, probably for the first time. We both knew only his secret separated his world from my own—and how easily he could fall.

"Yeah, well, I've been having trouble seeing the board sometimes. I think I need to get my eyes checked or something. Thought I'd sit closer to the board this time around."

"Yeah, well, you sit any longer next to gaybait there and you'll need an HIV test soon enough."

Marco tensed at this little exchange. While he appeared to be taking it with grace, he was holding onto the frame of the table with a white-knuckle grip. The whimsy of reclining back in the chair had stopped. He gently eased the chair back down.

"You trying to say something already, Beau? You got a problem with where I choose to sit?"

Beau raised an eyebrow over this small breach in jock etiquette. It was a flag, a big flappin' red one. I wasn't so sure I was worth Marco having to take a stand so early on our first day.

"Look, uh, I can sit up front." I began to gather my things.

Marco held up his hand, palm facing me. His body language was clear—*Elliot, you don't move a muscle; I got this.*

He stood slowly. He wasn't as tall as Beau but he carried himself like a warrior of equal stature, if not greater. Was he their captain? Quarterback cred, maybe? I wasn't sure which, but it was sort of awesome to watch it all unfold.

"I said my eyes need to be closer to the board. You got some sort of problem with me needing to see?" Marco cocked his head to the side a bit to emphasize his point.

Beau's gaze flattened. He was about to come up with some sort of retort when Mr. Crowe walked in, sensing tension in the air—probably because all of the students who were already seated were just as wide-eyed as I was over the verbal exchange.

"Nah, it's your funeral, Sforza. You can sit wherever the hell you want. Just try not to catch anything." He moved off.

"Gee, thanks for the vote of confidence. I hope it extends to the field, Hopkins. Have a blessed day."

Marco sat down again, waved to Mr. Crowe who seemed to accept Marco's signal that the world had indeed righted itself again. He began to sort out his desk and write up the day's plan on the board, though I noticed Mr. Crowe's gaze kept bouncing up to Beau and Marco, trying like hell to decide if he needed to watch those two.

Yeah, I am right there with ya on that one, boss.

Marco pulled his phone out of his letterman's pocket and tapped a message out. A second later my phone buzzed in my pocket. I tried to hide my smirk as Marco chuckled softly.

I pulled the phone slyly out of my pocket and tapped the unlock code and there was a pic of Marco naked, completely hard in the bathroom after a shower. It was dated this morning. Under it simply read: *I so want to fuck you, sexy*.

As if the phone sent a shock up my arm, I threw it into my backpack, my hands nervously shaking from the little exchange. It buzzed again. I let it buzz.

"Look again," Marco whispered so softly I nearly didn't hear him.

Though I was thoroughly frightened of what I might spy this time around, I reached into my bag as if I were searching for a pen and punched in the lock code to find a picture of Marco's chest with a heart drawn on it in gel soap. Beneath the picture were the words: *I love you and I'll behave now.—M.*

Marco slipped his phone back into his jacket as the other kids filed in with the bell chiming in the hallway. Mr. Crowe called the class to attention and their voices dissolved.

"All right, everyone, let's take our seats so I can get roll taken and the syllabus out to you for this semester's work."

The class went okay. Actually, better than I'd hoped. Mr. Crowe had assigned a couple of research projects on Shakespeare and Marlowe and had paired up the students according to where we sat in the room. This left Marco and me as research partners, a perfect ploy for us to fly under. I left the class practically walking on air, though I noticed the dark stare between Hopkins and Marco as we made our way to our next class.

American Civics was next on the docket and I made my way to the class with all haste. Since the halfway seating seemed to work in the last class, I thought I should keep to the tactic that hadn't failed me yet. Marco followed suit and our little ploy seemed to even out. Thankfully Hopkins was a no show for this class so things were a lot easier to manage. Until Cindy Markham showed up and took the seat on the other side of Marco and proceeded to occupy his time with idle chit-chat over things only an air-brained cheerleader would think had any relevance to this journey we called life. *The bitch*.

I secretly hoped our near hits and misses weren't going to go like that all day. As we departed Civics, my phone buzzed. I grabbed it and found Marco making a sad face with the word *sorry* under it. I shook my head before stopping at my locker to pick up my calculus book. I made my way to class and found Marco had been trapped by a group of girls who ate up all the seats around him. Marco's eyes found mine, without anything he could do about it. I gently shrugged at Marco and took the seat next to my only friend on campus, Greg Lettau. He was a hawkish looking kid with thick horned-rimmed glasses magnifying his eyes, the quintessential math geek cum wizened owl. Summer had been good to Greg. Gone was the rail thin body. He'd filled out a bit; solid muscle tone lay underneath the T-shirt now.

Did everyone have a bang-up summer?

The one good thing about Greg, well at least to me, was no one seemed to know what a wickedly fast sense of humor he possessed. I'd studied with him before last year in Trig, so he was a known entity. Seeing how geeks couldn't often afford the luxury of choosing who to be friends with, he didn't seem to mind the loner gayboy status raining down on me 24/7. Greg seemed to enjoy trading the verbal barbs. His pop-culture refs were nearly as good as mine—and he could riff esoterically as much as I could. Though he did have to Google Maria Ouspenskaya when I threw that one at him. He actually knew who she was from all of those classic horror movies from the early Hollywood days; he just didn't know her name. Now he tried to drop her name whenever he got the chance. By this new barometer, if someone our age knew about Maria, then they were fucking golden to Greg and me. There was a point where I thought Greg might be gay too but then I spied a shit-load of girl-on-girl porn on his cell phone which put him squarely in the straight boy camp. More metrosexual (or post if you took into account the whole metro thing was so passé now), actually. But things were cool between us.

"Heya," I said flatly as I plopped my backpack down on the table and turned sideways in the chair to chat him up.

He nodded, a slight twinkle to his eye. "S'up? Good summer?"

"Yeah." I glanced back at Marco who still was chatting up a few of the cheerleaders but caught my gaze and chanced a wink in my direction. "Actually not too fucking bad." I took a gander at Greg, letting him see my eyes roll up and down the length of him. "You sure seemed to fill out. What the fuck, dude?"

"Yeah, decided I was through with turning sideways and disappearing altogether. Had my big brother show me a few things in the gym. Busted my ass there most of the summer. Seems to have paid off. Well, 'cept for the horns around my eyes." He tapped the glasses. "Gonna have to address that if I hope to get a chance at scoring with a girl this year."

"Nah, your whole Clark Kent thing sorta works for you now. You can definitely see the Superman bubbling underneath."

Greg leaned in slightly to me. "Dude, it's way too bad you aren't a girl. You are *so* good for my ego."

"Hey, I got your back on this. I hear any girls who might be interested and I'll steer 'em your way. Cool? 'Sides, with the work you've been putting in, I bet your backside is one of your better assets now." I wiggled my eyebrows.

"Hey, now. Appreciate the merch all you want, but from a distance." There was a gleam in his eye, though. I think part of him was fairly cool with someone thinking he had achieved some sort of hotness cred on campus, even if it was from the gay guy.

I smiled broadly. I glanced at Marco. He never stopped staring in my direction, choosing to dart back to whatever girl had addressed him with a question than to avert his eyes from me. Something to his gaze caught my attention. Was he jealous of my chatting up Greg? I should test that—I know it sounded evil but hell, he had a gaggle of girls around him trying their best to garner his attention, why should he have all the fun?

I leaned forward a bit and Greg caught on it was a private moment. Well, as private as we could get in a classroom environment.

"Yeah, well my summer was hella hot and sweaty too. Just not in the same way."

Greg's eyes widened a bit. "Dude, really?"

I nodded, not bothering to hide the lascivious smirk Marco had put there.

He bumped my fist. "Fuck, who'da thought the gayboy would score before the straight geek did? That's gotta be some sort of coup, right?"

He glanced around. No one was paying any attention. Geeks and gays fly under the social radar for the most part.

"Anyone I know?"

I shrugged, rolling my eyes to the ceiling for emphasis that he most definitely did but I wasn't saying.

"Fuck? *Really?*"

Greg never missed a beat. I liked that about him. His eyes darted to the ring on my finger. The wedding-band ring finger.

"That from him?"

I shrugged again.

"Is it real?"

I calmly nodded.

"What is it? White gold? Looks like it cost a chunk of change too."

"Platinum, actually. And I'm fairly sure it did."

"Dude, that's some serious shit." He turned a bit to stare at his opened math book. "Donahey ain't virgin meat anymore," he murmured as he looked at me again. "Does your mother know?"

"That I'm not, yeah. Who? No. Gotta keep it on the DL, though. Sorta sucks but it's the way it has to be for the moment."

"Are you sayin' what I think you're sayin'?" His eyes widened a bit where his mind raced with the implication. "Fuck me."

"If you insist," I smiled.

He shoved my shoulder. "Shit, you wish, Donahey."

"Yeah, well. Actually, what I got goin' on definitely takes me out of the market. Not that there was much of one before. But fuck me if it didn't turn my world upside down when it happened. Still *is* sort of upside down."

"Yeah, well, that rock star ring you got there is proof it's serious. Right?"

"Hope so..."

"Well, at least you learned from the trophy wives of Beverly Hills to get the rocks before you suck the cocks."

The bell rang and we started to sort ourselves out for the next droll hour of Mr. Barrett's monotone lecture on all things Calculus.

It was pretty much how the day panned out. PE was better as the first half of the semester I had signed up for tennis, something I was actually quite good at. At one time I'd even thought about going out for the team but couldn't seem to get over how I'd be ranked in with the jocks and I wasn't quite willing to go there on principle.

This was, of course, all before I started banging a jock, but still, the principle somehow held. Marco decided to sign up for tennis as well, though it was painfully clear with all of his athletic prowess—which he had in great abundance—he had never held a tennis racket in his life.

This struck me as a bit odd. Marco came from a rich family; didn't all rich people play tennis? Wasn't it a prerequisite for being a member of the club, right up there with golf?

Whatever the reason, it gave Marco a great opportunity to learn how to play with me as his teacher. By the time the period was over I taught Marco how to serve consistently and we had quite a few rounds of great volleys going back and forth. I could tell Marco really enjoyed that we could do something athletic together. No doubt my revelation of playing multiple sports with my dad was still percolating around in the back of his mind. I rolled my eyes when the shower buzzer went off and we hastily made our way back to the locker rooms.

"Wanna do lunch off campus?"

"Well, I did bring something, but yeah I guess we can."

"Great. Howzabout eating out on the cliffs?"

"Can we make it in time if you gotta pick up something for yourself?"

"Who said anything about picking something up? I got a picnic cooler all set up for us."

I blushed. I should've known Marco wouldn't let it slide. I looked around to make sure no one could hear our conversation. "Are you trying to get a nooner out of this?"

"One can only hope, sexy."

I put a hand out to stop him for a second. I whispered the next part to make sure we weren't overheard.

"Okay, new rule. No sexy talk before showers, cool? I so don't need the extra attention."

"Yeah, I get it. Okay. But it doesn't mean I won't be thinking it."

"Yeah, okay, big guy. I getcha."

"Are you ever…" he purred.

WE SHOWERED, CHANGED, and were out the door nearly five minutes before the lunch period bell rang. I took off walking to a part of the stadium furthest from the campus as if I were going to eat lunch on the bleachers. Marco pulled out in the Impala and navigated to the same part of the student parking lot where no one could spy me slipping into the car and we were off down the road for the five-minute drive to the clifftop bluffs.

After parking in the lot at the far end where it bent at an odd angle from the entrance, we thought we would be safely secluded from any would-be onlookers. The moment the engine was off Marco hiked himself over the driver's seat and was pawing to bring me back with him. I giggled and Marco laughed as we collided in the backseat in a clash of bodies, mouths, and tongues. Marco got his nooner of sorts and fifteen minutes later, only because we were on a tight schedule, we were sitting on the hood of the car with our backs against the windshield eating some cold fried chicken and potato salad and drinking Cokes Marco had packed for us. I offered one of the two green apples I brought to Marco, leaving my simple PB&J to wilt in the bag for dinner at the shop later.

We ate in silence until Marco finally commented on our day so far. "Well, all in all, I think we got something good going on here. I think we can get through to November without too much interference. And the nooners definitely are a plus." He wiggled his eyebrows leaving me with the obligatory eye roll.

"Well, I don't know 'bout Hopkins. He seemed to be pretty put out by my being so close to you. That could still be a problem."

"What? No way. It ain't gonna happen—not on my watch." Marco said it with such finality I knew better than to contradict, but only because I didn't want it to be the cause of our first real argument. "I got you on this, Els. He ain't gonna come near what's mine. I'll take care of it. Okay? No one is gonna touch a single hair on your beautiful head as long as I'm around."

The last part of the day passed with relative ease leaving us with English being our one class where anyone could cause a commotion, though Marco didn't think Beau would. We had our say, and Marco thought it would blow over. I thought maybe it might not be the case and Marco was being a bit naive in how he viewed Hopkins' raging homophobia. But then again, a guy like Marco never had to deal with homophobia ever being directed his way. No one would ever see it, not even if he showed up in bright pink tights and a feather boa. They'd all laugh it off as some joke. He had the cred to pull it off. Cred enough to burn and still have an abundance left over. But his line of cred in no way extended to me. In the words of my boyfriend: ain't gonna happen.

Chapter Eight

Time Keeps On Slippin'...

THE NEXT COUPLE of days seemed to slip by. Just like one of Marco's favorite classic rock songs, we were *flying like an eagle*. Things moved along at a fairly decent clip.

Because of this we lapsed into a carefully controlled, but regular routine. No one seemed to be the wiser. Even Hopkins had tempered himself into a gentle ribbing of Marco each morning, telling him he needed to get his eyes checked soon 'cause he couldn't see the riffraff surrounding him. The edge to his ribbing surprised me, but both guys seemed to laugh it off with ease. Maybe it was a macho thing I couldn't translate—but I didn't think so. All I could do was accept Marco had been right, and the tension would blow over.

Yet, every time I let my gaze wander to the back of the room, Hopkins' glare was intense, focused, and undeniably virulent. And no mistaking it, it was pointed solely at me.

THE FIRST FOOTBALL game of the season was coming up this Friday and as it was a home game, Marco kept asking me if I was going to show. Typically, I was working when the football games were going on but sensing how important it was to Marco, I begged Mom to take my

Friday evening shift, trading a Wednesday to be fair, so I could attend the games under the guise of trying to be a bit more active in my senior year.

She was so surprised at my sudden interest in school, she openly welcomed my asking for Friday nights off to attend the football games. I suspected perhaps she was suspicious about this new boyfriend of mine and the possible tie to my sudden interest in the football team, but if she was, she didn't make any inquiries to suggest she was onto me.

I sent a text to Marco Wednesday afternoon that I was definitely on for Friday's game. I hoped it would make his day to find out I was *so* in. A few seconds later, the phone rattled on the store counter and I got a reply in the form of a picture with a breathtaking ear-to-ear grin of Marco with the caption *"11 on the F-O-M, babe!"*

I grinned at the phone, content I could make Marco's day. I promptly texted back, reminding him we had to restrict our fun before a game; it was bad luck, though I thought it probably was a myth, or it only applied to boxers or something like that. The phone vibrated in my hand.

Marco: *Yeah, but I am so gonna score after the game. I don't care how the team does—either way I'm a winner!*

One-hundred and two characters representing my boyfriend's bliss. It made the slog through my shift at the Q a bit more bearable.

I found I already missed the days where it had only been the two of us and our plans were the only thing we had to consider. It was just like when I was all by myself, but with major bennies. I pulled out my iPhone and stared at the picture of Marco's big smile.

"Eleven on the fuck-o-meter," I chuckled to myself. "I broke the scale, hon." I smiled softly as I ran a slow thumb along the image of Marco's face. "I still don't know what you see in me, babe. But"—I sighed heavily—"whatever it is, I hope you never lose sight of it. I'm really counting on it, big guy." I couldn't help it when my eyes misted up over the sentiment. I didn't know how I'd ever be able to cope with losing Marco. It was unfathomable, overwhelming in the extreme.

The back door to the store popped open and shut and my mother's slip-on heels clicked as she made her way from the back. I liked knowing my mom had some sense of style. She was in a '60s chic retro phase, but it seemed to suit her toned figure. Today it was her pink pedal pusher Capris with a simple button-down white blouse with her blonde locks tied off with a pale pink scarf. Very JFK Camelot wonderful. A blonde version of Mary Tyler Moore from *The Dick Van Dyke Show* era. It always sort of amazed me how much of an amalgam I was between my parents. I got my waifish pale body from my mom, but my height and darker features from my dad. She smiled warmly as she glided in my direction. I clicked my phone to off and slipped it in my pocket. I hurriedly grabbed a wet towel and began to wipe down the tables and chairs for the umpteenth time today. It was something to do.

"How's my boy doing this afternoon?"

"Great, Mom. We actually had a small rush about thirty minutes ago. Family of six wandered in lost but, thankfully, hungry—evidently happy to find food they could identify with, I guess. All on a road trip through California from Ohio. It figures our only shining business of the day had to come from out of state. No one else ever seems to stop by. Ya know, I think when Grandpa died he took the real business with him. Sorta put the spook on the place, don't you think so? I mean, I remember you bringing me here every now and then. It was never empty like it is now."

She sighed, obviously conceding my point. "Yeah, I know. I've been thinking of selling the franchise to someone else. I just don't know the first thing about it. Do I take an ad out on Craigslist? It used to be so much simpler when I was your age."

"Well, duh, you didn't have me to contend with for starters, so, uh, yeah."

She flicked a towel playfully at me. "Yeah, well, I wouldn't trade it for all the business in the world. So, it's not crazy busy here. With what your dad sends we're getting by."

She looked a little wistful. I wasn't sure she wanted me to see that, so I tried to look busy. Neither of us were very good at this.

"And I guess it gives me something to do."

She seemed a little down about that. I figured it was hard for her to do this alone, even if I was putting in nearly all of my available spare time into the shop to give her some much needed downtime. It wasn't so bad working at the shop, really. She even let me do my homework while on the job if things were slow enough, which invariably they were.

"So, the boyfriend, is he on the team?" she asked coyly as she faked wiping down the counter, waiting for me to surprise her with a revelation she could cling to.

"Not sayin', Mom, so you can stop asking. I said when the chance of drama blows over, then we'll come clean.

Until then, I am giving him his peace of mind. It's only for another month and a half or so. In the grand scheme of things, I think a little longevity in our relationship is worth a month and a half of sacrifice, don't you?"

She stopped and leaned against the counter, a look of awe blossoming across her face. "Well, that does settle it. He is on the team. The football season ends right around then."

I opened my mouth to say something to the contrary, to deny the obvious. It was pointless; I knew that. But I needn't have bothered.

She held a hand up to stop me before I began. "But I'll respect both your wishes on it. *For now.*" She said her last a little pointedly. I got the message. She was biding her time, but only just, though there seemed to be more.

"But what I'd like to know now, when did you get to be so grown up?"

She didn't say it sarcastically; she meant it. It was as if what I'd said suddenly allowed her to see me for the man I was becoming. She walked around the counter and sat down at the edge of the bench of the table I was wiping down. I'd been rubbing the same spot for so long I was sure the white was going to strip away from the Formica. She reached out and grabbed my hand, stopping me. I rolled my eyes, trying hard not to wince at her mothering. My mom didn't have a long list of things to do during her day. I shouldn't be so quick to remove me from it.

"Hey, from the way you talk about him, well, what little you have, anyway, I can tell he means an awful lot to you. But I don't want you to think you have to hide, okay? I'm good with it; we're good with it. I mean, even your daddy figured out there was someone special."

"Yeah, and I'm sure he was just over the moon about that one."

"Now, don't be too hard on him. He loves you very much. It's just, well, you never plan on your children being that way."

"That *way*? Really, Mom? Gay, the word is gay. You better get used to saying it, 'cause it's not a phase. Ma...uh, we...uh, have been talking about long term plans between us. After high school sort of plans. He's very old fashioned. He's already said he wants to marry me at some point. Though don't worry, it's not like it's gonna happen tomorrow. Well, I don't think so, anyway. But with him, I dunno. He could pop the question in the next hour. He's quite taken with me. Lord only knows why, but he is." I shrugged, more to myself than to her. "I kinda like it."

My mother bit her lower lip and her eyes got a little misty. She tugged on my hand which I knew by now meant she wanted to have a heart-to-heart so I might as well put away all pretense of working and sit my butt down. Like an emotional pit bull, there was no way to talk Kayla Donahey out of something once she sank her teeth into it. I plunked myself down and blew the hair out of my face to watch her fully.

"Sweetie, I know the world is beautiful to you right now. Everything is golden and he makes everything so special. I get it. But the world can be a very scary place. Especially for..."

"I know, Mom. Big baddies around the corner—I got the memo on it. The thing is, I truly feel he has my back. We both are aware of how weird this whole school thing is. Keeping things on the down low. He doesn't want it either. He truly doesn't, and I believe him. He's only asking for a little time to get out of the limelight. Then he said all of it will come out. He'll accept whatever happens with his friends and teammates. That what we have is what matters to him. He's looking beyond high school already. I believe him; I really do. You'd be impressed with him, Mom. He comes from a good family. He said he wants to meet the both of you and he hopes he'll be able to show you how much I mean to him. So, it's good, Mom."

She looked at me for a bit. Her eyes still wet with what was surely anxiety over the road I faced. She sniffled and tried a smile that made her eyes sparkle.

"So, marriage, huh?"

I nodded, pouring every ounce of seriousness I had in me the subject warranted. She didn't want me to hide, so there it was—in all its naked glory. Well, almost. I still hadn't confirmed who he was.

"Hey, it was a surprise to me as much as it is to you. He's even said he wants kids. I sure as hell don't have any idea on how I'll manage that one."

She patted my hand.

"I think you'd be a very good father. You've got a good heart, Elliot, a natural propensity for compassion. You see things very few people do. I suppose it's because of your quiet nature."

I ran my thumbnail along the edge of the tabletop, not looking at my mother's face—afraid of how she'd take any more information about Marco. Then I thought, if she meant what she said about not hiding, she should get used to hearing about my life. Very quietly, as if testing the waters, I added, "He said he's loved me for two years now and it took him that long to work up the courage to ask me out."

I couldn't help myself; my eyes darted to Mom's face, curious on how she'd react.

"Really?" Mom frowned in the way people do when they get a bit of news they didn't expect. Not in a bad way, just from out of the blue sort of news.

I nodded. "He said he checked out the store for three weeks in June this summer after school got out just to figure out when it was slow so he could be alone to talk to me."

A quirk of a smile colored Mom's face. I couldn't take it, her thinking something that went unsaid. "What?"

She shook her head. "Your daddy did sort of the same thing with me. He was so scared to talk to me—afraid of what, I have no idea. I was about as quiet as they came back then."

"You? Quiet? I'd love to have seen that!" I snickered to the point where I ended up sputtering and choking on my own spit.

"You laugh, but yeah, you're not too far off the mark from how I was back then. You get your temperament from me, mister, but you get your heart from your daddy."

"If that's so, why'd he leave to go work in Alaska, then? I know it was because of me, of what I am." I was a bit surprised I actually went there. So not the time to bring up Dad's departure to the wilds of the Alaskan coast. She seemed nonplussed by it.

"Now, baby, it's not like that. Not in the way you think. Yes, your daddy has had to figure out what your coming out means to him. But he still Skypes with you on a regular basis, doesn't he?"

I sort of nodded and shrugged. I had to concede to her point. And despite my anger and resentment over my dad leaving just when things got heated, I did look forward to those Skype calls. Despite all my grumbling, I did miss him so.

"He still wants to stay connected to your life. It's just something he's never had to grapple with, that's all." She held a hand up to stall the words bubbling at the edge of my lips. I waited, ceding what I wanted to say to hear my mother out. "Not that he's tormented over it. Actually, it frightens your dad. Frightens him in ways I don't think he knows how to deal with."

"So, he up and runs away."

"I know it seems like that."

I snorted, despite my trying to remain neutral for her. "Only cause it is."

"Cassiel Elliot Donahey, you know it is not how it all went down! Don't you make me pull the Mom card on you, young man."

"Yes, ma'am," I replied sheepishly.

She nodded curtly once, accepting my implied, though unspoken, apology. She pressed on in his defense.

"Your daddy is a big burly guy. A man's man, as they say. But inside, he's very soft. Gentle. His fear for you overwhelms him at times. The job in Alaska was an opportunity too good to pass up. The money is too good. The contract is almost up and he'll be coming home soon anyway. I can tell he can't wait to wrap it all up and come home."

"And what will we do then? Not like we can live on the fine life the Q can provide."

She nodded, acknowledging the obvious. "Well, he said the company he's contracted with has an engineering position in the project management side in their corporate office in Monterey. They've offered him the position if he wants it."

"And does he...?"

"He's negotiating the deal as I sit here with you right now. So, see, baby, everything will work itself out. Heck, by the time you and your beau come out of hiding or the down low, as you kids say, we'll all be back together again. Win-win, right?"

I rolled my eyes. "Yeah, okay. One big happy gay family. Got it."

She shook her head but accepted she got what she wanted from our little talk. I started to get up again when she suddenly grabbed my hand, stalling me.

"Is it Stephen Lowry?"

"What? Uh, Mom...no! That's so—OMG, ewww. We used to have sleepovers in elementary school. That's so many shades of wrong."

"Okay, okay. It was just a thought."

"One you can put out to pasture 'cause that's bucketloads of crazy. Stephen Lowry—ehhhhgh." I shook violently from the thought of being intimate with my one-time best friend from elementary school. But it didn't have anything to do with the fact Lowry started to ditch me around the time I began to admit my attraction to other boys.

It didn't. I swear.

FRIDAY DESCENDED INTO a quagmire of gray and grisly with the threat of a raging storm heading our way. There was talk the first game would be hell on wheels on account of the rain. By 2:00 p.m. the clouds had definitely blackened a bit but so far not a drop had fallen. Most people were positive it'd be cold as hell, but the forecast was the game was still a go no matter what.

Great.

When the final bell rang a half hour later, I rapidly made my way out across the stadium to the far edge of the school grounds. By the time I scaled the ridge, navigating between the redwoods and cypresses covering the hillside that ran alongside the road behind the school, the dark purr of Marco's car was heading my way. The car slowed briefly, and like a well-oiled pep crew at the Indy 500, the door popped open and I slipped inside and we were off to spend a little downtime before the big game.

Marco drove us back to our small parking lot along the cliffs. Given the nature of the weather, we weren't too surprised ours was the only car in the lot. Marco took our favorite spot at the far end safely tucked from view. We spent the next hour cuddling and kissing in the back seat. I was able to keep Marco at bay, promising he could have his way with me all night if he wanted. My mother was running the shop until nine and then was going out with a couple of girlfriends up to Carmel to hang out for the night. She probably wouldn't be back until early morning.

Marco's eyes flashed brilliantly at this news.

"Baby, I can't tell you how happy you make me, that you're coming to my game. I am gonna play so hard for you. I'll make you so proud; you'll see. Everything I do out there, it's 'cause I'll know you're in the stands watching." He kissed me deeply, his fingers gently stroking my face, my brow. Marco's lips moved from mine along my chin to nuzzle upon my neck. I gave of myself freely, allowing Marco to take whatever he wanted—well, nearly everything he wanted. There was a point in our making out where he made a valiant effort to strip me out of most of my clothes, but I was adamant about the no-sex-before-a-game rule.

"Look, if I'm gonna freeze my ass off watching you get pummeled on the field, I think you can hang onto your libido for a few hours. After that, I'm yours to do with as you please, as many times as you please."

"You know what I want to do?"

"What?"

"I wanna take a bath with you."

I quirked my lips over his request. I wasn't expecting it but it was definitely something to look forward to later on. "Hmmm, okay, done."

"Really, baby? Just like that?" He was practically giddy over my granting his little wish.

"Yup, just like that. Mom won't be back until morning so, yeah, and you know what? I'll even throw in an after-game massage just because you're being so patient with my whole no-sex-before-a-game. Deal?"

"I can't believe we've reached the stage in our relationship where I have to barter for sex now," he said in a mock pout.

"Hey! Only while you're playing football. I don't want to be the cause for any poor performance on the field, ya know."

"Uh-huh," he drawled.

"I'm serious. It's hard enough Hopkins despises me for continuing to sit next to you during English."

"Baby, I told you, it's all behind us."

"No, it's not."

"You're kidding, right?"

"Not in the slightest."

Marco pulled back and sat up, running his hand through his long curly locks. He so had this hot Jon Snow thing going on. Very noble swordsman sex-on-two-legs sort of look. Manly, alluring. But the look on his face was nothing but anger.

"What do you mean—not in the slightest? He's eased up. I've seen it."

"Yeah, when *you* look at him. But not when I happen to glance his way. I've seen it, babe. He loathes me. That's pure hate there. No doubt about it."

"Then why haven't you said anything?"

"Because it's been cool so far. It's not like he's cornered me in the hall or anything. He may not like me, but he's figured out something about us. Maybe not to its true extent, but he knows something's going on. And it's more than the fact Crowe set us up as research partners. Which, by the way, we do need to get our strategy wrapped up on our Marlowe project."

"Yeah, I know. I've got some research to show you." He propped his elbow onto the knee he had hiked up with his foot resting on the lower frame of the car. He ran his fingers along the small soul patch he had growing underneath his bottom lip. It was so damned sexy to me I often masturbated just thinking about Marco's mouth and his little patch of hair.

"Fuck! That pisses me off!" Marco slammed the side of his fist against the door, making me jump.

"Babe, don't do anything. It's cool. Just leave it."

"You need to tell me these things, Els! Don't let me fall into a false sense of security. I can't protect you if I don't know something's out there."

"Well, lover, something will always be out there. The world's a pretty fucked-up place."

"Yeah, you know what I mean. I'm serious, baby. Let me know if something crosses your path that shouldn't be there. I couldn't bear it if something happened to you." He was looking down at his lap as he said it. "You're my world now, Els. Everything. I want to spend all my days making you happy. Every fucking one of them. Arrggh!" He banged the side of the door again. I knew I needed to calm him down. I languidly reached for him. It took a couple of hard tugs to get him to finally come back to my arms, but he did. I soothed my lover's qualms, kissed away the anger—at least for now.

An hour later Marco dropped me off at home telling me where to find seats in the bleachers, so he'd know where I was in the stands. I promised I would do as he asked and I'd find him after the game. I waved, watching a pensive Marco pull out before turning the corner and slipping away.

Chapter Nine

Raphael, My Avenging Angel

I'D LIKE TO say the ensuing hours till I headed for the game were worry-free. I'd like to, but I can't. I was a twisted bundle of nerves lying in a puddle of water under a thunder and lightning sky. Oh, and with a huge lightning rod stuck in the middle of my gut and riveted to my spine. Ya know, virtually guaranteeing beyond all doubt that yeah, I was so gonna fry.

Mom called about an hour before I left to tell me she prepped one of her healthy rabbit-food inspired meals in the fridge for me to finish preparing and eat. I didn't have the heart to tell her I had no stomach for it. There just wasn't any way food was going to enter this mouth without coming out the way it went in. In the end I just dumped it down the disposal. To be honest, it didn't look very appetizing at all. But I fully copped to the fact with the mood I was in I probably would have barfed up the best meal Bobby Flay could whip up. I was a mess.

It wasn't just that I was going to see my boyfriend play. I was actually very excited about it. I'd've been more excited if only it was him and me. I'd watch him play as long as he'd like. I could never tire of watching him. I know he said every move I made captivated his imagination. I heard his words but really I had no idea how on Earth there could be any truth to them. There was nothing but boring old me. He was the magical one in the relationship. I was just enamored with the fact he even noticed me in the first place. I was always waiting for him to wake up and figure out what a terrible mistake he made in taking me into his arms. So far it hadn't happened, but we had a number of years ahead of us—if I had anything to say on it—so any number of things could come along and break whatever preposterous spell he thought I put him under. But I told him I'd be there, and I meant it. I would.

But that's where things got murky for me. I was like the proverbial Christian entering the lion's den or the gladiatorial arena. Or like I had been chafed raw and bloody and then dragged through a tank full of hungry sharks. These were the very jocks, their friends and hos (yeah, I said hos—every last bitch who hangs onto those boys like the vaginal social parasites they are) I spent every minute required of me to be at school trying like hell to avoid at all costs.

I bore the scars, physical and emotional alike. Like vipers they would strike out from their conclaves and gatherings and take a piece of me in order to appease the insecurities and fears they carried. Better to draw some poor schmuck out into the light than face their own shit. And here *I* was, walking right into their world—*willingly*. I seriously needed to have my head examined. Fucking heart and its gooey love-riddled middle making me do icky things to please my guy.

I don't know if Marco understood what he was asking of me. But I also knew I said I would endure anything for him. And so, I found myself scrubbing like mad in the shower—more to wash away nerves than to actually achieve any degree of cleanliness. It wasn't lost on me how my scrubbing had left me a flush rosy hue (subconsciously chafing myself into chum, I suppose, virtually guaranteeing they could smell blood). By the time I found myself before my full length mirror trying on outfits—once again making an enormous pile of cast offs which hadn't made the grade—I realized how unsuccessful the entire exercise had been.

In the end I opted for black jeans Marco had bought for me, a gray pullover sweater, and a thick Mercy High gray with blue accent sweatshirt zipper hoodie. As my guy was the star attraction, I figured I should suit up in school colors. I thrust my feet into my scuffed-up blue and white trainers and grabbed my keys and made for the door.

A half hour later I was a few yards from the merriment of a world I knew nothing about. I was the proverbial stranger in a strange land. I got the meaning of the phrase now. For all of their revelry, I couldn't help but see the absurdity of it all, raising these boys to the status of gods of the modern age. They were titans of smaller worlds—most would never achieve the glory of a career in the sport—so yeah, this was it for them.

I couldn't wait to be rid of them all. I was a prisoner here. I felt the irony of the town's name like a weight upon my shoulders. There was no *mercy* here. None for me at least. Well, I knew that wasn't entirely true—I had Marco.

At least for now. My inner Gollum/Yoda niggled me.

The thought snaked through my mind. I desperately beat it back from where it came. I had no doubt about it, though; I was totally out of my element. Walking among the students, their parents, and the few teachers who bothered to follow the team, or at the very least, felt obligated to make a showing at the first game, was a surreal experience. And me? This wasn't my world. Then it occurred to me: *it wasn't before, but apparently, it is now.*

I moved purposefully between the cars, the students carrying on as if tonight was the highlight of the Mercy social season. Given the small-minded and simple folks who called it home, perhaps it was. Like I needed to bring my armor inward, shore up any gaps in my defenses, I hitched my hoodie closer to me, wishing I brought my thicker scarf and my Giants baseball cap. It was getting to be brutally cold. The wind coming off the ocean was beginning to kick up. I didn't know how I was going to deal with a couple of hours of these brutal winds. I should've at least had the good sense to bring a blanket. How could I have been so stupid? Say nothing if it actually rained—for fuck sake I didn't even have an umbrella, though the stands were covered with a great awning so maybe I was good there.

Fuck, I'm such the butterfly in the beehive with this one.

Any sane person would have realized how woefully unprepared I was as the boyfriend to a football star. Maybe I should see if there were any football wives blogs I could gain a few tips from. It was a thought. Even if Marco's pool of stardom was the small pond of Mercy High, I'm sure there were some corollaries that might help a gay brother out.

Yeah, dream on.

Employing my usual modus operandi I kept my head down, trying not to gain anyone's attention. I was good at this. I had years of practice of flying under the radar—sometimes I failed miserably, but usually I got by. If you don't see them, then they tend to not see you. I maneuvered between people, doing my best not to even touch them as I turned, glided, and inched my way through the tailgaters up to my goal: the senior parking lot.

After reaching the waist-high chain link fence of the lot I waited, feeling like a vagrant looking in the alley for some crumbs or refuse I could scrape together to sustain myself. I just wanted him to show up. If I knew he was here, then things would sort of be okay. At least I'd know he'd ultimately come to my side. Well, at least I hoped he would.

Of course he would. Why wouldn't he?

Fuck, I hated that I kept debating this. I knew better. I really was my own worst enemy. I shook my head to clear it. I was over the doubting. Of course Marco would defend me. I had the fucking ring for Chrissake. He didn't do it on a lark. And he got angry whenever I even hinted what we had wasn't permanent. Yeah, I was a dick. He was my guy, the man who said he wanted the whole damn enchilada: the big-assed house complete with two maids and a nanny (yeah, I bargained hard for the nanny, 'cause even the Bradys had Alice), then we add the kids, the marriage, the 401K, the health plans, the business—holy fuck, we hadn't even discussed what we were going to do to keep everyone alive with a roof over their heads and food in their tummies. I didn't know how to deal with any of it!

Ah, Christ, Marco, why'd we have to say we're gonna have kids? I'm so unprepared for that world.

I took a deep breath. *He's worth it.* And it was what he wanted, and I knew I'd do it. I'd do anything for him. But fuck, kids and a house. I was drowning in domesticity and I hadn't even walked down the aisle yet. Wait a minute! Was I going to be the one walking down the aisle? Or was he? No, it would be me, right? Or would we both stand together from the start? Would my mom give me away? My dad? Mental note to self: I had some serious gay husband research to do when I got home.

But I would do anything for Marco, obviously because I was standing here, among the enemy, trying to stay in the shadows while watching my man, my hero, from my familiar dark recesses. I trembled with the horror of who I was and what it could do to his world, shattering what should be the best year of his life. I was a risk. But I couldn't let go, I just couldn't. I needed him desperately.

Not that I'd kill myself or anything if it went away. I didn't think I'd succumb to that. At least I'd like to *think* I'd rise above it. I wasn't too confident about it, though. So, I chose to hide—it was easier. It reduced the threat I posed to his perfect world. I took whatever I could get from him and was happier than I'd ever been whenever he thought of me.

The rumble of his car off in the distance brought me from my pensive thoughts. I found it funny how the roar of the Impala soothed my soul like no other sound—well, except the sound of its driver's moans in my ear when we made love. Yeah, that sound was infinitely better. I was safe in his arms. Within them I knew no fear. I soared. Being with him was like walking on clouds. It was beyond anything I could even dare to imagine.

I sensed the rush of wanton women running to fawn all over my boyfriend. I admit it; I was a tangle of emotions on that score. I realized, for my boyfriend's sake, it was a much needed level of security, for the layer of female adoration kept suspicion off of Marco. It helped keep our rendezvous secret, and therein lay the rub: our relationship was secret—had to be. I understood the why of it. I understood the need to protect us both, but it didn't make it any easier to deal with. I contemplated Marco with a steady eye as he exited the car. He spared only cursory glances at the girls, waving and smiling like the local celebrity he was, but his eyes always came back to mine. Faithful to a fault in his own quiet way, my guy was.

A gaggle of hos ran up to the fence, watching his every move. Part of me relished how I was the one to know him intimately. The other part, the one stewing in its own jealous secret sauce, was hurt how I couldn't claim what we meant to each other out in the open. For a moment I railed against the thought of those "it gets better" videos. But I already had something better in my life—yet I couldn't publicly acknowledge it. And even if we came out, we would always have to deal with closed-minded morons whose fear might lead them to do something horrific that could turn my world, as fragile and precious as it was to me, upside-down in a matter of seconds.

The girls displayed themselves, hoping with what they had on offer they'd be the one to catch his eye. And then there was me. The one who had captured his eye as well as his heart, but didn't have a chance in hell of having the satisfaction of having it acknowledged, much less accepted by their lot. So, I simmered in that jealousy-ridden secretive stew Marco and I had brewing. Somehow, I figured all of the spices and good intentions in the world couldn't make it taste any better or help it go down.

He moved purposefully. He was probably running late. Marco was forever dashing between appointments. He was fairly punctual whenever we'd planned anything, so I was thankful I rated so high on his list. He painted on a charming smile for the girls along the fence. He begged off that he was late, and the coach was going to have his ass if he didn't get suited up. Then he was beyond them. Our eyes met; my breath hitched as it always did. I couldn't help it; my man was breathtaking to behold, even more so I imagined because of the aura he exuded in this setting. He was in his element; I could tell. Little I would know about it. As much as I spied on him before we got together, it had never occurred to me to come to one of his games. I guess I knew how removed this part of his world was from mine and had no reason to think I would ever have been a blip on his radar. How funny it was to know he had been watching me all along.

God, sometimes life is so strange and surreal.

As he passed by me, winking and mouthing he *loved me*, my heart soared. Privately, though, in solitude. For my eyes and heart only. In a way it was nice, in another way—not. I schooled my expression, blinking hard so he would know I sent my love back. It was a thing we'd agreed to. A wink for a little love; a blink if it was more intense, and a hard squinched blink if you were really wanting to shout it for all to hear. I was screaming it. He shook his head, smiled, and with a humorous roll of his eyes, he was gone.

I sighed as he took off at a decent clip to the locker room; no doubt he was going to walk into a brusque browbeating from Coach Ostrich on the ethics of timeliness in team sports. Marco would probably be properly reprimanded and would hastily suit up, transforming himself from my mild-mannered boyfriend into the football demigod the school proclaimed him to be.

Though I didn't follow the sport as avidly as most at school, I was aware they'd had a great season last year—securing the championship game and taking league and divisional championships. Why I had committed it to memory was beyond my gay sensibility—but hey, I guess we fags had our hands in all sorts of baskets, never knowing when a particular bit of information might come in handy. I attributed it to my innate survival instinct—*knowledge is power*. And, often being perceived as one down in society, I intended to hoard power wherever and whenever possible.

Focus, Donahey, for fuck's sake, focus. You're a fag in enemy territory!

I could be so random when it was totally not the right time to be. I knew it worried Marco. I needed to get better at this. He expressed to me on a number of occasions when I had let my mind wander off on some random tangent and I wasn't paying attention to the here and now; I needed to learn to focus.

Of course, invariably, I'd counter with the fact he was still negligent about Hopkins' dissatisfaction with my sitting so close to him in English and he hadn't even bothered to notice. But I had to concede it was the only one I could drum up in my favor against the litany of my mental wanderings. He had a point. I needed to pay more attention. He was my guy; I needed to listen to him more. He knew what was best.

Odd thing was, I usually did pay attention. I only started to really mentally ramble when he entered my life, as if my survival instincts had dulled because I put the trust in him so I could carry on unimpeded by any real threats to my health. He said he'd protect me, and I took him at his word. Case closed, right? Yeah, he had a point, though; he couldn't be everywhere at once. Maybe not so case closed after all.

I stood there long after he had slipped into the locker room. Part of me wanted to wander in after him. If it were just between us, he'd want me to as well. I knew that. Just being here brought to light how much of my life was out of sync with his, how much of his world revolved without me. Sure, I had the Q, but lately he was there hanging out in the back of the store whenever he could. He knew the restocking drill and prep setup as well as I did. So really, he'd immersed himself into my own little existence. I could never be a part of this world. Not really. Just the proverbial fly on the stadium wall, to be honest. I finally moved off from the fence and began the slow trek to the stands.

Out of habit whenever I was around the other students from school I kept my head down, my eyes to my own feet and the heels of the person in front of me. If anything, only to ensure I didn't bump into them as I made my way up the steps to the stands.

It seemed like a half hour to make the hike up to the walkway along the top of the stands but after glancing at my watch I realized it had only been a little over seven minutes. I turned right once I reached the top. The stadium was filling up swiftly. I was trying to work out where Marco had suggested I sit so he could find me, but I was sort of turned around and still trying to work it out when a vaginal bullet train whisked right by me, nearly taking me out in the process. I huddled against the press box, hoping no one would take notice of my milling about.

Attention all Angel revelers. We have a gayboy fish clearly out of water on the home field upper walkway. You'll no doubt be able to pick him out of the crowd by his large deer-in-the-headlight eyes and his keen fashion Abercrombie & Fitch sense of style clearly indicative of the type of boys he'd like to bone. Rumor has it he is boning our star quarterback, Marco Sforza, and his favorite position is on his back in the back seat of bad boy's Impala Sforza is so fond of. Sorry ladies, titties and clit-laden gashes between your legs hardly seem to satisfy our beefy quarterback who is a bona fide tube-steak-loving A&F homo. Yet Sforza says he plans on making our resident fairy boy an honest househusband with a well-negotiated two maids, a nanny, and a whole gaggle of rug rats running around their rustic Italian villa so they can spread their America-destroying lies to a new generation. Let's give it up for Satan Spawn himself, Mercy High's own, Cassiel Elliot Donahey.

Okay, so the announcer didn't actually say it over the stadium sound system. Each eye, however, roving my way and spied what a glaring misfit I was at these occasions, all seemed to have the very expression as if he had.

And yeah, my bitch gayboy was raging hard. But hey, you have to know my life is constantly tormented by the girls of this school. You can't trust them. Not. One. Damned. Bit. I'm not proud of how I feel about it, but until they let up, I won't.

I hesitantly walked up to the railing overlooking the stands below, still not sure where to go. A lovely male voice caught my ear, but more than the tone, I was taken by the soft lilt to the clipped English that spoke of foreign birth. Italian, if I wasn't mistaken.

"You looking forward to di game, no?"

I turned to find a haunting pair of eyes staring at me over a gray, white, and black woolen scarf. Stunningly familiar these green eyes were as they flashed and held my gaze—mesmerizing eyes. I weakened from the pull they had upon me. But that was entirely impossible, as I'd spied my boyfriend entering the locker room only twenty minutes before.

Absentmindedly, I casually nodded, lost in the stranger's brilliant verdant fire, so achingly familiar. Yet something was off, though what it could be was beyond me—with only a small patch of face to gauge everything by I realized I'd have to figure out a way to get my mysterious new friend to reveal a bit more.

"Ah, *scusi*, pardon my rudeness. My name is..." His vibrant green eyes flicked past me, to something just beyond where we stood, focusing on something in the far off distance. "Eh, Angelo. I am foreign exchange student, from, eh, Milano."

Well, it would explain the accent and his slightly strange manner. But I found it powerfully alluring. Something tugged upon my conscious. I was here for Marco, the love of my life, and yet I found this young man was flirting with me—and what's more, I was enthralled he was. There was no mistaking the gleam in his eye, the sparkle. It was exactly the look Marco had when he walked in the Q that fateful day in July.

Marco...

Cassiel Elliot Donahey, grab a fucking clue and get your shit together and stop with the flirting, already!

I shook my head to get the cobwebs out. I was reading too much in this boy's stares, the manner of his speech. He was just European, that's all. Italian, for Chrissake. They fucking ooze love and romance—it's in their DNA. Hell, if anyone should know, it would be me. I'd parted my legs on numerous occasions for my own Italian Stallion. I needed to focus. *Marco is my world; Marco is everything*. With renewed focus and a smile, I offered my hand. "It's nice to meet you, Angelo. I'm Elliot Donahey."

I couldn't help but notice his eyes as my hand slipped from his, as if he was missing the contact. That was absurd. There was nothing to the handshake. I needed to stop reading into it.

"I am new to the school and do not know many people. Perhaps we could watch the game together?"

I wasn't so sure what to do here. My eyes darted around. I knew there was fear lacing them, and rightly so. But it was just a game. He wasn't trying to put anything else on it. He didn't know anyone, probably just as lonely as I was, maybe more so being foreign and all. Was I really going to be an asshole, confirm for this Italian that Americans were rude, obnoxious and self-centered? Well yeah, most Americans were, I suppose. But I didn't have to confirm it for the guy, did I? He didn't have to come away from this experience with that sort of impression. My mother would kill me for being so rude. It wasn't how I was brought up, say nothing for what Marco would think. The thought I'd do anything to disappoint Marco in any way cut me deeply. I knew what was right, what I should do. I decided I better get to know the guy a bit more if we were going to watch the game together. But his face was nearly obscured by the thick woolen scarf wrapped around his head.

"You uh, seem to have me at a disadvantage. You can see me, but uh, all I get are your eyes."

"Ah, I have a bad cold. I do not want to make you to get sick, you know?"

"Uh-huh..." I didn't know why he was being so considerate for my health, but from the small wrinkles around his eyes, I could tell Angelo was smiling.

"You look, eh, *freddo*—eh, uh, cold. Yes, cold. I have blanket. We could use it together, no?"

He produced the blanket he had tucked under his arm as if to sway what small amount of reticence I'd built over the course of our conversation. I couldn't help but be taken with the young Italian. Maybe Marco would be pleased I made a friend with the Italian foreign exchange student.

"Sure, why not?" I said softly, allowing myself to smile openly with his suggestion.

Sure, why not? Really, fucktard?

I couldn't believe how easily the words came out. Once I'd committed to it, things seemed to flow between us. Okay, so the guy was foreign; he didn't have any real friends—right? He needed to make some. I was just helping a foreign brother out, that's all. Besides, I'd show him a little American hospitality then the guy would find out what everyone said about me and he'd slip away from the local gayboy like any sane straight boy would—European or not. So, I'd make a new friend for the night. It was nothing more than a diversion. Maybe a little cultural exchange. Who knew, maybe the guy was even more cultured than the average American male, so that had to be a plus—didn't it? It wasn't like he was gay or anything.

And yet, and yet...

Angelo eyed the stands. "Eh, so where are we to sit?"

"Fuck me, if I know," I muttered before catching my slip of the tongue, and saying more clearly, "I can't really say. This is my first football game, as well. But I know someone on the team, so I came to cheer him on." I shook my hands in a mocking flimsy cheer. "...Yay team..." I chuckled at just how much of a deer in the headlights I was. The whole situation was absurd. And that extended to my relationship with Marco and this seemingly nice Italian boy asking to join me in watching the game. All of it was surreal. But there was no denying Marco loved me. I was here for him. That was real. It was tangible; it had weight.

Angelo held out his hand and before I could stop myself I took it before I even realized it. For a brief moment I forgot what others would think of two boys holding hands and gave in. I let myself go with the flow, with the sheer adrenaline of not hiding who I was.

Everything for those few seconds felt golden. I had made a new friend, a boy who wanted to share watching the game with me. Why? I didn't really care; after all, he would surely slip away from me once someone explained who I was, what I was.

Angelo pulled me along the bleachers, finding a seat. I plunked down next to him as he unfolded the blanket and spread it out over our laps. The seats were ice cold even through our jeans, but the blanket helped. I leaned into the moment, and chuckled at the sudden turn of events.

It turned out despite being a foreigner, Angelo seemed to have a love of American football. He was able to explain, in his adorably fractured English, how the game was played. By the time the teams were assembled to enter the field Angelo had successfully worked me into an eager anticipation to get the game rolling.

In truth, I found Angelo's impassioned explanation of American football quite endearing. The way I figured it, if a foreigner could get excited about the game then maybe there was something in it I could find appealing. I wasn't a complete gayboy when it came to sports.

Angelo was a patient and attentive audience member, and I couldn't help but be impressed with my new friend. He was an energetic individual with a gentle, guiding soul. I found myself watching him from out of the corner of my eye far more than I probably should. I couldn't help it. There was something innately familiar about the man, which troubled me a bit because I couldn't understand how that could possibly be. It was a strange feeling, and one I wasn't sure I should be entertaining. After all, my boyfriend, the man who held my heart in his hand, had even put a ring on my hand to signify how much he cherished my love, was right there on the field.

And yet, Angelo's presence stirred something deep within me.

It was hard to shake, though I knew outwardly I was simply enjoying the company of a foreigner who wanted some company during the game to feel like he was acclimating to life in America. Nothing more.

Still, I found it hard to explain why Angelo held such interest for me. A couple of times as Angelo discussed his love of American football, he touched me. They were simple gestures, no hidden meaning I could discern from Angelo's caress: a hand on my knee, or on my shoulder, a brush of Angelo's knee against my own under the blanket we shared. All were small instances that really didn't seem to mean anything in and of themselves.

But Angelo's eyes were riveting, inviting engagement from me. Effortlessly, I found myself engaged. Their brilliant green spark and intensity held me spellbound—not too unlike how Marco's gaze entranced me. The arch of his brow, eyes as captivating and riveting as the verdant conifers dominating the landscape. It all seemed so—right. Between the brim of the cap, pulled so far down on his head it was nearly impossible to determine the guy's hair color, to the maddeningly curved line across his face from ear to ear over his nose from the damnable scarf, there just wasn't enough facial real estate to make any real determination if what I saw was as near a copy of my boyfriend as I thought. I knew it was utterly impossible.

I'd seen Marco walk into the locker room to suit up. But the guy next to me drew me in, provoked these small caresses, the engaging personality, the warmth that seemed to flow between us, as if we'd always been with each other, had always shared this camaraderie. Something worn in with history, palpable, weighted.

"So, eh, you okay with sharing the watching of the game with me?" Angelo inquired, not bothering to hide the hope glimmering in his eyes.

"Sure, Angelo. I have to confess, though, it's like I've known you for some time. But that can't possibly be. I mean you just got here in America—right?"

"Eh, yes. Only about a month now. You know, eh, to get with the family here."

I nodded I understood, and I did. I hadn't inquired which family he was housed with, though I suspected it might be the Sforzas, but maybe that was a huge supposition on my part. And really, how cliché would that have been? Let's put the Italian with an American-Italian family. But maybe it worked that way. Hell, I didn't know.

In my four years of going to Mercy High, I'd never met another foreign exchange student. It didn't mean they weren't there, I just never crossed paths with one. But living under my rock probably explained it. So, this was all so new. He hadn't offered any information about the host family he was staying with, and it seemed impertinent if I asked. I guess I would let him take the lead on it. Or I might hear it down the geek grapevine from someone later on in the week. I understood the logistics of coming to live briefly with a foreign family. And yet, I still couldn't shake the odd feeling of familiarity—of a shaded truth hiding just there, under the scarf and beneath the cap.

The fanfare of the game revving up broke the flow of our conversation. My gaze was drawn magnetically to the field, scanning it with every fiber in my body to see the Sforza name emblazoned on Marco's jersey. Like an idiot, I realized I didn't know Marco's number. It had never even occurred to me to ask. How odd it seemed to me just then. For fuck's sake I was only dating the star quarterback. What a serious faux pas in the boyfriend department I'd made.

I looked for Marco in the lineup as the boys made their way to the field. I made a silent vow to myself to take a greater interest in the things that mattered to him. A small pang of regret in it had never occurred to me to take a great interest in what he liked to do. This was compounded by the fact I knew Marco had done everything he could to find out what mattered most to me. Hell, just the fact he trailed me for the better part of two years before plucking up the courage to even speak to me spoke volumes on what a better boyfriend he was to me. Just contemplating it weighed heavily upon me. I hadn't even bothered to ask about Marco's family, or what he did on his own time away from the football field or when he wasn't with me. Jesus, I was such a fuck-up when it came to being there for Marco.

"No more..." I muttered sternly to myself. I felt like such an ass. No, not felt like—I was an ass. He was so going to score tonight. It was up to me to devote every ounce of myself to make it up to him. If he was truly mine, as he said, then it was up to me to honor that, to know it intimately.

I looked askance at Angelo who, in turn, had been watching me as my thoughts percolated over how bad of a lover I had been to Marco. My brow furrowed as Angelo's eyes seemed to darken with concentration—as if trying to lift my thoughts. Odd thing was, I somehow thought he could do it, this mysterious and engaging Italian sitting next to me.

"I'm sorry. I guess I let my mind wander just then."

Angelo nodded once to acknowledge me but didn't contribute to my line of thinking in any way—for which I was thankful. I thought it best to change the course of our conversation to less personal matters.

"So, uh, do they do some sort of ritual or fanfare for the players?"

"Eh, usually, which I have always found rather amusing. I mean, when you look at how you Americans hold football players as the supreme titans on the field, it is not too unlike the gladiators of my country. These are up and coming warriors of the sport. A lesser coliseum, perhaps. Where, eh, the quarterback is like the supreme gladiator. And the two teams oppose each other in a battle of sorts. So not too different, you see?"

"I never thought of it that way. Sort of makes it come alive for me when you say it like that, the historical aspect and all. Makes me look forward to the game in that context."

Angelo's eyes flashed brilliantly. I blushed a little at the hidden meaning behind his interest in American football, and maybe a tiny bit in the way he was flirting with me. My boyfriend was the star player meeting our school rival's advancing army. I guess he was a general, of sorts, a warrior of prominent status. A sexy thing when I gave it some consideration. I was so going to give my baby one hellaciously good fuck tonight. He had already earned it, and they hadn't even kicked off yet. I couldn't help myself; those thoughts caused me to blush further.

"Eh, you see your friend on the team, yet?" Angelo spoke loudly over the din of the press box announcer kicking things off to thunderous applause from the stands as he announced the arrival of the Carmel High Padres, the Padres' cheerleaders doing their best to get the visiting crowd engaged in the festivities. My mouth became a grim line at finding myself unwittingly at a crossroad of sorts—should I tell Angelo about Marco being my boyfriend or should I just feign ignorance of not knowing enough to have even asked what number Marco wore? Which wasn't much of a stretch to the imagination, because I hadn't.

"Uh, well, it's sort of embarrassing. You see, I never asked my friend what number he played. So, uh, I don't know where to look."

"They have, eh, their name on..."

I finished his sentence for him. "On the back of their jersey. Yeah, I know. I realize how stupid I've been in not even asking what number he wore. Sort of makes me feel like an asshole. I should have asked."

"This boy is more than a number to you, no?"

In the heat of the moment I panicked. I shrugged and nodded, making it fairly obvious that while I was trying to play this very nonchalantly, very noncommittal, I was sort of letting the cat out at the same time.

Angelo's gaze became far more pointed. He seemed to be waiting for some additional confirmation from me about the nature of my relationship with the team member who brought me to the game.

"Well, they get called out soon, so you get to see him then, h'okay?"

I tried to smile softly and nod. I was thankful if Angelo suspected anything going on between me and the mystery footballer, he wasn't going to make a big production of finding anything out he probably could do without knowing.

"Ah, *bene*..."

That seemed to signal he was letting it go—at least for the time being.

The Mercy High marching band began to play a raucous engaging number while the announcer began to rattle the cage as the booming voice of Ben Ostrich, the head coach's brother and a local radio announcer, started to call the team members onto the field. The Ostrich boys had attended Mercy High, so they had an affinity for the football team bordering on the religious, a passion even I found hard to deny given how everyone was sort of into it. Mercy's boy cheerleaders held a huge paper banner with the school logo across it while their female counterparts did their best to whip the crowd into a fighting frenzy. The banner took up the far corner of the field near the locker rooms as Ben announced the arrival of the Mercy High Avenging Angels. Ben's powerful bass voice rumbled from the expansive speaker system getting the home crowd riled into all the frenzy of a raging Viking raid upon an unsuspecting English village. The mood was definitely infectious. Angelo ran his arm around my shoulders and pulled me into him, shaking me into a rush of adrenaline that seemed to captivate the crowd around us.

The electricity of the crowd, the feel of Angelo (far more palpable than I'd expected), along with just knowing the love of my life was out there on the field had all of the synapses of my brain firing in ways I never imagined possible. I suddenly got why these events sparked such fervor. It was heady, intoxicating, and deeply alluring in its own right.

I spared a look at my new Italian friend just as the scarf nearly slipped off his nose, revealing a very familiar rise and fall of it. It made my eyes widen and hitched my breath all at the same time—sapping the very air out of my lungs. That was Marco's nose! I swore it was. I knew every curve, every inch of Marco's face. I'd memorized it, etched it into my subconscious so I'd dream of my lover when I slept alone in my bed at night. How could that possibly be? Before my mind could do anything with this new information, it was gone as Angelo pulled the scarf maddeningly back into place.

But the flash of his nose left me needing to figure out a way to see this boy fully. I didn't know quite how to do it without seeming like I was coming onto him. Angelo said he had a cold and didn't wish to spread it. On one hand I accepted his explanation at face value. Perhaps he was just an overly considerate guy when it came to his health. He certainly seemed robust enough; his body contours defined in the rise and fall of his muscular frame as it was encased in the tight knit dark blue sweater appeared to be just shy of Marco's build. A close second to it, a very close second, now I looked at his physique with a gayboy critical eye.

This too had my imagination running rampant with conflicted feelings. As the roar swelled, we both sprang to our feet along with the masses as the Angels took to the edge of the field with all the ferocity of heaven's army, longing to smite the Padres. These Angels did battle; they were exuberant and voracious in their display of masculine aggression. In fact, the audience did nothing but encourage it. Like the gladiators of old, the Mercy High Avenging Angels had supplanted them and achieved stardom in their own right. They moved as a very impressive cohesive unit.

I beheld them all in wonder, for they were like an army, armed to the teeth to do as much damage to the other team as possible. Something stirred within me, something I hadn't expected at all—a real sense of pride. I was truly astonished by the sensation. A sense of pride in the team, in Marco, coursed through me deeply. Indignation surged through me that anyone would dare challenge my man to combat. Every fiber of my being didn't want Marco to simply win—I wanted him to annihilate them, decimate their ranks, pulverize and exploit their weaknesses. Where had this overwhelming desire to have Marco dominate come from? It was as if this awakening had split my personality into two beings at war with each other. One half of me was the same as it always was: the jocks were the enemy. They were the guys to avoid, to be granted as wide a berth as possible so as to avoid their menacing gaze. But this new faction within me held my attention now—and this half was highly competitive. I wanted to witness Marco's victory. I was nearly bloodthirsty for it. The conflict roiled within me as my eyes scanned the field of battle.

I knew how deeply moved I was by how much Marco loved me, how much he expressed it whenever we were alone. He always went out of his way to make me feel like I was the center of the universe and all things in it had to relate to me. It was just how Marco viewed the world. It always left me feeling overwhelmed when Marco said those things. He would hold me close, particularly after we made love, and gaze for long periods of time into my eyes—silently, sometimes unerringly in that I thought he could really see into my soul. In those moments Marco was such a gentle giant of a man. But not now. Now Marco was a titan, ready to do battle. The unexpected pride I felt for him at that moment swelled within me, flushing me with such admiration I was lightheaded and slightly intoxicated by it.

"...and now, your Mercy High Avenging Angels!"

The crowd roared and chanted to the players as they crashed through the banner and hit the field, working their way out to their warm-up exercises before the game got started. The warm-ups allowed me to find Marco's jersey. A new wave of emotions assaulted me at seeing my guy all suited up for battle. Around me a few of the girls remarked on how sexy Marco appeared in his football gear. The mix of emotions at hearing them coo over him was like a quick jab to the gut followed by the euphoric bliss I experienced after we'd fucked. The whole sensation had me feeling off-kilter, making it hard for me to regain my balance.

Angelo leaned over to speak to me through the audience din, asking me the most obvious question. "Do you see him now?"

I flushed a tiny bit and with a small upturn of my lips, I nodded. "There, number 7—Marco Sforza."

"Eh, my own countryman!"

He held up his hand and I high-fived him, the blood rushing to my face again.

The crowd settled down and the team captains made their way to the center of the field. It shocked me to find out Marco was not only the quarterback but the captain of the team as well. How had I not known that? This evening was proving to be informative in how I had really fucked up in the boyfriend department. It seemed I was a far more selfish lover than I originally surmised. I was definitely going to hold myself to my vow to learn everything about Marco going forward.

The toss ended up in Mercy's favor for the kick-off and Angelo explained that Marco would obviously take the receiving end of the coin toss, which he told me was the usual choice but wasn't always a given. After I thought about it, I realized it would give the advantage of first strike in my boyfriend's favor—an odd I found to my liking as well. I marveled at how instantaneously I had become personally invested in the outcome of the game.

The kick soared into the night air, so high I could barely detect it before it came crashing down into the roar of the crowd, sounding a lot to me like waves crashing upon the cliffs, a force of nature rumbling upon the Angels' emerald field.

The ball came down to number 18, Martin Connolly, who caught it and had the good fortune to have his team work a path for him to get into the midfield before he was tackled. The offensive team of the Angels took the field. My heart began to race as Marco advanced to his position. The whole of the universe seemed poised on edge for the next play of the game. It was as if God himself had taken a personal interest in the game and the battle between Angels and Padres.

The analogy between my boyfriend and a military general turned out to be an apt one. The Angels moved into position but at the last second Marco called something out and his teammates started to change it up on the field, like a general realigning just before the battle was engaged. Marveling with rapt attention at the control Marco exuded on the field, my pride in my boyfriend swelled.

In a moment so taut, like the bowstring pulled back to the point of breaking, with only the haunting sound of air moving about the people in the arena, Angelo's whisper floated upon the breeze. I don't know if he intended for it to be heard or not, but as it fell upon my ears I realized there wasn't a hint of broken English in it.

"Excellent, Marco. *Good move...*"

I didn't know what to make of the whispered approval. This boy seemed to have as vested an interest in Marco's play as I did—perhaps even more so. I was sure there were many who were just as enraptured with Marco's star-like poise on the field, many who had come to watch and cheer him on in leading his team to victory. But Angelo's quiet tones, muted but focused with a precision that spoke of a familiarity with Marco, caught me off guard. I really didn't know what to make of it.

What I did know was watching Marco in action was like watching a master at work. Every move of his body had the grace and agility of a hunter cat, evident in the small patch of skin along his calf muscles, calves I'd touched, licked, and held close to my own body in the heat of passion. On the field, Marco seemed untouchable—a Titan. Part of it, I was sure, was the license I was taking because of our mutual love for each other. But it didn't remove any of the allure of seeing Marco in his element. Watching him in motion, I fell in love with him all over again—it was as if a totally new side of my lover had been revealed to me. The ball was hiked and Marco had it for but a few seconds before in a scramble of bodies it went sailing long to an end linesman who had shoved past the defensive line of the Padres. Marco's pass connected cleanly and as if his heels sped upon Mercury's wings the boy sprinted to the first touchdown of the game. The home audience surged to their feet—roaring with renewed fervor. I was a mess, so many feelings going through me. I was euphoric and wallowing in nausea with worry of what was to come. With my tangle of emotions, I panted as if I were the one exerting myself, when in reality, I had simply forgotten to breathe during the whole play and my lungs were simply aching for oxygen.

The rest of the first half went pretty much like that. Peaks and valleys, watching Marco take to the field each time the team had the advantage to score another goal, my heart soaring to heady heights, only to come crashing down when the Angels' advance was stymied by the Padres. By the time the half was called, nearly fifty minutes in, I was a puddle of nerves and adrenaline. There wasn't enough time in the night to make up for how much I needed to do to make things right with him.

For his part, Angelo had been a welcome crutch for me to metaphorically, and sometimes quite literally, lean upon. He was a rock of man, exuding a sophistication I found myself drawn to despite the need to keep my distance. The odd thing was I thought Angelo was actually encouraging the pull between us. It was vastly confusing in my topsy-turvy state.

During the half-time Angelo excused himself to use the restroom, giving me a bit of time alone to ponder what the evening had brought so far. I really was starting to like coming to the game. I didn't know if I could count on Angelo being a constant audience companion, but I'd worry about it later. Maybe we could meet up during school and talk about it—provided, of course, he wasn't run off by the lurid talk of my being the school's resident fagboy. That drama had yet to play out, something I readily admitted to myself could change the dynamic of any future games I decided to watch Marco play.

Just before the game started back up I happened to look back toward the top of the stands. I spied Angelo talking to Dr. Sforza. I knew the doctor as I am one of his patients, and he was one of only two general practitioners in the town. Watching them from a distance, I could tell Angelo did know the Sforzas after all. I just wished I could get a fuller view of Angelo because it appeared he wasn't so concerned talking with the doctor with the scarf pulled down from his face.

The conversation between the men had started to become a bit agitated, with Dr. Sforza indicating down the stands from where they were talking. Angelo simply shook his head and after a few more terse-looking words, he repositioned his scarf and turned around to make his way down the steps to where I stood under the pretense of wanting to stretch my legs a little. As Angelo descended, I turned my gaze back to the field so as not to give him any indication I'd been spying on him. I really didn't know what to make of the odd exchange.

I'd comment on the rest of the game, but since it was such a roller-coaster ride, I'll spare you the parlaying back and forth. Suffice to say by the fourth quarter only three points separated the Padres and the Angels with the heavenly fathers slipping by my man's Angels.

The roughest patch had been in the second minute of the fourth quarter when Marco got himself sacked—and rather hard too. My stomach did so many somersaults I nearly tossed my cookies, which would've been a big accomplishment because I didn't have much in there to begin with. It took my eyes like thirty or so seconds to come back to me because I had them firmly planted against my palms, not wanting to see if he was really hurt. Angelo, with the sweetest amount of concern in his voice, talked me through the worst of it.

The audience cheered and I finally released my palms from my eye sockets, only to wait a maddening half minute before I could see my boy moving shakily off the field. His father, the contracted physician for the school, took a look at him and within a few minutes Marco was back out onto the field to a further round of applause and cheers from our side. I was sick with worry. All I wanted to do was run out there and hold him; daring anyone to come near him again. I knew it was overdramatic. By now Angelo had to know the depth of my connection with Marco. I wasn't that great of an actor to pull it off. I was too emotionally distraught over the whole thing, far more than an average fan would be in the circumstance. To his credit he seemed to take it all in stride. It actually didn't seem to faze him at all.

By the last play of the game the Angels were triumphant in scoring an additional touchdown and goal kick to come out four points over the Padres. Not quite the trouncing I'd hoped for but I'd take it, nonetheless. From the tired ambled gait of my boyfriend I could tell he was hurting and I had quite a bit of work ahead of me to work it out of him.

A WEEK BEFORE, Marco had gifted me with one other thing of great importance in his life: the key to his beloved Impala, on a lovely leather-clad Chevrolet emblem key ring. This, he told me in no uncertain terms, was the key to the second greatest thing in his life. He pointedly reminded me I was the first. I didn't know how the car felt about my supplanting its position at the top of Marco's ranking of important things in his life, but I was quite pleased.

Here is where the whole key thing came into play: I was supposed to make my way down from the stadium before the fans had started to clear, head out to his car, climb into the back and wait it out until he came so we could leave. Cheesy in a weird spy/horror movie kind of way but he said he thought it would make things easier if we didn't have to answer any questions about my going home with him if anyone happened to see me get in the car.

I told him I could walk home but Marco wasn't having it. He became so angry with me for even suggesting it. He was adamant about my being safe at every turn. I had to promise him I'd get a ride to the game to begin with. I'd lied and said Greg was going to the game with me and he was my ride in. I didn't like lying about it, and truth be known, Greg was actually at the game, so it wasn't too far-fetched. His older brother, Kevin, had played for the team in our sophomore and junior years, but his parents hadn't given up the ghost that there weren't any more Lettaus playing and felt like they had to make up a reason to go. So, he was roped into going as a family outing sort of deal. And I guess I could've gone with them and not lied about it, but honestly, I wanted the alone time to sort things out. But walking home in the dark on a stormy night did pose certain health risks Marco was right I shouldn't be taking. So, he won our little debate. I sort of knew he would. He said he wouldn't ever risk something so precious to him—he always wanted to see I was covered, I was safe, though I well knew life held no guarantees for safety.

I didn't have any pipe dreams about it. I knew at some point our luck would run out in some way. I just hoped we could deal with it and move on. It wasn't a matter of if, it was a matter of when and what. I don't know if he ever gave it much thought.

Knowing Marco and his ever-the-tactician ways, he probably did, which was why he was so damned persistent about my being safe at all costs. With the game ending in the next fifteen seconds I knew it was my signal to depart ahead of the crowd. I turned to Angelo and held out my hand which he shook without hesitation, though something in his eyes wanted me to stay, was asking me to stay with him.

"I have to head back home. I told my mother I wouldn't be out much past the game."

"Sure. Eh, hopefully we shall see each other again soon?"

I smiled at his suggestion, not knowing for sure if it would ever pan out—the reality he could hear about me by the morning would probably change everything. And in truth I was a bit saddened by the prospect. My smile was a little strained as I told him how much I would like that. He pulled back allowing me to head up the stands. Once I reached the top I found he wasn't paying attention to the game any longer. He had turned so he was solely watching me take my leave from him. Those eyes, so maddeningly familiar, so intent on keeping me close. I probably was reading something in them that truly wasn't there.

That's ridiculous. It's just gayboy wishing on my part.

But I spared a look back again as I slipped between a few revelers who had the same idea I had. Damn him if he wasn't still watching me, the gaze even more intent—riveted was the word I'd use. It couldn't be, yet there he stood, facing me while every other person in the stands was glued to the action on the field. It only made his gaze more defined, more pointed.

The crushing part of the whole experience? I never got to see him fully. He never took that damned scarf down from his face. I wasn't so sure, aside from those eyes piercing me, leaving me raw, I'd be able to sort him out in a crowd of students at Mercy High. Then again, there weren't many guys who had green eyes. It wasn't as common a color for eyes as one might think. Quite rare, actually.

A few seconds later and I was descending the stairwell leading out of the stadium. My emotions were all over the place. I was excited beyond all measure that my boyfriend would be in the car soon; I'd have him back to myself. As giddy as I was at the prospect, I couldn't help but be conflicted over Angelo's attentions throughout the game, the way he was so easy with me, touching me, pressing our knees together under the blanket. When he made to scratch his leg under the blanket, I knew I wasn't mistaking the small caress along my leg. When his hand strayed just a little onto my thigh, his fingers moving so gently to brush the inner part, my breath hitched. But it was when his eyes looked directly into my own—a look so maddeningly familiar I found I couldn't look away. I couldn't move at all. The touch was even familiar, as if Marco were right there, next to me, the caress of someone who knew me intimately. I remember swallowing hard as his fingers inched so slowly toward my crotch. I remember everything fading for a brief few seconds—to where it was just Angelo and me in the stands. Then the Angels had scored, and the crowd rose to their feet in an enormous wave and the caress was gone; the gaze retreated from where it came.

We stood up and cheered with everyone else. Angelo never made that particular move again. He acted for the rest of the game like it had never happened, up until we had shaken hands and he gifted me with a soft caress of a finger against my palm. I thought I'd imagined it in error—thinking I was with Marco. Even if we weren't going to fuck, he always slid his thumb against my palm whenever we held hands, even if the pressure barely registered one or two on the Sforza fuck-o-meter. It was his way of letting me know he'd always make himself available to me, he always wanted to be naked and in my arms, he always desired me in that way.

Always.

And what had I done? I openly flirted with Angelo. I'd allowed it to happen. *What the fuck was I even thinking? Focus, Donahey. Get your head in the same place as your heart and for fuck's sake focus for once in your fucking life.*

By now, my eyes were moist with shame. How could I have let things get to where they were with Angelo? I should have rebuffed him the moment it happened. I knew it was the right thing to do. I was Marco's and I knew it. I wanted it.

I unlocked the car, slipped into the backseat, and collapsed onto my back, staring blankly at what Chevrolet had called beige but was more of an ecru shade interior. Like an enormous drive-in movie screen, I imagined the ceiling interior showing my time with Marco over the last several weeks, especially the night of my eighteenth birthday. That one was a particular favorite of mine. Over the following days Marco and I had sex numerous times, but I always cherished the first time in the cabin as my go-to when I wanted to feel close to Marco. From now on I did my level best to concentrate on what I had to be thankful in Marco calling me his. I snuggled into myself a bit, relishing the very thought. I was his. I wanted nothing more.

And yet, Angelo's stare was so haunting. I couldn't help my thoughts roving to those eyes, the brilliant shock of green against the darkest brown hair that nearly went black. Such an unusual combination. The same combination I had in Marco. His familiar arch of the brow. Women would kill for his kind of a painted brow, yet it took nothing away from his masculinity. He was definitely all male. Those intensely pointed brows emphasized and enhanced his soul-piercing gaze, the green ablaze like an ethereal fire, like Greek fire—only on an Italian. I shook my head. I wasn't making sense any longer. I was trying to put words to my observations, but I was getting way off field.

I started to slip off into a light nap when people started wandering near the car, possibly other seniors who had parked in the lot for the game. I was glad of the angle of the parking lot lights in relation to Marco's Impala. For all intents and purposes I was obscured from any passerby if they didn't really bother to scrutinize the interior of the car too much.

Marco happened along soon enough, in a rush, tossing his bag into the backseat with me, his eyes all alight from me tucked in against the seat so as not to draw attention. He plopped in the driver's seat and adjusted the mirror, no doubt checking himself out.

"Hey baby...you ready for our hot date night?"

I rolled my eyes and noted he wasn't checking himself in the mirror. Instead it was angled so he could watch me in the back seat.

"Anything for you, lover boy."

"That's my man...We'll be out of here in a jiffy."

He cranked the car over and gunned the engine. He waved at someone passing nearby before muttering some sort of curse at something he wasn't too happy about. He briskly shucked himself out of his jacket and tossed it over the seat at me.

"Tuck under that, will you? I'm sorry—I don't think I can back out so quick and some of the cheerleaders are heading this way. I heard Stephen Lowry's having a team get-together at his place. They're probably coming over to ask me to go."

"Oh," I said as I threw the jacket over me as best as I could to obscure myself in the dark recesses behind him. "'S okay—you can drop me off outside the lot and I can walk home."

"What? No fucking way, babe. It's you and me tonight. I just got some dipshits behind me who haven't moved on yet so I can't back out and make our getaway. What makes you think..." He didn't get to finish his sentence when a tap happened upon his window.

"Heya, Marco."

Cindy Markham—*fucking great, that's all I needed to hear*. Even muffled under the jacket her voice irritated me to no end. She was so gunning for him it made my stomach turn to even think of her putting her hands all over him.

"Hey, Cindy."

Marco kept his voice even, no hint of pleasure in it, but then again, I was sure that was more for my benefit than what he really thought about being pursued by Cindy and her gang. A small part of him had to enjoy being chased by girls. He was just that kind of guy—so beautiful in his masculinity others couldn't help but be drawn to his allure. Hell, no one understood it more than I did. But it didn't make dealing with it any easier.

"So, uh, several of us are getting together over at Stephen's parents' house. They're gone for the weekend—can you imagine missing your son's opening game? Anyway, so uh, we were wondering if you would be going?"

"Ah, gee, Cindy, I'm sort of seeing someone right now, and we sort of have plans tonight. But you all have fun, though. Don't miss out on my account."

"Wow, you're with someone? When did that happen?"

"Over the summer. Not from around here which is why I gotta get going. Heading up north to Carmel." He turned his head out the window and yelled, "If I can ever get out of this fucking parking space…Yo, Cramer—tell her that's what cell phones are for. Some of us already have dates!"

A couple of Cindy's friends sort of laughed at Marco's plea. There was an awkward ten or fifteen seconds where I wasn't sure what was happening because no one was speaking. Then a car pulled away from behind us.

"Well, see you around, Cindy. Ladies…"

The car begin to back out. The gripping spell this situation had on my lungs let go and the trapped air pushed past my lips. My head spun from the lack of oxygen. I breathed in deeply to clear it.

"You okay, lover boy?"

"Peachy," I mumbled.

He sighed heavily. "Fuck, I hate how we gotta go through this too, baby. I can't wait till football is over. I don't want us to hide anymore."

"Uh-huh…" I drawled. I hadn't intended for it to slip out, nor with the cutting edge that went with it.

"We're out of the lot; get up here where I can see you."

I climbed out from under his stuff and clumsily slipped over the seat and buckled in. His hand searched mine out, gripping it far harder than I thought was warranted. He brought the back of my hand to his lips and kissed the ring he gave me I always wore now—though to avoid suspicion, I had started to wear it on a chain around my neck when I was at school. Tonight, like a lucky talisman, I wore it on the finger he'd placed it on. The wedding finger. I was his. He made no bones about it, even if he had told a few lies to avoid any drama coming our way. Didn't mean I had to like it. For that matter, it sounded like he didn't either.

"Baby, don't you ever doubt my love for you. It's only you. 'Kay?"

"Uh-huh." He arched an eyebrow over my noncommittal comment. "Hey...it's cool. I know we talked about it. Doesn't mean I have to like it."

"I know, sweetheart, I know."

He kissed my ring again and twirled it absentmindedly around my finger as the awkward silence grew between us. I turned my hand in his and brought his hand to my lips. I kissed it gently, reverently, taking time to kiss each finger before I laid my cheek against it.

"C'mere..."

I unbuckled as we turned onto my street. I slid over to him, sitting uncomfortably on the hard console surface, and he wrapped his arm around me and held me close as he guided the rumbling car into my driveway.

"Pull around back...just so you don't have to worry 'bout being seen here."

He glanced at me, pointedly.

"I just am trying to control the drama, like you said. Like we discussed, remember? *We* decided this."

His mouth formed a grim line. Yeah, he hated this shit as much as I did, evident in the way he didn't like my reminding him of our pact. I leaned over and ran my tongue along his neck, nuzzling a bit before settling on sucking on his earlobe, one of his particular favorite things I liked to do for him.

"Baby, you know you drive me crazy when you do that."

I chuckled darkly, my voice husky with lust. I wanted my man. I pulled back just far enough to watch him.

"Good, 'cause I was so proud of you out there. I never knew, baby. I never knew how sexy you were on the field. It made my heart race; it made me want to crawl under the bleachers and hide. When you got sacked, babe, I was so fucking scared for you. For us."

I pulled him tighter against me as he rounded the back of the house. He cut the engine and turned in the seat to meet my reach for him. We kissed hungrily, gnashing teeth, lips, and tongues. I pulled him toward me, falling in my usual position, on my back, though this time in the front seat. It felt odd and familiar all at the same time. Completely upside-down and normal.

Marco laughed softly, his eyes probing mine.

"Seems to me, I recall, though I admit I may be mistaken"—he gave me a mock frown as he pondered the careful choice in his words; he loved to toy with me like this—"after all, it was in the heat of our making out so my body was high with all of the wildly hot things you do to me. So yeah, I *may* have not heard it right, but I *think* you promised me something. Something that..." He leaned forward to drink from my lips deeply, the blood rushing from my head to my cock. I was dizzy with the way he could manipulate my body. We parted briefly, both panting with lust. "Something I have been pondering—

just there, in the back of my mind. Even"—he kissed me softly, running his tongue along the part in my lips, making me ache for him to take possession of my mouth—"when I was getting sacked on the field. My only thought was of your promise to me about tonight. Something about, uh, a *win-win* for me?"

"Yes, love of my life. You remember correctly: I owe you a massage"—I kissed him back—"a bath, and believe me, I am so going to take my time washing every part of you from your head to those precious toes I love to suck upon."

"Ah..." His brows went up along with a finger he was now using to signal something was still amiss, what he thought was an omission on my part.

"Ah, nothing. You can put your finger back down. I remember. I plan on having you ravish me as thoroughly as you want. I remember, baby. In fact, I'm counting on your being *very* thorough about it."

The smile between us lit our eyes with the lustful possibilities the night held—we couldn't wait to get to them.

FIFTEEN MINUTES LATER and my boy was on my bed, naked, just the way he should always be. *God, how I love his body*—the feel of those muscles under my hands as I massaged all the kinks out of him. He moaned softly as I worked the lotion into his lower back, my gaze moving lower to his fine muscular ass. I moved around and slipped between his legs, running my hands down from his lower back to the globes of his ass, parting them. I leaned forward and gently blew upon his hole. He shuddered under me.

"Ah, baby, you really know how to take good care of me."

"Lover boy, I'm just getting started with you."

I playfully slapped his ass, drawing a small yelp from him.

"C'mon, lover. I've a bath to give."

Chapter Ten

Being There

ONE OF THE few benefits of my house was while my room was small, it did come with its own en suite bathroom. Not grand by any standards, but it was mine. The added benefit, from my perspective at least, was I had an old-fashioned claw-footed bathtub. I loved it beyond anything else I had—at least as far as the furniture went. Certainly not more than my drawings, but as for the meager possessions I used on a daily basis, the tub was like a bit of old Hollywood right here in Mercy.

Before Dad had skipped off to the wilds of Alaska, I had him help me change the lighting in my bathroom to include a recessed lamp above the tub. I'd asked for it with the excuse of being able to read/study while taking a bath if necessary. In reality I just wanted a bit of old time glamor when I took my bubble baths. Yes, you heard that right, *bubble baths*, something that gave Marco no end of the giggles as he pondered the bottle along with my other bath toiletries. No doubt he was imagining me dramatically lit up to my earlobes in bubbles. So, to get back at him I drew a really hot bath to soothe his tired muscles, and just before he got completely settled I tipped the bubble bath solution into the water and giggled as it slowly enveloped him, his pinched dark stare as the aromatic foam gently consumed him, mentally berating me for my twisted sense of humor.

"Now who's laughing?"

I stuck out my tongue, which got me yanked into the tub on top of him with water and bubbles flying everywhere. It was like a Lawrence Welk nightmare. I yelped a bit at the temperature of the water, and he told me it served me right for plying him with bubbles.

With our laughter diminishing along with the bubbles, he gently pushed my bangs behind my right ear and stared silently into my eyes, tracing his finger along my brow. His eyes followed his lingering, ghosting touch along my skin. I was overwhelmed by the enormity of him—I usually am. I can't help it; he just does it to me every time. His eyes came back to mine. I often found it hard to keep his gaze, as I did now. There was just so much love there. I always felt inadequate when that tidal wave would come pouring out of him.

He pulled me to him, chest to chest, and tucked a finger under my chin, forcing me to find his eyes again.

"You always look away, baby. Why is that?" he asked me quietly, turning his head at a slight angle as if I were a puzzle to him.

I shrugged. It was a bold-faced lie—I knew why; I just didn't want to upset him. He absolutely hated what he said was my short-changing myself. I didn't want to deal with it right now. But I never could get anything by him.

"You love me, right?"

That was easy; it came out of my mouth automatically. Never had to think on it.

"Of course, with all my heart. Always. You mean everything to me."

I looked up at him in absolute wonder.

He nodded just once, accepting me at my word. He swelled at my words, his cock thickening, pressing against my own—what I said obviously pleased him.

"Right, so why would you think I would give my love to someone unworthy? Do you have such a lowly opinion of my love?"

"No. But..."

He lifted his chin, raising a brow with it for emphasis. I wasn't supposed to argue with him. He was trying to give me something. I needed to listen.

"There's nothing to discuss here, baby. No one has ever made me happier than you. I knew it was you from the moment my eyes drifted to you two years ago. I watched. I waited, wanting to find out anything I could about you. Your soul warms me, babe. The whole world could go away but as long as I have you, I'm complete. My world is full. You don't need to rationalize it, or understand it. Just trust that it is. Trust that it always will be. I wouldn't lie to you, Els. Not ever. You are the most sacred thing to me. If something ever happened..."

His lips trembled; his touch faltered. He clenched his eyes shut, blinking tears he'd suddenly formed before he could bite back whatever horror he beheld. He clamped down on it; he couldn't finish the thought. I was truly touched with how my absence would affect him. His voice became hoarse, thick with emotions he didn't want to consider. I was overwhelming him. I kissed him, deeply, profoundly. It was the only thing I could think of to take what he was feeling away from him. It seemed to have worked.

The moan in him rumbled between our chests as the kiss deepened. He gently rolled over until I was on my back against the tub and he was on top of me, his muscular frame easily eclipsing my own. I loved that about him—that I could melt into him, pull him around me, consuming me, all of me. As soon as he had me on my back, my legs went around his narrow waist, my feet resting upon the small of his back. I hissed as he probed for entry.

"Baby…I don't know…"

"Shhhh—trust me?"

I moved my eyes lazily from his chin, with its slight dimple, to the fullness of those lips that look like they were sculpted by Michelangelo himself, to a nose that had captivated me from the first time I spied his profile those two long years ago. But it was the eyes, those eyes penetrating past all my defenses. He pulled them aside as if made from simple tissue paper. I was powerless against him. The enormity of him was as much comfort as it was awe inspiring. I clung to him, letting him guide me—I knew he'd never fail me. Not really. I knew this no matter how much I fought the reality of it. He was patient, god, was he ever patient with me. But those eyes, the brilliant green dazzling and fiery eyes. He scorched everything within me, burnishing me.

He entered me—the soap my only lubricant. I hissed and moaned loudly, clinging to him tighter.

"That's it, baby, trust me. I have you."

I nodded, past any use for words. Even as he said this I opened to him as I always did. The dominance of his large frame, his prodigious cock, and the power they contained within. It always felt as if he were cleaving me in two. But I'd learned to accommodate him. My body knew him, knew of his power, knew of his desires. He said when he was fucking me he felt like he was home. Only when we were together did he feel complete; every moment we were apart he was always aching to take me back to him. The few times we actually had slept together, real sleep, he often did it fully embedded within me.

My mind sometimes wandered when we were apart, trying to imagine what we must look like together when we made love. My thin waifish body—he said swimmer's body, but I never really bought it—wrapped so delicately around the hard contours of his masculine frame. Porcelain against burnished brown. Ice blue to verdant green.

He never wanted me to look away while we fucked. He said nothing got him so worked up as my gaze while he moved within me. It was hard at first, meeting his penetrating stare as he burrowed deep within me. Probing every part of me; he was a formidable force to reckon with as he took me. But I learned. Every ounce of pleasurable pain from him, he wanted to watch, he wanted to commit our lovemaking to memory. He often said he wanted to film his making love with me because he knew nothing would get him hotter than watching me react when we fucked. I blushed deeply at that. He hadn't got around to filming any of it, yet. But I knew if he talked about it, then he'd do it. Marco seldom mused about something that didn't end in actually doing it.

"Sweetheart, so deep, make it last...'kay?" I murmured, between moans and hissing as the friction of his cock massaged my prostate.

"Baby, we're just getting started. I haven't even jacked off for a whole day 'cause I wanted to be so amped up to make love to you as you should be loved."

I panted into his mouth as he continued.

"Deeply"—we kissed—"profoundly"—he thrust, snapping his hips in the way that made me cry out in ecstasy, cocking my head against the pillow when we'd fuck in bed, my mouth slack with lust—"and most importantly, for long tortuous hours. I haven't made love to you like that before. We will tonight."

This time I stared back, just as intently as he always wanted me to. This time I wanted him to know I wanted to be there for him.

"Just make sure you do it until you're satisfied. I want to be there for you. I'm all yours."

I ran my hand along his face, the ring catching the light from above. He turned his gaze to it and kissed it.

"You might be a little sore come morning."

"Baby, I'm counting on it. I want to ache from it. Now get to it, lover. Make me burn."

And he didn't disappoint.

For the next hour or so we made love in the tub; he came twice. By the time we abandoned the tub, after I'd washed every square inch of him, sucking on his precious cock and every one of his manly toes, he told me he wanted to make our way back to the bed. We stood and showered to rinse off. Before we left I produced an enema bulb I filled while he was rinsing off. I found it online from a site specifically for gayboys like us. With his glorious backside to me I inserted the long flexible tube into his ass. He jumped about a foot in the air but I told him to take as much as he could then expel in the toilet. He said I better not be thinking about doing him but I just laughed, telling him I had other ideas. He said it was weird but he took over and continued to clean out as I grabbed a towel and made my way back to my bed to wait for him.

A few minutes later he came to me—no towel, dripping all over my floor. God, was he ever glorious. Each little rivulet of water coursing over his fine muscular body drove me wild with passion for him. He wasn't joking when he said he wanted to make love all night long—his cock was raring to go. I laid back, with my legs spread, running a finger around my well-fucked hole, teasing it as

I eyed him lustfully. I wanted him again. I'd always want him.

His eyes became inflamed with passion again. He came to me in a rush of muscles and water. We laughed and I rolled him onto his back, straddling his chest before I began to slide down the length of him, kissing, suckling and nipping before my cheek was rubbed by the length of his hard cock. I ran my tongue up the shaft. He moaned as I laved and took him briefly into my mouth. I smiled at the whimper I got from him as I moved past his balls, taking a moment to suckle upon each one, driving him crazy with the sensation. I moved further south and I caught his eyes widening as soon as he put together why I had him evacuate himself earlier. I spread his legs as my mouth took possession of his ass, burrowing my face into him, fucking him softly at first with my tongue. As soon as I sensed him relax into the feeling, I hoisted his massive legs forward, pressing his knees onto his shoulders as I did so, exposing his hole to me so he could watch me as I ate him out.

He moaned, thrashing his head from side to side as I tongue fucked him. His eyes bulged widely for seconds at a time as I continued to lap at him—brilliant flashes of green and amber. I breathed him in—god, I loved the smell of him. He smelled of water, soap and the particular scent that was definitively him—musky, heady, *male.*

Within a few minutes he yelled he was about to blow; I hummed hungrily as I renewed my assault on his hole with intense vigor. Marco was nothing if not a man of his word; within a few more seconds of my intense efforts, he moaned loudly, crying out how much he loved me with his hands gripping the bedding so hard he was pulling it off the bed as he shot big thick ropes of cum up his chest, neck, and face. Light from the small table lamp next to the bed caught the cum glistening up his torso like liquid jewels. I released his legs and promptly crawled up the length of him, lapping him up as I made my way to his face, savoring the taste of him in my mouth. I kissed him, letting his load move between us in the kiss. God, did we ever kiss that time.

He rolled me over and consumed my wiry frame with his, nearly taking the light with him as he did so. With one hand, he retrieved the lube from my headboard cabinet. Generously slicked up, he moved me into position. We only broke the kiss as he drove into me, never really losing his erection—he was so turned on. That's my guy, ever the ardent lover. I knew I had opened up a new avenue of things I could do to him to drive him wild.

I tasted the cum from our kiss still on my lips, on my tongue as I opened up to him, never really waning much from when he came, because he said when he was with me, I never failed to make him hard. He began to fuck me in earnest, reaching under my ass to pull my hips up to meet his thrusts, our hips smacking together in loud cracks of flesh.

"So. Fucking. Love. You. Baby." He punctuated each word with his forceful probing of my ass, pounding my prostate into oblivion, making my eyes roll back in my head as he did so.

"Uh-uh, look at me, babe. You know you need to watch me. I know it drives you crazy. But let me see it, please, baby. Let me see it."

I fought my way back from the back of my head to find his gaze, warm and inviting despite the thrashing of my hole from his cock. We were of two minds. Frozen in our lust with our eyes, caught spellbound, with a resounding voraciously cracking assault as he pummeled me, ensuring I felt the measure of his body.

"Burns, baby."

"I know."

"More, 'kay?"

"I know."

"Make it hurt."

"I know. I got you."

And he did. And this time he made it last. I don't know how long the fuck went on. He moved me into many positions, each more intense than the last, bending me in intense positions that forced me to exert more pressure on his probing cock. For once I was thankful how much I had spent stretching my body into weird Pilates-type positions I found online. I did it for core strengthening, but it seemed there were other benefits I hadn't considered. I made a mental note between Marco's powerful thrusts to become a more dedicated devotee of that particular set of exercises.

We were all over the bed. I came several times from the thorough plowing he was giving me. But he never relented in his assault. He marked my body with intense kisses, blossoming hickeys, and light bruising from how his roughened hands had positioned me while we fucked. I was a mess when he finally blew his wad deep within me. I was on my back again with his forehead against my own, his eyes watching mine as he shuddered violently and spent within me. He murmured his love for me, a bit of spittle flying from his lips, sweat pouring off him, bathing my face. It was literally raining Marco and I luxuriated in it.

Lazily, in the afterglow, because he had exerted himself so thoroughly, he ran his hands, those large rough hands of his I loved so, along my face. He kissed me. I was so moved by him, by his love for me. He said he wanted to show me how much he loved me. And he did.

"My poor baby. You're so exhausted."

He leaned down and rested his head in the crook of my neck, somehow finding the energy to suckle upon it. He didn't do it to mark me, but to show he still wanted me. I slowly massaged him where I could reach, soothing his body, cooling him down. I toed the sheet from under our bodies and pulled it over us. I let him fall asleep on top of me. I could barely reach the nightstand for my phone and set it for 3:30 a.m. to wake us before allowing myself to slip into a restful sleep. Marco's warm massive body was better than any blanket I could have wished for. He burrowed into me, only allowing himself to completely let go when he was assured I was safely tucked under him.

We slept.

WE NEVER MADE it to 3:30. I awoke to his prodding his entrance back into me. He wanted to fuck some more. We're teenage boys—it's what we do. So, we did—slower, far more erotically tortuous and grueling. I say grueling because he made sure I felt the breadth of him. He made me ache, moaning quite loudly with each thrust—not from any real pain, but more because I couldn't imagine the absence of him I knew would come later. I loved him even more, if it were remotely possible, when we were moving together like this. He bit, he suckled, nuzzled, the whole nine yards.

When he came sometime later—who really had time to look at a clock when fucking heaven on Earth was all around me?—it came in the form of a guttural rumble from deep within him. There was no frantic thrusting of hips or thrashing of bodies. It was just one long protracted thrust into me as his cock throbbed with release. I welcomed him, whispering into his ear how much he meant to me as he expended himself. I drank him in, literally. It was truly one of the most heart-wrenching moments I'd ever experienced. Probably because it wasn't rushed, like the constant lapping of waves upon the shore, it was lasting, and deeply moving. I relished the languishing pace he'd set for us both, the way he manipulated my body to sweeten the fuck, taking care to ensure it was the right balance of pain and pleasure two men could share. This is what my mother could never understand about Marco and me. She may sympathize in her own way; she may even rationalize it to her own experiences. But there was something transcendent when two men shared this level of intimacy. For me it was the personification of truth. Truth in who we were, truth in the courage we had to be there for each other, truth in that I'd never deny him and I knew, after tonight, I need never doubt he'd be there for me.

He pulled my ring finger to his lips and kissed it, telling me how much I meant to him. His eyes glistened with how vulnerable he was just now, blazing brilliantly in the darkness, a flash of intense green and amber. I leaned forward and kissed each eyelid, before bringing his head to rest upon my chest. We dozed for a short while before finally extracting ourselves from the tangle of bedding and moving to the shower for a quick wash. He lathered me and I him.

Once he dressed, we went out into the frigid cold morning, damp with the rainstorm we hadn't even noticed before. I was already hurting knowing he was leaving. He closed the door to his car after we kissed so many times I thought the sun would rise before we'd part. But he saw me shivering in the cold dawn air—even with his thick sweatshirt on me. He panicked and abruptly stopped the car just as I reached the back porch steps. I turned around to spy him running from the car—which he hadn't even bothered to turn off—as he made for the house again, moving swiftly past me. I reached out to stall him and he smiled.

"Forgot something from your room, ya know…"

Oh, yes, how could I forget? His collection from my room…

"You know, you're gonna strip it bare before I graduate at this rate."

He leaned forward to me and we kissed briefly again.

"I promise to leave you the bed."

"Well, good 'cause I don't fancy fucking on the floor."

He smiled darkly. "You'd let me fuck you just about anywhere so don't give me that…"

I smiled impishly at him, a smile I knew drove him balls to the wall crazy with lust when I did it. He shook his head, adjusted his crotch, and started to go into the house when I called him back.

"Love of my life…come back."

He turned to catch me pulling a necklace from around my neck. It was a simple gold chain—something I'd splurged on myself the first summer I was slaving away at the Q, one of my few indulgences. But it was time I made peace with casting my doubts about us aside.

"Here, you can have this. It's mine. Not like my mom or someone in the family bought it. But I've had it a while. It might as well be yours now. This way I'll know it's always safe."

His eyes became wet again as I removed the chain from my neck. He leaned forward and kissed me as I slipped it around his neck and latched it for him. He ran a finger gently along the strand of gold.

"I'll never take it off, babe."

"I know."

Another kiss and he pulled me tight at the waist into him, nearly taking the breath from my body in the process. I curved into him like those glamor poses in old time movie classics. I didn't care, really. He could have his way with me and I'd take whatever he could give. Was it selfish? Or low self-esteem? I didn't really have an answer for either question because in truth I didn't feel any of those things. Oh, I know I said I felt like I didn't deserve him, but that didn't mean I didn't want to deserve him or I thought I was trash or something. I was just baffled: *why me?* But after our last fuck, yeah, I knew there was no going back. I would be his and he would be mine until we took our last breaths on this earth. This was forever kind of love, a written-in-the-stars sort of thing, just as he'd said.

I knew it now. Accepted it, even.

He released me, our breaths caught upon the frigid morning air.

"I better get going."

I whimpered as we started to part, pulling a small snort of approval that he knew I was so against his leaving me.

"I know, babe."

He ran his fingers softly along the necklace around his neck. I could tell he liked wearing it.

"I feel the same way." He kissed my forehead. "Just a few more months then I swear, you'll never have to be apart from me."

"What the hell do you mean?"

He'd obviously been working on something he hadn't told me about and decided as he was heading to the car to spring it on me.

"Marco Raphael Sforza, what have you been up to?"

"Stop...you're sounding like my mother."

"Mmmm, 'kay, uh, *eeew*. So not wanting to dredge up that visual for you."

"Careful...that's my mom. But yeah, I get you."

He laughed at my wacky sense of humor and the odd times it decided to show up.

"I just meant..." Not really knowing how to rephrase it I muttered, "Ah, fuck me."

"You want to go another round?"

Now, there's a thought...

I nodded vigorously, bringing a loud belly laugh from him. He lazily shook his head at me. For some reason, I could see how he'd never let me slip away from him. I knew I spied such things before, but this time there was a confidence threaded there, saying very plainly, I'd never get away.

He stepped back up so his face was even with mine and kissed my forehead again.

"Bye, baby. See you later on today?"

"I gotta work."

"I know." *Cocky bastard.*

He smiled which transformed into a yawn. It drew a smirk from me. I looked up at him from underneath my lashes—something that also drove him bat-shit crazy with desire. I was pulling out all the stops.

"Behave..."

He gave me a pointed stare. It went right to my dick.

"I have you to see that I do."

"Damn straight."

"Darlin', there just ain't anything straight about us..." I drawled at him.

He smiled.

He got back in the Impala, revved her up, and her power vibrated deep within me before he backed out of the driveway around the house to the road. I closed the back door as soon as he cleared the house and ran like mad to the front window. He waved a hand as the taillights glowed ominously in the dark. She was a beautiful car, radiating power. I understood Marco's attraction to the classic vehicle. My man was one of the good guys, and at that moment I knew how lucky I was.

From my bedroom my phone vibrated on the nightstand. He was already reaching for me. I ran back to it, picked it up, and tapped it to connect the call—he reached and I was always there.

Chapter Eleven

You're Killing Me, Smalls

THE REST OF September went on in fairly the same manner. I never did see Angelo anywhere. To be honest, it was several days after the first game before he even formed a thought in my head. I have to admit, having Marco as your boyfriend tended to eclipse just about any other rational thought stealing across your mind. Only when Friday rolled around and another game was on the horizon did my thoughts circle back to Angelo. However, he turned out to be a no-show at the other games.

No matter; I figured as much.

And while Mercy was a fairly smallish town, we only had the one high school so practically every kid from miles around went there. It was easy to disappear.

As for the games, I was left to my own devices to watch my boyfriend do battle on the field of grass. Other than those moments when I was utterly alone in the stands, I was happy the team was doing well—everyone was saying it was another banner year. School was progressing, I guess, as it should. I went to school, dealt with Beau Hopkins' glares that seemed to penetrate the back of my head, regardless of how little I interacted with his precious captain. *Hell, he's my fucking lover!* So just what the fuck was I doing bowing to freakazoid preacher-boy Hopkins?

Yeah, well, that's how I raged inside. Outwardly, I cowered, like I always did.

For the most part, I just got by. Marco and I still had our lunches every now and again. He wanted them more but acquiesced to my point that he needed to make appearances at the Jock Plateau at the lofty Olympian heights in the center of the quad garden during a few lunchtimes here and there. Otherwise, things could get far more suspicious. He agreed but he was very grumpy about it.

"Els, I don't wanna be around those assholes. You *know* that. Fuck me, all they do is bad-mouth everyone else. It's so fucking obvious what fucking dicks they are."

I smiled, trying not to gloat as he railed against his own. Then he'd catch my suppressed smile and he'd chuckle, realizing the irony in his conflicted position.

"What?" he asked me.

"I know it's a necessary evil, but I just marvel at how wrong I was about you. It wasn't fair of me. It's probably one of the greater shames I carry. I should've given you the chance to show me who you were before I made any decisions as to your character. I was such a fool."

He shrugged, though the firm set to his jaw, the thin line of his lips said differently. I'd struck a nerve. I knew he somehow knew what I'd said about him before. He'd never said a word about it. Not once. But the look on his face, the stern wall of something utterly painful to him, something I'd put there, added salt to the painful wound of shame I carried. Inwardly I cringed at how badly I'd behaved, regardless if it provided me a modicum of safety that would eventually save me from harm from lesser enlightened jocks and their ilk. Watching him now, with the walled-off pain he carried, was almost too much to bear.

Then he'd pull me close and consume me again, if anything, just to solidify the fact his world hadn't changed, that I was still there—and I was. Since the night after his first game, I never wavered. I was a rock for him. I think it surprised him how much I'd adjusted to an "us" after that night. On one hand he relished the change, the level of commitment I was pouring into our relationship. On the other, I think it troubled him—not because he didn't like it, because he did. It was because for the first time the threat of something moving in from the side, something not seen, not anticipated, could upend our world.

I felt the same thing; I was just careful not to let him see it. He was carrying it enough for both of us. I decided to lean into him, metaphorically and, at times, literally, because it gave him a foundation to work through his fears.

On any given day I might be harassed a bit by a couple of the football thugs whenever I was unlucky enough not to have Marco around—usually as I was making my way to Psychology after Art class. It didn't happen often, but I detected their ever-closing ranks enough to know it for what it was. Like a well-oiled vise, they were doing their best to squeeze me from Marco's life. Only they hadn't counted on Marco's hold over me.

Hell, I knew the threat was real. Fuck, it was my world up to the point where he'd entered it. Now he was a part of my world, somehow it had made a small difference. I didn't have as many encounters with the jocks, cheerleaders, or other society twats who called Mercy High their academic home. They were still there, lurking in the shadows. Though their presence had lessened, they hadn't gone away entirely. Just when I thought they'd eased off, Mackenzie and Willem, two of the most brutish boys who ever were and who seemed to gather strength from terrorizing the gay kid on campus, cornered me as I made my way from Art to Psychology, like I was their personal Energizer Bunny or something. They didn't specifically warn me off Marco—at least not directly, just a moment of motivational harassment before they moved off to class. The threat of how easily it all could come tumbling down shadowed me throughout my day. I just couldn't quite shake it yet.

Such a point in time thrust itself into my world the first week of October. It was a gloomy day, which generally I liked. I happened to be Gothic in nature to a great degree, given my particular style and general proclivities toward the more darkly dramatic things in life. My world existed in a very Tim Burton sort of way. An off-kilter, darkly humorous, twisted and angular perspective was home to me.

Then Marco came along. What Marco brought to me was clarity, a more uniform and balanced world. He still allowed me my darkness, my inner Goth-Emo wallowing until he had enough of it and then he'd throw himself bodily in the mix, and like a supernova, he completely obliterated my dark moods with the enormous amount of light he brought with him.

Fuck, he could always turn my world upside down and it was glorious. It spun me around each time he did it, but that was completely okay with me. Like a child being twirled around on one of those spinning jungle gym turnstile things (if they have a name for them, it escapes me—funny, because I like words and all), the way he'd swoop in and clear away the dark clouds was just the same as the feeling I used to get lying on those turnstile platforms while other kids kept spinning them around and around as I stared up into the sky. It was dizzying and satisfying all at the same time. Marco was often like that. I liked how much power he exuded over my world. He was my Marco, radiant, illuminating and all-encompassing, a force to be reckoned with. And with him, I did a helluva lot of reckoning.

Well, our gloom-ridden Monday began as any other. By now we had progressed to getting to school earlier than most of the other students. It was Marco who did the driving these days. The cool part? I didn't have to hide because no one was really around.

We'd talk for a while, mostly about our future, and gods of Olympus, was it ever his favorite subject. By that week in October our future had been laid out for the next few years. He even knew exactly where we were going to get married, though he didn't want to share the location with me. He said he wanted me to be taken there with a hood over my head so I wouldn't see a thing until I got there. He was going to plan it and execute it down to the last detail. I laughed at how serious he was about it all. I know he got why I laughed; it was a nervous laugh because I knew everything he was saying would come to pass. I just had to show up.

I know I should be railing against it. It was all laid out for me. Who would walk into that? I know how it sounds. I get he comes off as he is some sort of Svengali obsessed with controlling every aspect of my life. But what I am not saying, what I should credit him for, is all of our plans were discussed between us. And he heard me, he valued what I wanted—hell, sometimes more than I did. The decision he would put into play was one we had discussed at length, with careful examination of how I felt about not only what I wanted in life, but what he wanted. He's a good guy, remember? Not a tyrant.

Anyway, that morning I awoke to my phone rattling as much as it could on the pillow next to my head. Marco—our daily morning call. This is where the bomb was dropped. This is where my man, my rock, faltered. There was such fear in his voice I thought something bad had happened. I'd never heard a tremor in his voice. I went from sleepy daze to fully awake within the matter of seconds.

"Hey, sweetheart," he barely murmured. And the *sweetheart* came out something akin to a whine. *WTF?*

"Baby, what's wrong? I can tell something's not right."

He chortled, but there was absolutely no mirth in it. The lack of humor troubled me.

"We know each other too well, don't we? Look, I don't want to hide anything from you."

"Oh, God." This was it: he'd decided we weren't going to work out after all. It was a ludicrous thought—for Chrissake we had just spent several hours last night working out our plans for when we'd get married and he would go to Stanford. There was certainly no indication from him things were going south for us. *Why did I run to that?* I hadn't entertained those thoughts since before the night after his first game.

We are solid. I just need to stop running back to old habits!

"No baby, not an *oh god*. Not really, anyway. But it is something we have to deal with, something we have to discuss. It's kind of a family thing; them fully inserting their plans for me. Something we haven't talked about much. Well, it came out at dinner last night. I knew about it when we talked before bedtime but I didn't want to trouble you. I wanted you to sleep well."

"Sweetheart, you can't do that. You can't *not* tell me things because you want me to have a good night's sleep."

I tried like hell to keep my voice down, but it wasn't easy. It was 6:30 a.m. but I didn't want my mom to come barging in wondering who I was arguing with at this early hour. I took an audible breath so he would know I was regrouping.

"Babe?"

"Yeah," I sighed.

"FaceTime, 'kay?"

"Okay, but I look like hell..."

"Never. I think you're the most gorgeous thing I've ever seen."

"Not when I first wake up...fucking death warmed over. Remember, I'm the pale one?"

"I love that about you, though. Like porcelain bisque."

A beat. I was busy chewing on a thumbnail, fretting over what was to come.

"Hon?"

"Huh? Oh, yeah. Talk to you in a sec."

We switched over to a FaceTime video call. And of course, he was fucking radiant. I could hear the choir of angels singing his praises in the background.

"So not fair..."

"What is?"

"You..."

"Huh?"

"You're so fucking gorgeous when you wake up it hurts. I'm gonna have to get up an hour earlier than you just to compete. I've got sleep in my eye still, my teeth aren't brushed and they taste like ass, and my hair is all over the fucking place. Whereas *you*..."

"Whereas I have been up for over an hour, worked out a bit, showered, shaved, and put myself together for my man, but you, on the other hand..."

"Look like death warmed over...we've covered it already."

"Stop...you'll hurt my feelings."

"*Your* feelings? Hey, it's me we're talking about here!"

"Uh huh, and you happen to be the center of my universe and you're trashing it so you just better check that, mister. I don't love trash. My man is the most beautiful person who ever walked the Earth. I worship you. I don't care what you say about it. And that's final. *You're killing me, Smalls.* Now stop it."

"Okay, okay...message received. So, what's the bombshell? Out with it. If we had to switch to FaceTime, then I know it can't be good. So just give it to me. I take my bad news like my coffee—black and straight up. Out with it."

"Then why do you have me put a crap load of cream in your coffees when I get them?"

"Because you make me happy. Cream equals happiness. I know it doesn't make sense, but stop evading the subject and just get to it already!"

He sighed, and now I really was worried because I could see how conflicted he was about whatever it was.

"Marco..."

"Okay—two words: Homecoming King."

"Homecoming..."

"Yeah. And I don't want to do it but Mom was all over my ass about it. Said I'd totally regret it if I didn't do it, 'cause I'm the fucking *star football player*; I'm *going places*. This will *look good for my college application*—which you and I know is utter bullshit because Dad's already fucking locked that up."

"What? When?"

"Babe, it's why we've been talking about Stanford as much as we have. I know where I am going. I'm not even applying anywhere else. Mom wants me close but she also knows I need to go to a great school. So, it's either Berkeley or Stanford. Dad graduated from Stanford so there you are. And we are so way off course here; stop sidecar driving."

"Okay, we'll talk about it later. So, homecoming."

"Not just homecoming—but Homecoming King. She wants me to run. You know where that'll go."

"Yeah, and you're so popular it's virtually a shoo-in."

"Right, I know. I fucking hate this shit."

"So, don't do it."

"I wish it were that easy. Dad got involved at dinner and it got kind of heated. Even my…"

"Even your…what?"

He paused, ran a hand through his hair. "Nothing, not important. What is important is I don't see a way out of it."

"Okay, so we deal with it. We knew some shit like this was bound to happen."

"But it's so not fair to you, sweetheart."

"I know. I get it. But it's not like you can take me to the dance anyhow."

"That's so not the point. I wanted to slip by all that shit. Yeah, I had to play the game but fuck me, I didn't want to have to play that sort of game as well. Just Mom's going on about it. Fuck, you'd think she paid for me to win it and she didn't want to be out the cash."

"Wait, you don't think she...?"

"Be real, Els."

"Yeah, okay. So? What's the worst that could happen?"

"I'd win and have to escort whoever is the fucking Queen to the damn dance. I so don't want to do that when I could be making love to you. That's all I want. It's what I *want* to do."

"Well, ditto from my court as well, babe. It's what *I'd* rather we were doing that night."

He grumbled and even roared a bit in frustration. This had really upset him.

"Babe, look, we gotta deal with this. It obviously isn't going away."

"Yeah, I know. Doesn't mean..."

"We gotta like it, yeah, I know. But it's only one night. I think I can handle it." Though inside I wasn't so sure. One thing I could count on was his seeing right through my fears.

"Els, you don't have to worry. I'll do my fucking duty and then I'll get the fuck outta there and come straight to you. You know that."

"Yeah, I know. I don't doubt it."

"So? What's eating at you?"

"Nothing."

"Els? Out with it."

"It's nothing, I *swear*."

"You're so full of shit like a Christmas turkey. Tell me. No secrets, remember?"

"Hey, you didn't tell me yours last night...that's a secret."

"But I told you this morning and I take your point and will not do it again. So, we're square there, right?"

"I guess. It's just..."

"What?"

"That fucking bitch, Cindy Markham, is *so* gunning for you and I just bet the cow is going to get Queen and she'll have her paws all over you the whole fucking night. She already does far more than I like." I mumbled the last bit, but I knew he heard it.

"Baby, you know I don't like her doing that. It's you, Els. Only you, babe."

"I know."

He smiled and there was such a light in his eyes, brilliant flashes of emerald and amber.

"What?"

"You're *jealous*."

"I am not..." I gasped like a southern belle clutching her pearls.

He quirked a brow. The move went straight to my dick, which didn't need much encouragement as I already had morning wood to begin with.

"Oh, my baby is *soooo jealous*."

"So? What if I am? I think I have a right to be. You're mine!"

His mood instantly changed from smiling to a more serious tone.

"Yes, I am."

"I need to protect what's mine!"

"As you should." His lust was palpable; he wanted me. He obviously liked it when I got possessive of him.

"I better go. It's going to get all sorts of weird here."

"Okay, I'll let you off the hook...*for now*. But I am so getting a nooner out of this."

"Uh huh. Whatever, big guy."

"Babe?"

"Yeah?"

"You know I love you more than all the stars in the sky, right?"

I blushed, picking at a loose thread on my comforter. "Yeah, right back atcha."

"'Kay, look, don't pack a lunch. I got you covered, okay?"

I yawned. "Uh huh. Okay."

"Love you, sweetheart."

I tried to say "I love you too" but it came out as one long yawning drawl—"Ahh uhhv ooo tooh."

He smiled and blew me a kiss. I caught it in my hand and blew one back. Though just before we clicked off I caught his attention. "Babe?"

"Huh?"

I flipped the camera direction on my phone to show him my rock hard cock as I stroked it, then flipped it back around, raising an eyebrow of my own. "See ya..."

"You're soooo..." I clicked it off and tossed it aside. He rang right back but I forwarded it to voice mail just to tease him. I knew he was going to pay me back at lunch, and I was *counting* on it.

A QUICK HALF hour later I was sitting on the tree stump by the road around the corner from my house. I think my mom was looking forward to driving me, mostly because it was our usual Mom-checking-in-with-her-boy-to-make-sure-he-was-okay-time, rather than my actually needing a lift to school. But lately Marco had taken up the mantle and while I loved my mom, I'd much rather be with my guy whenever possible. Sorry, Mom—the little boy is all "growed up," and then some...

Marco was looking rather dashing in a black tee about a half size too small, emphasizing his sculpted torso so well it left little, if anything, to the imagination. It was practically painted on. Knowing Marco's mother, it was probably of Italian design, from Italy no less, and very expensive for a T-shirt. Some of Marco's clothes as individual items cost more than nearly my entire wardrobe. I know 'cause I looked them up online after. Not that I had a Cinderfella complex or anything, but I was curious if the Sforzas had as much money as I imagined. They didn't, they had more.

He was a vision in the taut black microfiber T-shirt disappearing into his narrow waist and those fucking outrageously sexy cherry red jeans hugging every contour of his ass and powerful legs. This was his *Elliot you are so fucked* outfit. He wore it the night he gave me the ring on my eighteenth birthday, and we all know what happened then. I hadn't seen him wear it since. But he'd commented the last time he wore it that it was one of the outfits he'd wear to put me on notice. I stood at the door of the Impala. Suddenly I wasn't so sure how much eating would get done at lunch today. Seriously, though, when I thought about it, Marco didn't re-wear many of his outfits. His closet must be one giant Kleenex box of clothes. Wear and toss. Must be nice, but it did underscore what a disparity there was between my world and his.

But he didn't care about any of that. He told me as much when we talked about our future together. He said he expected us to live in some small flat near Stanford and we'd share our clothes, but he much preferred clothes to be an option when we were home. He said I should plan on being naked around him a lot when we got our own place. Once he had me completely to himself we'd be spending an awful lot of free time fucking. I knew this was his hormones doing the talking. But I also knew whatever got going in his noggin would eventually become a reality. I guess we'd have to have bathrobes on the coat rack near the front door for when either of our parents decided to show up. I put all of these musings aside as I slid into the car.

"C'mere, you." His giant hand went to the back of my neck and he pulled me to his mouth. He deep tongued my tonsils to his utter satisfaction. I was merely along for the ride. And what a fucking hellacious ride it was.

We were both left panting when he finally let me go.

"Good morning to you too."

He smiled and gunned the engine. "I am so going to make love to you later."

"Uh huh, I know. I see you're wearing the *you're fucked, Elliot* outfit. Consider me officially on notice. You and your nooners."

"Oh, like you don't get something out of it?"

"I do. I just don't like it to be so damn quick. I like when you make it last. But then, I guess we'd never make it back to class on time, would we?" I said it sheepishly, looking up from under my lashes. He melted in the driver seat, twisted his head a bit, with a slight jutting of his jaw as if he was really struggling to keep driving us to school. A beat later and he had pulled his hand from mine to readjust himself.

"Pants getting a little too tight for ya?" I said as I looked nonchalantly through my emails on my iPhone.

"Careful, or I'll just keep driving to Officer Langley-Pierce's fuck point. I have no problem ditching for the day."

"Can't, babe. We both have a quiz in American Civics. Supposed to be a surprise but I spied the draft on Grant's laptop when I talked to him about my paper at the end of class last week. So, *nooner* it is."

I said all of this without even looking his way, very noncommittal, as if we were discussing the economic ramifications of the government shutdown going on in DC. He huffed and puffed at how easily I was playing it. He reached over and gripped my crotch hard, finding I was sporting a stiffy as well.

"Yeah, you talk a good game, Donahey. But your other head is talking louder."

I finally turned to look at him. He kept his attention divided between me and the road.

"You should hear what my ass has to say on the subject, then." I smiled and he laughed.

"Careful...quiz or no quiz, Els, I will pull into the woods right now and bang the fuck out of you just 'cause you're giving me lip. Then you can explain to Crabapple why we weren't at first period."

"Marco, we are not going to fuck before school. That's final!" I said it a bit more pointed than I should've. Marco didn't like ultimatums or challenges going unanswered. I'd just challenged him. The trouble is my family lived on the outskirts of Mercy. It meant there were more than a half dozen places where he could easily pull off the road behind some fallen trees or dense blackberry canes capable of hiding the Impala while we did the dirty in the back seat.

Three minutes later and we were in the backseat and he was fucking me for all his worth, using my spit for lube so I could feel what I got when I challenged him. He made sure I burned with it. But I got a new hickey out of the deal—which was cool. When he came, it was violent and deeply satisfying, though I think he scared off a nearby deer when he howled through his orgasm.

"It's a good thing I'm wearing my black skinny jeans and athletic boxer briefs. Otherwise you'd have to take me home to change," I mumbled in his direction, not bothering to hide the gleam in my eye because I knew this was how he liked to have me—in the afterglow of a good fuck.

"You better do your best to keep it up in you 'cause I'll need it again around lunchtime."

"Yeah, I got it."

He hoisted my legs up so he could inspect my well-fucked hole. He fingered it for a while. "So fucking wet, baby. Just the way I like it."

"I know. Makes me wonder what'll it be like when we do live together."

He waggled his eyebrows and I knew the answer. I'd be butt naked and well fucked. It's what turned him on about sex with me. He liked seeing the fruits of his labors on me. I suppose it is why he marked me as he did. Who needed tattoos when you had Marco the body marker for a boyfriend? My eyes found his again while he continued to finger me.

"You're so beautiful, Els. I think I'm gonna make us ditch today. I just can't give you up now."

The wet tip of his cock at the base of my spine made me hunger for him. He was fully aroused again and rarin' to go.

I smiled. "Well, I'd better make it worth our while then..."

He laughed as he had another go with me.

Halfway through our lust-filled abandon the clouds let loose with a torrent of water, as if God really was throwing out the bathwater. It was a fucking deluge. We even paused in our fucking to listen to how hard the rain was pummeling the Impala. But she was a strong old gal (as Marco called her). Not like these new tissue paper cars on the road today. He was such a classic muscle car snob. I loved that about him. Like Dean Winchester, the only songs he permitted in the car were classic '70s and '80s rock. I had to relearn old classics from my parents' heydays. "Carry On Wayward Son" was high on the list of his favorites, as was "Eye of the Tiger"; pretty much if it played on *Supernatural*, it was on our playlist too. I once mentioned how Dean scoffed at his little brother Sammy's adapting the cassette player to play from an iPod but Marco just told me he and Dean had differing opinions on the topic. He wasn't letting his entire music library go for nothing. To be fair, he had one of those older classic iPods, so I kinda got how he was seeing it.

He had me lying on top of him in the back seat after he'd flipped to the battery and turned on the iPod so we could hear some music. We didn't crank it up, more for background while he continued to stroke my back.

"We should get to school sometime today, lover."

He looked at his watch. It was approaching 8:45, well into our first period English class. I told him I thought it was a mistake. Ol' Hopkins wasn't going to let it go unnoticed if he and I were missing on the same morning. He said to drop it. He'd figure out something to set it straight. I snorted at his choice of words, but he didn't rise to the bait.

I was leaning against my elbow with what I guess was a dreamy sort of look because as he ran a finger along my brow he asked me where I was wandering off to.

"Nothing. I'm just trying to see us down the road, that's all."

"Oh, that's all. That's fairly important stuff, Els."

"I know."

"And? What do you see?"

"Well, I do see an us. That much is solid. I see it, babe. I really do. But I dunno—everything else around us is in such turmoil."

I just shrugged and laid my cheek to his chest, listening to the most magical sound of all—his heart. I could listen to him forever. It calmed me, soothed whatever ailed me. Funny how something so simple, so pure, could hold you spellbound. When he held me like this, I didn't want to leave. Not ever. I could grow old like this, in his arms. I knew what he meant by saying I completed him. Because he did with me.

WE FINALLY GOT to school in time for American Civics—but barely. You have no idea how hard it was to go through my day worrying each time I sat down and got back up I'd have a wet stain on my ass. Luckily for me it didn't happen but I smacked the shit out of Marco when we were alone at lunch at the cliffs again. He just smiled and took it on the chin. I ended up gifting him with an exasperated look, realizing there wasn't going to be any change in what we'd do when we were alone together. It's just how we were. Immutable, unchangeable—he'd always take me to his arms and I would always submit to the power within him. It's what we did. It's what made things complete in our world. He was my brilliant sun; I was his warmth.

After lunch the bombshell from this morning became a force to be reckoned with. Posters of Marco appeared around campus. His jock buddies were all fist bumpy with him and the cheerleaders were exuberant if a little reserved with Cindy obviously spreading the word Marco wasn't a free agent when it came to dating. So, I guess I had a little something to be thankful for—though it wasn't much when she kept not so subtly pawing him whenever she got the chance.

We coasted through the rest of our day though it was surreal seeing your boyfriend plastered on nearly every wall and door in the joint. Here's the strange part about it: the posters were professionally done. I mean, his mother was obviously funding his little campaign. But that photo, the one that made Marco look like Antonio Sabato, Jr. from those famous Calvin Klein ads that went up in Times Square back in the '90s? It was a bit racy for a school poster but it was presented in a distressed way to hide most of the titillating bits. What unnerved me so was the photo was mine. I took it one afternoon after we'd just had sex—obviously keeping the lens above the actual crotch but with just enough to hint at his sexy curved muscle along his hip pointing to his prodigious gifts. No more than you'd see in low slung jeans for god's sake. I guess his mother wasn't above hawking her son's skin to get what she wanted. But I knew what worked in that picture, what gave it the "it" factor. The look in his eyes, the look that was supposed to be reserved just for me—only now it was *everywhere*.

I felt enormously invaded. Violated, even. Girls were gushing about how sexy he looked and how they knew he was destined for super-stardom: he was going to be discovered and then be surrounded by Hollywood starlets at big celebrity parties. They had his whole world planned out for him. It was my fucking picture, but everyone else's story.

You bet I was fucking bitter.

Far more than I should've been, but hey, I'm only human. When Marco picked me up at the back of the school in the Impala, he reached out for me; I didn't melt into him like usual. He immediately pulled over to the side of the road. I told him to keep driving; we were too exposed being so near to the school. He said to fuck the school; he wanted to know what my shit was.

So, I told him.

"I have had it up to here"—slamming my hand hard against the roof of the car—"that I am some dirty little secret. I am the one who you *say* you love but *no one* gets to know it but me! While I may take you to my bed, or for fuck's sake the back seat of this car, everyone else has planned your future and it doesn't include me. I know it doesn't make sense. I know it's my own fucked-upness about it. I get it. I do. But fuck me, I don't know if I want to anymore."

His eyes widened with the fear my words brought to him. On one hand, I immediately wanted to soothe him. I wanted to tell him I knew my feelings were utter bullshit; but on the other hand, I wanted him to feel my pain, if even only for a moment, just so he'd know exactly how fragile my world was without him. I knew I was wielding it like a weapon—and I was using it stupidly on him, the man I loved more than anything. I knew that. If I did it, if I really opened my mouth and told him how scared I was, then he'd see what a fucking basket case I was and he'd leave. I wouldn't have to imagine it, 'cause he'd make it true. Of course all of my musing didn't mean I was going to be smart about it. My mouth got ahead of me again.

"I can't help it; it's how I feel. Everything is coming at me from all sides. And the only person who can hear me, the only person who says they understand is you. But don't you see? It's what hurts so much. Those posters, this stupid fucking contest, all of it, fuck, even your own parents are driving you to do this against your will and you're going along with it. All of it cuts, Marco. All of it hurts one person: *me*. 'Cause I can't be a part of this. I was a fool to think I could even put a toe in your world."

God, the fucking tears really started to flow now. Marco reached for me, tried like hell to bring me to him. I fought; I pushed, finally bringing my foot up between us and shoving him back to his side of the car. I opened the door and climbed out so fast—choosing to move through the oak forest to only god knew where, but I needed some space.

"Elliot! Baby! Wait!"

He turned off the car. He sprinted after me. I ran, tripping and falling over small flora debris that wouldn't have presented an obstacle to a more coordinated individual. He kept calling after me. Like Snow White I couldn't get through a fucking forest to save my life. My backpack caught on a branch and I tugged on it like the wildly over-emotional gayboy I was. Swatting at it like a big ol' girl, I struggled for a few seconds but couldn't figure out how to unhook it and keep my distance from Marco's advance, so I just shrugged out of it and left it.

I tried to pick up speed but I knew it was a lost cause. I simply wasn't that kind of an athlete. He was gaining—and fast. I took a sharp right and tried to sprint, caught my foot on a fallen log, and went head over heels down a steep ravine. Before I knew it, it was too late. Everything was a jumble. I was cut and scraped; Marco cried out, thinking I'd really hurt myself, which I have to admit as I tumbled to the bottom I thought was so spectacularly ironic I actually hoped I'd break my neck or something so I wouldn't have to deal with the aftermath of my little drama. I was far more embarrassed about making a complete ass of myself in front of him. Then the worst happened: I flipped one last time and my head came down on a decent sized rock. The world lurched; my stomach heaved; Marco yelled my name in absolute terror and then...

Nothing.

Chapter Twelve

Once More Unto the Breach...

I DON'T KNOW how long I was out.

But fuck me, did my head hurt when I came to. My face was wet, something dripping all over it.

Is it raining?

There was a rumbling or rolling sound, no, more like rocking motions around me.

What the fuck is all of that? Can't someone make it stop?

And the noise—fuck, I just wanted to sleep.

Does it all have to hurt so damned much?

"Baby? Oh, please, baby—Els, please. Sweetheart, look at me. Oh, fuck, baby—that's it. Open your eyes, Els. Open them."

"What?" I mumbled—slurred, more like.

Marco. I found comfort in his voice despite the hurt and the fear in it.

Who made him so upset?

I struggled to open my eyes, thanking the rain gods the sun wasn't shining down on my face. Why wasn't it more wet if it was raining? As my vision cleared and things came into focus I discovered it wasn't rain. It was my man, crying like a baby with the biggest grin on his face.

"What's so funny?" I murmured.

"Not funny, baby. I was scared. I thought I'd lost you. Ah, God. My whole heart came out of my chest. You fell and went tumbling down the embankment. I have never been so scared in my life," he sputtered, spit and tears and fear pouring out of him.

"Then why're you smiling?"

"'Cause I'm happy you're okay, sweetheart."

He ran his hand along the side of my face. Even though his fingers were rough, it felt amazingly good. I wanted to curl up against him and go to sleep. I found myself doing just that. He wasn't having it, though.

Damn him.

"Uh uh, Elliot, baby, you can't. You gotta stay awake, sweetheart. Please? C'mon, Els. Come back to me. *Elliot!*"

"*What*? Ow, baby, that hurt! Stop with the yelling, 'kay? I'm right here, for Chrissake!" I rubbed my temple and my fingers came away sticky.

"No baby, don't. You'll probably make it worse. Can you stand up?"

"I don't want to stand." And I didn't. He was so warm all I wanted to do was fold myself into him and close my eyes. But instead he started to get up and pull me with him.

"What are you *doing*?" I cried out, hearing the whine in my question.

I didn't fucking care. Everything hurt; I was confused, and discombobulated. Once I was on my feet the world spun for a second and Marco gripped me a bit tighter around the waist. I wanted to retch. He hooked my arm around his shoulder and I let my head lean into the crook of his neck; it was still wet from the streaks of his tears. Geez, I must have really scared him. He just wasn't the crying type. I don't know why, but I found it so strange just then.

"I got you, baby. I'm never letting you go. You hear me?"

I nodded and murmured my agreement. I couldn't really remember what drove me out into the woods anyway.

"Everything hurts..."

He snorted but I could tell he wasn't very happy about it.

"Yeah, well it's no wonder. You went ass over head down a fucking ravine. Scared me shitless. You're so not a dexterous kind of guy, sweetheart."

I sort of remembered we got into some sort of discussion and I got pissed but being so close to him now, smelling of the particular scent distinctly him—hands down, my absolute favorite smell on the planet—was comforting. I wanted to melt into him. I kept kissing his neck and he smiled as I did. My feet kept stumbling as we moved toward the car. We paused briefly as he seemed to sort out how best to carry me forward. A few minutes later and he had me safely tucked and buckled in the passenger seat and he slid across the hood of the car to shorten the distance to the other side. I smiled, looking at him cock-eyed with my head lolled to the side, leaning against the window. My super-hero boyfriend was truly amazing when he used that body he knew so well.

I started to close my eyes, just to rest mainly. But Marco, it seemed, had other ideas.

"Hey! You keep awake, baby. I know you probably want to rest but it's not a good idea right now."

"But it hurts—all over." I yawned, mostly because I wasn't really breathing fully. I was simply too tired to draw a deep breath.

"Fuck, this is when I regret having a classic car with no power windows. Elliot, baby, you gotta stay awake." He flicked on the iPhone and cranked up Boston's "More Than A Feeling" which he knew was one of my favorite tunes.

"Turn it down; it's too loud."

I lunged for the controls on his stereo. He batted my hand away.

"Uh-uh, nothing doing. You need to stay awake until we get there."

"Yeah, just drop me off near the store and I can walk it from there."

"Walk it from...What the hell are you thinking? You aren't going to any store, babe. I'm taking you somewhere else right now."

"Where?" I yawned again.

"Deeper breaths—you need more oxygen. It'll help wake you."

I breathed in like he said and my side hurt from the exertion. "*Ow*! Oh, I don't think I should do that again. It hurt, Marco."

"Okay, then breathe as deeply as you can until we get there. Okay?"

"Where are we going anyway?"

"To see my dad. We need to get you checked out."

That woke me the fuck up.

"What? Are you crazy? I am so not ready for that."

"For what? He's your family doctor, right?"

The threat of being in the same room with Dr. Vincenzo Raphael Sforza and my boyfriend, his son *and* my lover, wasn't so appealing to me just now. I wasn't ready for that sort of meeting.

"Yeah, but I can't, not with you there."

"What? Now's so not the time to bring up our relationship and my parents, Els."

He reached across and ran a couple of fingers along the side of my head. It hurt like a son of a bitch when he did it. I hissed at him and batted at his hands like the sissy little gayboy I am. He smirked but then showed me his fingers which were now stained dark crimson.

"We need to get you checked out, baby. I'm not chancing anything happening to you, even if you were being a little crazy a few minutes ago. Don't ever run away like that, you got me? That scared me enough. You wanna hurt me? Truly cut me? Then do what you just did. I felt like my fucking heart was being torn out of my body. Then when you went down the ravine, I thought...well, I thought..."

I reached out and placed my hand in his. He rubbed my palm very lightly, more of a soft caress. He wanted to hold me, bring me to him. I was simply too embarrassed how it had all turned out.

"I'm sorry. You know that, don't you? I know I made an ass of myself. I didn't mean to take it out on you. It's just..."

"Shhh, I know. Actually, I'm glad you told me. Just could do without all the shoving and hysterics, that was a bit hard to deal with. But whatever it is, baby, we can always talk about it. You know I listen to you. Whatever goes on in that head of yours, whatever is troubling you. I listen. Whatever it is, we'll deal with it—together. 'Kay?"

I nodded, recalling how childish I had been earlier. It was all sort of coming back to me, the rush of completely irrational emotions—not that I had them, just the way they all came out. It wasn't fair to dump my insecurities on him. I was sure he was feeling fairly guilty giving into his parents the way he did anyway. I know he was a take-charge kind of guy, but obviously that came with some limitations. I knew it wasn't his fault. And that was the embarrassing part. I made it his fault. It *was* his fault, but for completely different reasons than what I'd mistakenly attributed to him. He was guilty of being such a gem of a guy, of everyone liking him as much as they did. Another reminder Marco truly was one of the good guys. He never spoke ill of anyone. Sure, he groused about someone being in a bad mood or being snitty with him. He was human, after all. But never did a malicious bone in his body make itself known to me. I liked that about him. Why shouldn't others? I knew I was just being selfish.

"I'm still sorry. You didn't deserve that. And I'm sorry for scaring you. I'd never leave you, Marco. Never." I tried to leave it at that, but my mouth keeps getting ahead of the line in the sand my mind keeps drawing for it. So instead I mumbled, "It'll be you who leaves me, one day. I know that." I uttered the last bit to the window because I couldn't look at him as I put words to my deepest fears. I believed we were solid. I wanted us to be solid. But I couldn't control the other half of us, the half crucial to providing our sense of stability. The trouble was, I hadn't mumbled enough.

"Well, that day will never come. It's us, baby. All the way to our last breath on this earth. Grumpy baggy bones and wrinkled flesh and all, surrounded by our kids and even more grandkids."

I chuckled a little bit to think of us as old grumpy men who still would be chasing each other around the bed butt-assed naked, walkers and all. He smiled as if he was picturing the same thing.

Yeah, okay, we're good.

The Impala took the driveway slowly. I guess he was trying to be gentle with me in my bashed up state. I was thankful. The Impala was a fuck beast of a car but she wasn't so gentle where the shocks were concerned. Normally I didn't mind. He pulled into one of the two reserved spaces his father had in front of his medical office.

"So what do I tell my mother?"

"Let me take care of that."

Aw, courageous, if misguided, boy that he is. How sweet he wants to walk into his own funeral for me. I put a hand out on his arm to stall his getting out of the car.

"*You're*—going to call *my* mother, and tell her you took me to the doctor? *You're* going to do that?" I inquired with a fair degree of skepticism.

"Yeah, why?" He had this wide grin as if I were the one being silly here.

"Obviously you've never had a conversation with my mother when my health was concerned."

"It'll be fine. I need to start talking to her sometime."

I sat there looking at him like he'd sprouted two heads.

"Yeah, well, it's been nice being your boyfriend. Let me know where you'll end up, so I know where to bring the flowers when I visit your grave."

"You seriously doubt my good looks and manly charms?"

He shook his head and glanced at the front door of his father's office, noting as I did Mary Farnsworth and her five-year old daughter, Macy, leaving. Macy was quite pleased with the strawberry lollipop her good behavior seemed to have netted for her troubles in visiting the doctor.

"*That*, no. But just where do you think I get my hysterics you mentioned earlier? And just to be clear, I don't doubt for one second the allure of your charming good looks. Hell, they snagged the fuck outta me."

"Literally..." he chortled which earned him a Clarey Greenbaum-flavored slap on the shoulder.

I quirked a brow at his teasing me.

"Yeah, well, Superman—good luck with hugging Kryptonite Mom. Should be quite the spectacular event. I should sell tickets. YouTube the damned thing."

He leaned forward, which I thought was either really fucking courageous or really fucking stupid of him, and placed a soft kiss on my lips. He had this big ol' dopey smile on his face as he gazed at me through glazed half-lidded eyes. They were wondrous to behold, even at half the brilliance.

"Eh, sweetheart, you *do* realize *where* we are?"

His green eyes drank me in and it went straight to my crotch, still keeping the same dopey I-am-so-in-love-with-you look on his face. I have to admit, I caved a little and responded with a small smirk to let him know he'd achieved his goal of getting to me.

"Uh huh. I don't care right now. I have you back and I am just allowing myself to enjoy that right now. Fuck everyone else," he said in a dreamy haze of his being so in love and truly not caring.

"Uh huh..." I drawled, adjusting myself. He chuckled softly.

"You ready to get checked out?"

"Uh, Houston, we got a problem there..."

"As in?"

"Just how *much* of me is he going to check? You've been fairly possessive today, not to mention the serious fucking we've done. And by last count I have about four new hickeys gracing my upper body. Not something I think I want to answer to just now."

"Yeah, let me sort that one out. I'll come up with something."

"You're the boss."

He rolled his eyes and slammed the flat of his hand on the steering wheel, thankfully not hard enough to beep the horn.

"Yeah, it's about time you figured that one out."

"I never doubted it. I just like jerking your chain every now and again. Keeps things fresh."

He waggled those prominent brows again. "And you jerk it so well, baby."

"*I soooo don't need a boner when I see your dad!*"

I winced. It hurt in so many places.

"C'mon, sexy boy. Let's get inside so he can see to your head."

DR. SFORZA'S OFFICE was ultra-modern in what I imagined was chic northern Italian decor. The Sforzas wore their Italian heritage as if the flag were sewn down their spine so it could billow behind them. But not in a tacky *Jersey Shore* kind of way. Proud, but definitely tasteful. European to the hilt.

Don't get me wrong—I fucking relished my Italian boyfriend, so I was good with it. But Dr. Sforza was about as European as you could get and still legally be on the American continent. The decor was further accentuated with a cousin of Marco's (from the old country, no less) who was their receptionist. Her accent was as thick as the long raven locks billowing in come-hither curls down her back. From the way she reacted to my boyfriend she seemed to have a particular soft spot for Marco. If the world admired Marco, his family bordered on fanatical adoration.

Then there was me: standard American belly-lint. Only with my rough and tumble landslide this afternoon, it was bloody belly-lint on offer today. Marco's cousin positively glowed as she came around and planted a European-style kiss on each of his cheeks, talking a blue streak in Italian. After her radiant adoration of Marco, she cast an eye to me like he'd picked up gum on his Bruno Malis. Maybe I was reading too much into her look. While I'd gotten good at reading Marco's unspoken musings, I wasn't so sure I could apply the technique to another member of his family, let alone one of the opposite sex.

"Eh, Francesca, this is Elliot Donahey. Elliot, you remember my cousin, Francesca Donatella Sforza."

I didn't know if we were supposed to do the cheek kiss thing or not, so I just stood there like a bloody wide-eyed deer in the headlights. She must have sensed my complete lack of etiquette or manners because she painted on a half-smile before lavishing her attentions back to Marco. As she curled into him, he kissed her forehead. It all seemed a bit too cozy to me.

I took a moment to eye her. She was slightly shorter than Marco's 6'3" height—though it was really hard to tell in the four-inch heels she was wearing. She was impeccably dressed in a gray suit with a fitted skirt hugging her curvaceous body. The jacket was single-breasted and tailored to cling to her small waist and ample bosom. The mustard silk blouse brought out the amber flecks in her eyes. She had the fiery green and gold eyes of my boyfriend.

Lucky sons of bitches.

I found it really hard to hate them for it, though. It was as if I were walking amongst gods and goddesses of the classical Roman era.

So, here's the thing, I know you're probably wondering where the formulaic beard is in my story? Well, to be honest, women confound me. Francesca epitomized and crystallized it for me. You'd think I'd have the cliché straight girlfriend with whom to share my deepest secrets and we'd talk about boys, fashion, movie stars, and things like that. I'd do her hair and we'd go shopping a helluva lot.

Yeah, so not going to happen for this gayboy.

I tried it in junior high with a girl named Carrie after my world with Stephen sort of collapsed with my coming out. We tried the whole GBF thing and I just couldn't find any way to relate. I mean, aside from the whole liking boys, there really wasn't much else. We didn't even have the same taste in music. She was bubble gum pop with boy bands and there I was with my darkly amorous Jay Brannan. Thank the stars above her parents moved to another state taking her with them when we made the migration from Helen Keller Junior to Mercy High. Frankly, after that failed experiment I couldn't see the point. I required men in my life. I was only comfortable with them. I understood them, even if they often didn't understand me. My mother currently fulfilled any and all requirements I had for the female sex. This is why Francesca rattled my cage. I was responding to her in a way that had never happened to me before. To be honest, it was pissing me the hell off.

Marco's retelling of my dramatic antics brought me back to the moment.

"He fell on his way home from school and hit his head on a rock. He's one of Papa's patients. Is there any chance of him taking a look at his head?"

"Eh, sure. I am sure we can fit him in. Your papa is having a very light day today." She eyed me with a great deal of suspicion, a slight narrowing of the eyes like some jaguar eyeing prey before a kill, or maybe she was trying to ascertain why someone like me would be in the presence of *his divine glory,* Marco Sforza.

She walked in that high fashion model way—okay, I'm totally exaggerating here but seriously, the whole fucking family was drop dead gorgeous. Even if I had a modicum of good looks, I'd still come up as belly-lint with this crew. Ear wax, at best—*maybe.*

She slinked back in the feminine way that used to irk the shit out of me but drove straight guys wild with lust, but on her it seemed to work. Wow, did I have a straight boy gene in me somewhere dying for some boy-on-girl action? I huffed as she moved back to the receptionist desk.

"She thinks I'm lint," I whispered.

He raised an eyebrow at me. "What?" he whispered back, clearly not getting my reference. *Where was he when I was having these serious conversations about our lives? Can't he read minds like I need him to?*

I shook my head to let it go and he just rolled his eyes. "Tell me later, then."

She looked up from the books she was perusing, the quizzical arch to her brow I'd come to expect from this familial line. Seriously, did they rehearse these gestures? They were more in sync than the acrobats of Cirque du Soleil. Obviously, I wasn't as quiet with my speech as I thought. Or über-model Francesca had supersonic hearing to go along with those sexy Roman goddess looks.

I wished I could leave it alone but something kept nagging at me. Francesca was far too shrewd to put up with our story of Marco just being a Good Samaritan who happened to be nearby when I took my fall. We weren't that good at hiding our familiarity with each other. It was definitely working against us.

"Your insurance is on file with us, eh? Up to date?"

"Cassiel Elliot Donahey. And, uh, yes. It should be."

Marco raised an eyebrow. I hadn't shared my full name with him. Not that I was ashamed of it. I just knew my first name wasn't something you'd see on a coffee cup. It was a bit old school. I was cool with it. In fact, I'd thought about using it as my pen name for when I broke into comics. Just Cassiel. Nothing else. I wanted to disappear into that name for my art, if I could. It's why I never said it to him. I thought once I let it out fully into the world it wouldn't hold its special allure any longer. But it was Marco; I should entrust everything to him, shouldn't I? My inner Gollum/Yoda gave up any poetic pretense and just cursed me out.

Oh for fuck sake, Cass. It's not like it's the end of the world. So, he knows your first name now. Big f'n deal.

Francesca eyed Marco's face with cat-like precision.

"Date of birth?"

I told her, "August 2nd, 1994." I knew she was verifying she had the right file on her computer.

Again, with that familial quirk of the Sforza brow. This time between them both. I was surrounded by Sforzas. I looked around the waiting room, the lone Irish Catholic amongst the Italians. Even though we shared the same church, I was so out of my element with them. I wanted to cling to Marco something fierce. He had to see it in my eyes.

"*Un attimo controllo se il papà è pronto di vedere Elliot.*" Francesca nodded once to Marco before she moved from her desk to the back.

We were alone. Trapped air escaped from my lungs, making me go weak in the knees from the oxygen deprivation. Marco's hand gripped my arm while his other went immediately to my waist.

He whispered very softly, "Easy, sweetheart. I need you to be well. Papa will take care of you. Don't worry."

I made a harrumphing noise. "*He's* not the one I am worried about..."

"What do you mean?"

"Well, your cousin for starters. She's suspicious of us."

"She doesn't know anything. You've got such an imagination, baby."

"Shhh! Stop saying those things! Jesus, we're in your dad's office for cryin' out loud!" I was whispering so loud I was rapidly going hoarse.

He just sexily smirked at me and I knew he wanted to bone me. He always wants to bone me whenever I get flustered. He told me once it was like an aphrodisiac with him when I got worked up over something. I rolled my eyes, took as deep a breath as I could, putting my hands out at my side, palms facing the floor—you know, the general pose one takes when you want to step back and regroup, but in a big gayboy-like way? Yeah, well, me and my group were thinking of walking out, concussion or no concussion, and taking my cookies all the way back to the Q. Instead, I pressed on to the more compelling matter.

"Then, there's my mother."

"Oh, yeah. Thanks for reminding me."

He pulled me to him in a tight embrace with the hand at my waist while the other reached into my back pocket and pulled the phone out—even taking a second to cop a feel of my ass in the process. My guy was a full-on multitasker. I made to take it back and he held it out of reach and with one of his big manly muscled arms held me firmly away from it.

"Marco, give me my phone!" I rasped. "You are not going to call her. I will."

"No, I said I'd do it, and I am."

Francesca said something behind the frosted glass partition wall. It brought our lovers' antics to a stop. I made one last grumbly face at him and he smirked and walked toward the front door of the office. I could see he'd already found my call list, no doubt liking the fact he was number one on my favorites list, ahead of Mom, Dad and the store—in that order.

"Hello? Mrs. Donahey? Yeah, I'm aware this is Elliot's phone. Me? This is Marco Sforza. Yes, he's fine. But he had a bit of an accident."

I gingerly pinched the bridge of my nose with the fingers of my right hand. *Why'd he have to go and say it that way?* There were some things you simply didn't say to Kayla Donahey; one of them definitely was *Elliot's had a bit of an accident*. I was *never* going to hear the end of it. Sometimes I think my mother secretly aspired to be a Jewish mom, though I was sure Irish moms could hold their own by comparison. She had the whole guilt thing down pat.

"Yes, ma'am. He's okay. He hit his head when he fell. He's a little banged up but he's awake and conscious."

"Mister Donahey?" Francesca's sultry sirenesque voice lured me away from my boyfriend working out the details of his premature demise with my mother. *Oh, great, Juno in all her Sforza greatness has descended from Olympus to sweep me into an examining room.*

I turned to find Marco, smiling and chatting with my mother, waving me off as if they were having such a lovely conversation. He pulled the phone away from his face and covered it with his hand. "Go, I'll find you later. I got this."

I turned my attention to Francesca from the fear and panic I had forming watching my boyfriend "handle" my mother. Naive guy, he is.

"Yes?" I replied.

"Come this way, please."

She turned and led me back to the examining rooms. I had been here many times before over the years, yet this time it all felt different. Now when I turned the corner, I swear the hallway resembled the one JoBeth Williams had to run down to save Carol Anne and Robby from the Beast in *Poltergeist*. It just went on and on. It suddenly felt like he had private rooms for every citizen in the town. After we reached room 426, Francesca stopped, opened the door, and waved me in.

"Doctor Sforza will be with you in a moment. In the interim, I need you to sit there next to the thermometer stand and I'll take your temperature and we'll get your weight. Okay?"

Fuck, I didn't know how to react. I mean, if what Marco wanted to come to pass for us like he said he did—er, we did—then this chick was going to be family as well. Hell, I couldn't even look at her directly. I was gay and *she* was appealing to me. The same fucking allure Marco had. *What the fuck is that about?*

She smiled, genuinely this time. I found it was just as disarming as Marco's.

"So, Elliot," she started demurely, though a bit of lioness lingered in her gaze. I was still prey, it seemed. Would it ever be any different with this family? Then she dropped the mother of all bombs on me—with no warning!

"How long have you two been fucking?"

She said this with all the matter-of-fact inflection that oozed from her when she was turning someone's world upside down. She was a goddess. Her powers seemed to have no end. The room spun—clearly my hearing was now being affected. I swallowed and breathed at the same time, coughing and hacking like I was going to hock up a lung.

Well, that certainly went smooth. Yeah, Donahey, you are so going to sail through this river of denial.

"We're, uh, we aren't..."

She produced a thermometer with one of those plastic wand covers on it to make it hygienic or something. And before I could really reply she popped it in my mouth.

"Don't bother denying it. Marco's in love. He glows with it. And it's you. I know it when I see it. Mama said it's a gift. I tend to think it's a curse. You love him too. That's very clear. A life and death kind of love. Am I right?"

I tried to say something, but she put one of those exquisitely manicured nails to my lips.

"No talking. You think you're supposed to say something here, eh? No. I know these things. Marco has had eyes for no one. Boy or girl. But he's been thinking about it. I've watched him—family gatherings, holidays, you know—like that. Only rarely did he ever have that warmth in his eyes. Then lately I would see it, just glimpses of it, usually when he was looking at his phone. Fort Knox should have tight security like that phone. It never leaves his side. I knew whoever was on his phone was the center of his world. Then here you are, and he is—how do you say it? Eh, *radiante*—radiant. Yeah, that's it. He's fucking glowing. It's you. I know it. His whole face lights up and glows when he looks at you."

The thermometer beeped but she hadn't removed it from my mouth yet. Probably wouldn't until she'd had her say. *I knew we were fucked coming in here.* My eyes widened as she leaned in for the kill.

"So, I gotta hand it to you. Marco's a catch. But if you ever hurt him, I'll destroy you, eh? You got that?"

I nodded, fear coloring my face, scared as shit. I knew she could do it. No Mafia hit or nothing. She'd enjoy doing the deed herself.

"Okay." She pulled the thermometer, noted the reading, and ejected the plastic cover. I was rather impressed by how she did it all with her eyes never leaving mine. "Can you stand up?"

"*Si*, er, uh, I mean, yes."

"Ah, *bene*. He's teaching you, eh?"

"Italian, eh—" *Shit! Get it together, you fuck!* "Uh, no. But I've been paying attention some. I've watched some Italian movies. Tried to learn. Figured I better."

"*Bene*. Step to the scales, please."

I did as she asked. I could tell she wasn't someone you fucked around with—unless she let you.

She went on, "You'll have to watch out for his mama. Sofia is a tough one to crack. Hell, even I watch myself around her."

When I stepped on the scales I caught her sizing me up like a side of beef.

"One hundred and sixty pounds. Not bad. You're a bit on the thin side for Marco, though. We'll have to do something about that."

"Can we *not* talk about it? I don't want..." My gaze darted to the door. I was sure my future father-in-law was going to walk in on this catastrophe.

"Don't want what? Oh, eh, his papa?" She waved a dismissive hand. "He don't see what he doesn't want to see. No worries. I won't tell him nothing. It's between family, right?"

She indicated I should take a seat on the examining table, so I did.

"He'll be in, in a minute, I'm sure."

"Should I take my shirt off or something?"

"If you think he needs to see something, sure."

"I'll leave it on unless he asks. It's sort of cold in here." I shivered, though I think more from Francesca's cross-examination than the actual temperature of the room.

She arched one of those inquisitive brows at me. So like Marco. I think she knew how much of Marco's lust was under my shirt.

"*Bene.*" She held her arms out. I didn't know what she wanted to do. "Hug, you silly boy. You're family now, even if the big guy doesn't know it yet."

"Who? Marco? He..."

"No, not him. He knows, that I know for sure. I've never seen so much love in someone. You're like air to him. He needs you. Desperately, right?" I nodded, calmly—she didn't wait for my confirmation. "His papa is another matter. Give it time. They love Marco like the sun. He's life to them."

"Yeah, that's what Marco said about giving it time." She nodded once to confirm Marco had it right.

She held her arms out again and kissed me once on each cheek before turning to leave. As she opened the door, she turned to me and said, "I will give him this, he picked an angel for himself."

She smiled in that warm Marco kind of way and then winked at me. Suddenly I didn't feel like belly-lint any longer. As she started to exit, while my mouth was hanging down about a foot, Marco slipped past her and into the room. She swatted his ass as she left in a swirl of raven curls. He yelped at her swipe, but giggled nonetheless, and closed the door behind him.

"We're all set. She's upset but was so thankful I was there to help you out. I like her. She's gonna close the store and make her way over here."

"Oh, that's just great. One big happy Sforza-Donahey reunion. Wonderful. I can't wait for the clash of the titans between your father and my mother's hysterics." A beat passed between us. "You wanna run to the store for me?"

"Why? What do you need?" He eyed me suspiciously.

"Some microwave popcorn," I replied matter-of-factly.

He rolled his eyes.

"What? I think it's gonna be movie-worthy. You still got my phone? You might wanna YouTube it."

"Stop. She was fine with it. I mean, not about you. She was upset about that. I told her so was I. She asked me to stay until she could get here. I told her I would."

The pinching of the bridge of my nose ensued again.

"What? I told you I'd charm her," he cooed softly as he walked toward me. I held a hand up to stall him.

"It's not that..." I sighed heavily. He waited with a smirk for my drama to pass. "Francesca knows."

"What? What do you mean she knows?"

"Well, we aren't Academy Award winning actors, Marco. We're too familiar with each other. I guess it just... *showed*."

"Nah, maybe you're mistaken. Maybe you misunderstood her. She's from Italy; they're used to men being far more affectionate there. It's probably nothing."

I held a finger up to gain his attention. "And I quote—*How long have you two been fucking?*—end quote. Doesn't leave much to interpretation there, lover boy."

"What did you do to convince her we had?"

"I didn't. Fuck, I didn't even have a chance to speak! She dropped that bombshell before popping the thermometer in my mouth while I was hocking up a lung. It surprised me. No greeting, like, *isn't it a nice day*, but rather, *how long have you two been fucking?* Pretty straight to the goddamned point, wouldn't you say?"

He just smirked at me.

"We are not having sex in your dad's office, Marco. This is *not* how this is going to go down!" I rasped at him again. I really was going to go hoarse if I kept this loud whispering up.

"Maybe not right now, but..."

I inhaled so large a breath my ribs hurt again and I ended up coughing. He held out my phone and I swiped it, a bit more harshly than I intended. He shook his head at my spinning drama as I pocketed the phone again.

There was a gentle knock on the door and Marco's father, my larger-than-life future father-in-law, walked into the room. Like his son, Dr. Sforza was a hellaciously good-looking man. I suddenly saw him with new eyes. I wondered if my baby was going to mature into someone like the good doctor. My whole world spun for a moment. My head became light and dizzy; I thought for a second I was about to faint. Marco held out a hand to steady me. I pushed him off, not harshly, but sternly enough I hoped it was believable to his father.

"Marco, nice to see you, son. Would you care to wait out in the lobby while I check on Elliot?"

"Uh, if you don't mind, Doctor Sforza, I'd rather he stayed," I murmured.

Both Sforzas quirked brows, though for differing reasons. It was a very surreal visual. *My life is so fucked up.* Again, with the regrouping. I seemed to gather my group up a lot these days.

"It's just I don't remember much of what happened. Marco was there; he saw it all. Maybe he can fill in the gaps."

"Oh, I see. Well, if you're okay with it, then yes, he can stay. Marco, I don't have to remind you..."

"About patient confidentiality—yeah, Dad, I remember." He spoke with a touch more sarcasm than I thought was warranted. I shot him a pointed look and he held up his hands in surrender. He knew I didn't want to make waves around his father. He wasn't helping.

Marco took a seat near the window on the far side of the examining room.

"That's quite a gash you have on your forehead, Elliot. Can you tell me how you got it?"

I glanced at Marco out of the corner of my eye. I realized we wasted all our time alone talking about Francesca and not about how we were going to do this.

"Well...uh..."

Marco came to the rescue again. "He was walking close to the Oak Creek ravine. You know, the one behind our school?"

His dad nodded as he cautiously poked at the cut on my head. I winced and pulled back a bit as it was extremely tender. Dr. Sforza made some notes on the iPad that no doubt contained my file. With the exception of the old style datebook on Francesca's desk, he ran a very hi-tech office, one of the things I admired about his being my doctor.

"I think he tripped on something."

"A tree branch," I offered.

"Yeah, that's it. It was a tree branch. And then he went head over foot down the embankment. When I saw it happen, I stopped my car and ran to see if he was okay. I found him at the bottom of the ravine lying on his stomma-ch."

He faltered. I could hear the emotion welling up. I was shocked; my guy never falters. He could attribute it to some random bodily function like spit not going down right or whatever. But I knew it for what it really was: I had scared him. Badly. I decided it was my time to do the rescuing while Marco got a grip on his emotions.

"I remember falling, tumbling like crazy and then coming to a stop, and then just a hard pounding on my head. Marco said it was a river rock or something. Nothing sharp or jagged. And then he scrambled down and helped me get back up to the road. He thought we should come see you."

Vincenzo glanced at his son, who seemed placid enough, noncommittal, even. That gaze from his father, though not quite inquisitive of the scenario we'd painted, was searching his son for something. Probably because my whole presence practically screamed gay, *gay, gay*! I mean, I wasn't effeminate or girly, but I wasn't necessarily screaming hetero-macho jock like Marco and his crew did, something I could glean the doctor expected of his son—and more importantly, those who associated with him. I didn't think I quite made the grade.

"Well, then let's have a look-see, shall we?"

He took out his penlight thing and checked my eye reflexes. He seemed to be satisfied they were up to par. He asked me about my vision which I said was fine. I got a bit woozy if I moved too fast but otherwise all appeared to be normal.

"Except your breathing. He can't take a deep breath without wincing," Marco offered.

His father looked at Marco with no small degree of interest.

"What? He's my study partner in English! Half our project is in his head. I can't have it cracked up and ruin my grade, now can I? I mean, aside from just being a Good Samaritan about it and all."

That seemed to make some sense to both of us. Boy, my guy really could think on his feet—or his butt, as the case may be. A small sense of pride swelled within me. He really was going to pull this off. Then came the words I dreaded since we walked in.

"Well, why don't you lift up your shirt and let's see what we have."

I tried like hell not to look in Marco's direction as I began to lift my shirt. I'd like to think I was successful. But Dr. Vincenzo's glance in his son's direction didn't give me the impression I was.

I pulled my shirt over my head, knowing along with whatever bruises had formed since my great tumble down the ravine, the marks he'd put there were on prominent display for his father to see. I couldn't help but notice the good doctor's eyes wandering over four rather prominent hickeys. One on each side of my neck along the tendon Marco seemed to favor while we fucked. And one near my right nipple and the last near my belly button. It was followed by one on my inner thigh but I was thankful we'd spare Marco's father that further embarrassment.

Dr. Sforza arched a brow at those little love nips. No doubt he realized I wasn't a virginal teenage boy. But he kept it strictly professional and concentrated on the bruises around my right ribs. He gently applied pressure and I hissed in return. My eyes darted to Marco who tried to look away but I could tell he was fighting it too. We were just drawn to each other. It was palpable—at least for us. I didn't know how much his father would notice. Francesca commented he didn't see what he didn't want to see. Maybe we could rely on that now. *I could only hope.*

Marco tried to play it off by scratching along the back of his neck so his face was turned to a lovely poster—I'm using the term sarcastically in case you didn't notice— extolling the virtues of proper heart health. He didn't fool me for a minute. Marco was already thinking of how we'd sneak in to bone on this very table. *Yeah, good luck finding room number 426 down that* Poltergeist *hallway, babe.*

He had turned himself back to us, resting his forearms onto his thighs but there, I saw it. His hands were together and he was rubbing the palm of his left hand with the thumb of his right—so hard I thought he was trying to draw blood. I rolled my eyes and luckily all of this sailed right past his father. Small miracles. I was thankful for those little miracles wherever I could get them. Dr. Sforza indicated I could put my shirt on. I did while he gave me the rundown of how it was all going to go down.

"Well, it looks like some general bruising. Nothing taking it easy and some rest wouldn't take care of. Now, let's get that hell of a gash you got on your head all cleaned up."

The door rattled as Francesca poked her head in, saw Marco, looked at me and arched the trademark Sforza brow at me. Me! Like I was at fault for all of this! *Really, woman?*

"Your moth..." She never got to finish.

My mother, like the hurricane force she can be, sailed right through the door and practically pushed me off the table in her desire to reach me.

"Mom, geez, lighten up, will ya? I'm not three anymore!"

"What the hell happened to you?" she practically wailed.

I stared at them. My family. Though to be fair, only three out of the five of us knew it. Funny how parents can be so clueless at times. Marco looked slightly taken aback, clearly aware he needed to heed my warnings where my mother was concerned because she no doubt was very different from the composed gratified woman she presented to him on my phone earlier. Now, she was Mama Bear—in all the wrong ways possible.

"Ah, ssst." She gingerly touched my damaged head and I batted her away. "Elliot, what the hell were you doing out near the ravine? You know you're not the most graceful boy." She was hovering again.

"Mom..."

"Well, we'll get you cleaned up and I'll get something good in you and you can rest. Oh, wait, probably not, huh? Yeah, on second thought, you're not supposed to rest, are you?"

She finally broke her gaze from me to the good doctor who just stood there with the rest of his family eyeing mine as if we had goat legs sprouting out of our foreheads.

Yeah, I realized then how far out of my league I was compared to Marco's family. Even he had a look of fear seeing my mother in all her whacked-out glory.

"*Mom*! Christ! Give it a fucking rest, will ya?"

She snapped back like I'd just bitch-slapped her. Which, I guess, I had.

"I fell, got a boo-boo, and the doctor is gonna stitch me up. You could, however, thank Marco." I almost added "your future son-in-law," but after looking at his face and those of his father and cousin, I wasn't so sure it was a given anymore. "After all, I would still be lying at the bottom of that fucking ravine if it weren't for him stepping in like Superman. Now, I'm thankful you came to pick me up, but seriously, can you just give it a rest and grab a seat in the lobby and slap around a magazine like any other mother would, and let the best damn doctor this side of San Francisco do his bidness? For fuck's sake! Sorry, doctor, I'm just flustered." *Shit! Marco's surefire aphrodisiac...*

Marco and Francesca were both suppressing big smiles. Those two were too much alike; it frightened me. Dr. Vincenzo, on the other hand, didn't quite know what to make of my peculiar brand of love for my mother—in a way only the Donaheys can express. My gaze darted back to Marco, who had moved to stand behind his father. The lust in his eyes said I was in *sooooo* much trouble. He was so going to bone me now—and on this fucking examining table. The worst part? I caught Francesca's stare between us and I think she knew!

"Eh, yes. Perhaps you should all wait in the lobby while I get Elliot cleaned up."

He began to usher everyone out. My mom looked shocked beyond belief. I knew I'd hear about it for the next thirty years or so. I could wait it out for a few more blessed minutes while the doctor took care of my noggin.

NEARLY A HALF hour later, after thanking Dr. Vincenzo for his patience and his good service, I promised Francesca I would phone in a couple of days to update her on any change in my recovery. I didn't expect to call her with anything important. I didn't think she expected to hear from me anyway. She did, however, write a six-digit number on a piece of paper.

"What's this?" I asked, staring at the numbers in absolute confusion.

Marco came up behind me and looked over my shoulder.

"Ah, that's for me."

He snatched the slip of paper from my hand before I had a chance to commit it to memory. He and Francesca did the Italian cheek-kissy thing and then she came around the desk and did the same to me. My mother really didn't know what to make of it all. Probably the first time she'd ever been sidelined in her life. The guilt I'd be feeling was mounting up so I had to get her out of here. I might avert her blowing up and going postal on my ass if she could let off a bit of steam on the car ride home.

I turned to my rather pissed off but subdued mother, leafing through a *People* magazine extolling the non-productive and pointless celebrity of the Kardashian twits, as I'd come to call them—*I mean, seriously what do they contribute to society?* The thing that caught me about my mother's behavior was how rapidly she was leafing through the magazine. There was no way she could absorb a single piece of text on those pages at the rate she was flipping through them. Yeah, the needle on the postal meter was rising rapidly. I turned to Marco.

"Er, um, thanks." It seemed so empty a way to express to Marco the depth of how grateful I was that he was in my world—as whacked out as it could get. I couldn't hug him. I couldn't touch him. And I'd scared him. If anyone deserved a hug, a kiss, and some love, it was him. But he took it in stride. He just looked up at me from under those dark thick lashes, those radiant green eyes, the quirk of his lip—his oh so sexy smirk he reserved just for me—and I knew we were good. But the draw to fall into his arms was so great I ached for him. So close, but it could easily have been miles separating us. For a split second, I leaned forward—only to catch myself and stop. He sighed softly, a little upset we didn't feel free enough to just go through with what we felt.

I knew my body was blocking him from my mother's view. He mouthed "love you" and smiled again. I nodded and said softly, "Yeah, me too."

I turned and faced the dragon lady herself, a force of nature I somehow found the nerve to bottle up. And the bottle was shaking—she wanted out. I rolled my eyes. "C'mon, Mother. I'm tired. Let's go home."

"Yeah, well, we'll talk about that." I had no idea what that was in reference to; actually, for the first time I found I really didn't care. Maybe I was becoming my own man, so to speak. But I wasn't out of the woods just yet. I still needed her. And my father too, now I thought upon it. I guess a little humility may be called for here.

Marco went to the seat next to my mother and offered me my backpack. He'd retrieved from the forest. When had that happened? Did he pick it up when we were making our way out of the forest? I didn't recall any of it.

Wow, my guy was far more resourceful than I'd realized. I was in good hands. I sort of always knew that, but to feel the measure of it, undeniably, embodied in my backpack there in his hands, was deeply gratifying. It was his way of letting me know I didn't have to have a handle on everything around me. He'd take care of it, probably part of his training as a quarterback, having to be ultra-aware of his surroundings. Having watched him play several games now, I could see my guy was extremely vigilant, his gaze precise, eagle-like in its reach and observation.

God, I just wanted to fold into him just then. He knew. It was there, in his eyes, his stare now undressing me as I held his gaze—ice blue to his verdant green.

"Later..." he whispered as he handed me the backpack. I shrugged it on.

"Mrs. Donahey." Marco turned to her and lifted a hand to wave goodbye to her. She walked up to him and, standing on tiptoe, gave him a hug and a kiss on his cheek, surprising us all for her grace when she was still so clearly perturbed with me.

"Thank you, Marco. I don't know how to thank you enough for being there for Elliot. You handled it far better than I have."

Ever the diplomat it seemed, my guy had one hell of a reply. It's what my mother needed to hear, something she didn't get from me: acknowledgment, validation of her fears. "You're his mother; I would expect nothing less."

She smiled a strained smile, filled with gratefulness, but reserved. He seemed to accept it for what it was. She then turned to Francesca and nodded at her a quick goodbye. Francesca just painted on one of those placid but warm Sforza smiles that could charm a cuddle from a viper. *Damn, this family is golden. Stranger in a strange land* kept creeping through my head as I observed them. I was so out of my league with them. The gulf between their graceful beauty and what meager presence I could summon made the Pacific seem like a stagnant cesspool just then.

I opened the door for my mother who bolted out. I smiled to them both as Francesca wrapped an arm around her cousin's waist, leaning her head against his shoulder. Those raven locks, dark lashes, flawlessly radiant olive complexion, stunning white perfectly aligned teeth, and brilliant, engaging, and mesmerizing green gazes. I was so hopelessly lost in the Sforza world at that moment. I longed to be with them. I aspired to their grace—their powerful but measured poise.

I turned to follow my mother when Francesca called to me, "Cassiel." I was surprised she chose to call me by my first name. She obviously had an affinity for it as I did; I knew there'd be no secrets between Francesca and me. "*Non mi sbaglio. Tu sei l'amore della sua vita.*"

I quirked an eyebrow between them.

They both smiled, shared a soft laugh, and I knew. I knew right then I was a part of them. I was solidly in their world. I was accepted, at least by this generation of Sforzas. I'd probably have to work harder to gain the affection of the elder Sforzas. Given Old World sentiments, it would likely be a lifelong effort on my part to ingratiate and make myself invaluable to them. But it would be a task I'd undertake with such verve and vigor I'd make these two proud. I knew I would. And they would love me, for who I am, for being the center of Marco's universe. Today hadn't been so bad after all.

Marco chuckled, shaking his head at my lack of Italian. Language lessons would soon be on the horizon. "I'll tell you later, *bebe*." Francesca laughed heartily at that one, her head lolling back so the light cascaded in highlights and shadows from the high window behind her. I blushed something fierce.

"Elliot!"

Oh, yeah. *Her*.

I looked out of the door and rolled my eyes. "Yes, Mother."

I turned back to them one last time, blew them a kiss, and started to walk out. Just as the door was about to close behind me I caught the sound of Vincenzo calling for his son. That couldn't be good. The brightness in my chest lessened a little from what pain I could still cause my man.

THE RIDE HOME was somber, far more disquieting than I'd've liked. She was obviously saving her rage for the more solid confines of our home. I guess I was cool with that. Gave me more time to regroup—yeah, even *more* with the regrouping. Marco had so upended my world that fateful July 17th. I wouldn't have it any other way. I'd endure anything for him. Even my mother's overprotective instincts and her building rage at how I'd snapped at her.

We pulled into the driveway and it was then she decided to crack—to let me have it. Not in a torrential downpour of hurricane forces like I knew she could. No, instead she pierced past any teenage ambivalence I'd prepared to protect myself with, with a simple tear and a voice so soft I scarcely heard it.

"I really don't understand you sometimes, Elliot. The little boy I knew, the one who kept to the shadows, who never caused a moment of worry or pain, the angelic gaze from eyes so bright they could blind anyone in their path. You have no idea how much you affect those around you, how much you'd be missed if something happened to you."

Somewhere in the back of my mind I marveled at the precision of her strike. I hadn't meant to reduce her affections for me to a cold postmortem type analysis. But I guess that was my gayboy sensibility and survival instinct. It even applied to family members it seemed. But it didn't mean I didn't feel for what she was going through, the real fear something could happen to me. It was highly probable; despite the fact I had a super-boyfriend watching my back. Even he couldn't be everywhere at the same time. I knew he had limits.

"Mom," I began. She put up a hand—not harshly, but rather, reverently—as if she were concerned any sharp emotions would damage me, would drive me further from her.

"Elliot, just promise me, whatever it is you have going on in your life, you won't shut me out completely. Okay? You're the only son I have. My only boy. I can't pretend to understand what you're dealing with. But I am trying. But it has to go both ways, you know. You gotta be willing to meet me halfway."

I nodded, unsure of what else to do. She hastily wiped a lone tear from her face and began to gather her things. I unbuckled my seat belt and reached for her and pulled her into a fierce hug. She seemed to need it. She folded, collapsed into me for a moment, thankful in that instant to have me back, if only for a small quiet moment. We were simply mother and son. It is who we are. No matter how far I'd go, how much I'd push into the warmth and solidity of Marco's arms, a part of me would always be tied to her. We rocked together in the car. Like the tears we silently shed between us, outside a gentle rain began to fall.

Chapter Thirteen

The Unholy Trio

WHILE THE DRAMA from my ass over teakettle fall down the Oak Creek Ravine was behind me, I did have to eat some major crow with my mother. I knew this was going to happen. I thought it would be armfuls of guilt topped with a heaping scoop of I-told-you-sos but nothing doin'.

Instead, she was kind, thoughtful, and didn't once pester me about whether Marco was *the one*. I don't know if it was because she had it firmly entrenched in her head he was given the way we could barely keep ourselves from, well, ourselves. I never realized the full breadth of how much Marco's presence tugged upon me until my visit to the doctor. It was like I was smacked in the face by a Mack truck. It was monumental how a single office visit had turned what I thought was an upside-down world around again. Did that make it right-side up, then? I wasn't sure.

As I put my head down at the end of a very arduous day I got my nightly phone call from my guy.

"Hey good-lookin', what'cha got cookin'?"

He quietly giggled at my corny, and very dated, greeting.

"Depends on how adventurous you are. How *are* you feeling? I should have asked that first, sorry."

"Yeah, be the caring boyfriend I know you to be."

"Yes, babe. You know I always care about you. God, Elliot, when you went over the ravine, my heart—don't ever do that to me again, 'kay? Well, the whole fucking conversation tore me up, actually. But I hear you. I get it. I just wish my parents would stop with their grandstanding about us. It gets old real fucking quick."

"I didn't know it was like that. Why didn't you ever say?"

He huffed into the phone. Whatever it was, he was still raw with it. God, I wanted to be there to soothe him, bring him back down like he liked me to do whenever he got riled.

"You have no idea how hard it is, Els. They can be unbearable sometimes."

"I sorta figured when your dad called you as I left. And there was the way Marcel spoke about your mother."

He sighed audibly again. Yeah, that was what I thought it was: he'd been under the Sforza microscope after I'd left.

"Yeah, Dad wanted what he said was the *real* rundown of what happened."

"And what I was to you...why *you*, right?"

Silence.

"You might as well say it, babe. I heard it in his tone. I knew I'd fucked it up for you."

"You didn't fuck anything up! You *never* fuck anything up! Stop saying that! You're perfect."

"I beg to differ on that score. I am *far* from perfect..."

"I meant, you're perfect for me. In *every* way possible. Those aren't just words I bat around, sweetheart. You're it for me. If something happened to...baby, I couldn't handle it. That's all. I just couldn't. I'd follow you anywhere. Even in death. I will not abandon you, ever."

"Wow, we went down a really dark alley."

"I know. I'm sorry…I just…"

"Shhh, it's okay. I'm glad you told me. I can't say I'm overjoyed at the prospect of knowing if I do have my last moments on Earth they'll be filled with *oh, shit, now Marco's gonna suicide on everyone and it's all my fault*. But I get what you're saying. And right back atcha. I can't live without you, either. I know you're the one. I'm actually grateful to know that. Thrilled I don't have to spend all of my young adult life doing the dating thing in college—trying to find someone I'm compatible with. I know it's you. I do. Especially now, knowing you dealt with my mom for me and all. Hell, I should marry you on that point alone."

He chuckled. We seemed to have moved on from our dark *one-not-being-able-to-cope-without-the-other* the conversation had careened into without much warning. I understood our feelings on the subject. I got it. I knew he did too. And perhaps it was good we had our say on such a difficult subject.

"I need to see you, baby."

"Oh. FaceTime, then?"

"Uh-uh. I'm outside your bedroom window."

"What the fuck…?"

We both hung up as soon as I caught sight of him. I got up from my bed and there he was, shivering in his letterman's jacket and tight dark jeans hugging every contour of his body. The light from the moon as it peeked between the clearing storm clouds gave his broad, powerful frame an ethereal glow. Thankfully, my window screen hadn't been replaced from a year ago when I popped it out to clean it properly from outside and never got around to putting it back. Since my room was along the back of the house, it didn't seem to be a big deal. I'm sure my mom grumbled under her breath about how I hadn't gotten around to doing it. But now Marco had availed himself of it, I was never going to put the screen back.

I slid the old-school double-hung window open as quietly as I could. Mom was sleeping with Prince Valium tonight (which she solely reserved for those times when life was truly tiring—like today when I really had tried her patience) so I wasn't overly concerned with the sound of wet wood scraping against the frame. She'd be out cold, sleeping the sleep of the undead, as it were. But still, I didn't think we needed to take unnecessary chances.

He heaved himself up onto the ledge with little effort on his part and a slight chuckle as I helped drag him in. He was cold and wet but I didn't care. He was mine and as soon as he stood up I folded right into him. He chuckled softly, turning his head into the crook of my neck, inhaled me deeply before finding my earlobe and pulling it between his lips to suckle upon it. I relished the feel of him against me, cold and wet as he was. His large rough hands stroked my backside and slipped down past the waistband of my black boxer briefs to grip his favorite part of me—my ass. The cold air from outside finally caught his attention as he realized I was nearly naked. After being intimate with my man, I usually now slept in the nude but as I hadn't fully turned in yet I was still wearing my underwear. He kissed my lips briefly before he moved back to the window and slid it gently back into place.

"Get into bed, sweetheart. It's freezing," he said quietly as he slowly slipped out of his clothes. I pulled off the underwear with my ass facing him, being sure to bend over so he had the best view possible. He paused briefly after removing his shirt and leaned down and took a small nip of my right ass cheek. I started to move fully onto the bed when he slid his arm around my waist. He spread my cheeks with his other hand and his tongue begin to lap at my hole with intense vigor. I bit my lip to strangle the moan trying to escape. After I'd opened him up to the erotic pleasures of rimming, he was always feasting on it—before and after we'd fuck.

I whispered, trying like hell to hold in the burst of yelps fighting for release, "Babe, let's get under the covers, 'kay?"

He lapped a little deeper for a moment, provoking a deep intake of air from me as he worked the particular brand of magic only his tongue could do before he released me and finished stripping himself. A second or two later and he joined me in my bed, a human blanket like no other.

The only other thing I had of any real worth was one of those memory foam beds. I made a mental note to be extra kind to Mom for having the foresight to get me one when she and Dad bought theirs. It made my lovemaking with Marco much easier to control tonight—at least from a creaking bed perspective. All we had to worry about was our mouths, which was going to be plenty.

He pushed me onto my back, his all-time favorite position so we could lock gazes while he screwed the daylights out of me. At first, it was so hard to meet his penetrating stare but he'd schooled me to do it every time we'd fucked and now I couldn't think of any other way to do it. He said my eyes were his guiding light while we made love. His studied gaze picked up unspoken signals from me of what to do with the delicious cock of his that tortured me so. And I was happy to give him what he desired most. He could have my body anytime he wanted. I would never refuse him. I think even if we went to bed angry with each other (which I couldn't believe would ever happen) and he wanted to fuck, I'd be right there for him. Can't say it wouldn't be downright aggressive, but it could be fun too, I suppose. Might even break the ice in whatever we'd argued about.

"You really okay, baby?" The powerful length of him drove my passion as he began to grind his cock against my own. The sword play had already begun. I nodded that I was fine. My eyes staying with his, he smiled, confident he'd reach and I would be there, like clockwork. We were a great team. He leaned forward and lightly kissed the two small stitches his father had put there.

"Was it so bad, your father and all?" I was truly concerned I'd made a mess of things. I recalled all of it, my panic over our small argument regarding the Homecoming King thing in the car before I stormed off like some air-brained cheerleader girlfriend, to his having to deal with my crazy (if well-intentioned) mother and everything in between. He was hands down a bona fide god in my book. And I worshiped him, would do anything for him. He had to see it. I tried like hell to let it show in my steely gaze.

He didn't answer my question directly, just sort of shrugged and then took my mouth captive with that magical tongue of his. I smirked a bit during the kiss, only because his tongue had just been in my ass and anyone else would've thought twice about French kissing after he'd been lapping at their hole, but when you had a boyfriend who liked to fuck as much as he did… I gotta tell ya, wiping and washing took on a whole new meaning for me. My ass was so clean nearly all the time you could practically eat off it, which I guess he had. Thus, the smirk.

He was chuckling softly too. I knew he was thinking the same damned thing.

"Do you want to?" He eyed me intently.

I could tell he wanted to—he always wanted to. Yet, I knew if I said I was tired and still hurt he'd pull back. He was such a gentleman about it with me. It's why I'd never refuse him. Because I knew he'd never complain if I did. I just couldn't say no to him. Ever.

"Always, baby. With you, always."

We kissed deeply, slowly, though I winced just a little with my sore rib. He nodded he'd watch it while we made out. I lazily inched my hand up above my head to the cabinet-like cubbies that made up my headboard. I slid one of the panels aside and retrieved the lube. He closed the door for me without looking. We could seriously do this completely in the dark and blindfolded—we were that practiced at it. He stopped kissing for a second and leaned over to reach the light and flicked it off before resuming our lovemaking.

I popped the top to the lube and put a decent amount into my hands to warm it up for him. He propped his hips up so I could reach down and stroke the length of him.

"Gonna go slow, baby—just so we don't make too much noise. 'Kay?"

I nodded, knowing full well what this meant. Whenever we'd fuck slowly, it would take him quite a long time to release himself within me. He'd build and edge for quite a while, fucking me with his full length, making me hiss slightly as the enormity of him cleaved its way into me. It would burn; it would inflame. And it would be long, arduously long. I knew what he was asking.

"You sure?" he asked me again. That's my gentleman of a guy.

I didn't answer, just pulled my feet alongside his hips, guided his slicked-up cock to my hole; then I let him do the rest. And boy, did he ever.

I could take Marco in just about every way imaginable, and we tried every combination of moves and positions; my boy was an adept lover. We were very adventurous when it came to fucking. But this, the simple act of his cock, the length and girth of it, stretching me repeatedly in the slow full stroke action of his hips, being sure to gyrate his hips when ours collided, mercilessly bruising the fuck out of my prostate, undid me every time. I'd shoot my wad at least two or three times during it and he'd keep right on fucking me. I relished how he had schooled me to want him more if I came before him, working through the after-burn and letting it morph into a stronger desire to keep going. For him it would be a one-off and it would be a big load too, an earth-shattering type of orgasm. And this time, we had to be quiet about it. That was something we'd never tried before. It was the real challenge tonight.

"Just, uh, bite down on me," I whispered to him as I looked to the mark he'd made on the tendon from the right side of my neck to my shoulder so he knew what I was talking about, "if you need to when you shoot. Okay? It'll probably be easier for you to keep it quiet."

"I don't want to hurt you. I might have to bite real hard—you do that to me when I shoot in you, sweetheart. The pull from you is the sweetest thing you give to me. Your ass is so talented. That's why I love to fuck you as much as we do. I keep chasing that rabbit."

I flushed, unseen in the darkness as I kissed him deeply; he began those long strokes within me. Yeah, even more than Alice, he *loved* going down that rabbit hole.

"I don't mind, baby. If you need to, I can take it. I want to take it. Whatever you need, it's yours. You don't have to ask, you know. Just reach for me and I'll be there. Always."

His gaze was pointed, riveting, electric.

I hissed as he moved within me. It was a quiet protracted hiss, as he burned his way into me.

"More lube?"

I shook my head. "Uh-uh, I like it like this. Just keep going."

"Baby, I love you so much."

"I know. I'm all yours, lover. I love you too. Now do your bidness and fuck me till it burns."

He smiled and we kissed as the fucking took on a renewed quiet vigor. Nearly an hour or so later, as he'd been edging for quite some time, I could feel a load beginning to take form for him, just the way his body would begin to tense slightly. It was my signal we were coasting in for home. My hole was accommodating his thrusts to where he could pound my prostate, making me bite my lower lip again. His eyes would flash slightly in the dark of my room each time he found that spot within me. We were sweating something fierce. I relished it when we got slick with our controlled, measured movement as we fucked.

"I'm close, baby," he murmured softly in my ear as he nuzzled deeply along my neck. He gradually inched down as his cock bore down deep inside me, grinding his hips in a slow circular action pressing firmly against my p-spot. My eyes watered from the pleasurable pain he was causing deep within me, the sweetest torture he could do to me, and he knew it. He fucking relished that he knew this. He loved giving it to me. And when he did, when he tormented me as deeply as he was doing now? I took; I fucking hoarded it whenever he gifted me with his intense pleasure. This more than anything would bind me to him. He knew every single cell in my body and, more importantly, how to ignite them. Other men may know how to fuck and bring that much pleasure to another man, but I knew it was the love between us, the difference to which they'd never measure up.

I bit him back, gnawing on his muscular shoulder. He chuckled.

A soft murmur broke from my lips. I bit it back as best I could but he was torturing me in ways that hadn't happened before. I don't know if our having to keep quiet had put it into a different sensation now, but I was so hot for him to empty himself in me I wanted to scream like a banshee for him to let go.

Then he bit my lower neck along that tendon—hard, incredibly hard, vampiric in its voracity. He sucked at it savagely, yet never managing to break the skin. His spittle oozed down my back—secretly I imagined he was a vampire and he was feeding from me. If he were, I knew I would let him—without question. He could have that much from me. I could tell from the way he was sucking on it, it would be so bruised it might border on being black. It hurt but when the pain mingled with the deeply satisfying pleasure his cock was giving to me—in short, it was heaven, the intense pleasure and pain.

I held on. When he came, I did as well. We rocked with each other in perfect unison, our bodies so comfortable with each other in the throes of our passion. It seemed like he came forever. Half a minute later and he was still shuddering a bit. He continued to fuck me purposefully as he came down from it all. I let him pull me tight against him as he broke from biting my neck and nuzzled in with soft kisses and heated panting breaths like fire against my skin. I ran my hands along his back. I was surrounded by him, his massive body easily eclipsing mine. I loved this part the most, where I could disappear into him and just be a part of him. I knew he loved this part too.

"That was incredible, babe. Thank you. Love you," I spoke to him softly into the dark quiet of my room.

He whispered softly—something about his loving me too, but I shushed him. Half of it sounding Italian, though it was so muted I wasn't sure. I gently stroked his hair and face, letting him fall into a light doze. Minutes later his cock finally slipped from me. I was always saddened a bit from his absence. I was happiest when we were joined, when I was connected to him like no one else in the world, when he was mine and I was his. And we were one.

Always.

THAT BEGAN A series of his coming over late at night and we'd repeat the process. We actually got to the point where we sort of preferred these long, quiet, intense fucks. I figured somewhere we would change it up again, keep it fresh, but for now, I was enjoying how he could take my body and bend it to his will. He'd reach and I'd be there.

As the days ticked by at school I began to become acclimated to seeing my man all over campus. His mother, ever the closeted marketer, rotated a different set of posters around, again using a photo from my phone I'd shared with him. This time he was suited up, helmet off, sweat plastered across his brow, a *Game of Thrones* Jon Snow geared up for battle pose—heroic. Who knew I had such an eye for capturing my man? He confessed later when his mother asked him for photos he liked of himself it had been he who suggested them. He said it was his way of letting me know he *only* wanted everyone to see him through my eyes. He only felt sexy and desirable when I said he was. I snorted and said he always looked that way to me—even on the crapper with his underwear around his ankles leafing through an *SI* magazine on his phone. Yeah, we had achieved sharing a bathroom and being unaffected by it all. We really were solid.

It was two weeks before Halloween—which fell on a Wednesday this year. My ass over teakettle wound along my hairline had segued to a light yellow-purple bruise. Thank the gods I didn't have any permanent scarring over it. I so didn't want to be called the gay Harry Potter. Thinking about this brought me back to the morons and social troglodytes who peppered my school and their bass-ackward way of thinking and all things Homecoming.

I don't know why I never paid any attention to the other competitors in the Homecoming race. Beau Hopkins was also up, but even with his stunning good looks (and yeah, even I had to admit the guy was good-looking), everyone seemed to think he didn't stand a chance against the radiant star of my boyfriend. No guy did. There was an underground campaign to write in my geek buddy, Greg Lettau, as King and secretly Marco and I were pulling for Greg to pull an upset at the last minute. Marco said it would be so sweet for Greg to win that he wanted to offer to pay for his campaign posters.

I'd like to say I was surprised by the posters of Cindy Markham going up everywhere a poster of my guy was, but I can't claim ignorance there. Somehow Marco's mother, in her drive to get her son a lock-in for the title, had financed not only his campaign but shelled out quite a bit to give Cindy the leg up she seemed to need against some of the other girls in the running. Sonya Lawton, who went by the delightfully dreadful name of Sony (pronounced *saw-knee*, not like the electronics manufacturer, even if she liked to spell it that way), Cindy's best friend and my arch enemy, was also up for the title of Queen Bitch on campus. It was the two besties vying for face time with my boyfriend, each hoping somehow they'd be the one to catch the attention of the student body to get voted in as Queen Bee over her best friend. I thought I should start a campaign to have myself as a write-in for the title. I joked about it to Greg one day, just as a lark, saying with a fair amount of cynicism to my voice that we'd make quite the Homecoming couple. I don't think he was the one to do it. Maybe someone overheard us, but word got around quickly swiftly the local gayboy wanted the title of Homecoming Queen. It had disaster written all over it.

 I cornered Greg on the subject one morning in Calculus and he flat out denied it. He said he'd never do something so callous and sort of resented that I even considered him. I ended up apologizing to the point where he stopped short of literally gagging from all the conciliatory gayboy ooze I was giving him. He finally accepted it. He said he'd rather accept my apology than my slathering more gayboy love all over him. But he had an ear-to-ear grin and a sparkle in his eye when he said it. We were still good. I then told him to behave or it might just end up being the two of us as write-in upsets. As soon as it left my lips, I wished I hadn't said it.

Because, you see, the universe tended to listen to me at all the wrong times.

SOMEHOW, I STILL managed to fly under the radar and did my level best to stay so. Or so I thought. On my way to my art class from a lunch spent with Marco, I was intercepted by Cindy, Sony Lawton, and Stephen Lowry. Evidently, Stephen was Sony's latest in a long line of squeezes. I guess he never got the memo from the other guys on what a cock block she was. She didn't need anyone else to do it. From what I'd heard she had quite the sham going to tease the hell out of a guy only to block any progress on his part. She was the package deal: hook, line, and suppressor.

Sony prodded me by my shoulder into an empty classroom two doors down from the art room. From the looks of it I could only think it was home economics or some sort of lab room I'd never been in. The two girls rounded on me with Stephen standing guard at the door. It was obvious to me I wasn't allowed to leave until they had their say.

"So? What now Cindy?" I deadpanned.

"What's *now*, Ladybird Donahey, is I just want it clear there's no way your little faggoty ass is gonna swipe that crown from me."

She often thought she was the original Santana from *Glee*. She wasn't even remotely intimidating in that hardcore cholita way. Nor with her ladybird moniker was she even *that* original.

"Well, it's not like I'm campaigning for it or anything."

The look of shock on their faces that I'd even bothered to open my mouth was kind of amusing. Never in all the years of their torment had I said anything to defend myself. I usually just stood there and took it. Whether it was because of my being with Marco or not, I wasn't sure. But I realized that guy wasn't me anymore.

"Excuse me?"

"What? You didn't think all the time you two were barking at me I ever had a thought in my head that would run contrary to what you were saying? I do have a brain, you know. A fairly good one, it seems. It actually gets me solid grades. God knows I'll be at a great college while you're still trading your fading looks for some guy who'll be sorry he married you once the *I-dos* are over. But by then, it'll be too late. He'll be an alcoholic before he hits thirty, and that's if he's lucky. God knows he'll need the distraction. But you'll be good. While he languishes at work because he wants to spend more time away from you than back home, it's not like you'll care because you'll be banging the pool boy rather than the pot-bellied alcoholic hubby who's probably schtupping his secretary anyway. So, all's fair, right?"

"You little faggot. You think you know what my life is gonna be like? What gives you the balls?"

I chuckled darkly, confounding them both. I had to admit, I was sorta in my element all of a sudden. It was rather liberating.

"'Cause I got them, that's why. Look, I don't want this whole Homecoming thing. So, it ain't coming from me. I'd so rather not be bothered, to tell you the truth; it's just too fucking *embarrassing*. I'm not the one you should be focusing on. And you can tell Beau that as well 'cause I know he's the one behind this."

I indicated with a swipe of my finger to the three of them.

"Well, him and Marco's mom. It's clear your sudden rise in poster population is being bankrolled by her. Lord knows you don't possess the wherewithal to come up with something original. The similarity to Marco's posters is too fucking close to be denied. She may have the money but clearly not the imagination. By the way, did you ever wonder who took those pictures of him gracing those posters? I think you'd be surprised where they came from, if you knew."

It was the closest I'd come to completely outing Marco and me. Perhaps it was too close. Then again, this was Cindy *I am lucky if I can spare two brain cells to rub together to keep a thought warm* Markham. What the fuck was I worried about? Oh yeah, Stephen was in the room. He wasn't a lame jock. The guy was quick. I probably bit off more than I could chew. I spared a glance his way—no dice. There was no way my remark was getting by him. Fuck. I'd have to tell Marco I'd fucked up.

"You gonna let queer boy get away with that?" Sony spat, more at me than her bestie.

"I said you don't have to worry about anything coming from me. It's just a fucking rumor for Chrissake. I don't put much stock into it, why should you? Worried I might actually win? A fag like me would score higher than the head cheerleader or her lackey?" *Wow, I really had grown a pair. Marco'd be impressed.*

"Watch it, Donahey," Stephen said through clenched teeth. Clearly he was the guard dog on site for Sony's benefit.

"Or what, Stevie? You know you touch a hair on my head and my mom will be all over yours like white on rice.

And we know how much your mother prides herself on being a model family to the church. You willing to risk that over these two? I pegged you for being smarter than that. Sorry to see you disappoint."

"I don't give a fuck about what disappoints you, faggot."

"Maybe not, but *I know* how you toe the line with Mommy." I sighed. I needed to wrap this up as cleanly as possible. "Look, again, I'm *not* the one to focus on. I told you I don't want it. Never did. So, you won't see me vying for votes like you two are. It's really pathetic, you know, the competition between you two, hanging all over Marco like he gives a rat's ass."

"And how would *you* know?" he asked me pointedly.

He was narrowing in on what Marco was to me. I needed to divert them all.

"I do study with the guy, you know, English Lit project and all. We talk and not always about the project. I might know a thing or two about what he really thinks. *Not* that I'm saying. That's between him and me. I respect his opinion too much to ever say what he talks about. I wouldn't do that." I spared a glance at Stephen. "Even if you drag all the team in here to beat it out of me, I wouldn't ever betray him. I know the rules. I'm far smarter than you give me credit for. A jock confides in me for any reason, my mouth remains shut. But believe me, he has opinions about it, *all* of it. And we've talked about the rumor of me as a write-in. I told him I didn't want it, that I hoped it was a lie. And I do. It wouldn't serve me in any way to win. So, you're safe there. I'm out. Totally. I just want to get to graduation and put the whole lot of you far behind me."

I started to move past Cindy when she put a hand on my shoulder.

"You better not do anything to swipe this whole thing away from me. Marco and I will be crowned like it's supposed to be. And your faggoty little ass isn't going to ruin it. And you better see to it you don't either."

"Wow, you really are as stupid as people say. The rumor is it's a *write-in* candidate. You get what that means, don't you? I don't have a say. If people write my name down, then that's it—game over. Since the votes are tabulated privately, it's not like I can slap their hands as they vote. I'm not in the driver's seat: total sidecar passenger along for the ride. But I'll tell you this, if by some odd alignment of the stars I do win the damned thing I'll withdraw. Will that satisfy? I want out—jeez, how many times do I have to say it to get it through all that spackled makeup you slather on your face to achieve any degree of beauty?"

She slapped my face, hard. Sony chuckled. Stephen looked anywhere but at me.

"You keep your fucking opinions to yourself. Faggots like you don't have opinions. This is my school. I own this fucking place."

My eyes narrowed causing hers to widen. She clearly wasn't used to the new and improved Elliot 2.0.

"Yeah, for what? The next few months and then it's over. Haven't you figured it out yet? Once school's out and you're let out into the world, all of this"—I indicated the room around us—"will not matter. You don't own the school, Cindy. At best, you borrow it. Once you're out, you're gonna find out how wrong you were about all of this. The world is a pretty big fucking place. The social strata you reign over here will dissolve the moment we toss our graduation caps into the air—a pretty fucking empty victory if you ask me. But hey, I guess you might see something in it that escapes me. Good luck with that. But I don't think I'm wrong. And you know? You *are* right about one thing, fagboys don't have much sway in high school. We are lowest rung on the totem pole here. I get it, believe me; you and Sony have made it abundantly clear over the past couple of years. But you know what? Once we're out in the world, we gayboys blossom. More of us have far more disposable income to spread than most married couples. And get this, here's the rub in your direction. In that big wide world out there, there's a helluva lot more guys like me who won't bow to your petty narrow-minded ways. So, you might want to think about becoming allies with guys like me. Interior decorators, hair stylists, hell, even your fucking doctors—we're into pretty much everything these days."

I glanced at Stevie to drive my point home.

"Even in *sports*. So those little YouTube videos are right; when I get out it will get better. If anything, just because I won't have to deal with close-minded sexually-backward individuals like you who think their looks alone give them the right to hold sway over everyone else in the world. Does it mean I won't run into your kind out there? No, absolutely not. But after dealing with you twisted..." I thought better of my current situation and regrouped. I smiled. "Two, for the better part of eight years, I've learned how to get by. It hasn't killed me, so I'll come out stronger in the end. So, thank you for that. You've given me the edge I'll need later on in life. Bet you never saw that coming, did you? You helped this faggot cope better in life. Gave me the thick skin I'll need to navigate those waters out there far better than you ever thought. Life outside? Ain't high school, sweetheart."

I walked right up to her and got in her face, making her take a step or two back and into Sony. "It's big, and it's messy, and it *certainly* doesn't give a rat's ass about your petty ideas. So, as we near the finish line, a word of advice. Start learning to work with the people around you instead of trying to control them. I'll bet you get a helluva lot farther along in life."

She stood there gape-mouthed, as did Sony.

"If you don't mind, I'm really late for my art class." I made to shove past her only to run into Stephen who puffed himself up a bit. "Really, Stevie?"

"Dude, you don't get to call me that any longer. We ain't been friends since you made a pass at me back in middle school."

"You flatter yourself. I asked you to be my first boyfriend before I even knew what it meant. To your credit, you were nice about it, even if we never spoke afterward. But you gonna get all jock boy on me now? I meant what I said about my mom calling yours."

"So, the faggot has to run to Mommy to do his battles?"

"You're *really* gonna go there?" I leveled the steeliest gaze at Stephen I could, hoping it would prove my point. "The three of you gang up on *me* and *you're* gonna pull the mommy card? The way I see it, with a three on one I get to pull whatever's at my fucking disposal. All is fair in love and war, right?"

"It doesn't end here, Elliot. You know that, right?"

"I'd expect nothing less." I turned to all of them. "You accomplished what you wanted and I told you I have no vested interest in winning. I don't want the fucking thing anyway. So good luck with that. I hope you get what you want. I really do. I don't need the distraction. I've got other fish to fry."

I nudged him and he glared at me for a second, his breath pulsing on the side of my face. There was a small flicker there of something from our shared past. Had he ever been tempted by my offer so many years ago? I had to wonder. But he must have seen some recognition in my face because he stepped aside and let me through. As the door closed, Sony went off on him for not standing his ground against me.

"You made your choice there, buddy. And *I'm* supposed to be the weak one?" I whispered to myself as I opened the door to my art class.

THE FOLLOWING FEW days leading up to Homecoming were a dizzying array of emotions for Marco and me. At times we could laugh loudly about the absurdity we found ourselves in, only to have it come crashing down around me, and I couldn't deal with it.

I was being silly; *he* knew I was being silly. But he never blamed me for it, never accused me of being so. He stood steadfastly by my wildly erratic behavior. At times I'd crumble a bit and then curse it was my mother he could blame for my mood swings. I told him I was trying to cope; he just chuckled and said he wanted to make love, that it would soothe me. And he did, and it did. It would always be okay if I could end up in his arms. Safe. Secure. Loved.

The bombshell of all bombshells fell on us midday the day of the Homecoming Game. Principal Silverstein intercepted me on my way to my art class as Marco made his way to Spanish.

"Mister Donahey, a word, please. Mister Sforza, I believe you have a Spanish class to get to, do you not?"

Marco watched as I was led to the Principal's office where I found Greg Lettau sitting outside.

Oh, shit.

Sure enough, within moments we were seated in front of the principal in his office—simultaneously reprimanded for our disrespect for the long tradition of the Homecoming ceremony and to congratulate us, informing we both were required to be at the stadium at half-time as the votes were in and one of us had actually achieved the title while the other received enough votes to make the court. But given the sensitive nature of the upset we weren't being told who. The school board was meeting at the school within the hour to discuss how they were going to respond to the way things had turned out. He suggested we both prepare to be properly attired as no matter who won, the other would be a member of the Homecoming Court. Our presence was required regardless. Greg took it a hell of a lot better than I did.

I felt sick to my stomach. Not just over what was to come tonight, but were it me who won the title of Queen and Marco as King, how that singular event could cause everything to spiral out of control.

Needless to say, I never made it to my art class.

Minutes later I was walking out onto the track within the stadium, trying to fathom how in a few hours my whole world would come crumbling down around me. My beloved Marco, the man I could never find it within me to do any harm, and yet my being who I was, what I was to the students of this school, would do just that. I would be the instrument of his undoing. Not just the whole gay thing tainting his reputation, but smiting the whole of Homecoming, forever recorded in the annals of our school. The star quarterback and the fagboy voted in as Queen as a joke.

That's the sum of it: I am a joke—always have been.

What had I been thinking? *Hot jock boys and artistic fagboys don't mix and they certainly don't fuck.* I had the right of it back then and I refused to listen. I wanted to believe we could get by, we'd somehow beat it. I was so wrong to put my faith in that. A mistake of epic proportions. Either way I was going to hurt him.

I took a seat high up in the arena, tucked under the dark recesses of the large awning covering the stands. I let go, letting the tears fall, my frail body rattling from head to toe. I knew my sobs were probably echoing from the far corner of the stands. I didn't fucking care at the moment. Fifth period PE didn't seem to take heed of my dissolution, the eroding of my confidence that any of this would come out okay.

I was so lost in my grief I didn't even notice when fifth period lapsed into sixth. About halfway through it, though—my eyes red and puffy from all the crying I'd done—a movement to my right caught my attention.

Marco.

"Shit."

I started to gather my crap together, fully ready to bolt. I needed to get away from him. I needed to leave. Yeah, I'd beg Mom to send me away to my Aunt Tilly in Sedona for the rest of the school year, somewhere I could begin again. I'd be an unknown. I could reinvent myself. Maybe even date a girl and see what the fuss was about. I could become an artsy hippy kid, visit Mom and Dad on the holidays. It could be okay. It'd be hard giving up Marco, but in the long run it would be better for him.

Deep concern blossomed across his face as he approached me. He knew I'd been crying.

"Shit. You weren't supposed to..."

"Supposed to what? See you're hurt, or upset?"

I got up and started to move to the other end of the row to take the stairs down. He easily sailed over two rows and closed the distance to where I was heading. I changed course and turned down another aisle, running as fast as I could.

"Babe! Are we really going to do this?"

"Leave me. I need to get away. Far away. I'll only hurt you."

It was useless. I could never escape him. He knew it; so did I. Realizing this, I stopped where I was, defeated. Deflated. My shoulders sagged in resignation and I fell to my knees, the pain in them redoubling before I knew it was upon me. He was on me within seconds, those strong arms taking me in. I tried to shrug him off. I pushed, I hollered at him, telling him he needed to leave me. I would only bring him pain.

"What? What are you saying? No, Els, no. Baby, listen to me. I don't know who did this to you, who hurt you this way. But I'll make them pay. I swear I will."

"Well, then, let's start with *you*! Because *all* of it, all of what I stand to lose, what *we* stand to lose would never have been if you hadn't come to me that day back in July! And now, now...ah, fuck, now I stand to ruin it all. And I never wanted, never! Never wanted to be the one to harm you. But I will. I *swear* to you, I will! I will be the cause for your whole world falling apart. I can't go on lying; I can't go on with the half-truth. I thought I could. I thought, as you said, it was only for a couple of months."

"Yes, exactly. And we're nearly through it. Don't you see, baby? Please." He was crying now, his worst nightmare rising before him.

I was hurting him, cutting him deeply. But it'd be better this way. He could have his family. He could have all of his dreams. Just not with me. I'd only bring pain. I reached out and stroked his face, the pain I'd put there. He thought he was losing me. I could see how much it hurt him. God, how I hated myself for this.

"Forget me, sweetheart. Your life will be better if you do."

I got up haltingly and picked up my backpack. The pain intensified knowing we'd just had one of our nooners, not knowing it would be our last.

"I'll never let you go. You think my world would be *better* without you in it? It'll kill me, Els. I ain't playing here. It. Will. Absolutely. Kill. Me. You can't; you just can't."

"But I have to. You don't understand. This..." I stood so close to him he only had to reach out and pull me in. And I knew I'd still let him. I knew what I had to do, what I should do. But this was Marco. I'd never refuse him. Didn't that warrant him at least having all of the facts? I couldn't even finish my thought. It hurt too much.

I sighed and sat down on the seat closest to me. He stepped up and slipped into the seat next to me.

He ran a finger along my face, catching a tear still pasted there. "You're such a drama queen, sweetheart. Now will you calmly tell me what we're dealing with?"

I opened my mouth to speak but stopped at the singular finger he held in my direction.

"Calmly. We'll deal with this *together*."

I leaned into his touch. I couldn't help myself. Maybe. Maybe we could do this? I was his. I was. I shouldn't be. It was improbable, impossible. But I was. He smiled; he knew he had me again. The confidence in his eyes. The fire to fight for me. For us.

So, I told him.

I can't say he didn't feel the enormity of what would probably be the outcome.

"Actually, not probably, it is me. I know it is."

"Did he say so?"

"No."

"Well, there you are."

"But think about it. If it were Greg who won the title of King, then what would be the big deal? It has to be me. I think he did it because he thought I wouldn't sort it out. I think he doesn't know I knew about the rumor. He probably thinks I was a write-in for Homecoming King. But really, again, why would it be so controversial if I won the title? Because I didn't. We both know the only thing bringing the school board to our doors is if I were controversial. That's the title of Queen. And what greater joke would there be at my expense?"

He thought about it. The anger built within him, back-burning there deep in his eyes. The fury that I was about to be targeted, that I was going to be harmed. The tension in his approach.

"It's okay. I sort of expected it when I heard the rumor. I wanted to believe it wasn't true, that I'd heard it wrong, but deep down inside I knew it was. True, I mean. But it's okay. I can deal with it. I've been dealing with it since I came out."

"No, Els, that doesn't make it okay! It doesn't excuse what they're doing to you. To us!" The anger in him was palpable. I needed to talk him down. Talk him down now.

"I know. But I can take it. I'd take anything for you. But that's the easy part, when it's directed at me. Because, like I said, I've been dealing with it already; it's old hat. But, even if I do, I can't stop the association it will bring.

I can't stop how deeply it will cut into your world. How the cohesiveness of the team will suffer from it. I can't have that. It's why I have to leave. They can't crown the joke that isn't there."

"Not an option, babe. No." I was about to protest but he put a finger to my lips. "I. Don't. Care. About any of it. There's only you. There's only *us*. Okay? I'll own it. I will. So, let's turn it back on them. I got a hell of a lot of school credit to burn. Let's cash in...all the way. As long as I win the game tonight, and I'll make sure we win, then they will have their fun but we will turn it back on them. We'll come clean, take the wind out of their sails. Stun them all. I'm out, I'm with you and no one can say anything, not at a school sponsored event. There'll be too many people watching."

"And what about tomorrow? Or the day after?"

"We'll deal. No matter what. Even if it means you and I get away. Far away."

"Oh yeah," I snorted. "'Cause we have a boat load of cash at our disposal to do so."

He turned to look out onto the field. For a moment I thought he was actually seeing it for the first time from my perspective, as a fan of the sport rather than one of the hallowed players. I had to remember his whole experience with football was from the field. He whispered his next words, more to himself.

"Actually, I do. I have a trust fund I have control of from my grandparents from the old country—favored of the grandchildren, and all. Mom and Dad are no longer the executors once I turned eighteen. They wanted the age to be higher, but my grandmother evidently didn't see it that way. So, we can do it, if it comes to that. I'd like to think it won't, of course."

"It will."

"Ever the personification of the good in man, that's my guy."

He leaned forward and kissed me. I panicked and pushed him back.

"Marco! What the *fuck* are you thinking?"

"Babe, we're going to own it in front of god and everyone in a few hours. I think I can kiss my guy whenever I want now."

So, he did again, out in the open. No one out on the field seemed to notice us. If it weren't for the dark clouds gathering around us, that moment could've been kind of hot. We gradually broke the kiss. He ran a hand down the side of my face.

"C'mon. Let's go home."

"I still think I'm bad for you. You know that, don't you?"

"Baby, it'll never work. You can run, but I swear to you I'd tear the whole world apart to find you. You're mine. *Always*."

Chapter Fourteen

My Trip to the Museum

WE HAD A plan. I thought deep down inside it was a foolish plan, but it's what my guy wanted to do. It was how he was going to come out and turn it around on all those guys, those jocks and social elites who mocked me. In a perfect world it just might work. Or in a made-for-TV movie on a premium cable channel that message might come through. Hell, didn't *Glee* make Kurt a Homecoming Queen or something? So, there was a pseudo-precedent, right?

Yeah, okay, I wasn't so sure about that.

He took me back to his house. It was the first time I'd ever been there. As we turned onto the long tree-lined driveway leading to his two-story Italian villa-style home, I began to get butterflies in my stomach. To say it was impressive would be a major understatement. Its landscape was manicured to perfection, not so much as a leaf out of place. The tall equally spaced Italian cypresses standing between tall narrow-paned windows were trimmed like a helix spiral, each reaching to the top of the building. This was a house belonging in one of those *Architectural Digest* spreads of dream homes. This house exuded money; it exuded power, pretty much the Sforzas' main calling card. They might be big fish in this small pond of a town but, from what I could gather from Marco, their family was fairly big in any town they occupied. He didn't say it with awe or devotion. I could sense how much he detested it.

"Wow, Marco. You sure I don't need to get tested or something before I go in? Prove I ain't gonna bring some sort of pestilence into the place?"

His mouth became a grim line. I'd offended him, or at the very least, I'd said something in haste I probably shouldn't have.

"I'm sorry. I didn't mean…"

"Yes, you did," he said through slightly tense lips.

I didn't like the darkness creeping across his features, either. House of horrors, much?

"And you're right. This isn't a home. It's a museum. I live in a museum. I don't keep you away because I'm ashamed of you, *or* of us. I keep you away because I don't want you to become afflicted with our…" The pause as he searched for the right word was more than pregnant, it was soul searching—and not what I'd expected at all. "Familial disease. I keep you away to protect you. You have no idea the pressures that come with the family name. To be honest." He sighed deeply. The walls went up in him, like he was arming himself, prepping for battle. "It's everything I don't want *our* home to be. This place is cold, austere. I want what you bring into my life: warmth, love, compassion."

He slowed the Impala along the front of the home so I could look out at the intricately carved old world influenced masonry decorating the front. "This isn't a home—it's just where I eat and sleep. Those things I take from your room? The ones I never fail to ask you for? *Those* are my home. *You're* my home, babe."

I turned to look back at him. He wasn't spying me looking at the house. His gaze was straight ahead, as if he couldn't look at it any more, at least not with me present. I realized he was being honest about what he said: it wasn't me he was ashamed of, it was his family life. Out of the corner of his eye he caught me watching him—a strained smile blossoming into a real one lit up his face as he took me in. I *was* life itself to him. He pulled the back of my hand to his lips and caressed the ring he bought me on my finger.

"In spite of my family issues, you're never getting away from me. Never, babe. Let's never have a conversation like the one we had at school again. Okay? No matter what. We'll be okay. We'll find a way to be okay. Just you and me."

I nodded, mostly because there was a lump the size of my neighbor's cat and just as hairy lodged in my throat. I didn't think I'd be able to speak without breaking.

"Don't worry. No one's home yet. But we gotta work fast if we're going to be in and out without anyone else being aware."

"Oh, uh, okay."

"No, *not* what you're thinking. I'm not gonna hide you from Mom and Dad. It'll just be faster time-wise if we can get you rolling and I can get back here so I can get to the game before it gets too late. That's all. You wait; after tonight, you'll be obligated to family dinners here. Believe me, I'm sparing you that as long as I can. It isn't something pleasant I look forward to. My parents can be...challenging."

"Well, if Francesca can be there that'd be a help. I think she kinda liked me." He rewarded me with a wicked smirk. "Well, okay, maybe just a little," I said, holding my fingers up in a pinch-like manner.

"Are you kidding? She told me after you left I better not hurt you or she'd kick *my* ass. How's that for having an ally? She's firmly in your court. Said if I didn't treat you right she'd find a way to turn you straight. I told her ain't no way that was gonna happen."

I blushed at his words. *We can do this. We have to do this. It'll be okay. It has to be. Just has to...*

He pulled the Impala into the five-car garage sitting behind and slightly to the left of the palatial home. No bang on of lights when we entered Marco's parking space. No, with the Sforzas evidently subtlety was key—the lights gently ramped up to full illumination as we pulled into the garage. Once inside the Impala purred slightly before he turned her off. It was eerily silent without the beloved car rumbling underneath us, the only sounds being our breathing and the small clicking noises old cars make as they cool down.

"Ready for your future? Please don't be scared. I've got you."

"Jesus, Marco. You make it sound like I'm going to the gallows or something. It's just your house, for Chrissake."

"If that were only true."

I looked at him, my eyes trailing down to his hand laced with mine. There was definite fear in his whole demeanor. He wasn't mincing words. He truly dreaded my coming to his house. What sort of family horrors waited inside? I suddenly had a fuller appreciation of how my guy put on a brave front, plastered on a smile, and made it all look effortless. Clearly it wasn't.

We casually made our way from the garage. I wasn't sure if we were going to enter from the back, which was closer, or... My guy, ever the mind-reader when he was with me, decided to give the full tour.

"C'mon. You might as well get the full-on Sforza effect. It's what drives Mama, your future mother-in-law, to put forth as our statement to the world." We took a few more steps. "I really can't wait for you to take me away from all of this." He took my hand in his own again. I think more for him than any comfort he thought he was providing me.

"Baby, you know no matter what they think of you, I'll never abandon you. You know that, right?" he said softly, though there was a definite edge to his words.

"Of course I do. I never doubted it. Just doubted whether I was worth it or not."

He stopped us just before we reached the corner to the front of the house, his hands coming up to cup my face, his gaze probing mine.

"You are worth everything I will ever have to endure. As long it's you I curl up with at night or hold hands like this"—he reached down and clasped mine again and held ours up to emphasize his point—"then everything I go through is worth it."

"Yeah, yeah. I gotcha, big guy. I'm golden—the chosen one. And I know"—I stalled him as he opened his mouth to protest—"it's not for me to understand. It just is."

He smiled, leaned in, and kissed me lightly on the tip of my nose.

"I can do anything if you're beside me," was all he said. It was enough.

The "house" was indeed more like a modern-day palace; it truly was spectacular. The entryway was an atrium encompassing two stories of the home. A large stained-glass dome no doubt cast brilliant hues when the sun shone. On a day like today all I could do was admire the workmanship that went into it. It was a religious scene of what appeared to be the Archangel Raphael descending onto a Tuscan landscape. Or what I imagined was a Tuscan landscape—but in truth, I really wouldn't know one if I wandered onto it.

A grand curved staircase wound its way along the opposing wall leading up to what I had to imagine were the bedrooms. To the right was a formal sitting room or library. I wasn't schooled enough in the ways of mansions, this being the first I'd ever been in, to make a definitive call. To the left I spied what could only be described as a music or ballroom of some sort. Did Marco's family throw parties? He never spoke of them.

He allowed me to move off from him, taking it in in my own way. The entire downstairs seemed to be of a slightly cool off-white, gray, and the palest taupe I'd ever seen. Neutral colors, austere colors, seemed to allow the paintings, the artwork, and the furnishings to pop against the cool theme. Marco was right. It had no warmth—we might as well be in a wing of the British Museum for all the difference it would make. I could sense the ironic smile on his face. The smile because it was me quietly taking in his world—and whatever I did seemed to amuse him to no end. The irony was it was a world he wasn't all that enamored with. In fact, he seemed to loathe it. *Not like our house will be,* he said. Now I knew what he meant.

"You can go further in, if you'd like, you know. It won't bite. Well, *not much*, anyway."

I glanced his way out of the corner of my eye. His smirk was positively brimming with lust. *"Really? Now? Here?"*

He just nodded, before ultimately sighing. "But we haven't the time."

"Small miracles," I replied and he snorted. Embarrassment averted, or maybe not.

"*Don't make me* press our luck..." he countered darkly.

I turned my head to him more fully and he was leaning his backside into the wall by the front door with his feet crossed while he ran a pocket knife under the nails of his left hand. He was eyeing me between tending to his nails. Lust built there—weighted, heavy. I knew what I'd done to bring it on. I was flustered. His house, the *museum* as he called it, had me walking on tenterhooks. My nerves were like a beacon to him in the dark: *let's fuck*. It probably didn't help that I was practically tiptoeing, walking ever so gently like I had snuck in and was about to be discovered for the street urchin I am.

Finally, he took pity on me.

"C'mere, sexy boy." He slipped his pocket knife back into his letterman's jacket pocket and held his hand out. "We have a couple of minutes before we run out of time. Let me show you around for a bit."

"What if your parents come home?"

"What if? They're going to have to meet you sooner rather than later anyway. We *are* stepping out of the closet—so to speak."

He turned me in his arms and pulled me close. He kissed me softly. When next he spoke, his lips still hadn't parted fully from mine. It tickled a bit, the sensation of his talking directly into my mouth, but the sexiness of it far outweighed any of that.

"Besides, Mom is getting her hair done for homecoming and she and Dad are meeting at Fiorelli's in town for an early dinner before making their way to the game. Mom will only be popping in here to change about a half hour before having to be at the restaurant. That gives us at least a good ninety minutes since we cut class. Dad doesn't come home when they eat out. He has a shower at the office, so he takes a change of clothes with him. He goes straight from the office to meet her."

My turn to puff into his mouth as he kissed me between words. "But what about the staff?"

He chuckled, kissed me deeper, then pulled back to an achingly sexy movement across my lips. "You catch on quickly."

I pulled away from his lips and spoke a bit louder than I'd wanted to—the echo from this foyer/atrium only intensified my being slightly offended. "Hey, I've seen *Downton Abbey*. I'm not a total social-class moron, you know."

He gripped the back of my neck with force, making me catch my breath—bringing my lips into contact with his again. "We were kissing, lover—don't pull away when we're kissing. And I never said you were socially inept. Isabella is off for the evening—no dinner tonight. I have to fend for myself. Beatriz has already departed from her routine cleaning, and Manuel, the gardener, doesn't come on Fridays. We're quite alone."

He stalled whatever other thought was crossing my mind by pressing his tongue back into my mouth, making my knees go all jelly-like. He rumbled with laughter inside, feeling me succumb to his temptations. I don't know how I ever entertained the thought of leaving him. It would never work. No matter how far I ran, he would come after me. He'd pound and break and bend anything in his path to get to me. I required his strength in the way he was holding me to him. I was trapped, just the way he liked to have me. Pliant, forgiving, willing. He reveled in dominating me—but never so far as to emasculate me, just so my body did what it did best when he was near. I molded to him, fit him comfortably. He knew how much I relished being held by him. He always worked it to his advantage. He loved the chase, the capture, but more important, the fact I'd press at the edges—keep him on his toes. I may be pliant—but I was also crafty. He loved that most about us.

"Um, should we, upstairs?"

He practically purred into my mouth and I swear I nearly came from that alone.

"Now, you're talking. I need to fuck you in my bed now we've broken in yours—more than once." He started to pull me upstairs but I held him back for a minute—tugging on his hand to stall him. He turned to me in a huff, his desire for me creating that lustful bulge arching from the base of his cock as it wrapped to one side of his hip. I fucking loved that look on him; it said he wanted me.

"You remember our rule."

"Ohhhh, no you don't. Not today, baby, please?" He was pleading with me, down on his knees and everything. He really wanted to fuck right now. That was not going to happen this time. I didn't fancy coming out of the closet to the world and his parents by our giving into our base desires before his Homecoming game.

I stepped up one stair and knelt down as well to face him.

"Baby, you know the rule. Especially today of all days. You have to win—you have to. There's no choice here. Besides, I don't fancy getting us all worked up and lose track of time and then your mother comes home to change. Wouldn't *that* be the best foot forward on my part? Uh-uh, nothing doing, babe."

"But pleeeeeease, baby. I swear I'll make it quick."

"Oh, so now I'm some cum-dumpster to you, huh?"

He dropped his mouth open in mock horror. "I would *never*..."

"Uh huh," I drawled. I pinched the bridge of my nose. I never refused him. Not really. And the thought of doing it in his bedroom was really appealing to me. I sighed again, peeking with one eye at him, seeing such hope there. "How did I ever think I could leave you?"

"Beats me. But you know it'd never work, right? You know I'd *never* let you get away with it. I'd find you, Els. I'd find you and I'd win you back. No question."

"I know." I cast my gaze down and then looked up at him through my eyelashes. He knew he'd won.

Without a single word he jumped up and as I scrambled up after him he gripped me about the waist and hoisted me onto his shoulder Tarzan-style and proceeded to take the stairs two at a time. I was seriously impressed at his stamina, even if it left me bobbing around on his shoulder like a wounded impala.

"Wow, nice view from up here..." I warbled as we bounced up the stairs.

"Yeah, the stained glass was by some famous Bay Area artist in the East Bay—Berkeley, I think." He said all of this like a tour guide on crack. "Paintings are originals from the old country. Cost Dad a fortune. Shit, most of the art in this house cost a fortune. I hate it all so don't expect me to walk you through it. There are name plates on each piece. I'm sure you'll have plenty of opportunity to read them later. Here's my room."

It was the third door on the right—well, his right, as I was backwards over his shoulder. I'd have to remember that so I didn't walk in on something I shouldn't later. I could still see the top of the dramatic staircase as we slipped into Marco's room.

It was very clean. Where the rest of the house seemed cold and austere, Marco's room had the same clean lines the Europeans favored but this was done in warm colors. The carpet was a pale apricot, very like a dusty peach, with the walls having dark wood wainscoting rising halfway up the sides of the large room and finishing off in a slightly warmer color of the carpet. The thing I noticed most about Marco's room was how big it was. How big everything was in Marco's house. Seriously—a third of my house could fit into his bedroom alone. He plopped me unceremoniously onto my back as he started to get out of his clothes. A gradual salacious smile blossomed on his face as he spied me looking around his room instead of stripping. He started to pull mine off for me. I finally gave in and stripped, choosing to leave my short athletic socks on just because I knew it would bother him. He had my legs up—catching my socks still being on, he ripped them off with a deep growl and a pointed glare. To which I just giggled at his frustration that I was slowing him down when we didn't have time.

"Sorry 'bout it being so fast, baby. I swear I'll bone you real slow in here sometime soon. Do it right, ya know?"

"Uh huh." My man swung into action. He hoisted my legs forward to my chest and lapped at my ass—applying quite a bit of spit. He chuckled and smiled.

"Still wet and moist from the nooner. Best fucking lube, babe."

I barely got my next words out when he slam fucked himself into me in one long thrust. "Yeah, well I like to keep my guy haaaa-pp-yeee, ssst, fuck, Marco—ease up, baby. Give me a few to get used to you. You're no wilting flower, you know."

He was ignoring my words as he was on a mission to bust a nut. He began fucking me in earnest, kissing me deeply—probably to keep me quiet while his hips slapped the fuck out of mine. He pulled back for a second, his eyes making sure I was locked to his gaze, the way we did things when we fucked.

"Like churning butter, babe. So fucking wet and sweet inside you."

"I know, babe. Go to town, hon. I'm good."

It was a sloppy fuck; it's what he liked. Hell, it's what I liked too. We're boys; we liked messy, especially when it came to sex. And he was right about the butter part. I caught a glimpse of his cock when he pushed my knees onto my shoulders, so my ass was pointed straight up, giving him the best leverage possible to fuck me silly. My gaze took in his muscular body as he pounded into my ass—his engorged cock slick with a frothy mess from the load he'd planted there at lunch. I was pretty damned good about keeping it in when we did it. It was how he liked it. I was good with that.

As he edged for the better part of fifteen minutes while doing me, I began to talk dirty to him, saying how he must have fantasized about screwing me on his bed so the stains from lube and cum would be on the bedding, to piss off his parents. That got him going. I began to see parental issues here. Control issues. Marco liked being in control—I knew that. His football career demanded it from him. But the one place he was subservient, where he had to toe the line to someone else's wishes, was here in his museum-like house. I'd deal with it in my own good time. But it did give me clarity into why Marco did some of the things he did. Not that I was judging him, but just being here, watching him as he fucked me furiously, I found I understood him.

"Shoot for me, babe. I'm ready."

I knew what he was asking me. When we fucked fast and furious, nothing put him over the edge like me letting go and shooting onto my own face while he spent himself. It was one of his favorite ways to blow a wad. So, I got into the fuck as he screwed the hell outta me. I moaned, relishing the slap of our flesh as he tore into me. He pressed my knees so hard into my shoulders the head of my cock was less than an inch from my lips. I burst, hard and in copious amounts, fucking brought the rain down on my face. Bukkake boy: party of one.

That did it. He moaned so loud I swear a flock of birds took off from the tree outside his room. He panted how sexy it was as I spent my juices all over myself. I knew how it affected him, and I worried. Because this type of sex usually led to more boning after he'd lap the cum off my face and we'd kiss with it passing between us. We didn't have the time.

"You know," I panted as I gradually came down from my orgasm, my face a painted mess. I was very impressed none of it had gotten into my eye—'cause that woulda been a real fucking nightmare. His cock was still throbbing deeply inside me; his orgasm was still subsiding—filling me.

"So fucking sweet, babe."

"Yeah, but you know we can't do another round, right? You *do* know that, right?"

He nodded slowly as he let my legs down to fold themselves gently around his hips. He stayed firmly planted as he began to lick the cum from my face. We kissed, snowballing it between us for a few moments, until I finally made to swallow it down to get us going again.

"Hey, so not fair. I wanted that. Was gonna be my protein drink before the game. Ya know, rejuvenate me?" He wiggled his eyebrows. I rolled my eyes and then showed him I still had it in my mouth. I laughed and it sputtered and he set to sucking back up from my mouth. It was a fucking mess. Literally.

He got up and pulled me up with him.

"C'mon. Quick shower then we gotta find you something amazing for you to wear for your crowning."

"Oh yeah, *that*," I intoned drolly.

Forty-five minutes and another furious fuck in the shower later—so much for my rules before the game—we'd dried off and he found me some designer threads to put on. They actually didn't look too bad on me. I needed a jacket and his were all too big for me but I said I had a nice black one at home that would work. He seemed satisfied with it. He had me put on one of his über-tight dark blue shirts. Since it was a size too small for him—he bought it that way because he knew it would drive me crazy with lust for him if I could see every contour of his body—it sort of fit me.

He had this trick of using a small chain with tiny roach clips I could clip in the back to tighten the shirt a bit under my jacket. I was okay with that. He gave me a necklace to wear made of platinum—a very delicate sculpture of an angel. It was quite captivating. I usually didn't go for religious iconography, but he said it would look good in the pictures.

"It's Raphael, my namesake angel, my middle name. I want you to wear it, so I'll be with you tonight when you need it most. Against this shirt, and those eyes that cut me like diamonds, you look quite stunning."

"Or just stunned, more like."

He ignored my slight.

"It never fails to catch the light."

He slapped one of his black jackets on me. It was way too big but he wanted to see the lapels and dark fabric—even if he had to pinch the backside a bit to create the effect. He then took my simple studs out of my ear and replaced them with half-carat blue diamond studs he had. He said they'd set off my eyes to perfection. They did.

They weren't clothes I'd have picked out and worn, but just like the wedding outfit he'd put together during the summer, my man knew how to make me shine. I wish my mouth hadn't gotten ahead of my brain again. I should've been more appreciative when I spoke.

"Wonderful, I'm your cum-dumpster fuck doll you get to play dress up with," I said as I turned slightly to take in the whole effect. He snorted, choosing instead not to rise to the bait.

One size we did share in common was our shoe size. My feet were large for my frame and they matched his to nearly the same proportions. He pulled out some Kurt Geiger spider killers in a muted black. My ensemble for Homecoming Queen was complete. I just hoped it wouldn't go all Stephen King *Carrie* south on us when the time came. I mean, Carrie's dance was chaperoned and look what happened there.

The hottest part about this whole ensemble change? My fashion designer did it all completely naked! Fucking aces in my book, standing in his large walk-in closet with mirrors everywhere and his delightfully muscular body on display at every angle. It was a feast for my eyes.

Yeah, I sucked him off in the closet before I let him dress and we could make our escape. I don't know how we managed it, but by the time he dropped me off, he still would have forty-five minutes to spare getting to the game to suit up. I told him I was getting a ride with Greg's family—which was true. Greg had offered it as a half joke but then softened and committed to picking me up when he detected how scared I was about the whole thing. I told Marco I would see him there.

Alone, in my house, I crumbled for a bit. I sat and stewed. I actually poured myself a tumbler of scotch from my parents' bar. It wasn't locked, mostly because I detested the taste of alcohol, so they figured it was safe.

Yeah, well, not tonight.

I was feeling fairly composed and slightly numb by the time Greg's car rolled into my driveway.

Chapter Fifteen

(Halloween + Homecoming) x Sforzas = Disaster

WHOEVER THOUGHT A Halloween-themed Homecoming was a good idea should've been hauled away and had extensive electro-shock treatments applied. They could get their Halloween yah-yahs and leave the rest of us the fuck alone. We had bigger shit going on.

I mean, I understood while it did fall the weekend before the holiday nearly everybody loved, to apply its trappings on a stadium event was just beyond ludicrous. All it did was promise a bizarre mix of costumed festivities looming large for both the fans of the game and the Homecoming participants. Word had spread that the tailgating theme was a zombie fest—since the "Walking Dead" were all the rage thanks to the popular television show of the same name. All the serious fans came to the school in full-on costume. It was a wild conflagration of colorful costumed revelers everywhere you looked. Vampires sat next to zombified princesses. There was even someone who came to the game in a T-Rex costume—what the fuck did he think was going to happen, a costume contest at half-time? Not bloody likely considering the scandalous turn of events I knew was coming my boyfriend's and my way.

My eyes searched the crowd but I never did catch Angelo at a single game again. As heady as our first meeting had been, part of me didn't want to find him. I mean, I went back and forth on it. At times I really wanted to know what part of the school he called home, whom he hung out with. The other part, the reasonable part, wanted nothing more than to not have that particular temptation around me. It was far too familiar: the electricity, the warmth and dazzle of those familiar green eyes, right down to the arch of his painted-looking brow. Way too fucking familiar. And it shouldn't've been. Not really. It was best to leave it the way it was. It was safer, right? It was fairly easy for me to do; when I was at school I tried like hell not to get noticed. Say nothing of how Marco would react. I shuddered to think about how it would all pan out.

Yeah, having Angelo relegated to my past was probably a very good thing, despite how much he seemed to desire me like my boyfriend did. That was a thought my inner Gollum seemed a little too gleeful over.

Give Marco a run for his money, he would. Wouldn't he, precious? I mentally shoved that baldy bitch back into the ether before his way of thinking got to me.

Giving up, I looked around the stadium. Those thoughts were familiar to me. I spent time trying to gauge what that first meeting with Angelo meant, what it cost me in being faithful to Marco. But I couldn't help thinking these thoughts as my eyes scanned the stadium. With all of the costumes on display it was a surefire way of not finding him, even if he bothered to show up. That was until an arm slinked around my waist.

"Eh, bet you think I had forgotten all about you."

Angelo.

I turned to face him, thinking at last I'd finally get to see him fully, even if he was wearing a little greasepaint. I was so wrong about that. As I turned to greet him, I discovered he went full-out as the Red Death from *The Phantom of the Opera*. It was an over-the-top crazy-good copy of the costume used in the Broadway play my mother had taken me to see when it played on tour through San Jose a few years back. His costume was perfection personified, right down to the skull-like mask covering the top half of his face. I never seemed to catch a break on seeing the whole thing as one.

"Where have you been? I've looked for you at *every* game—even the away games."

"Yeah, eh, well I have not been to any of them. The school work is, eh, much harder when it is not in your own language, you know? I was struggling for a bit. Is better now."

"It's..."

"Uh?"

"It's better now. You said, *is* better—*it's* better..."

His eyes flashed radiantly from within his garish makeup and any pretense of why I was instructing him in his English went right out the proverbial window.

"Eh, never mind." I smiled and so did he. Those lips—fuck, I knew those lips.

"Marco?" I whispered softly to this made-up boy, this studly Italian from Italy.

"Marco?" he echoed back to me, confused—but in a slightly amused way.

"Yeah, never mind that."

I was aware he hadn't removed his hand from the far side of my waist. Nor had I shrugged it off, as I should. His haunting familiarity, I struggled with it. For reasons I couldn't begin to explain, it was as if Marco had stepped from behind the guise of his life in football and was standing next to me. But my conscience got the better of me and I gently extracted myself from Angelo.

"Uh, with that hat we probably better sit along the back of the stands."

"I suppose I could take it off."

I know my eyes must have lit up at the suggestion. He cut off any potential reply with his next words.

"You look really nice tonight. Going somewhere special later?"

I looked down at the floor of the stands for a moment, unsure if I should spill it now, or if I should allow him to be just as surprised as the rest of the school was going to be. I decided to come clean.

"I'm up for one of the titles at Homecoming." His eyes went half-lidded, apparently scrutinizing my situation as best I could determine under his rather dramatic mask. It was there: green fire shimmered through the shadows, intense, beguiling, familiar.

"Eh, so the uh, Homecoming King? You think you will win?"

I knew I quirked my mouth in a way that surely conveyed I wasn't too pleased with having to be here at all, let alone dressed in Marco's designer clothes. "Something like that. I have to at least make a showing. Just in case."

There, that wasn't completely a lie; more of an omission of the facts.

"Should we get seated then?"

He guided me with his hand at my lower back. I knew I should probably shrug him off, but to be honest, I missed his camaraderie. There was an ease when I was with him, picking up right from where we left off—as if the intervening weeks hadn't happened at all, a mere turn of the day at most. We sat high up in the stands, near the far aisle as I would have to make my descent about ten minutes before the end of the second quarter as the Homecoming announcement was to be made during half-time.

Fifteen minutes later, Angelo and I were immersed in a heavy conversation about religion and its effects on society. He for, me against. While we debated our positions, I could tell he was doing it all in good fun. It didn't keep him from pressing his point, but he seemed to approve of the good-natured play we had going on between us. Even though I couldn't see his face clearly, I did spy how bright his eyes were while we debated. He was having a fair amount of fun with me.

The marching band started up as the teams took to the field. My stomach did flip a little knowing the impending drama was really going to get going at half-time. It would make this hootenanny look like a kindergartner's Christmas pantomime.

I leaned forward in my seat a bit—a breath caught at my ear, red sparkles percolated around the edges of my sight.

"You really are quite beautiful tonight, Elliot."

Not a trace of accent in his small compliment. As flat in tone as any American.

I turned to look at Angelo. Surely I hadn't heard him right. But he was sitting back against the seat, nowhere near my ear. He was looking at me, but I couldn't quite come up with a way he could have whispered to me without a rustle of all those feathers and sequins. I'd have noticed, wouldn't I? But there he was, simply watching me as I took in the entrance of the Avenging Angels. I smiled and was warmed when he returned it. I turned my head back to my boy as he made his entrance onto the field to a wild round of applause. My heart raced as it always did. He was truly glorious in this arena. He muthafucking *owned* it, my guy did.

"I love you so much, baby. Make me proud..." I whispered softly to him, hoping by some miracle my voice would linger down to the field and caress his ear. I knew that was a pipe dream and a half. But I could at least let myself believe in the fantasy of it. I'd tell him about it later and he no doubt would say he thought he heard something caressing him inside his helmet just to tease me.

Despite the attention I was receiving from Angelo, I lapsed into becoming a bit melancholy as I realized to get to that intimate moment, I'd have to share the stage with him in what *he* thought would be our moment of triumph. I still wasn't so sure. Perhaps we'd make it through the night without any *Carrie*-like effects and mayhem. He was probably right. But as for when school renewed again the following week? Or the week after? With seven months left to go for the school year, I didn't like how long the road stretched out in front of us, unsure and with twists and turns that could come our way.

I was so caught up in it I found I was only half paying attention to the game, that half being how much I became riveted to my guy whenever he was on the field and not paying any attention at all to the other half of the game when he wasn't. In those times I amused myself by sitting back and watching Angelo in his wild-assed get-up.

"So, why the extravagant costume?"
"I thought you would be pleased."
"Me? Why me?"
"I think you know the answer well enough."

I smiled at his flirting with me. Okay, so maybe he wouldn't run away if he found out about me. In fact, looks like he already had and wasn't too put off by it. Perhaps a bit too much.

"But aren't you hot underneath all that? I mean, most of the people here only have a bit of greasepaint on. Whereas you, you look like you stepped right off the Broadway stage."

He laughed in a silvery melodious way I found very charming. He was far more playful tonight, more so than I remembered.

"I am, eh how you say, very *hot* underneath all this..." He wiggled his brows just a bit. I involuntarily flushed with excitement of his open flirtation.

Why now? Why has he returned to me now? Of all days he could have chosen why would my lovely Italian companion, my foreign friend, choose this one?

His hand sought out mine and laced my fingers with his. I wanted to pull away; I did. He was just being friendly, I convinced myself, though I found it hard to ignore the electricity sparked by the simple touch of his hand in mine. My eyes darted to just beyond his shoulder to spot an older woman who was probably a relative of one of the players. She wasn't in costume but I doubted even makeup could improve upon her sour visage. It wouldn't have hidden her disgust over two boys holding hands like we were. Angelo caught the line of my gaze and whipped his head around to see her one seat over from him.

"Problem?"

She appeared startled at Angelo's challenge, to something he must've conveyed in his stare, because she then wrinkled her nose just the tiniest bit but said nothing and turned her attention back to the game. Once satisfied we were left to ourselves again, Angelo turned his attention back to me, those piercing green eyes like searchlights through his maddening prosthetic mask. I noted throughout the whole ordeal he hadn't released my hand. In fact, his hold had become far more possessive.

As he continued to hold my hand, occasionally running a thumb along the top of it, my head swam knowing here was another boy who was interested in me. You can't imagine how happy I was his grazing touch wasn't along my palm. I think it would have spooked me far too much at the moment. It was a simple enough caress. At the first game I thought Angelo wanted to get closer. Now I was sure of it. But I knew where my loyalties lay. Though I sort of liked the attention—it gave me something to focus on as the seconds of the first half of the game ticked by.

I returned my gaze back to the game for a while. The heat from Angelo was palpable. I tried my best to ignore it—well, the sexual tension I felt from it. I was a right shit for taking it from Angelo, leading him on with no way I'd ever follow through. But I was an emotional mess the closer we drew to half-time. I knew he could sense my being restless, but thankfully he did nothing but caress my hand every now and again—letting me know he was still there beside me.

Finally, I turned to him and leaned forward so there could be no mistake about my words.

"Angelo, I have to go down to the field now. Homecoming is going to be called at half-time. I don't know if we'll see each other afterward. I think it might get a little crazy. I hope you understand I'm not leaving you because of something you said or did. Okay? But I have to go do this. I really do like being your *friend*."

I tried to emphasize the friendship part of the equation. I think I was successful. I hope I was. I really did value what I came to know of my Italian friend. He pulled my hand to his lips and kissed the back of it. The white makeup of his painted skull features left its imprint where his lips had grazed my hand.

"*Ciao, mio amico.*"

"See ya..."

A part of me didn't want to go. Maybe I could stay and spend some time getting to know him better? But to what end? I had Marco. Marco would definitely not understand. Shit, it was ludicrous I was even entertaining a thought like this.

He unhurriedly released my hand, but I sensed he truly didn't want to let me go, as if he were fearful for me and what lay ahead. Finger by finger he relinquished me to what was to come. I hadn't said a word, yet he seemed to sense my unease. I finally pulled away and made my way down the stairs far faster than was probably warranted. I was flustered. I turned and looked back at Angelo. His gaze never left me. I waved once more to him and then turned the corner and made for the field.

One of the assistant PE teachers was there and he acknowledged me as if I was expected at this point in time, which I guess I was. I spied Greg already gathered with the girls on the field. They were all dressed to the nines—the whole lot of them. I had to give it to my buddy, Greg. He actually looked every inch a member of the Homecoming court. That small notice cut me more than I expected. Even he appeared to be abandoning me, leaving me behind to fend for myself. I didn't get too close to them all.

Though I was sure my clothes from Marco cost more than all the girls' dresses put together, I kept my distance. I needn't have bothered. My proximity, no matter how much distance I put between them and me, was too big a bauble (at least to my way of reckoning) for the Queen Bitch of Mercy High to ignore.

"What are you doing here, Ladybird? Trying to improve your social status?" Sony Lawton hissed with all the venom of the viper she possessed. This, of course, brought me into the sights of the worst possible person imaginable to make my gnarled nerves and stomach twist and hurt even more: Cindy Markham.

"You really think you stand a chance to take the title away from me? Is that what this is about?"

"What do you mean from you?" Sony taunted.

"Cool it, Sony. You've always been second fiddle, whereas this little faggot is trying to muscle in and take my glory."

Half-time was only seven seconds away. Marco would be joining us soon. Glancing in his direction, I realized the opposing team had the ball, so Marco turned from the bench to spy the little tête-à-tête going on. Not liking what he saw, he got up and made steady, purposeful strides to get to me. His gaze pointed. My eyes darted in his direction, hoping against all hope he couldn't see the fear in my eyes, how I just wanted to run and get away from all of this. I thought I could handle it. I did.

But with Cindy's words clawing into me, and knowing how everything was about to change, I didn't want him to witness this small exchange. I wasn't concerned about me; I could take the pain. I was only thinking of him.

Greg tried to intervene on my behalf. "Look, he's here because Silverstein said we had to be. Something about it being an upset of some sort."

If it weren't for what he actually said, she might have bitten his head off. Yet those words had sunk in—she was a shrewd one when her survival depended on it. She put it together with what I did when the principal had put it that way. No other way to take it. I knew then I had the right of it. I was dead on with my assessment. Sony and Cindy just exchanged a look that said they knew my presence meant trouble.

Marco had jogged over to us by now as the half was called. A team member handed him a large bottle of water; he dumped half of it on his head to wash away most of the sweat. The rest he took in a long draw to quench his thirst. He smiled at me, his eyes only for me. I was the instrument of his undoing, and he simply didn't care about the damage I could cause.

"Hey..." He came up to me and said softly.

"Hey yourself," I replied.

"What the fuck, Marco? You friends with the faggot boy now? Fucking Beau is going to be over the moon with that one."

Marco flipped Cindy the bird without so much as taking his eyes off me. So much love there. So much.

Greg chuckled at Marco's salute to her Supreme Bitchness, and the girls gasped in surprise at how Marco was treating them. Castoffs. He was so sure of how it all was going to go down. I guess I had to trust him.

Beau Hopkins and his lackeys from the team, Willem Hawthorne and my old elementary school friend, Stephen Lowry, had shown up for the Homecoming announcement as well. With the lone exception of Greg, all the other guys on the Homecoming court were on the football team. My heart went out to just how odd this whole thing had hit the two of us. I admired Greg for hanging in there even more. He was a truly great guy. I knew some lucky girl would snag him one day. I hoped she knew what a gem of a guy she'd be getting. I caught his eye for a moment and he rolled his eyes and had a smirk for me, letting me know he was hanging with it all.

"Mister Donahey, a word, please?" I turned to find Principal Silverstein looking down his nose at me, though not out of pity or scorn. No, just because he was a tall man and there really wasn't any other way for him *to* look at me.

Marco and I exchanged a quick look before Marco nodded and I moved a few steps away from them all with the Principal. I glanced back at Marco as we came to a stop to find he was watching me with all the possessiveness he could muster from where he stood. Cindy and Sony, on the other hand, seemed to have regained their lofty airs, no doubt believing I was in some sort of trouble for thinking I could eke into their closed world. I spared a thought for Greg who sort of had fallen to be background noise to the whole thing. It was truly one of the biggest things to happen to him and yet even I knew, and deep down he had to have done the math as well, being the true math geek he was, he hadn't won the upset title. That was me. Still, I had to hand it to him. He stood up to Cindy and Sony and the three other twats whose names I couldn't recall at the moment. I admired Greg for that. He didn't have to say a word. We were both trespassers in their world. Passing urchins. Cinderfellas on borrowed time.

"Mister Donahey," he began.

"Uh, Elliot, please. Mister Donahey is my dad."

He tried a small smile at my correcting him. It was strained and I immediately thought, *oh shit*.

"I tried to reach you on your cell but I guess we don't have the correct number and the house phone went unanswered. I wished to have spared you the embarrassment, you see. The board met over the issue we discussed this afternoon in my office. Do you remember?"

"How can I forget? I knew it was me once you said it."

I glanced over at Greg who couldn't help but look skeptical at this turn of events. *Yeah, me too buddy.*

"Yes, well. In truth you did win. But the board couldn't see fit to give you the title."

Part of me was completely relieved at this, the other part was actually kind of pissed off. But I decided to take the blessings where I could get them.

"What?"

That came from Marco who had stormed over to stand next to me. The sudden anger in his tone was evident to everyone around us. He was crackling with the wrench Silverstein had thrown into his plans.

"Mister Sforza, this is a private matter between the school and Elliot. Do you mind?"

He rolled right over Silverstein without even a small thought, "In fact, I do mind. You see, Elliot's my..."

"Friend..." I hastily inserted. I could already feel Marco's pointed gaze at how I was playing this forward. "My *friend*. We're study partners in Mister Crowe's English class. He's just concerned, that's all." I gave him a pointed stare of my own, trying to convey he should just wait it out to hear what Silverstein had to say on the subject first without jumping into the fray.

"I see." Silverstein's eyes darted between Marco and me. No doubt he was trying to ascertain just what was going on at the moment.

Yeah, good luck with that. I'm not so sure we know either.

He continued warily.

"Well, in any event, the board couldn't allow you to take the title because, given your situation—you are gay, aren't you? We had that part right at least, didn't we?"

I nodded, it wasn't like it was some big secret on campus, after all.

"Yes, well, the board decided given the rumor mill—don't look so surprised, Elliot, we have our own ways of keeping tabs on the students. But as I was saying—given the rumor mill, we thought the title was a form of bullying and what with our zero tolerance policy we thought we'd spare you the embarrassment over it. I hope you understand the board's decision wasn't meant to slight you. In fact, we were trying to spare you any unnecessary embarrassment on your part."

"That's kind of you."

"Elliot…" Marco gritted through his teeth. He was clearly not pleased at this turn of events.

"Marco, please. It's better this way."

I turned from Marco to our principal who had nothing short of a confused look at how easy Marco and I were conversing. Even he knew the social rule-breaking going on at the moment, despite the excuse I'd provided on why Marco and I were on such friendly terms. He knew something wasn't adding up. They all did. I was doing further damage just being here. I needed to pull up stakes, and get the fuck outta Dodge, like *now*.

"Thank you for telling me this before I made a fool of myself up on the stage."

He nodded once to let me know our business had concluded before he moved off to ensure the small stage the booster club was putting out in the field was ready for the Homecoming announcement.

I pulled Marco aside and we walked away from everyone, well, about as far away as we could considering we were right along the stands anyway. Marco jerked his arm out of my hand—something he'd never done before. I yanked my hand back as if I were stung by his abrupt move.

"What the fuck, Els? We had a plan. This was how we were going to do this and you just let Silverstein kick you to the curb like that?"

"Calm down, sweetheart," I hoarsely whispered as best I could given the din from the crowd. He had to lean in toward me to hear. I was aware of the entire Homecoming Court watching us with eagle-like gazes. So much of our conversation was being analyzed by each of them and for varying reasons. With the sole exception of Greg, I didn't think any of their conclusions would help Marco and me out. I needed to make a clean break and fast.

"Look, I know what we planned, but think about it. This way we just proceed with what we had planned all along. This isn't plan B, it's still plan A. Nothing's changed. In a way, it's even better because you don't lose any cred in the process."

"I don't give a *fuck* about my cred, *sweetheart*." He intoned his last word not as a term of endearment but to emphasize how upset he was with me. It was the first time he'd ever used a term of endearment as a weapon. It cut me deeper than I think he realized. But he wasn't focusing on that at the moment. Right now he was upset with my going along with the school board's decision to sweep me under the rug. I was okay with the rug. Hell, most of my school experience had been trying to stay under that damned rug. It was familiar; it was safe.

But I supposed maybe that's what Marco was tired of—playing it safe. He wanted us out and known to everyone far more than I did. I wanted to give him that; I truly did. But I also knew far better than he what it would cost him. I think he'd be surprised at how fast his wad of school cred would burn up and he'd be left in the negative with all of them. A social outcast, a pariah of sorts since until tonight, he was one of their own. Is *still* one of their own, I reminded myself. I also needed to remind myself of what I was trying to accomplish now I didn't have to push our relationship out into the open before god, the Angels, and their fans to see.

"I know *you* don't, but someone has to think about you. I don't think you really understand what's at stake here."

"And *I* don't think *you're* hearing *me*. This was supposed to be about us not giving a fuck what everyone else thinks. That was the whole point. You didn't want us to hide. Now it seems like all you want to do is deny us, what we are to each other. I never would have thought you'd do that. It hurts, babe. It really fucking tears me up to know you'd go there."

His face glistened in the lights from the stadium. It took me a few seconds to realize it was because I was crying from his words. The pain he felt when he'd said them plain upon his face. It didn't mean they weren't true for him. I'd thought before when we'd argued that we'd had a fight. But now I realized how wrong I'd been. This was our first real fight, because this one went where the others hadn't—this one hurt.

"No, you're turning my words around on me. It's not what I meant at all! I'm just saying we stick with the original plan we set out at the beginning of the school year. It was your idea. We only have a few weeks left to ride it out. But if we do it now, if we let this out, then it will affect the team, your status at school—which is far more important to you than you know. I know the circles you move in...I know..."

"You know *dick* about it! Christ, Els! Give me some muthafucking credit here! You think I don't know what these assholes think about you, what they'd think about us? I know, and *I don't fucking care*! How many times or ways do I have to say it? I'm done. I don't know how else to get you to see what I want is *you*. What I want is *us*. Jeffrey, Marcel—the kids? Any of this ringing a bell?" He stretched his hand out toward the football field. "I don't give a rat's ass over this bullshit! It's all over in a few months anyway. Think long-term here. Think about, as you said to me when we left the Greenbaums, do you remember what you said? How what we do now will affect how we choose to live our lives as we move forward?"

I was shaking from how hard his words were hitting me. I wanted to run away. I wanted the safety of my room, to grab my pillow and cry my motherfucking eyes out. I wanted the anonymity of my old life, if just to gather my wits and take a much-needed breath, mostly because since he started his rant I hadn't found a way to breathe at all.

"You still see a way for us to move forward?" Never had ten words caused such fear in me than after I asked that.

His gaze was hard. It was pointed. I tried like hell to find *us* in his stare. There were moments flittering around back there—trying like hell to catch fire. He huffed from frustration, running a hand through his sweat-laden hair.

I couldn't stop the tears from falling. His hand twitched; he was fighting the ingrained impulse to reach out and touch me. In the subtle move of his hand a glimmer everything could work out revealed itself to me. *If* he wanted it to, that is.

"You make it very hard sometimes." He deflated, resigned to let it go. "I'm just surprised at this whole turn of events. But this hurts, Els. That wasn't fair."

I nodded to let him know I understood and I wanted to tell him how sorry I was but his gaze stopped me. He was still angry with me. I could tell.

"Friends, then?" My lips were trembling no matter how hard I was trying to control myself. Somewhere Cindy and Sony laughed. I didn't want to look; I didn't want to give them the satisfaction if it had been at my expense. Given the two cunts in question, I didn't think it could be anything but my being the butt of some joke they were sharing.

"I think you should go. I think we need some time to cool off, that's what I think. Maybe it is best you bow out now. I don't know how I feel about it all and I don't want to say something I will deeply regret," he murmured. The pointed gaze softened a bit.

I tried to smile. I painted one on though it didn't seem to have the effect I was after. His gaze was just as pointed and hard as before.

"Look, I'm, uh, gonna go home. I, uh, don't need to witness this. Cindy's gonna gloat more than usual about having you for the evening."

"We don't know I've won, yet."

"Get serious, Sforza."

He attempted a smirk, but it came out more of a grimace. I could tell it was merely icing on the hurt-filled cake, nowhere near the normal smile he reserved just for me.

"I got shit I gotta do. Unlike *you*, I don't get to shirk *my* responsibilities. Not an option for me." He glared at me, very hard. I hated being on the end of that. "I guess I'll call you later so we can talk. 'Kay?" He asked it like a question, unsure of how I would take it.

"I still don't like this. I fucking hate it, actually. Just so we're clear...You *denied* us. Nothing short of it. That hurts me far more than I thought you'd *ever* do to me. I can't be with you right now. So, go. Just go."

I nodded. I thanked the stars above we were angled in just the right way no one from the court could truly spy what we were saying to each other.

"Yeah, okay." I turned to leave.

I glanced back to see him as he walked backwards to the group, keeping his eyes on me. Pointed, glaring, so much anger there. An anger I didn't know we'd ever be able to put behind us.

He nodded once before turning back to the festivities. So easy for him to forget me, it seemed. *Why did I think there'd be an always for us?* They were just words. Words and promises. Promises were made to be broken...wasn't that the saying? Wasn't that what he'd implied by telling me to leave? Yeah, well, I wasn't sure which of us was breaking our promise. But I knew one thing—something had broken. Badly.

I nodded and waved a small wave he didn't bother seeing and made for the parking lot as fast as I could, Cindy and Sony's laughter echoing at my back. I hoped we might be good; we might even be great after this fiasco, but I so didn't want to see a moment of it. He could tell me about it later if he chose, if we were still talking. Or I guess someone would post it to YouTube and I could always watch it there.

Yeah, probably not.

THE ROAR OF the crowd swelled as the Homecoming ceremony began—like an emotive scrub brush chafing me raw. The tears flowed freely. I ran the back of my hand across my running nose. I was rapidly becoming a mess. I tried to hitch my jacket closer to me but the cold sliced through me something fierce—adding another level of pain I had to endure. I dashed through the senior parking lot trying to figure out the best route that wouldn't have me walking along a busy dark road wearing black and blue, not to mention the crying made navigation a challenge to begin with.

I jumped when a pair of bright lights caught me crying like a baby. With a new rivulet of snot trying to escape my nose unnoticed, I snorted. I paused mid-step like the potential roadkill I was. The car sat there, not honking or anything. I casually hunched my shoulders up in the jacket, trying to hide my disheveled mess. I got to the other side and held a hand up in thanks to whoever it was pausing to let me by. I continued to move through the next aisle when the same damned car caught me again near the exit of the lot. This time I stopped and waved them by, but they didn't move. Instead the car pulled up alongside me.

"I'm trying to pick you up. Get in. You look like you could use a friend."

Angelo, and driving no less. I didn't even know if that were possible, or legal for that matter. Why that oddball thought wiggled across my mind when so much other bullshit was screaming for my attention was beyond me. I needed to stop with the fucking sniveling and man up.

Marco's name bellowed from the stadium to a swell of thunderous applause, and a completely new round of tears came forth. I just couldn't hold it back any longer. Marco was right. I should have fought it. He wanted us to do what we said, and I put a stop to it. I was a fucking fool. Marco was what was important. He was right. But now I really messed things up. Even if he still loved me and thought I was beautiful, I had abandoned him.

Angelo threw the car in park and was out and at my side in seconds. He carefully hugged me. I noted he had stripped out of his monstrosity of a costume. While I truly thought it was spectacular, the sight of him now was jaw-dropping. He was bare to the waist in gym shorts. His face still had some prosthetics obscuring it, dammit, but his body was *un-fucking-believable*, tight and bronze and muscular all over. Not too unlike my Italian stallion who was no doubt wowing them in the stadium.

Then Cindy's name was called amid screams of joy.

I mean really? She thinks she can pull that off after how hard she grilled me about stealing it away from her marshy ass?

I held my hands to my ears and Angelo wrapped his arms around me and gently guided me over to the passenger side of his Audi. I slipped in and thankfully he had the heater and some tunes cranked in the car. It immediately took the edge off everything.

He climbed back in on his side of the car. I glanced in the back seat and saw the mess of his costume there. It looked like a high-priced drag queen had exploded in the back seat. Angelo, on the other hand, was heat personified. I didn't need the heater. This boy was smoking, even with his ghoulishly marred face.

Focus, Elliot. You just left your boyfriend with a school of piranhas while you took the chicken way out. And now you're checking out this boy next to you like some bitch in heat. You're still wearing Marco's ring for fuck sake. Focus!

Angelo, in all his revealed masculine glory, turned to me and put a hand around my shoulder and pulled me to him. The warmth from him was incredible. The noise of the crowd penetrated the window a bit and thankfully Angelo turned up the music to help drown it out but it was too late. An avalanche of tears came out. He held me to him and rocked me as he ran his hands down my back.

"It is okay. I saw it. I know."

Now how could *he* possibly know? Even if he saw what he said he did—which I had my doubts—there couldn't be any way he could spot anything like that. We simply were too far away. Not unless he had some sort of spy camera or something. And I had to admit in the melee of the Homecoming, I wasn't really looking for him. I was fairly sure something so massive and glittery would have caught my eye—or I'd like to think it would—but with everything going on, I may have missed it. It didn't matter either way. Not really. I needed some comfort other than my pillow at home. Angelo seemed to be there and he said he understood—on some level maybe he did.

And I needed that. I needed someone to hear me.

Not because I didn't think Marco didn't. I knew he did. In fact, if truth be known he was probably beating himself up over it while all the craziness of the fucking event was swirling around him. Then he had to play the second half of the game. Meanwhile, where was I?

In the arms of a hella hot hunk of Italian man-meat.

Okay, that was a bit uncalled for, I berated myself.

Angelo was truly a very nice guy; and he was here for me. He certainly didn't deserve my fag boy angst. I slowly pulled back from him. Our faces were so close. My eyes searched his in the midst of all that makeup. Brilliant green to ice blue. Hauntingly familiar. But there wasn't any way it could be true. I knew where my guy was...

And where he was, was without me.

Don't get me wrong. I knew how much of it was my fault. And how much of it truly was his.

"So where to?"

I raised an eyebrow, sniffled. He produced a Kleenex from the glove box for me. I blew my nose, and we both laughed a little. The tension, sexual or otherwise, seemed to dissipate. I sniffled again and then grabbed my seat belt and told him how to find the way to my house. Instead he turned along a different street; I guess we were going for an out-of-the-way drive. I realized he was taking the scenic route, to give me some time to come down from my insane waffling between whose fault all of this was to not caring and just wanting Marco to come back to me.

We didn't talk much. He did put out his hand out between us and so help me if I didn't put my hand in his. Without thinking. Automatic.

What.

The.

Fuck?

"I know you just need a friend, right now."

We were passing by the Q and for a brief moment I thought about asking Angelo to drop me off there—thinking I could have used a little Mom and me time. But then I realized I'd have a lot of explaining to do and thought better of it. Which brought me to another point of discussion with the mysterious Angelo.

"So how is it you can drive?"

"I know how to drive..." he said drolly, as if he thought, in the middle of all my drama, it was an absurd question.

"But is it *legal*?"

He just sort of smirked again, making me focus on the fact of how much Angelo reminded me of my boyfriend.

And he's still your boyfriend, you twit, grab a fucking clue and start acting like it!

Using my thumb I absentmindedly started to twirl the ring on my finger between our entwined palms. The ring Marco gave me—*our* ring.

What the fuck was I doing here?

The tears started to form again. I wiped them away and painted on a smile as best as I could manage. It was a pained expression I was sure.

"Let's just say I can drive. Okay?" His eyes kept trading glances between me and the road ahead. Somehow I kept pulling his focus as well. He sighed and squeezed my hand a little bit for emphasis. "You don't have to hide your hurt, you know?"

I nodded.

"Thank you, by the way. You didn't have to..."

"Why do you do that?"

"What?"

"Apologize for things you have no need to apologize for?"

I shrugged, the pain still no doubt evident upon my face.

"He is pretty lucky, you know?"

Here it comes. He knows.

"Marco. I saw you with him. It is clear you both are in love."

"If that's so, then why is he *there* and I am here holding your hand, seeking comfort with you instead of him? Just feels like I'm being dishonest. Insincere. I shouldn't be doing this."

"Doing what? Seeking friendship while you are dealing with something hard?"

Again with the shrugging on my part. I knew I wasn't giving him much to work with, but it seemed safe at the moment. He may say he was extending this companionship in the spirit of being good friends, but even I could sense the sexual tension between us. I wasn't imagining it. I knew he sensed it too. I glanced at him and smirked again.

"What's with the, eh, smile? Is something funny to you now?"

I started to laugh. I couldn't help myself. How I could find it within me to find something amusing when my heart was hurting this much was truly astounding to me. Nervous energy, I guess. Either that or my little choo-choo was going 'round the bend in a big way.

I couldn't help but notice the way we must look to anyone who happened to glance into his car had to be extremely strange. I mean, I was dolled up to the nines (which, compared to most, was probably closer to 7.5 on that scale), and he was bare-chested (and what a chest and rack of abs it was), gym shorts, bare feet (not that anyone else could see them) and his face plastered with odd bone skull prosthetics and greasepaint.

"Us...We look kinda ridiculous."

"Why you say we look like that?"

I arched a brow at him and allowed my eyes to scan up and down the length of him. When that didn't clear the confusion in his face, I waggled a finger over him and then said, "I'm dressed like a modern day fairy tale prince and you, well, either a zombie or a hot jock suffering from porphyria and the worst case of acne."

He laughed, finally realizing the odd pairing we made. I joined in before the sexual tension began to become too palpable in the car.

"You think me hot?" he whispered, trying hard not to look me in the eye.

"I have a *boyfriend*," I deadpanned, though I wasn't so sure of that anymore. Marco's glare still scorched onto the back of my mind's eye. It hurt me again and again each time I blinked.

"You did not answer the question, though."

I shrugged as we came to a lighted intersection. He turned to look at me while cross traffic proceeded. The heat in his gaze was biting. He really did want me. I knew that look. There was no mistaking it. Even past all of the bony prosthetics and greasepaint, his eyes were pointed—brilliant green. Riveting. Electric.

Marco—Marco wasn't here; Angelo was. And I'd allowed this to happen. Was I somehow using my time with Angelo to punish Marco for being who he was? Was I really petty enough to allow some part of me to be angry with his masculine beauty? With his charms? Wasn't that what I signed on for when he sought me out back in July? I had to know things like this might happen. Yet, some part of me wanted retribution, wanted him to be sorry…but for what? I didn't truly have an answer. I was better than that. He knew I was better than that. But it didn't mean I couldn't appreciate someone else who was beautiful as well. What would it hurt to tell Angelo I thought him beautiful? Wouldn't I want some sort of confirmation from people to know that, hey, I was appreciated too? What could it hurt? As long as I didn't act upon it. So, I decided to come clean.

"Yes, Angelo. I think you're very beautiful. Well, what I can see of you that is." I pointed in the general direction of his face. "You need to take those off. I'm tired of not being able to see all of you at one time."

"Ah, you wish to see *all* of me, *bel ragazzo*?"

"Uh, not in the way…arrgh, you're *so* not making this easy."

"But that is the point, no?"

"Are all Italians so forward?"

"Those of us who see what we want, yes. There's no prize for second place where love is concerned."

"What do you mean love? You can't possibly…"

"Love you? Why not? I know you do not know me…or me to you, but I am speaking about the game of love. All of it. Not just you and me."

"I see."

"I do not think you do."

The light changed again and we proceeded to cross the intersection to the road that would eventually lead to my house.

"I know what you meant."

"Well, that, yes. But there is a great deal you don't see. People have hurt you so much you do not see real love when it comes. Maybe that is what makes it…eh, what is the word…*prodigioso, magico*—eh, magic. Yes, magical. You are very magical, Elliot. Beautiful."

I blushed, and turned away from the heated looks he kept giving me.

"I will not make apologies for my feelings for you. For me, standing by and not telling you how I feel, I gain nothing. I know you did not see me around school but that does not mean I did not seek you out."

"I guess, from your perspective, I can see what you're saying. And especially on a night like tonight, I am glad I have that. While Marco…" A single tear escaped me again. I hadn't even felt it coming on, but like being lashed with a whip laced with iodine, my feelings were still quite raw.

"Marco Sforza is a fucking piece of shit for leaving you."

"Hey, he had a game to finish playing!" I bellowed back at him.

"Okay, but did he have to go forward with the Homecoming event? He could have refused, eh, withdraw—right? He could have stayed with you and let the whole stupid thing go by without him. But did he? No!"

I was a little taken back with how rough he was being on my boyfriend. But I could still see his point. And surprisingly, it was a point I hadn't considered. I'd just assumed he should go ahead and be the great and glorious Marco Sforza while I faded into the shadows where I belonged. It never occurred to me he could have told Silverstein and begged off the whole thing. To be honest, I bet it had never occurred to Marco either. I found it funny how something so obvious was lost in the personal pandemonium we were going through.

"I suppose you're right."

"Oh, you suppose? Suppose, nothing. It is the truth, no?"

"Yeah, but I guess we didn't think of it at the time."

"Oh, he thought about it. I could see it in his eyes. You need to ask him about it. It was not right what *he* did either."

It was sort of amusing and slightly emboldening to see him wave his hands about while he railed around what he thought my boyfriend should've done. *A passionate Italian, this one is...*

An awkward silence descended as he made the turn toward my house. I was just thankful that while I enjoyed the drive and Angelo's company, I wasn't so pro the whole I-am-sort-of-cheating-on-my-boyfriend-as-I-flirt-with-another-man thing. I pointed to the house near the end of the street, so he was clear where to stop.

He unhurriedly pulled up to the front of the house.

"Well, here you are," he said softly.

I reached for the handle to get out when what had been circling around in the back of my mind wanted out.

"Angelo? Can I ask you something?"

"I thought you just did..."

I would've rolled my eyes at that oft-used sarcastic response—but instead I found it cute that a foreigner would have thought to use it.

"I am sorry for my little joke." He was serious now. "What is it you wish to ask me?"

I found it hard to put voice to it. I just looked at him, with the odd pairing of bone-protruding prosthetics and white and black greasepaint simply fading away when compared with those riveting green eyes. They appeared to know me far more than I was comfortable with. But that was the point of my question: his familiarity with me.

"Why me?"

He looked confused. I needed to clarify.

"I mean, you said you had feelings for me. How? We only had that one other night, and at most we just held hands. How could you get anything from that?"

He held out his hand and without thinking I laced my fingers with his. There was a certain sense of home there, a feeling of belonging entwined with him too.

How is that even remotely possible?

But what it was, was completely undeniable. I mean, I knew there were such things as poly-amorous or open relationships among gay men, but hell, I was barely able to sort out my thoughts and feelings around Marco, let alone adding Angelo to the mix. It was all too much, but for some reason I really wanted to hear his answer.

"When, eh, you touched my hand, I had never known such depth. I know you feel it too. It is in your eyes, the way you swallow when you touch me. I notice everything."

I gifted him with a slightly exasperated expression because it sounded like a Hallmark card at Valentine's Day or something. But his pointed gaze shredded whatever façade the prosthetics were trying to project. Like Marco, he made it clear: it wasn't my place to talk. This was Angelo giving me what I needed to hear, a validation to completely underscore what Marco had been telling me all along.

"Listen to me, Elliot. I am not speaking to flirt." When I'd schooled my features to truly pay attention, he continued, "I know you felt it too, like electricity or a wave of emotion moved along your arm to your chest and then your head. I do not mean to make it so, eh, academic, but this little touch was magical. I knew you were with someone. I figured he had to be very special. Marco Sforza is special. If he is special to you, then that makes him special. This is why I kept my distance. I respect that. But"—he held up a finger in my direction—"things have changed. Marco has abandoned you when he probably swore he would not."

"But why *me*? My opinion can't matter all that much."

"Elliot, for a smart guy who thinks he sees everything, you sure miss quite a lot. It's just you. You are a light in a very, very dark world, so bright even Marco knows it will outshine his own. But he is okay with that. I can see it when he looks at you." He paused, trying to think of a new way to present his point. "Eh, you ever know about binary stars?"

I shrugged because I was aware of them but I hadn't had any real astronomy since the sixth grade. It wasn't a subject junior high schools tended to focus on let alone the higher grades. They were more about the frogs and the dissecting than the study of the cosmos.

"When these two stars pull toward each other they go kind of into a dance. They are locked together—inseparable. Then one begins to pull very hard upon the other, stealing its light, stealing who it is. That's what you are. Your light is so powerful but at this point it is eclipsed by Marco's. But the pull from you is so strong he cannot help himself. He's locked to you, in that dance."

I probably wore a disbelieving look—but I had to admit there was some truth to what he was saying. I did pull upon Marco. He'd said as much. I was completely aware of Angelo's hands encasing my own; the heat between us was rising. We were in very dangerous territory. I was never more thankful for Halloween than this moment. I needed to make light of it, break the spell.

"Oh, great. Now I'm the Death Star eating Marco whole."

"Elliot, stop. This is not something you can laugh away!" he barked at me. "You need to understand why Marco does the things he does. He would give you everything. He would let you strip him bare, shred him completely until he was raw and bloody if that is what you needed. And he would not complain—not one word would he waste on it! Not if it was what you needed."

"I know." I looked down at my lap, ashamed at how much I took from Marco. And he never said anything, just offered me more.

"No, I do not think you do. Like those stars, you pull from him and he gladly gives. For him there is no choice. You are his light. You are what gives him life."

I snorted. "How can you possibly say this with any conviction? You're not him."

"No, I am not. But I am like him. Far more than you know. I see your light. I see what he sees. And I cannot help myself either."

"Okay." I slowly extracted my hand from between his, gently so as not to raise any alarms. "No offense, but not like that wasn't like eight bags of crazy you just said there."

"Why crazy? Do you think the act of love is crazy? Who is to say what makes it catch like a spark? Some people see someone they are attracted to and that is it, they are the one. They just know."

"But you don't even know me, not really. We shared one game of football then, what? I don't see you like for several weeks. And when I do, then you come off and tell me you think you, what? Love me or something? *That's* the bag of crazy I'm talking about. I mean, how could you? No way. It just isn't possible."

"Why? In those two meetings I saw what a beautiful person you are, eh, man you are. Very gentle, very passionate, very quiet."

"Yeah, well, for gayboys like me, quiet and unobserved is what keeps us alive."

"Someone like you should never have to hide. Protected, cherished, yes. Hidden? Never."

I smiled. He was being really nice to me and I was acting like a jerk. He knew of my relationship with Marco. He knew how I felt; I made it clear—despite our flirting. But I didn't have to be a jerk about it.

"Yeah, okay, you're my superhero. I get it. And thank you. I mean it. You ever hear what they say about gift-horses?" He nodded. "Well, I guess I should take help from any quarter. Beggars can't be choosers and all of that. Ya know?"

He nodded.

"Well, thanks again. You've helped me far more than you know. Good night."

I reached for the door handle again, exited, and was at my door when his voice stalled me again.

"Elliot, can I ask a small favor from you? I will understand if you say no."

Ah, Christ, here it comes.

I knew immediately what he wanted from me. I just didn't know if I could do it. I slowly turned around to find him standing there in only his gym shorts. It was cold enough outside. I couldn't just leave him like that.

"What's that?"

"May I have one kiss?" Before I could protest or say any of the nine hundred million reasons why I shouldn't, he stammered on, "I promise it would be safe. Just one and I promise, I will never ask again." I unlocked my door and flicked on the light. He held his hands up in surrender, "Okay, forget it. It is crazy for me to even ask. *Scusi*. It is just..."

Before he could get away I turned and grabbed him by the hand and pulled him inside. I shoved him against the back of the door after I slammed it shut behind him. And I don't know why I did it. No, that isn't true; I did know why I did it. I was angry, angry at the world for forcing Marco and me into a difficult place, for my being the biggest wimp and not doing what he and I had planned to do in the first place. I was mad at how petty I'd become in wanting someone to love and stand by me. That's what this was all about, wasn't it? Me, me, me!

But most of all, I was angry with myself for hurting Marco, the man I swore I would love and cherish above all others. Even with that mess of makeup, the desperation glimmered in Angelo's eyes—catching fire. It was too familiar, there was too much of him reminding me of Marco—*this was madness*. I swear I knew it was.

But I found I couldn't refuse him. Perhaps there was something to this binary star analogy he painted for me? All I knew was before I could change my mind I turned and my hand was on the back of his head and I pulled his lips to mine. No chaste kiss either. If I was in, I was going to be in all the way. At first, he was stunned into just allowing me to kiss him. After the shock of it passed though, he caught on. The next thing I knew he had turned us around, so my back pressed against the door, his hands all over me. God, was he ever powerful. Like the rush of a tidal wave, he reached out for me and pulled me to him. He cupped my ass and lifted me up so I could wrap my legs around his narrow and all too familiar waist.

Within seconds my jacket was on the floor, his hands fumbling with my shirt. Some part of me was completely fine with this. I needed to feel his skin on mine. He was electric, so charged I tingled all over—his hands like brands against my skin. I hissed audibly, clutching him while he used the door to keep me in place while he worked my shirt off.

"So beautiful..." he murmured to me.

Skin to skin, the heat from his chest seared itself upon me; the heat of a thousand suns. His heart was beating so powerfully against it. Without realizing it I was accommodating his large frame as he pressed his weight upon me. This was going too far; I needed to put a stop to it. Every time I made a move to stall him he found a new way to drive my desires higher. I was buckling under the enormity of him.

Marco. I shouldn't be doing this. I'm still Marco's!

Then I thought of the look in Marco's eyes, the way he told me to leave, the look in Cindy's eyes telling me she was going to get her mitts on him. She'd have him. What would I have after? I didn't think I'd have anything. So, Angelo continued to tear at my weakening defenses.

"Stop thinking, Elliot. Where is your room?" he asked, his voice thick with lust.

"First door down the hallway..."

Why did I tell him that? No, no, no! Don't do this! You're Marco's!

But my body seemed to have other ideas. He had moved so he could nuzzle along my neck, his lips searching for my ear. Marco's ear. This was a baaaaaad idea.

Really? Ya think?

That was the problem, it seemed. Show me a little kindness and I was yours. I had only been protected from doing more damage because I stayed within the shadow of my totally awesome boyfriend. And right now he was the Homecoming King and no doubt, in Cindy Markham's arms—just where the skank wanted him. I knew she was gunning for him all along. Now it appeared he was right where she wanted him to be—and he'd agreed to it all. That's what hurt. I know he said we'd talk later.

Talk.

Angelo's tongue licked along one of the blue diamond studs Marco had put there as he navigated us to my room. He laid me down gently onto the bed and kissed me deeply while he speedily shucked himself out of his shorts. With the exception of his damnable prosthetic makeup, he was completely naked and exposed to me. He began to undo my pants while I toed off my shoes. Inside it was just as if my heart was watching this behind a thick pane of glass—walled off. Trying desperately to scream, plead, beg for my brain and body to stop what I was doing, each beat of my heart like a bloodied fist against that translucent barrier—desperate to be heard and coming up short. No one was listening—least of all me. I had but one goal right now; I wanted everyone to hurt as much as I was.

By now Angelo had manipulated my body so my legs were on either side of him as he drug me up the length of the bed, holding me to his body with one powerful arm—never relenting his possession of my mouth. It was an extremely awkward and slightly painful position to keep because of how fast it was all happening. He gripped the waist of my pants and underwear and pulled them down in one move and hurled them to the far corner of my room. He pressed himself fully on me, forcing my legs apart, and on an unspoken command, I opened up to him.

I was confused, overheated with Angelo's pressing into me. I couldn't help but compare him to Marco. It seemed the natural thing to do. Part of me was shocked at how similar they were. Something was off, something was adding up a bit too easy here.

"Angelo, I don't think..."

"Do not think, Elliot. Let me love you as you should be loved. Worshiped. You are so beautiful. So, so beautiful. I see that now." Somewhere inside I noted there wasn't a trace of Italian in his words, but what did that mean? Was he a quick student in ditching the accent? The enormity of him as he took possession of my body made those thoughts melt away.

With one hand he cradled the back of my head. I marveled at how even in his lust he had spared a thought for some comfort on my part. The other, however, had moved to cradle my ass, lifting me so he could apply himself directly in between my legs. He lunged forward, bringing his heated breath to my neck—igniting an inferno within me, melting any resolve I had against this whole moment.

"So beautiful...I understand now." His voice puffed gently against my neck, making the hairs upon it rise with renewed passion.

The largeness of him pressing hard against my own erection made my senses swim. That too was familiar—and wrong. I knew it was but the familiarity of his body, of the way he knew exactly how to push my buttons, fulfilling my every desire, was extremely powerful to push against.

And here's the deal: *I didn't*.

"Do you, uh, have something?" he asked between devouring my tongue.

I clumsily reached up to the cubby above my head. He lunged for it and seized the lube from there and within seconds had applied an ample amount onto his cock. It was the first time I'd actually noticed it. How familiar that seemed too. Suddenly I wanted him. I wanted Angelo to fuck away the pain, to annihilate the love still eating me alive. I wanted him to scorch everything inside me. I was hurting. I was angry. Angry for even contemplating what I was about to let happen.

Part of me wanted it over, wanted the anonymity of my previous life. All of this hurt too much: the anger in Marco's eyes, the harshness of his words—it cut me deeply. So, I should let Angelo take it all away. I knew it was foolish. I knew it was beyond absurd. It was only going to make things worse. But at that moment I wanted everyone to hurt as much as I did. And Marco was included on that list. I hated myself for it; I hated being so petty and weak. I knew this was a test of my love for Marco and I was failing. Epically failing.

I simply don't care.

In the span of thinking all of those things Angelo's lips found mine again and I knew it was going to happen. I was going to let another man have me. I was going to let him ravage me and tear me apart. I hoped he was brutal in taking me. I wanted the pain to break me. I wanted oblivion.

He entered me. My eyes rolled back into my head, as he tore into me. I hissed. I moaned loudly as he began to take me over and over. My toes curled from the intense pleasure he brought. Rough, so damned rough and voracious in how he ripped me to pieces. He tugged me down to the end of the bed so he could stand with one leg on the mattress and one on the floor. I held onto the end of the mattress as he pressed my knees into my shoulders—pounding me mercilessly. My toes alternating between curling and flattening out from the pleasure and pain of it all. He kept pummeling me. Brutally so.

"Harder..." I panted at him and he complied. "Hurt me, dammit!" I yelled at him. He brought the pain—nearly making me pass out from it all—and I still wanted more.

He kept repeating how beautiful I was—changing back and forth between English and Italian. I couldn't look at him—it was too damned familiar, even with the marred makeup smeared across his face. I just let him take me. It was a raping of sorts, if one could rape the willing at this point. Each time he prodded me with this thick prong, cleaving me open, I shuddered, letting him tear everything away. Tears flowed freely from my eyes—it was an emotional release I wanted most of all. I could tell he was very close. I began to bear down on him, pulling upon him—hearing the strain in his breathing. His cock was literally on the verge of exploding within me. He leaned forward and his tongue plundered my mouth.

When he suddenly stopped...

In a rush, his mouth retracted from mine. The next instant he withdrew. The pain of his abrupt withdrawal left me far emptier inside than I ever thought imaginable. I opened my eyes. He was staring at me, panting with exertion of what nearly happened.

He shook his head slowly.

"I can't."

"What?"

"I can't. This is wrong. *Non posso fare male a mio fratello così.*"

He pulled away from the bed and slid his shorts on over his engorged and slick cock. He stood there for a second, panting. He was massively beautiful. Even with the mashed-up state of his makeup, he was absolutely stunning to look at. So much like my boyfriend.

"*Scusi...*"

And he was gone. Seconds later the front door opened and closed, the car outside started up and pulled away.

Silence.

There was nothing but deafening silence and hellish emptiness.

It was like that for a few minutes when something welled up within me, the empty dark place I didn't want to deal with. It surged, an emotive dark tsunami threatening to overtake me. I tried to hold it back, but it was too big. What I had allowed to happen was too big. I began to shiver all over with how far I let it go, how much damage I wanted to inflict. To myself, to Angelo, to Marco.

Marco.

And I knew. I knew I loved him more than anything. I came so close to abandoning all of that. I came so close to letting Angelo take it away. I had to fix this. I knew it was going to be painful; I'd have to sort out whatever it was I did to hurt Marco and apologize and give in to how I had hurt him, take full responsibility for it. He could still walk away. He could still leave me.

I picked up my phone and texted him.

Can you come by to see me after the dance?

My finger hovered over the send button, shaking. Suddenly I wasn't so sure I wanted to face his wrath again. I knew how badly I'd hurt him. I didn't know how I would begin to address it. But I knew I had no pride when it came to him. I would submit to him and whatever anger he had for me.

I pressed send and let whatever was going to happen, happen.

Then I cried. I sobbed with what I had allowed to transpire tonight. So many tears came pouring out of me. I wailed, beat my fist upon the pillow. I raged loudly until my voice began to grow hoarse. I don't know how long I went on. I was naked, exposed, my ass still slick from Angelo's cock. I knew we didn't go there; before it went too far *he* put an end to this madness. It should've been *me* to stop it. But I didn't, and deep down in my heart of hearts, I knew it was the right thing to do. Only I hadn't been the one to do it.

If anything, I knew now Angelo was a man of honor. I could see how much he wanted me for himself. He wanted me, but he stopped. What was it he said? I didn't know Italian, but I remembered something of the sounds. Somehow I knew what he'd said seemed important. Whatever it was, I didn't think it was about me. The look in his eyes was for someone else.

SHOWER.
　Bed.
　Darkness.

1:30 A.M.
A tapping at my bedroom window brought me back out of my bed. "What the...?"

Marco.

I slid the window open and he was through within seconds and in my arms again.

"Baby...oh, my baby. I love you so much," he whispered into my ear.

I stood there in a daze, still not fully awake. I yawned deeply, widening my eyes to try to get them to work properly. He grabbed me into a fierce hug, those precious rough hands roaming over my bare skin. I smiled softly, shivering against his warmth and the raging breeze coming through the window.

"Uh, babe? Can we like, I dunno, close the window? I'm freezing here."

He chuckled and closed the window fast and pushed me onto the bed. He speedily toed off his shoes and stripped out of his clothes, not caring that they landed in a heap before joining me there. I noticed his eyes darted to the end of the bed; I didn't know why. His whole demeanor seemed a bit off, not totally there—like he was searching for whatever he lost in himself.

Only when he pulled me beneath him did I notice how wet his face was from crying.

"Babe? Whasswrong?"

He just shook his head. He didn't want to talk about whatever it was.

His eyes searched mine, desperation clouding his features as he kissed me. A tidal wave of emotion was poured into his kiss. When I was just getting into it, he broke it abruptly.

"Just tell me you'll love me forever. No matter what? Please, Els, baby, please. I love you so much I don't know what I'd do without you. I'd fall apart. Nothing would matter if you ever denied me."

"Why would I ever...Okay, now you're scaring me. What's going on? I mean, we only parted a few hours ago. I know we have shit to sort out but what's going on here? What happened?"

"I dunno. That's the problem. It's all so foggy."

"Are you on something?" I knew it was stupid to ask because I once had to argue with him when his body hurt from a particularly hard game and I wanted him to take a Tylenol (*for god sake—it's only Tylenol, Marco*) and he wouldn't budge. He was such a freak about drugs. His stern position didn't extend to marijuana when he decided to smoke it over the summer. But during football season, he was a saint.

This time, he wouldn't answer.

"Marco?"

"Baby, just hold me. Please?"

I did. But I also was deeply worried. What the fuck could he have done from the time we parted this evening and now? I needed to find out but he was so fragile in my arms. I was concerned I was going to push him and he might break. That was certainly not my Marco. Something drastically awful had happened. He was always there to protect me and he was so fragile now. I needed to step up and protect my man for once.

"Babe?"

"Hmmm?"

"Did you want to..."

"Huh? Oh, uh, do you mind if we just cuddle for a few first? I just need to be near you. I missed you so much tonight. Nothing went right. I hated all of it. I only kept thinking about you and how much my body ached to be near you. And then..."

"Then?"

He went silent again. The concern on my face was no doubt evident. Something was there and troubling him, deeply. It was then I discovered the thing that had been bothering me the most about him: he wasn't looking me in the eye.

"Hey, why aren't you able to look at me?"

His eyes moved to search mine, then darted away. Shame. What the fuck would he have to be *ashamed* about?

"Marco? Look at me!" I demanded of him.

"Baby, I can't. God, I love you but I can't right now. I'm so..."

"So what? Baby, you're scaring me. Now stop. What is it? You can tell me; you can."

"I dunno, sweetheart. So much went wrong after you left."

"You lose the game?"

He shook his head.

"Okay, well that went right."

"No, I wanted to lose. I wanted to punish them for pushing you away from me. I failed."

I smirked at his obtuse logic but decided not to draw too much attention to it. "Okay, so failure there, but I gotta tell you, I think I'm cool with your winning anyway. Just so you know. I'm okay with it. I definitely like my baby on the winning side."

A single tear slipped from his left eye. "I so don't deserve you," he mumbled.

"How do you figure that? It's me who should be worried. You're a god and I'm just me. Just Elliot."

"No you're not. You're so beautiful, so glorious and I try so hard to be worthy of you, and then I just..."

The same fucking wall he was running into he didn't want to talk about. It was starting to piss me the fuck off.

"What is it you aren't telling me? You keep getting to a certain point and then you panic and stop or change subjects. Just tell me!"

"That's what's wrong—I can't! Not because I don't want to—it's just *clouded*. I think someone slipped me something in my drink and then it gets all confusing. Something happened. I know, because everyone started acting a bit different after. But I can't put it together. Not really. I'm scared, Els. I've never lost it like tonight."

"So, you went to the dance?"

"Uh huh..."

"Well...Care to complete that for me?"

"Yeah. And you were right, Cindy was a fucking leech. Drove me bat-shit crazy. There's going to be a shit load of pictures, I'll warn you now. I'm smiling on the outside but baby, I was hating it—just look at my eyes. I was pissed about all of it. My mother was there and like a marketing demon she orchestrated the whole fucking thing. I was trapped. I plastered on that smile but every fucking moment I wanted you. I swear to you on my life, I was not happy the entire time. You have to believe me; you just have to. You just don't know what my parents are like. I didn't know Mom had volunteered her and Dad as parental chaperones for the whole thing. I should have guessed. It made me even madder that I couldn't get you to refuse to give up the title and take all of their fire away."

"Well, like I said, I don't think you understood what you stood to lose."

"And I said..."

"I know what you said. But you never had to live in everyone's shadow. You have no idea what it's like. I do. It has been my life. Still is, apparently."

"I hate that, you know. Nothing gets me angrier than your being slighted. I'm sorry I got short with you at the game. But I was railing against a lot of things just then. You just got caught in the cross fire."

"No worries. I'm okay."

He nodded, then kissed me softly again, his tongue only lightly probing my mouth.

"I'm spending the night, sweetheart."

"You can't, baby. You know what'll happen. I don't think we're ready for that meet-my-mom sort of thing, though she has been asking. Even tried to throw Stephen Lowry my way as a potential boyfriend, if you can imagine." I shook all over with the thought.

"Stephen *Lowry*?" *Yeah, even he couldn't buy that one.*

"Just because we'd been friends before. She thought somehow it would translate to us being boyfriends. Now, in her defense, Stephen and I had known each other since we were three, so we had quite a past."

"Don't tell me you two used to take baths together."

"Absolutely. Sleepovers and everything. Up until the summer before the eighth grade. Then it all went south. In this room, no less."

"Huh." He pondered my words for a moment before circling back. "Well, I don't care. You still had better lock the door because I'm staying. I don't care if I gotta hide under the bed or in the closet if she pops her head in. But I'm staying. No one is going to pry me away from you. Not tonight."

"Well as long as we fuck quietly, we should be able to get away with it."

"I dunno. I just want to sleep with you, babe. Maybe later. But right now I just want you to hold me, to keep me close."

"Wait, *you* don't want to fuck? I know we did earlier this afternoon, but when have you ever…"

"Dammit, Elliot! Just not right now, okay? Please, baby. I will later, I promise."

"Well, don't do *me* any favors," I said gruffly.

"Jeez, that's not what I mean. Fuck, Elliot! I always want to make love with you. Always. But I'm still coming down from what the fuck was slipped into my drink at the dance. I'm not totally here yet. It's still all a haze. I don't want to make love when I'm like that. I want to give you all of me. My head isn't where my heart is, baby. That's why I don't want to."

I sighed.

"Okay, I guess. I just don't understand how so much changed from when you and I parted last. What about your parents? Won't they be concerned you didn't come home after the dance?"

"They think I went out with Cindy. I dropped her ass off shortly thereafter. Then I drove around trying to clear my head. Sat at the cliffs for a bit just letting the ocean air shake it out of me so I could come over."

There were so many inconsistencies with what he said it confused me. But I didn't want to upset him further, so I let it go. There would always be time to sort it out later.

"Want you to hold me. Never let me go, okay, babe? Please..."

What the fuck did they do to him?

"Shhhh, I'm here. We're good. Go to sleep. I'll text Mom and tell her I'm zonking out and I got home safe. That should be good enough for her to ignore me when she gets in."

I grabbed the phone and sent her the message and then set the alarm for 7:00 a.m. Just as I was about to put the phone back in the cubby in the headboard Mom texted back she was getting ready to head home and would be here in about an hour and then she said to get a good night's sleep 'cause I had store duty at 10:00 a.m. I acknowledged I would be there and sent my good night.

"We're good. Sleep away, my prince."

He leaned forward and kissed me deeply. "I love you so much, Elliot. You are so good to me, so good for me. You're my angel. *Il mio angelo celeste.*"

Angelo. That singular word in Italian caught my attention. Suddenly, I knew whatever was bothering him would sort itself out. And I had to come clean about my night with Angelo. I couldn't live with myself if I kept it a secret. I didn't want secrets between Marco and me. I'd face whatever he threw at me. I deserved it. I knew what I was doing, despite how obligated I felt to give Angelo something for being there and helping me through a difficult situation. But there'd be time enough for that. I stroked his head and placed a soft kiss along his temple as he pulled me further under him, shrouding me within him. Just the way we liked it.

The warmth of him, the enormity of him, was everything I needed in a man. He was my life; he was my light. In our cocoon of muscle and bone, of mind and heart, I vowed I would always be his. The twisted events of this night had secured it. Grateful for his presence, I peppered his neck with kisses, lulling him into sleep. He murmured he loved me again and I let go in the special place he reserved for me—in his arms, surrounded by him, I followed my man into the depths of slumber. It was a peaceful, unburdened sleep.

A sleep of the Angels.

Acknowledgements

To my family, friends (both in real life and online), my fans and those beta readers who put in the time and efforts to help mold Elliot's and Marco's world. Mercy, California would not be what it is without you. You know who you are and I am forever in your debt.

Italian translations provided by Marco Guzman, J. Scott Coatsworth, Fabrizio Montanari, and Marco Munda. Their assistance with the tone and northern Italian vernacular of the Sforzas in my works is immeasurable and I am humbled by their generosity.

About the Author

SA "Baz" Collins hails from the San Francisco Bay Area where he lives with his husband, and a Somali cat named Zorro. A classically trained singer/actor (under a different name), Baz knows a good yarn when he sees it.

Based on years of his work as an actor, Baz specializes in character study pieces. It is more important for him that the reader comes away with a greater understanding of the characters and the reasons they make the decisions they do, rather than the situations they are in. It is this deep dive into their manners, their experiences and how they process the world around them that make up the body of Mr. Collins' work.

You can find his works at sacollins.com and as a co-host/producer of the wrotepodcast.com series.

Email: sacollins@sacollins.com

Facebook: www.facebook.com/sacollinsauthor

Twitter: @sacollinsauthor

Website: www.sacollins.com

Coming Soon from SA Collins

Before the Fall
Angels of Mercy, Book Two

I'll fight for you...
The phone buzzed and the screen was replaced by Marco's glorious face. I nearly dropped the damned thing because it surprised me when it went off, as if he could sense I was reaching out across the ether to him. I was reaching and as usual he was there.

His smile glowed ethereally from my phone and tears fell, blurring and obscuring his glorious and transcendent beauty. It kept buzzing, waiting for me to answer it—each throbbing, rattling motion pleading for me to answer his call.

One more ring and it'll slip to voice mail. I declined the call—hating myself to hell and gone for doing so, knowing he wouldn't let it go. A beat.

No voicemail.

Another call.

I let it ring through, sagging against my pillow and weeping like the fucking social retard I was. And I am not the type of person to use the word retard with ease. If I used it, I fucking meant it. And in reference to me, I meant it. Deeply. I was an inept and undeserving boyfriend. He was mythic; he was a god. A god who stumbled, but didn't they all in those mythic legends? Why should my guy be any different? I was the little fag boy who belonged in the shadows. I deserved to be cast back there – where I belonged.

No voice mail.

I should've answered. A reminder there were a great many things I should've...but didn't. I rolled over in my bed, clutching the pillow closer to me.

Silence, oppressive and weighted, pressed in around me.

The phone buzzed.

I picked it up and looked at the text from Marco.

Marco: *I get it. I'll leave you alone. Good night, my dearest love...miss you.—M*

I broke.

Also Available from NineStar Press

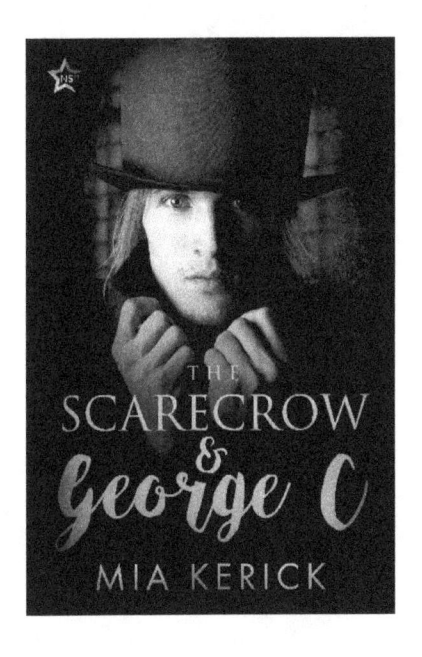

Connect with NineStar Press

www.ninestarpress.com

www.facebook.com/ninestarpress

www.facebook.com/groups/NineStarNiche

www.twitter.com/ninestarpress

www.tumblr.com/blog/ninestarpress

CPSIA information can be obtained
at www.ICGtesting.com
Printed in the USA
LVHW041503051120
670844LV00001B/100

9 781950 412853